Black Dog

Matt Syverson

Backstage Pass Publishing
Victoria, TX

For information, please contact:
Backstage Pass Publishing
P.O. Box 695
Victoria TX 77902
www.backstagepasspublishing.com

Author contact:
bowiefan1970@live.com

Cover Art conceived and designed by Tony Szatkowski.

Sincere thanks to my family for being so supportive.
Special thanks to Joe Dimeglio and Mantis.

Printed by Lightning Source in the U.S. and U.K.
Also available for Kindle from Amazon.com.
Contact author to purchase other e-formats.

ISBN: 978-0-615-42806-2
Library of Congress Control Number: 2011900171

Director's Cut

\m/ \m/

This book is dedicated to the musicians and writers who inspired me to create my own fumbling attempts at art. I hope it honors their endeavors and inspires others to explore the music of the 1970's and the writing of authors like William S. Burroughs and Hunter S. Thompson. That middle initial 'S' seems to stand for a lot. I don't have that going for me, but I assure you the letter 'S' has played a huge part in my life, regardless.

Please note: *Italicized* passages are the words of the story's narrator, who at this time wishes to remain anonymous. His speaking voice is eerily similar to that of Vincent Price or Vincent Furnier, although neither of them has agreed to take part in this exercise.

Introduction: A Word To The Student, Current and Former

Sometimes summer break sneaks up fast on high school students – a little too fast for good grades, a little too fast for the student body, and a little too fast for the student body's very own gangly and uncoordinated student bodies. Thirty day interludes that passed murderously slow in months like October and November are now speeding at them like a freight train that left Cleveland at 1:00 p.m., traveling 50 miles per hour in a vector aimed precisely at their (x,y) coordinates.

One student is particularly lost and finds himself standing motionless in the middle of a long, dark tunnel of confusion, knowing not where he is or how he got there. His head is down. He is confused and groggy, as if attempting to wake from a deep sleep or a miniature coma. He hears a roar, shakes his hairy skull, and looks up to see the aforementioned train entering the tunnel he stands in at top speed, its steel wheels glistening like a Ginsu knife thrown at him with impossible momentum. (Momentum equals mass multiplied by velocity, to quantify it in terms from Physical Science class.)

Essay question: Will the train reach this poor pupil faster than a Pony Express rider racing to deliver his English IV term paper to him? The horseback rider averages 10 miles per hour through rough terrain, 15 if he's on a dirt road. He was handed the assignment 34 hours ago in Chattanooga, Tennessee, and hasn't slept since. Well Poindexter, which one's gonna reach the boy first – the term paper or the train?

The answer is probably the train, unless the Pony Express rider has managed to get a fresh horse. Sorry kid, but things ain't looking too good. That teenager needs to get his 'you know what' together, but he just stands there, daydreaming. He doesn't even know his term paper is on the way. He is oblivious, unable to help himself. But, amazingly, the delivery man has made up ground and is approaching the tunnel entrance opposite the train.

The noble steed propelling the rider comes from a long line of thoroughbreds and wants nothing more than to complete his

black 1 dog

assigned task. He is a passenger pony and has galloped hundreds of miles. He cares not about himself – he has accepted that the heart in his heaving breast will likely explode seconds after the conclusion of his mission.

Tragically, the horse has run his course and slows, stumbling like a newborn foal. He buckles and lands on his front knees and his corresponding back hocks. With a shudder he falls on his side, throwing the rider, who is now mere feet from the entrance of the tunnel. The man leaps up from the fallen equine and enters the passageway, his eyes adjusting to the dim light faster than a Terminator's.

"Wake up, boy!" the anguished Pony Express rider wails at the tragic youth in front of him, who remains frozen like a marble statue. The mailman is no less driven to complete his task than his dying horse. He is within a hundred short meters of the student, intent on delivering the term paper at all costs, even if he suffers the same fate as his poor pony. The boy doesn't hear the exhortation over the roar of the steam train, though. He just stands like an effigy of Jughead carved from a petrified tree.

"Wake the heck up, son! I'm talking at ya, and you're asleep at the reins! Stop daydreaming, conblarn it, and concentrate!" Still the boy doesn't acknowledge the rider. He just stares at the train.

***

NOTE FROM THE AUTHOR – The creepy narrator's gonna talk now. He wanted me to remind you about the italics thing. I won't do it again, I promise.

***

Wow, this kid must have ADD or ADHD or some other acronym. A train's coming at him, just like in the movies, and he needs to get out of that tunnel before he becomes a steam engine's hood ornament. The jaws of the smoke-breathing iron beast are close enough for him to taste its bad breath.

Imprinted on the carriage's visage is an imposing logo – 'ADHD Railroad'. Irony is a 'b', huh? As any 7/16 scale model train enthusiast could tell you, this is a full-size, 16/16 scale steam-powered engine charging at him. The boy will be dead in a matter of seconds if he doesn't react.

black 2 dog

"WAKE UP DAMMIT!!!!!" the rider screams again, the words echoing down the walls of the tunnel from the opposite end of the chugging train. The boy starts awake and turns to see a man who resembles Davy Crockett, complete with coon skin cap, running as fast as possible toward him. The student's eyes focus for the first time, finally awakened from his daydream. "WAKE UP, fore yonder train kills ya, ya danged imbecile!" the Yosemite Sam look-alike cries out in a milk-curdling scream.

Is this dream or reality? The pimply teenager tries to wrap his mind around the unwrappable.

The boy jerks alert with a start and attempts to appraise his situation before it's too late. An instantaneous status report is delivered to his brain in unscientific terms – "I'm screwed!" He's off like a shot toward Mr. Coon Skin Cap and the term paper the mountain man carries, running like a cottontail on meth – fight or flight squared, maybe even cubed.

The cycloptic lantern of the coal-fired doom machine impends upon the boy unceasingly. He can't run any faster – he's bipedaling at top speed in hysterical exodus from the anonymous and unquestionable beacon of light, which bleats at him from the black hole. For some reason, the boy recalls Mr. Thompson, his Chemistry teacher, who taught him that light cannot escape a black hole's tractor beam of gravity. This gives the boy hope, as he realizes he may be in some sort of alternate reality where he can defy the laws of physics. He turns sideways and attempts to jump through the tunnel's brick wall and hits HARD, falling on his butt, almost knocking himself unconscious. Shaking off the impact, he returns to his body, which is now running again at a dead sprint, the train's whistle having scared him into Peter Cottontail on speed mode again. RUN RABBIT RUN!

Still, the locomotive careers toward the boy, pushing its lantern at 3.0 times ten to the power of eight, the speed of light in meters per second, the boy recalls deliriously. His Chemistry teacher taught him that, too. Amazing how his impending demise has spurred all these recollections from a class in which he has a 38 average for the second semester. He must be one lazy student, and Mr. Thompson must be one helluva teacher.

black 3 dog

The teenager sprints at a velocity of 5 meters per second toward Grizzly Adams, who is running toward him at 8 meters per second and seems to be the boy's only hope of survival. The mountain man holds his satchel in the air as he gallops to the poor pupil. His boots from time to time clank against the train rails and produce comets of sparks. He's wearing horse shoes, or rather, has iron 'man shoes' nailed to the bottom of his old boots. What kind of alternate reality is this? The boy wishes he had on ruby slippers to usher him home with a few heel taps, but he looks down and sees nothing but a blur of ruby red Converse Chuck Taylor All-Stars. His mind feels detached from his body, which feels detached from his feet.

He reaches the mountain man, who thrusts the leather purse into the teen's gut like Troy Aikman handing off to Emmit. Acting more like Brett Favre than Aikman, the Pony Express suicide bomber continues in the direction of the locomotive, screaming 1800's-era gibberish. "Camptown ladies ding my dong," is all the boy can decipher as the crazed prospector pushes himself toward his eternal demise in a futile, fatal attempt to derail the train and save the boy. His devotion to the teen's cause makes an Al-Qaeda operative look like some YouTube dork shooting a bottle rocket out of his butt.

Shaking off the morbid realization of the fate of the Pony Express man and his horse, the kid sprints toward the safe end of the cavern, carrying the pigskin like a running back from Odessa Permian. In other words – fast. RUN FORREST RUN!

As he prepares to start his trademark 'You Ain't Gonna Catch Me' high step, the boy looks down at the pouch in his hands and realizes it is not a Pony Express leather satchel at all. It is the beaten-up and beaten-down backpack that has burdened him for four long years of high school. WTF, he texts himself with his free hand.

Suddenly, incomplete assignments begin to leak from the backpack's failing zipper, rising on wind currents and fluttering behind him like ticker tape. "Those were due by Friday," he thinks to himself as a mask of terror embraces his face. His unorganized school binder spontaneously leaps out of the backpack like a deranged jack-in-the-box and lands on jagged rocks, exploding with a flurry of unfinished worksheets and corrupted class notes, which

black 4 dog

rise and see-saw to the tunnel floor like dying butterflies. Diplomas rain from the ceiling like hail, striking the boy and bouncing away wildly. Once again, he wishes he could clap the heels of his Chuck Taylors together and chant "same as it ever was". "I should've worn my Vans," the boy thinks.

***

Suddenly – thankfully – the real-life boy dreaming this nightmare startles awake, staring into the light of the movie projector he's manning, his chin resting in the cradle of his hand, which is supported by a knobby knee. He is not racing down a nightmarish hellhole, being chased by a train engineered by the truck driver from the movie, 'Duel' – he is only dreaming. He thinks he might be having a nightmare, but the light from the projector bulb looks like the train's light in the dream, so the boy knows not if he is asleep or awake. He is in and out of reality. The chair is uncomfortable, he thinks to himself as he drifts groggily to and fro.

An irritated voice screams up from the theater, startling him. Now, he's dreaming he's in Chemistry class, and Mr. Thompson is kicking the leg of his desk. He is being made an example for not paying attention.

"Wake up, kid, and focus the friggin' camera!"

"Mr. Thompson, what are you talking about? My phone is in my pocket," the boy mumbles.

"C'mon, dumbass, focus the camera! The previews are startin'." A faceless, agitated man is standing on one of the theater seats below, attempting to peer into the projection area where the tortured teen naps.

The boy shakes his head, bringing reality back into frame, instinctively reaching for the projector's focus control knob. This isn't the first time he's been called out like this, and he is unnerved, as well as a tad cranky, like most teenagers are when they wake.

"Yo, old man, chill the eff out! It's only the previews!" he retaliates, although he knows the patron has every right to be perturbed, as much as he's paying to watch this sorry crap they call a 'date movie.'

"I've got it under control!"

***

black 5 dog

Lately, these anxiety-driven nightmares are happening more and more, and the poor kid never seems to get any rest. The night gig at Cinema Two isn't helping, that's for certain. Meanwhile, his Chemistry grade's been sliding down the mountain like a globally-warmed glacier ever since he took the job. Maybe the free popcorn just isn't worth it.

His first semester report card should have been an adequate warning flare, but what happened? Same thing that happens to all of us – PROCRASTINATION. The word can be sung to a couple songs, to cheer yourself up. First try Carly Simon's, 'Anticipation'. YouTube it, if necessary, to get the melody down. The syllables match perfectly with the original version. Try it – "Procrastination, Procrastination is taking my grade. Keeping me failing, failing, failing."

You can also sing it to Rod Stewart's song, 'Fascination', but it's not nearly as fun.

***

Still reading, huh? I would have put this book back on the shelf by now when I was your age. It would have scared me. Does the scenario the author just related remind you of yourself? Maybe just a lil' bit? I'm sorry he decided to open the story with a lengthy nightmare and subsequent literary beat-down, but you need to be reprimanded – someone needs to scare you straight before it's too late. You don't play sports or take part in extra-curricular activities. Your parents don't care what you do. Most of your teachers barely know your name. Nobody seems to care. Mr. Thompson cares, though, doesn't he? And I care....

Look, I know school can be an overload. I went to school, too – Catholic school. It was hell. But if you think high school is tough, kid – wait until you graduate. Wait until you have to go to even more school, then you marry some crazy chick, and don't even get me started on your future mother in law.

See, I just want you to pass all your high school classes, so you can go to college and learn the True Art of Procrastination 101. College is the big leagues, and you want to stay as long as Nolan Ryan pitched in the majors. When you get settled into your dorm in the first weeks of your freshman tour, search out a seventh year senior and ask he or she how it's done. You are a rookie, and you need to pick a veteran to be your sponsor, just like in Alcoholics Anonymous. Pick the right one, and it'll be a decade before you see your first cubicle.

There is one major difference in the procrastination practiced in high school, compared to that done at the university level. Put simply, one keeps you from having to go to work, and the other keeps you from being able to get a job. I'll let you figure out which is which.

C'mon kid, keep your chin up. I'm not trying to discourage you. I just don't want you to end up digging graves like me. I've been through some tough times. I'm only trying to keep you six feet above ground.

***

So, we've established you have been made to quit your job, are attending multiple summer school courses, and are grounded for at least two months. What a perfect time to read an account of a couple teens I know who got a lot more than they bargained for on their summer break. This is known as a cautionary tale, which means: be happy you have it so good and learn from the mistakes and circumstances of others. Trust me – the boys I'm going to tell you about would have begged to be grounded for the summer and swamped with schoolwork. They had it really, really bad.

Get comfortable and relax – the movie projector is warming up. Pick a seat without a sticky, spilled Coke below it, grab some freshly popped and buttered corn, and do some wide-awake dreaming. Observe somebody else's nightmare, instead of your own. And learn from it. Keep your chin up, kid, and don't sleep on the job. Peace out.

CHAPTER ONE

"Hurry up, dumbass, or we're gonna be late for school!"

"Uggh," replied Jonah with a Shakespearean swoon. "Why dost thou plague me, vile, pre-pubescent tween witch?"

It was his little sister again, doing the bidding of the Mother. The Mother had no strength left with which to enforce her rule on her bitter little head-case son, Jonah. Being at the end of her rope, the Mother had enlisted Jonah's mini-Nazi little sister, Serah, to handle rule enforcement, and the bad seed enjoyed every minute. She was destined to become a prison guard.

Serah had a different father than Jonah, which explains the siblings antonym personalities. Jonah was the son of a vagabond, Serah was the spawn of a man who worshiped Hitler. In fact, her dad had been a devout member of the anti-everything group, 'The Germanazis'. He even had aspirations of being their Grandé Dragon but wasn't intelligent enough to pass the certification exam.

Jonah's dad was a surfer from San Dimas, California, and his only son had inherited his dad's sloth-like genes. Is it better to rise with the sun and the morning surf, with no other purpose than to chase the perfect crunchy wave, or to stay up all night snorting meth and devising conspiracy theories based upon racial hatred? It's all about good and evil and when the two shall meet on the football field in the sky. There is a war on earth for every heart and mind, and destiny will sweep you away in the rip-tide if you have no control over your own soul and pick the wrong wave to ride. If you get washed out to sea, swim perpendicular to the shore and tread water. You may prevent your lungs from filling with the saline liquid. And you may prevent yourself from drowning and being deposited in murky depths next to ancient shipwrecks, with no ability to profit from the lost doubloons you settle among.

***

"Let me sleep, Serah," Jonah managed from his hibernation.

"Whatever, zit-face," she replied, bringing a small aerosol can into aiming position with her right hand. "You're gonna get the pepper spray treatment if you don't cooperate. Don't make me waterboard you again." The little bitch was serious.

black 8 dog

Jonah shuddered at the recollection of the last punishment he had suffered at her tiny hands. Without invitation, she spoke once more, this time more sympathetically but no less emphatically.

"C'mon, Jonah. Mom says you better get in the car, pronto. We've been waiting outside for five minutes! Why can't you be ready for school on time for once?"

"It takes hours to apply my stage make-up, little girl, you know that." Jonah's voice rose to the volume of a Broadway actor projecting to the nether regions of an off-Broadway playhouse. "Prepare for my triumphant entrance, and behold 'The Transformer'!"

Jonah leaped from his miniscule 'dressing room'/bedroom into the mobile home's narrow, wood-paneled hall. He was glamming it up more than Ziggy Stardust.

Lil' Sis went ballistic at the sight of this. "Jonah, gosh-dammit, you are *not* wearing make up to school again! I can't take the trickle-down abuse!"

"Guy-liner is not make-up!" he replied with all the sarcasm his sleepy emo body could muster.

"Yes, it is, Jonah. They didn't call you 'Transformer' – they called you 'tranny'. Not good, unless you're playing Frank N. Furter from 'The Rocky Horror Picture Show' at a midnight movie. I may have been behind the bars of my crib drinking Benadryl Kool-Aid, but I watched all those crazy movies mom used to show you. I'm not an idiot. One thing I know for sure is, I'm the girl daughter, and you're the boy son. Get it straight! UGGH! You disgust me, Jonah! I'm embarrassed to be your sister."

"God, you *are* a 'b' with a capital 'B'," Jonah replied, although he was deflated by the harsh, but true, words of lil' Cruella. "Guyliner is not make-up!" he screeched at the top of his transitional voice, which cracked embarrassingly between the words 'make' and 'up'. "Nobody at school likes Lou Reed or The Sweet or David Bowie. Nobody understands me! I hate my life!! Where's the effing cold cream!?!?!?!!?"

Guilty feelings draped Jonah's little sister. She was evil to the core, but it was the result of training, like one of Michael Vick's pit bulls. At times she did feel sorry for Jonah, which manifested itself in a cramp behind the right ventricle of her little black blood pumper.

black 9 dog

She felt this pain now, knowing he was much weaker than her, and that she had played a major role in the breaking of the boy's spirit. She was a tortured soul at the tender age of twelve, and it was only getting worse. God help the people she will leave in her wake, but that is another story. (Preview: She will develop strong urges to cut herself and others during her mid-teens.)

"I know, Jonah," she strained through strangled lips. This was not easy for her. The words had to be forced out like Play-Doh being pushed through one of those extruders that make ropey lengths of star shapes and the like.

"I know how it is for a freak like you, brother. Let's get going, okay chump, er... champ? Use some of Mom's cold cream on that eye makeup – it's in the top drawer in the bathroom. We'll be waiting for you in the car. Pull yourself together, Jonah. Do it for both of us."

***

Jonah was 'emotional', which to me means 'pasty and weak'. I would have been beaten to a bony pulp if I had pranced around like a pop tart in high school, even if it was done behind closed bedroom doors. The bullies at my school would have assumed, or somehow sensed, that I was a private dancer. I would have been toast. I would have been burnt toast. I would have been croutons, for God's sake.

That was ages ago, though. Kids these days wear makeup, hair weaves, and the like, even if they aren't all that gay. They bleed pink and sunburn on the walk from the Wal-Mart exit to the car. They are conscientious to a fault about applying eyeliner, but never, ever remember sunscreen – the one thing they should never, ever forget. As pasty white as some modern teens are, twenty minutes at the beach could transform them into flaky little Lay's Original Potato Chips. That would be one bland, unseasoned chip and would not sell at any price.

Actually, the beach is a place you will rarely find emos. They can't skateboard on sand, and a surfboard requires far too much athleticism to master. Picture a pack of these albino living dead re-enacting the signature 'Chariots of Fire' scene, running down the beach in slow motion – bland on the run. Hmmm... sunscreen. I like that. Sunscream. Some screen. Some scream. We all scream for

black 10 dog

sunscreen. We all bleed pink and peel sunburned butterfly wings.

***

Jonah gazed into the bathroom mirror as he lethargically massaged makeup remover into his formerly glorious eye sockets. He was taking forever. He heard the Accord peel out as it left the driveway. The Mother was not happy.

"Eff school," he said to the image in the mirror. "Screw school." He was stretching his vocabulary, and he ached with every vowel. Jonah laughed, realizing he wasn't going to class today. He turned to gaze narcissistically into the full length mirror attached to the back of the bathroom door. He pouted his lips as he gazed into the looking glass and said, "I look like a negro." This was said by a person whiter than the paper this book is printed on. In fact, Jonah was so white he covered up his zits with a dab of Liquid Paper.

***

Jonah's statement was a joke. The kid had developed a sense of humor through the tribulations of his situations. The whole Flamboyant Freddie thing was an act he used to conceal his weakness from others. He wasn't even gay or all that metrosexual. He was just a normal boy in need of a father figure, and this was the way he got attention, albeit negative. He needed a role model. He needed a better mother. He needed a friend and a father. He needed lots of things.

The bathroom mirror had always consoled him when no others would. It had been his sanctuary from the external world since his early teens. This mirror had seen many American Idol-worthy performances, but not so much lately. Jonah had hit his awkward phase, and gazing lovingly into his own reflection had lost some of its appeal. Lately, he focused more on the pimples than the dimples. It had gotten a lil' bit depressing.

Don't misunderstand – he still loved gazing at his image, as those with little substance usually do. Those who can't graduate. Those who have no certifications, diplomas, or degrees. Those whose resume is a joke. Those with no checking account. Those who take pride in the only thing they have – their appearance, their mirror, and their camera phone. Jonah looked best from the elevated upper-left. If you don't know what that means, just consult any teen's

Facebook page. You'll see at least ten examples of the angle. Most of the time, their eyes will be gazing to one side, and they will be pursing their lips to the opposite side in a duckface, as if they are kissing an invisible ghost. I don't know how this caught on, but it is pervasive online and utterly vacuous.

Speaking of angles, Jonah's hair was a real-world Geometry lesson, zigzagging between the x, y, and z axes with abandon, depending on his mood. Salvador Dali would have been proud of him, as Jonah was the junior Picasso of hair sculpture, often changing colors while changing shapes in synchronicity.

Jonah applying Elmer's glue to his hair before a concert by one of his favorite little bands would bring to mind Rocky punching sides of beef, had you been privy to his pre-show preening and also seen the Sly Stallone movie to complete the reference. It was one of the only times he showed passion of any sort. The process was almost performance art, worthy of the Andy Warhol stamp of disapproval.

CHAPTER TWO

"Why can't white people who are pale as zombies remember to use sunscreen?!" Joe E. yelled at Jonah from around the corner of the back of the Wal-Mart, where his friend was attempting new skateboard moves. The echo from all the concrete amplified his exhortation to Zeusian levels. Jonah dumped from the board to the ground, looking around in confused bewilderment. He thought God was talking to him again.

This was not divine intervention, though. Devious little Joe E. had been spying on Jonah for fifteen minutes, waiting in repose for the perfect time to bomb his friend. He was tallying all the dirt he could dig on his best buddy during the process. At one point, Jonah had sung part of 'Oops, I Did It Again', which Joe E. would use most effectively at a later point in time.

Revealing himself from his hiding place around the corner, Joe E. strolled toward Jonah and said, "I knew you would be here. Why weren't you at school today? We had bacon bagels for lunch. They were terrible, as usual. If you don't believe me, taste this crap. I brought you one."

"Joe E., do you really think I want that piece o' dook?"

"You didn't have lunch, Jonah. Stop being so proud. Daddy Joe brought you food. Who's your daddy?"

"Give it to me. I hope it makes me sick!" He snarfed the food like a mongrel that has sniffed out some rotten bologna in a tipped-over trash can.

While Jonah ate, Joe E. attempted to perform an ollie on his friend's deck, very unsuccessfully. The result was painfully pitiful and vice versa, which caused Jonah to horse-laugh and blast a stray bacon bit out of his nose and onto his forearm. He quickly gurgitated the morsel, hoping Joe E. hadn't seen. He had – more fodder for more mocking. This was going to be a long summer for Jonah. His only friend was keeping a log of these types of things, which he referenced before bed each night to prepare humiliations for the following day.

"I saw that," Joe said as he locked eyes with poor, poor,

pitiful Jonah. They both started laughing. Joe E. put his arm around the other boy's neck and scobbed his knob. "Why weren't ya at school, kid?"

"I got into it with my little sister."

Joe E. shuddered. "Say no more." He had been brutally racked by Serah the last time he had visited Jonah's house, which had kept him away for the previous month. Joe recognized that it was her territory and was more than willing to concede it.

Joe looked with care at Jonah. "Dude, you are beet red. How long have you been out here?"

"Twenty minutes."

"Why didn't you put on sunscreen?"

"I always forget to buy it."

"Dude, you're in the back of a Wal-Mart!"

***

Remembering a grocery list is easy – you just have to figure out a way to recall the information in your time of need as you walk up and down the numbered aisles. It sounds much easier than it actually is. If it is vital to remember a list, mnemonics become necessary. Mnemonics are little shortcuts that help you recall vital facts like phone numbers, court dates, or 'buy toilet paper'. For example, you might say to yourself, "I'm gonna be Totally Pissed if I forget to buy TP." See – the Totally Pissed initials help you remember to buy a 48 roll pack of Charmin. That's a mnemonic.

You shouldn't need mnemonics for things that are easy to recall, like 'don't swim within one hour of eating', as stupid and unnecessary as that is to remember. I feel sorry for all those passengers on the Titanic who had just supped fine meals of escargot and T-bone tartare, and therefore, couldn't attempt to save themselves when the big boat went down. What a shame....

Fact is, Jonah was a teenager and needed mnemonics just to remember his own name, what with the changes his body and mind were undergoing. I'm talking about the Bermuda Triangle of Puberty – budding pubes, darkening armpits, and a medulla oblongata stretched tighter than a 5' x 9' Jackson Pollock canvas. It doesn't get any tighter, to explain the reference. Pollock was serious about his canvas and wanted it as tight as possible. He wouldn't be randomly slinging randomly selected colors on just any discarded old t-shirt stapled to a picture frame. His canvas had to be tight.

***

Jonah was in the midst of his 'blue period', like Picasso before him. The blue period for the average teenager is much different from the blue period famous artists go through – far less impressive. Jonah was sleepwalking through an Orwellian nightmare – his own little petting zoo version of 'Animal Farm'. To his left were rabid, leftist, Nazi miniature schnauzers, demanding to see multiple forms of identification – one with a signature, one with a photo at the time of birth, and one with a DNA swab. To his right were haughty ravens and vultures posing as teachers and principals, principally designed to give him grief and circle overhead, waiting for him to die a Pink Floydian tragic death, so they could rip apart and consume his carcass. Sweaty, drooling, pot-bellied pigs in blue uniforms of stretchy spandex swarmed around his legs, biting at his skateboard deck as he tried to escape their police tyranny.

On top of this, someone was endlessly texting him from 'Unknown Caller', 'U R Screwd'. How illegitimately prophetic in a knocked-up teenage girl sorta way. Pee on the pregnancy test tab – plus means minus and vice versa. I tutor on the weekends if you don't understand.

In the days of text messages, the 'Little, Brown Handbook' has been trampled underfoot. These grammatical infractions are extant, rending correct grammar extinct in real life – or 'moot' if you speak like Rick Springfield.

In addition to all these teenage problems, Jonah was on the fast track to becoming an unwilling pawn of the paranormal. He had always seen shadows in the corners of his eyes that weren't there when he reacted to them, but things were going to get real weird for him real quick this coming summer.

No TV camera crews raced to involve themselves in his situation, either – no imposing telescopic lenses of so-called 'reality' shows to document short, but intensely emotional, puzzle pieces of truly real human existence. Reality TV lives happen in succinct intervals, called 'Season 1' or 'Season 4', and last about two minutes in the big scheme of things, interrupted only by interventions and

black 15 dog

infomercials. Large egos, muscled arms on males, and huge mammary glands on the babes seem to be the only hiring requirements for these shallow cable networks. Oh wait, I forgot – reality show idiots must also have an addiction to unnecessary drama and violence.

No, I don't think VH1 and MTV are doing society any favors, as if you couldn't tell. In fact, I'll go on record as saying they are degrading our society to the point of MySpace MySpringer worthlessness. Any comments, Glenn Beck?

Mathematically, this can be summarized by my algebraic function, $f(x) = 40$-TV-internet, which defines the range of the y axis, which should always be positive in this equation. The value of $f(x)$ depends on the value of TV and internet, both measured in hours/wk. The measure of $f(x)$ must result in a positive number if we are to survive. If modern society becomes so consumed with vacuous attention whores that the value of TV and internet exceed 40, we are doomed. If I were to show you my other algebraic equation, which includes a variable for the cell phone, you might want to off yourself if you are over the age of thirty.

Please take advantage of the two cyanide gel-caps imbedded in the spine of this book and murder yourself, if you so desire. I don't want that, of course, but the option has been provided for you. (Disclaimer: The author of this book, herein to be referred to as 'Author' assumes no liability for the mass suicide of this book's readers, heretofore referred to as 'this book's readers'.)

***

Sometimes, the unwilling participant of a paranormal experience never even realizes the incident has occurred. The episode may be recovered through deep REM-state dreaming or hypnosis. Either way, the experience is almost always accompanied by a near-fatal state of depression, from which many do not exit alive. Don't even get me started on encounters with alien life forms and the probes they wield like Jedi Knights

The source of the paranormal event can vary – just as easily coming from inside the victim, purposefully, from the id or super-ego, or spontaneously, due to outside forces. As a quick example, I will offer the contrast of experience between fire-walking and sleep-

walking. One burns your feet, and one ends with you pissing in a potted plant. Both are unpleasant, which goes without saying.

Teenagers are especially vulnerable to paranormal and extraterrestrial episodes. They lack the intelligence to realize such incidents are a figment of their furtive imagination. In other words, Einstein never got probed – he was smarter than the Martian life forms that sneak into bedrooms at night. Aliens view humans like we view sheep. They'll sneak up behind some dumb-dumb, shear his hair, cut his balls off, brand him with an identification code, and throw him in a pen until the next time they visit. The average Joe Sheep is too stupid to write a book about living in an alien ant farm, so it goes undiscovered. It's a crying shame, but it keeps NASCAR in business.

In addition, narcissistic teenagers are the most susceptible to being contacted by ghosts and aliens. They exist in a haze of self-absorption and pay little attention to anything outside of high school musical movies and social network pages – they are prime targets. Self-absorbed teen girls become cheerleaders, and self-absorbed teenage guys play video games, make death lists, and wear black trench coats. I love it – 115 pound pseudo-masculine beings with no chest hair are ever so threatening as they pose for mock album covers, clutching Klingon swords with black vinyl studded gloves and an unfortunate mullet, face paint and all – weakness personified via their online profile pics. Don't get me started on the cheerleaders.

This book is not meant as a manifesto for the would-be school shooter or celebrity assassin. Holden Caulfield is long since fictionally deceased, and he and John Lennon will never be resurrected, ala Christ. Don't use this book to inspire the murder of classmates or prophets. In fact, I hope this book undermines any member of the Trenchcoat Mafia and his impotent combination of over-confidence and low self-esteem. I pray it serves as a deterrent to all those who aim to oppose authority with a rifle or revolver. To anyone intent on going out in a blaze of murderous glory: may a werewolf leap from your school locker and deliver a silver bullet to your trench face, you pathetic weakling. Come after me, instead. Make me immortal. Let your innocent classmates roam unfettered like the free range chickens they are. Try to assassinate me. I'm a man, you're a boy, enough said.

Having stated that, I will say I encourage and support conquering the bullies and the jaded teachers faced every day, but that is done with knowledge, not flaccid 2012 doomsday scenarios and semi-automatics. Take your wrath out on someone capable of defending themselves, like me or the ghost of Hunter S. Thompson. Go ahead and conquer the world online, but don't kill the fellow passengers in your real world life-boat, gamer. Life is real, and existence does not re-start like a petty episode of World of Warcraft. Boo to tha hoo, Elven warrior.

***

Mark my words, kids. High school will be over all too soon, and the real world will be breaking down your door, and I'm not talking about the MTV 'reality' show. Enjoy your life. Don't murder people or kill yourself. Don't count down the days until Christmas Break, until Spring Break, until Summer Break. That is unnatural and unhealthy and will turn you into a zombie searching for brains, which are few and far between these days.

In other words – don't worry, be happy. Let it flow and other surfer slogans. Listen to a favorite song every morning and feel good. Paint a clown smile on your face and enjoy your life, regardless of your circumstance. You only get one shot at this, unless you are a Hindu. (Your 209th life as a cockroach awaits you, Hindu pilgrim. Don't worry, though – number 210 brings you back as a porpoise with a purpose. You'll be solving crimes like Flipper!) Don't turn yourself from a happy-go-lucky tweener into a penitentiary prisoner, scratching marks on your wrist until your release for crimes committed against society, humanity, and an ex-girlfriend. Counting days down – wishing them away – is the true crime against humanity.

It's simple – don't steal any Snickers bars, don't plagiarize your English papers, and do relish in the life you have been given. Dogs love waking up every morning – why don't you? Don't wish away hours, no matter how bad your after school job is. One should not dread certain days of the week, hating Monday and loving Friday, only to cheat on Friday with a whore going by the name of

Saturday Night. Do that, and you'll end up cutting yourself like a low frequency tween-queen.

***

I've rambled on long enough. All I'm saying is, "Do what you want to do, just don't hurt other people." Almost makes me want to give up the 'death comes knocking' trade and start raising daffodils and driving a hybrid. On second thought – nah. Where's my scythe? I've got work to do. Gertrude – make me a Tom Collins for the road.

CHAPTER THREE

Alice Cooper and Led Zeppelin and Van Halen songs are the soundtrack for the dramatic vignettes of teenage joy and angst that accompany the final days of the school year and the magnificent and inevitable summer to come.

Alice Cooper in his prime was a very good songwriter, an engaging singer, and a marketing genius who wisely targeted those most vulnerable – angry and disaffected teenagers spending the allowances Mummy and Daddy bestowed upon them weekly, as long as the trash got taken out. Marilyn Manson attempted the same business plan and failed miserably and hilariously. Mr. Alice now spends his time perfecting his chip shot on Arizona golf courses, and Mrs. Manson is snorting Aleister Crowley's ashes off an Ozzy Osbourne CD and praying to remain relevant. Teachable moment – this is what happens when one attempts to profit off ideas not one's own. I'd be way more scared of a five-iron wielding Alice Cooper than a crappy Batman character rip-off who cuts himself when he loses a woman. Come up with your own character, kiddos. Be yourself. Be influenced, but do not plagiarize.

***

Back to the topic I introduced at the beginning of this chapter – beautiful girls and warm summer evenings. Teenagers, heed my words and rejoice in the voices of classic rock, which sing to you the songs you need to hear, but probably do not yet know. You can't find what I'm talking about in the music of new bands, so you will need to do research, mostly by reading books like this or hanging out with someone 'old' who knows who Jimmy Page is. God bless and may we revel in the Alice Coopers, Pink Floyds, and Van Halens of the world, for their words and melodies are manna from Heaven for the teenager passing through the metamorphic transformation from gangly, insecticide caterpillar into confident, well-rounded butterfly. Sing their songs together like the Nation of China, children – "School's out for summer! Hey teacher, leave them kids alone! I'm eighteen, and I like it! Wanna see my I.D., try to clip my wings – don't have to show you proof of anything!" You like that, right? Wait until you hear the songs those lines came from. They're gonna change your life.

It's worked for millions before you – just ask your uncle at the next family barbeque after he's had a six pack or two, and he'll tell you all about the songs and bands you need to know. Might even do a better job than me, but I doubt it.

* * *

Around the second week of June, school will have receded into the paneling. Then, it's summer nights and a radio, more than enough to provide the soundtrack to a million American Graffiti evenings for thousands upon thousands of angelic Spicoli's and their unholy apostles, all wreathed in halos of sweet-smelling smoke and munching out to a last supper of Chili Cheese Fritos and Pabst Blue Ribbon. Drink of the blood and eat of the body on a hot summer night, and turn the radio up, blasphemer – really loud.

* * *

Summer friends made over hot August days spent cleaning out garages and wrecking go-karts are what forty-year-old former Spicoli's like me love to recall while waiting for the charcoal to get hot. Staring at the glowing briquettes conjures distant memories of July 4th fireworks and flash pots at Iron Maiden and Judas Priest shows. That's what I remember, at least. I also remember Shelly Larsen jumping Suicide Hill in her Subaru Brat on July 5th at three in the morning and nosing it in the ultimate anti-climax, flipping six times and ejecting through the shards of a shattered windshield. I remember that hard. I also recall it never would have happened if her twenty-one-year-old cousin wouldn't have bought her a fifth of Southern Discomfort. Shelly was my girlfriend, in case that makes any difference to you. It sure as hell makes a difference to me. The reason I brought it up – sometimes bad things can happen during the summer, so be careful and wary of danger. Remember that. It's not all summer nights and a radio. It might just end up in a nose-dive wreck with a bunch of unconscious teenagers laying around a crumpled car, while a lame Creed song crackles through a couple of car speakers on life support. Excuse me while I walk around to the back of my trailer. I need a smoke.

* * *

black 21 dog

Summers and the beautiful evenings that accompany each day are when the best and truest friendships are made – in the dazed and confused years called 'high school'. You will never make a friend like that after the age of eighteen, not even in college. (Sorry to deflate your zeppelin, but it's true.) Experiences shared through the time of the epic struggle with puberty, fought in the front rows of heavy metal concerts and the backseats of hatchbacks, are the stuff of your life's legend. Sad to say, but those friends won't be talked to for many years after your mutual roads diverge. Fear not, though – the high road and the low road will converge someday, inevitably at a high school reunion or on some social networking internet site, and it will be almost like you never lost touch. You will be friends again, and it will be as if you never said goodbye all those years ago. Too bad John Lennon and Paul McCartney never got to become Facebook friends. They sang 'Two Of Us' and went their separate ways, to let it be and never to reunite or reconcile. They turned off the radio, got out of the Trans Am, slammed the doors, and their endless summer was over.

***

I'm long past those days of riding in the back of a pick-up going eighty miles per hour, throwing beer bottles at speed limit signs to elate in the explosion of a direct hit. Funny how many of those bottles bounced off the sign, rolled down the highway, and anchored in the ditch with a hundred other of their kind, just like me. We are all exactly the same, no matter how different we may seem on the surface. The missing link doesn't fall far from the tree, and it's time for this old orangutan to get off my soapbox, so you can read the story of two severely Caucasian, almost hairless, almost upright Homo sapiens named Jonah and Joe E. That's right – Joe E., pronounced Joey. Don't ask me why, ask his mother.

***

Jonah and Joe E. always had a good time together, as birds of a different feather often do, although they were undoubtedly an odd couple to be flocking together. Mr. Thompson's second period Chemistry class was the only common thing about the boys' high school experience – Joe E. was an honor student taking Calculus and AP History, and Jonah was in a Xanax coma, sleeping through his

black 22 dog

'education'. But, since their initial meeting in the courtyard before school on the first day of their junior year, they had kicked it together after class most days and on weekends. This was a blessing for each of them at this time in their lives. They needed each other. They weren't ready for interactions with girls – still way too awkward to be players in that game. They could barely enunciate simple statements to each other in the beginning, grunting like lowland gorillas for the first couple months.

Their initial meeting went as such:

Joe E. – "Where'd you get those checkerboard shoes, man?"

Jonah – "Dude. They're vintage Spicoli model Vans slip-ons." His statement was made with an incredulous air – as if everyone on earth should be privy to this information. "I found them on Ebay. They're original, not a reproduction. In fact, Spicoli wore these exact shoes during the filming of the movie – these exact shoes."

Joe E. felt immediately inferior to Jonah, at least as far as street smarts and knowledge of pop culture goes. Understandable, since Jonah had given Joe more than a hint of attitude with his answer – a little taste of the battery on his shoulder he dared strangers to knock off. Being teased mercilessly throughout junior high and high school and beaten up by his little sister on an almost daily basis had affected the boy.

People didn't understand Jonah. Although stereotyped as an emo, Jonah was more of a misunderstood and misplaced glam, preferring Ziggy Stardust-era David Bowie and Lou Reed to new bands, but nobody knew, since he didn't talk to anyone, and nobody went out of their way to talk to him. The words he had just exchanged with Joe E. were the longest conversation he had engaged in within the last two months. He had spent the previous summer isolated in his bedroom, playing video games, watching VCR tapes, and trying to avoid getting a tan.

Actually, Joe E. was the one feeling awkward during their first conversation – he rarely engaged anyone, either, being debilitatingly shy. Upon seeing Jonah's shoes, he had blurted out his admiration for them before he could stop himself. He thought they were checker boards at first. "Wow," he thought, "Portable sneaker

black 23 dog

checker boards. What'll they think of next?"

That makes Joe E. sound stupid, but he wasn't. He was very, very intelligent, but didn't have a lick of street smarts. After all, he had just moved to the big town, as a result of the unfortunate farming accidents which had claimed the lives of both his parents within days of each other. He was a 5th generation small town boy who could raise a barn or milk a goat, but had never been kissed or punched. He was a natural athlete when it came to primal sporting events like skipping rocks or knocking pecans out of a tree with a Nerf football, but he hadn't played organized sports, which was probably good for his mental metabolism and self-esteem. Jonah, in turn, wasn't one to be intimidated by Joe's scholarly record or athletic abilities – he didn't give a rat's you know what. Those were not things of concern to him. Jonah wasn't much concerned with anything, much to his private despair.

"Who's Spicoli?" Joe had asked with absolute innocence and earnestness.

"I'll show you after school," was Jonah's response. *God, what a rube,* he thought to himself snidely. "Meet me at the statue after seventh period if you're game."

The appointment was made and met, and the two boys spent the afternoon watching 'Fast Times at Ridgemont High' – Jonah's 112th viewing and Joe E.'s first. They had been constant companions ever since, thanks to Jonah's VHS player, his mother's collection of movies, and a thirteen inch portable TV – downloading pearls of cultural and sociological wisdom together through constant coming of age companionship.

I must emphasize that the internet could not be afforded by Jonah's mother and, thus, was of no influence. What was of strong influence, though, in addition to the VCR and TV, was a cruddy little CD player. They used the little battery-powered modern trapping as a secondary means to transcend their common loneliness, like refugees from a common nation. They hadn't hiked across an African border seeking sanctuary – this wasn't Darfur – but it was their life and it was important, for some possibly insignificant or possibly monumental reason, which remained to be seen.

These two boys had nothing in common, per se, except the

black 24 dog

sense of being alone in a crowd, although they weren't derelicts or outcasts for any reason other than being knees-knocking shy in a group. These feelings of inadequacy were always there, regardless of whether they were surrounded by over or under achievers. Neither of them was ugly, and thus, unfairly judged upon outward appearance, but they couldn't find their niche, regardless. Attending the second largest high school in the state can do that to a kid. Cliques of every description and affiliation, from National Honor Society to the Mexican Mafia, roamed the halls, and Joe and Jonah had an attraction to choice 'D' on the Scantron – none of the above.

They were crack-slippers – a pair of potentially great individuals sliding through the spider web fault lines in society's sidewalk, not realizing the decisions they made on a daily basis were laying the concrete foundation of their future. Step on a crack, hear your mother scream out in pain while clutching at her lower back. No prob, though – their mothers were so deceased or so anesthetized that they felt no pain – nada, nunca, nadie, nil.

Amazingly, a pair of size nine black and white checkered shoes had modified their world view and inspired the start of a story and a journey. The journey was theirs, but the story is ours. Maybe fate, destiny, and the Grim Reaper wear a size nine, too.

***

Contrary to most literary or cinematic stories of friendship, theirs was not an ultimate and instantaneous redemption song. They weren't initially enlightened to epiphany or overly infatuated with each other. They just, for some unknown reason, felt the need to be together and share their common experience. They both had trust issues. It started with baby steps but concentrated and distilled into almost constant companionship, although to best describe it would be to say they at first hung out alone together, if being alone and together at the same time makes any sense.

Although never verbalized, they were both timid and clutching at each other, in a friendly, non-gay way, of course. They had fears of abandonment hidden in the most remote pockets of their backpacks and tiptoed around each other like the spider and the fly for the first month of their budding friendship. Before they knew it, though, they were at the end of their junior year and were the best of friends. Two teenagers from opposite sides of the track had bonded on a deep and, typically obscured, cellular level. They were societal outsiders, like S.E. Hinton's Pony Boy and Soda Pop, but forged bonds between them that were unspoken, yet valid, and ended up deeper than most relationships married couples have by the culmination of their journey and the end of this story.

CHAPTER FOUR

Jonah lived and had grown up in a trailer house on the south side of town, and Joe lived with his Aunt Caroline, his deceased dad's sister, and her husband in an upper-middle class situation in the 'burbs, though the distance between the two boys' houses was a mere twelve blocks. Their adult caretakers were polar opposites, as well – Jonah's lone parental figure was a struggling single mom, and Joe E.'s were a couple of overpaid lawyers with nightly social engagements. Such are the disparate parental roles of families in the United States of America, and never the two shall meet, unless in a kangaroo court of custodial law – arbitrating demands and requests pertaining to the right to take the kid out to Chuck E. Cheese every other weekend. Sad, but in Mumbai they don't even have a Chuck E. Cheese, so let's keep things in perspective. We've got it good here in America.

Speaking of custody battles, after being charged with a minor marijuana possession and public indecency charge, Jonah's biological dad had abandoned him and his mother about ten years before this writing, and the two of them had lived a hardscrabble existence since. Jonah's father wanted nothing to do with custody of Jonah and the monetary needs of his wife and son. In fact, Jonah's parents battled over who would take custody of the poor boy, with neither wanting to win.

Eventually, Serah's carnie 'dad' came into the picture, but that's another story for another book. At least Jonah's mother didn't have to worry about the house being burglarized after the arrival of Serah and her father. The man was a loose cannon, hoping for and waiting to murder any minority who might try to enter their shack. He wasn't around for long either, though, so he requires no more attention in this story. I can't even remember his name. At least a permanent home for little Serah resulted from this 'man's' flight. It's hard to call thirty-something males like these 'men' without the use of quotation marks. Sad.

***

Jonah's mom walked to work each evening, to cover the night shift at a convenience store run by an expat Pakistani man who was caring, but also detached – understandable for a person who employed the unemployable. He was primarily concerned with his store's bottom line, rather than the multiple single mothers he had in his employ. He wasn't bad to work for, though – he even loaned Jonah's mother 750 bucks to buy a hooptie, to guarantee she showed up for her nightly duty at the convenience store. She had been harassed so many times walking to the shop after dark – he felt sorry for her and rewarded her loyalty. She wasn't loyal. She needed the money. But, she showed up on time and did her job and provided the best she could for Jonah and Serah. Thousands, if not millions, of women do the same for their children every day in America and should receive a medal for their tours of duty. Can I get an 'Amen'?

***

I've now presented these two boys and the opposite nature of their situations clearly enough. To put it simply, the origin of a mutual learning experience through friendship has occurred in a completely natural way, and it had nothing to do with status, caste, last name, possessions, or money. That's a rare and beautiful thing. Typically, opposite ends of our culture meet only in car crashes or penitentiaries, sometimes for good, usually for bad, but this meeting took place by blind chance and was all good. The moral is – one must be willing, at times, to embrace someone who may be, at least superficially, dissimilar to you. How else can one learn about other philosophies and opposing ways of life? Do you want to be the same person at forty as at sixteen? I think not. Opposites attract for a reason – it's social discourse amid cultural dichotomy. It probably has a name, but it would be too intellectualized and would embarrass me to use in the context of this story. Suffice to say, regardless of the name, Joe and Jonah were a great example of the concept. It's easily explained via simple examples – good meets evil, poor meets rich, skinny meets fat, ignorant meets intelligent, boy meets girl – and then something beautiful happens! Just like in a movie....

***

Opposites need to attract – it might be the truest axiom of life. Microcosmically, opposites wanting to hug each other is vital in the relationship between the nucleus and the electron. If the nucleus wasn't positively charged and the electron its negative equivalent,

black 28 dog

there would be no atom, and thus, no molecule, and thus, no us. Those are the basics on the subatomic and molecular level, but the attractions of the macrocosm are no less important. If our existence was not gifted gravity, the planet Earth would not be attracted to and revolve around our nuclear sun, and life on the third planet from the yellow star at the center of the Milky Way would not exist. As a consequence, rock-n-roll would not exist, which would be very, very bad.

Socially, the interaction of plus and minus human personalities is complex and difficult to understand. There is nothing worse than a bunch of people, all plus or all minus, thinking exactly alike in lock-step groupthink, not willing to accept outsiders and the valuable input they may bring. Pluses and minuses need to be thrown together, sometimes violently. Go to a punk show and play a round of 'spot the honor student'. Here's a cheat code – the honor students will be laying very low, occupying the shadows of the perimeter. Why are they afraid? They shouldn't be, but they usually are, and it's pretty easy to understand why – the honor students support the illiterate, whirling convention of floundering fathers gathered at the punk show, but are treated as outcasts, since they don't shove safety pins through their eyelids and snort Comet.

"Can't we all just get along?" I ask, to paraphrase someone, supposedly 'negative', who got beaten to a pulp by a bunch of supposed 'positives' on the side of a Los Angeles street. Like I said, interactions between plus and minus are often violent.

***

Jonah and Joe sensed all this but had no conscious awareness of such. Their need to support each other was buried deep in their psyches. They had gravitated toward one another like a moth to a bug-zapper, although in a far less fatal interaction. Much was hidden and not at all obvious – kind of like the backmasking on an old Led Zeppelin or Judas Priest record which has laid obscured for years by a thick layer of dust, like that on a freshly buried coffin. You can clean up the record, listen to the song, and think you understand its meaning, but when you act out the song's backward message, which you couldn't even consciously hear – you are a heavy metal zombie.

According to numerous lawsuits filed in the early eighties,

black 29 dog

backward messages on records *can* turn their listeners into automaton disciples of the Antichrist, bent on murdering their parents. The jury is still out on whether it's true, but I haven't seen any record-burnings lately.

Like the heavy metal zombies I speak of, the boys weren't experienced enough to motivate the things happening in their lives consciously – they were ingredients maneuvering through the agar of a giant, invisible Petri dish. Nothing was obviously stated, but everything was deeply implied on some sub-atomic, backmasked level – like a picture of a box of popcorn and a Coke at a 1960's-era matinee picture show that flashed for a millisecond and spawned a twenty-deep line at the concession counter.

Joe E. and Jonah were easily influenced. They were teenagers, after all, just like the others in line at the concession stand.

***

Jonah smoked weed regularly throughout these early experiences – a habit he had been obliged by over-exposure to the herb's effects, via second-hand smoke from his teenage mother and her acquaintances. Joe E. never judged him for it, though he never once partook. Joe never tried to stop Jonah from smoking around him, either. Denial may have been involved to a certain extent, as no brain could have resisted the contact high that came with their movie watching sessions in Jonah's bedroom, but there remains innocence in that, at least in the judicial sense. Joe chose to ignore Jonah's love affair with the weed, and Jonah ignored Joe's reticence to smoke it.

In ninety-nine percent of similar cases, such a profound difference in moral sensibilities would have resulted in an adversarial relationship or no relationship, at all. No doubt, their friendship would never have overcome such fundamental disparities in belief systems, but for the fact Joe was akin to some naïve apostle or saint. He was incapable of judging others, due to his own insecurities. One should know and believe in oneself to a fairly high degree if one is going to judge the actions of others, and Joe knew he wasn't up to doing that. Therefore, he was unwilling to be critical and cast Jonah as a societal pariah. He sensed that to condemn Jonah for his habit could never result in anything positive, only the loss of a potential, although unlikely, friend.

black 30 dog

Joe E. had wisely realized that almost every man on earth has some coping mechanism which could, in divine light, be viewed as an earthly crutch and a sinful violation of God's will. Joe E. had no such vice, it should be noted – he was too scared to indulge any intoxicant, although his attitude came more from fear than from any religious perspective or moral belief. The kid was confused and indoctrinated to the point of paralysis. Over time, he would question whether The Spiritual Being ruling our existence cared if someone smoked or drank a Guinness, as long as their actions brought nothing ill to bear on the innocent. Joe was, indeed, a wise young man.

***

Joe E. joined Jonah's world more than Jonah had joined his. Jonah grew up among the skateboard urchins that haunt alleys and loading docks behind abandoned supermarkets and decrepit dollar stores, smoking cigarettes by dumpsters and running at the sight of portly security cops. Joe E. had been home-schooled in a nurturing environment, yet was unfulfilled at the result, having been educated in the best modern interpretation of the phrase, but having remained socially inept, due to the isolated method of his instruction. He had been instilled or indoctrinated with an education meant to produce a future legislator or lobbyist, neither of which he was inclined to embrace or eventually perform. With education comes expectations, and he felt that pressure mightily. Show me a national merit scholar or 'most likely to succeed' recipient who hasn't won a Nobel prize by the age of forty, and I'll show you a human-shaped can of worms in need of major counseling.

***

Back to the present – the two boys had trudged through their junior year together, Joe E. tutoring Jonah in Algebra II and Chemistry, and Jonah assisting Joe in maneuvering through the machinations of modern life and complex social situations, as best one can within the modern high school context. Jonah showed Joe that even a famous surgeon can have lunch at a greasy Mexican food joint, catch hepatitis, turn jaundice yellow and croak, and Joe E. showed Jonah that having an education didn't mean one was mandated to become a condescending, professorial jerk.

This was not done in any formal manner. They infused one

black 31 dog

another with these human laws like some fancy chai tea concoction purchased at an expensive coffee house, meant to soften the cerebellum. Neither of them knew the lessons they taught each other would be vital to their survival, but this story would end here if that were the extent of their friendship. This book would be a 'novelita' you wouldn't want to read, rather than the 'novel' you hold in your hand.

The 'getting to know you, getting to know all about you' part of the boys' relationship has been established in the literary sense, so I will now proceed with the story of our two protagonists, two epic heroes in every aspect of the cliché. Though I recount their saga, I claim no responsibility or credit for their heroic actions. I am only one of the story's narrators.

The two boys and their quest are the important factors to focus on. Joe and Jonah probably saved mankind, although they did so in spite of their folly in handling decisions which should have been made by five-star generals or Kim-Jong-il. These two youths were participants, not victims, but their plight was as difficult as any pilot's on a doomed 747 ditching into the Hudson River, thanks to a fat, Central Park Canada goose in the wrong place at the right time. A better comparison might be to the passengers who fought evil on Flight 93 over the state of Pennsylvania on September 11, 2001. Like Jonah and Joe E., those people hadn't taken certification tests for their positions in the dramatic dynamic of that flight. They were true heroes – thrown into a situation for which they were unprepared. In desperation, they acted on instinct.

Check that – I'm wrong. Instinctual actions are done for the survival of the individual or to save the individual's offspring. The actions of the Flight 93 passengers were altruistic and selfless, the cornerstones of bravery – done to spare humanity further loss and done willfully by decision, at the cost of their own lives and the pain their families would endure. Those people sacrificed their existence and went down with the ship, to spare other innocent Americans. Let's observe a moment of silence in their honor....

***

Now... "LET'S ROLL!"

black 32 dog

CHAPTER FIVE

As the author has described so monolithically, these two teenagers became essential friends through their junior year. Jonah managed, with Joe E.'s help, to pass all his classes, and Joe E. was spared the humiliation of being elected Junior Class President, which could have happened, had he not been such a wallflower and confidant of fringer Jonah. (fringer, meaning on the fringe)

That sounds as if Jonah dragged Joe E. down to a lower level, but this was not the case. It is true his friendship with Jonah may have prevented Joe from attaining certain high school accomplishments, but that was what Joseph needed. He had sub-consciously sought Jonah, not the reverse. Joe E. was ill prepared for popularity or office-holding at this phase in his life – too green and unsure of himself. I could have said insecure, instead of unsure, but that would be inaccurate. Joe was discovering himself, taking one small step for his mankind every day. He wasn't a helpless snail. He was a boy learning how to be a man, but he didn't have anyone to guide him, so he needed to take it slow. He would be a leader of men some day, but not now.

At this stage in Joe's life, the intense scrutiny of being the focus of other people's attention would have doomed him to a life of Robinson Crusoe isolation and alcoholism – a shipwreck never to be salvaged. Jonah showed Joe that success was in the eye of the beholder, just like beauty, and one didn't have to graduate from Harvard Law School to be triumphant. Joe E. gave Jonah the validation he needed, as well, so it was a mutually beneficial, symbiotic relationship, like that of a hungry sea anemone and a starving clownfish.

Joe also taught Jonah not to be ashamed of your situation in life or where you come from, especially if you didn't cause your circumstances. Being born into poverty to a single mother doesn't mean one is destined to fail. And just because you check your mail at a trailer park correspondence cube doesn't mean your destiny has been predetermined to be an unwilling and, of course, shirtless star of an episode of 'Cops'. One must overcome before one can understand.

     One alone or two together – this was the choice these two boys were given the summer before their senior year of high school – a time that should have been theirs to savor and enjoy without such heavy decision making. They weren't mythical inhabitants of Eden, Utopia, Atlantis, or Xanadu. Nor did they dwell in Nirvana or Narnia. This was reality in the purist sense of the word amid the purest sins of the world. Tough choices lay ahead, and the decisions they made would become the ultimate climax or the dud firework of the year.

CHAPTER SIX

The last day of their junior year of high school came, which elated the two boys. Inwardly, they were aware they had completed their next to last year of public school and would soon be facing the hard truths that would accompany graduation. The head principal should give each kid a punch in the gut along with their diploma, like the drill sergeant from 'Full Metal Jacket'. That would best prepare the proud 'scholars' for what they'll face after graduating. It would be even more awesome to watch if the head principal was a woman.

Joe and Jonah were 365 short days from becoming another brick in the wall, both feeling more than a little anxious as they canoodled on their skateboards behind the Wal-Mart, where they once again went to be alone and talk. They could hear the names of that year's seniors being called over the public address system at the stadium, where the graduation ceremony was taking place three blocks away.

"Can you imagine how bad everyone is sweating over there?" Joe asked. "It's gotta be close to a hundred degrees. Why do they hold the damned thing outside? Everyone involved must be miserable."

"More like a funeral than a celebration," Jonah said. Joe stopped skating, realizing his friend had made a monumental observation.

"Wow. You can say that again, brother."

Joe pictured himself walking across the same stage among 1200 others and began to have an anxiety attack. "I feel sick," he said softly. He picked up his skateboard and threw it against the omnipresent dumpster that accompanied them like a smelly chaperone. The resulting 'kong' was loud, causing the people in the stands at the graduation to turn their heads in the direction of the sound.

"What's the matter, dude?" Jonah said as he picked up the resilient deck, unharmed.

"I don't need some piece of paper to tell me I'm a success. Big deal – a high school diploma. It's not an accomplishment, it's

black 35 dog

expected. It's only the first of a million other tests and certifications. We're never going to stop having to prove we're worthy of a job or a promotion or whatever. I don't even want to take the first step on that ladder. I should drop out and go off the grid – I'd be happier. Remember 'Mice and Men' from English class? We should travel around like that, Jonah. You'd be Lenny, of course."

Joe peered slyly at Jonah, wondering if his friend would catch the joke. They had read the book together for English 3, but Jonah rarely paid attention to things not on a video screen.

Jonah gave Joe a double middle-finger salute. "I may be a little slow, dumbass, but I don't pet dogs so hard I kill them!"

"I'm kidding," Joe said. "Just joking!"

"Yeah – Mr. Funnyman, as usual. You should drop out and become a comedian. 'What's the deal with this?' 'Did you ever notice that?' You'll be the next Chevy Belushi. 'Cheeseburger, cheeseburger.' 'Be the ball, Danny'."

"I'm sorry, dude," Joe said. "I'm just joking around, 'cause I don't know what the hell I want to do with my life, and I'm sure I won't have a better idea a year from tonight."

"It'll all work out, Joe E.," Jonah comforted. Jonah was the one who should have been worried, but he didn't have a care in the world. That's usually the way it goes, if you think about it.

Being a voluntarily enlisted Army soldier looked like the best option for Jonah, but he needed to toughen up before he'd be ready to wage war on a Muslim extremist.

Yes, it was becoming painfully true – their senior year was the home stretch of public school and the last they would spend together as day to day friends. At least Jonah *hoped* it would be his last year of school – some concern remained in the number of credits he had earned in math and science. But, odds were, like so many others, he would squeak by and graduate into the working world. Joe E. was destined to pursue an Ivy League post-graduate career, no matter how strong his reticence, so he was profoundly motivated to enjoy his last year of skateboarding and making straight A's without cracking a book.

"Let's go watch 'Fast Times' for old times' sake," suggested Jonah.

black 36 dog

"You're on, buddy," replied Joe E. They had viewed the movie on the first day of school, and they would do the same on the last.

As they screened the movie, Joe got deep, probably from his contact high. "This movie's about the loss of innocence. Those high school kids are making adult decisions, and they're not ready for it." He was slightly depressed by this recognition and let out a loud sigh.

"Well, we're *putting off* making adult decisions, exactly the opposite, so don't let it get to you," was Jonah's red-eyed reply. "Chillax, dude. We're gonna be fine. You're worrying about next year, when we should just enjoy our summer."

Joe took a deep breath, trying to still his anxiety. "Yeah, you're probably right. I'm feeling a ton of pressure already, though. I can't chillax."

"Just take a deep breath, dude – inhale. Phoebe Cates' boobs are coming up." Jonah was lucky – he didn't worry about his future. His idol was Jeff Spicoli, after all.

Joe transferred his attention from the dark-brown paneling to the little TV screen. "They *are* incredible," he said, breathing deeply the bedroom's tainted air. "Dude, I'm gonna buy you a big screen. That thirteen-incher doesn't do those puppies any justice. They look like mosquito bites."

"Wouldn't fit through the door," Jonah said without shifting his gaze from the TV.

"Oh. I guess you're right."

***

The following morning Joe showed up banging on Jonah's trailer door at eight, entirely too early for both Jonah and his mother. He had run the twelve blocks between their houses at a dead sprint and was panting like an over-worked Border Collie, rapping on the flimsy door with both hands, happy feet dancing below him.

Finally, movement was heard from inside. "What the hell do you want, Joe E.?" asked Jonah's blurry matriarch through the holes in the front door, her words dripping with irritation. "It's too early."

Joe's body moved spasmodically as he attempted to contain his excitement. He rushed up and down the three feeble wooden stairs at the door of the trailer like Richard Simmons on crack at a

black 37 dog

step class. "I've got to talk to Jonah. It's an emergency!" Joe whisper-screamed. He didn't want to wake Serah and face her morning wrath.

"Alright, you know where his room is," Jonah's mom replied. "I'm going back to Bill. I mean back to Bob. I mean back to bed."

"Yes, ma'am."

Joe E. reached through the largest hole in the door and unlocked the knob from the inside. He hustled to the rear of the long trailer, slipping silently past Serah's lair to Jonah's bedroom. He opened the door and launched his body onto the prone teen, who was sleeping the sleep of the arrestee in the drunk tank.

"Oh, my God! Help me! I'm broken!" Jonah exhumed.

"Dude, you're fine. Wake the eff up!!"

"Why are you doing this to me, Joe E.? It's summer vacation!"

"I'm leaving, and you're going with me."

"Where are we going? Are we running away?"

"We're going to my grandmother's house in Stringtown, Alabama. My grandfather just had a stroke, and they put him in an old folks' home. My aunt and uncle want me to help Granny transition to living on her own. Grandpa doesn't even recognize her."

"Sounds lame."

"What? God, you're a heartless jerk!"

"Whoa, I'm sorry. I meant living with your grandmother sounds lame. Sorry 'bout your grandfather."

"Thanks a lot, pal. I thought it would be an adventure. Be a little more open-minded for once, will ya? What the hell do you wanna stay here all summer for? Your sister is going to be a mini-Mussolini with all that free time. She'll make both our lives miserable. My Granny lives in a big old house by a forest. We could have fun. This is our last summer together, man! In fact, it's our only summer together. We didn't even know each other last year. And what's the best way to get to know somebody, young Jonah? A road trip. That's right." Joe took a deep breath to power his scream. "ROOAADD TRRRIIIIPPPPPPP!!!!"

Jonah put his hand over Joe's loud mouth. "Shut up, Joe! You're going to wake Serah!" He was as serious as a sergeant reprimanding a snoring private in a hot war zone. "You got a suitcase big enough for me to sleep in? Answer quietly, Joe, if you know what's good for you." He released his grip from Joe's cakehole.

"As scrawny as you are, I could carry you in my backpack," Joe whispered. "C'mon, Jonah. We've got a bus to catch. We'll leave your mom a note. She'll be glad to see you gone for a couple months."

"Screw you, Joe E.! My mom doesn't even have a cell phone for me to call her. She'll be worried about what I'm up to."

"That's definitely wishful thinking, Jonah. Mail her a letter."

The athletic one threw the pathetic one over his shoulder and carried him through the narrow doorway.

"Put me down you mastodon! If I'm gonna write my mom a letter, I have to write down the address to send it to."

"You don't even have your own address memorized? You'd forget your balls if they weren't attached to your crotch in that pathetic little sack," Joe E. cackled. "Pack something besides Cheetos, you albino, white-trash, emo punk!"

***

Two hours later, the boys were aboard a Greyhound bus thirty miles out of town, sharing ear buds and staring wide-eyed at the assembly of weirdos they traveled among. The derelict across the aisle from them was literally eating fried chicken bones from a KFC bucket, which looked like it had been salvaged from a dumpster.

Jonah removed his ear bud, motioning for Joe E. to do the same. "How far to Stringtown?" he whispered.

"A long way – couple more buses. Like twenty more hours or something."

"Grreeaaatt," Jonah said in his most patronizing tone. "Wonder who we'll see on the next one – Ted Bundy? Freddy Krueger? This is ridiculous! What the hell kinda name is Stringtown, anyway? They make tampons there, or what?"

"Nice, d-bag. They call it Stringtown because they used to lynch black people there – the name fit."

"Oh my God, they're gonna love me," Jonah offered.

"I'll watch out for you, as always. And you are far from being black, Jonah. Besides, we're just going to be lounging at my Granny's house, eating and playing video games all day. I don't plan on doing

black 39 dog

a lot of exploring in town. Neither of us has a license to drive, as you know. Maybe we'll hang out in the forest like a couple lumberjacks."

"I don't like the mental image of 'hanging in the forest' at the edge of Stringtown, if you get what I mean, Joe E. Let's just chill and stay outta trouble. I just got off probation."

Joe looked out the window at the shadows of the passing scenery. "Sounds like a plan. Maybe we can hold a séance in the old house and call up a ghost or two for you to compare tans with."

***

The courageous pair endured another twenty-eight hours of vagabond, Jack Kerouac 'On the Road' adventure, amid the cast of characters they mocked with nicknames, caricatures, and stereotypes, as most precocious teenagers will do. Wrinkleface, Sorethroat, and Chickenwang had long since arrived at their stops and disembarked the Greyhound, taking their various odors and sounds with them. The boys attempted hardened ridicule, but in the back of their minds, they realized they might end up like one of these road worriers if life took an unexpected left turn. In the middle ages, these people would be the norm – the commoners. In today's society, they were derelicts, worthy of scorn and derision. Everyone thinks they have to be a massive success in the modern social order, unless you happen to live outside the United States. In places like India, the Middle East, and Africa, expectations are, shall we say, a little lower – strictly survival. Americans without monetary wealth endure undue pressure to be a millionaire, when most of us are really natural slumdogs. And, the poorest of Americans would be considered wealthy in most parts of the world, like Rio de Janeiro or Mumbai. Why did they change the name of Bombay to Mumbai, anyway – an attempt to start over?

The trip was an eye-opener. The boys weren't dealing with high school cliques anymore. This was the real world, and they were growing up fast. "Just get us to Granny's house!" they were practically screaming by the last leg of their journey.

CHAPTER SEVEN

The tired bus driver shook the boys awake. They had reached the end of the line. The teens stepped off the bus in a fog and pulled their bags from the guts of the huge transport. They found the little bus station to be devoid of humanity, and the teenagers realized they had no means to reach Joe E.'s grandmother's house. All they had was a scribbled address written on the back of an electric bill envelope. They wandered back out the doors they had come in and saw no signs of life in the streets of the small town.

"What now?" asked Jonah.

Joe scanned the surroundings. "That looks like the center of town over there. Let's start walking."

The boys made their way from one working streetlight to the next, with multiple dark blocks between each. They saw no one, which they counted as both a blessing and a curse. Their minds raced like a lost dog's, wishing they had never dug under the backyard fence. Without warning, they were bathed in light. They leaped from the sidewalk into the shrubbery next to them like illegals spotted by Border Patrol floodlights.

The car slowly cruised by – a cop, stereotypically driving a Crown Victoria.

"Whew," Jonah said as the cruiser passed. "I hate cops."

Joe peered at the light array on the top of the vehicle as it crept by and read 'TAXI'. The car wasn't a Crown Vic after all. It was a Lincoln. And a Cadillac. And a Caprice. All at once. The car had more spare parts than Frankenstein.

"It's a cab, Jonah!"

The boys raced after the creeping Continental, yelling like shipwrecked residents of a Caribbean island attempting to flag down a passing freighter. The driver had his window down to take advantage of the cool night air, and the boys scared him. He thought he was being robbed, so he floored the gas pedal and roared off, sliding 'Starsky and Hutch'-style around the nearest corner.

"Dammit," Jonah said. "What now?"

"I'm sorry, Jonah. I didn't plan ahead on this one. I thought it would be easy to get to my Granny's house once we got to Stringtown. I didn't know we'd get here in the middle of the night. I guess we need to find a park bench and lay down until morning. When we wake up, we can figure out where we need to go."

As they stood on the sidewalk talking, history repeated itself. The cab driver had processed what had taken place and had come back around, hoping for a late night fare. He pulled up slowly behind the boys and aimed the spotlight he used to see addresses at them. This time, the boys froze like wilding weenie dogs in fear of a tranquilizer dart, unable to comprehend what was happening to them.

"Y'all needs a ride or what?" said a voice from the blinding light. Even a heathen like me has a hard time not comparing the scene to the burning bush.

***

It was well past the middle of the night when the cab carrying the boys pulled to the curb in front of Joe's grandmother's house, which sat on a property just outside Stringtown's city limits. The two teenagers gazed at each other in a combination of fear and confusion as they studied the fortress, which resembled a haunted house from an old Disney movie. As impressive and imposing as the hotel from 'The Shining', it stood alone on a property the size of a city block. A seven-foot high wrought iron fence, armed with deadly spikes, ringed the property.

Jonah wondered what the medieval barrier was meant to keep out, or keep in. The silence of the fog-drenched forest, which surrounded the property in the wretched darkness, was deafening. On top of all this, the moon was full. Clusters of clouds moved across its glowing silhouette, although no wind blew at ground level. If the boys had known anything about England's North Yorkshire Moors, they would have sworn they had been transported there. Suddenly, a lone wolfen howl ripped through the sound of silence like a Garfunkel gone mad.

"Who lives here, man, Vlad the Impaler?" asked Jonah in a loud, trembling voice. The old black cab driver glanced in the rear-view mirror at the two boys, terror flashing across his eyes. His toes dug into his worn Adidas sneakers, as if he was on the ledge of a thirteen-story building in a stiff wind.

black 42 dog

"Man, what you boys got me into? I needs to git!" He spoke with a deeply Southern accent that would have been endearing under different circumstances.

"What are you scared of, dude? You're only dropping us off! What do you know about this place?" exhorted Jonah. "Tell us what you know!"

"I know nothin'. I gots ta go! Get out my hooptie, please. The fare be ten dollars. Please tip generously, y'all. And y'all enjoy y'all's stay in Stringtown."

***

The boys reluctantly exited the cab and stood side by side in the street next to their bags, not knowing what to think or do. They procrastinated for two full minutes, standing on the old blacktop, staring at the house. Finally, they mustered the courage to make the single step up from the street onto the curb and paused again before going any further. The looming house seemed to speak to them – "Abandon Hope All Who Enter!"

"Joe E., why did we leave Rainbow Ridge? It was a good trailer park. I had a nice room for us to watch movies in. We could have taken down Serah if we worked together. What have you gotten us into?"

"C'mon, Jonah. It's nothing – just a big, old house," Joe E. said, mustering his resolve. "It's old, like an antique, that's all. We're on an adventure, and we're gonna have fun. We've just got to stick together, and we'll be fine. It's a learning experience. Everything will be better in the morning. The full moon is freaking you out."

"What was that howl?"

"Probably a coyote. Or a rogue Chihuahua."

"I hope so, Joe, but it didn't sound like either one of those to me. Can I count on you, man? We got to get each other's back. 'Cause I have a weird feeling about this, to quote Indiana Jones."

"Han Solo said that, Jonah, not Indiana Jones. Don't worry, though. We'll be okay, Short Round."

"I don't remember a Short Round in Star Wars. Was he the son of Boba Fett?" Jonah asked.

"Short Round was in 'Indiana Jones and the Temple of Doom'."

"What? We didn't watch that."

"We did, too! You were baked to the gills, Spicoli. You need to lay off the smoke."

"Oh. Okay. I guess so. His name was Short Round? That's weird."

"And Boba Fett isn't?"

***

The cab squealed away behind the boys in a fish-tailing rush, tires smoking, startling the boys. The driver had turned his car around and driven half a block down the road, pausing to watch Joe and Jonah before driving back into town. Although the cab driver didn't know them, he felt concern for their well-being. In fact, the delay before he left was the result of him saying a silent prayer for the two teenagers.

The boys glanced back at the taxi as it sped away, then turned to face one another, gulping dramatically. They took a mutual deep breath and turned their heads toward the house, exhaling simultaneously. They stood frozen on the curb, as if their feet were stuck in wet concrete. "We've got to do this," Joe said.

Joe took a baby step toward the gate. Jonah willed himself to match it after an extended pause. Joe took another step, and Jonah followed again. Joe took another step forward, but this time Jonah did not move. Joe looked back at his friend. Jonah smiled at him and snapped his fingers. "One-and-a-two-and-one-and-a-two," he counted, then did a zombie stanky leg jig up the walk like some kind of internet idiot.

"What the heck was that?" asked Joe, unable to keep from smiling.

"Texas Chainsaw: The Musical."

"You're a piece of work, Jonah. An unfinished piece of work – like Frankenstein's monster."

"I need brains," Jonah moaned.

"You said it, not me. I've got plenty of my own."

Joe laughed. The edge had been dulled. He followed his friend the rest of the way up the walk until he halted beside Jonah. They stood in front of an intimidating gate. The boys gazed upward at the house and then turned their bodies ninety degrees. They stared face to face, the antithesis of boxers attempting to intimidate each other with threatening stares. This was no title bout, and they weren't ready to go mano a mano until one cried, "No mas. No mas."

The boys felt like the exact opposite antonym to that type of behavior, but they couldn't admit it now. Unlike boxers staring each other down before a glove tap, Joe and Jonah were attempting to gain strength from one another. Joe reached out and moved aside the swoop of hair covering Jonah's eyes, as if to kiss him. He wasn't making a move on Jonah. They just needed to face the truth head-on in 3-D, eye to eye and mano a mano.

This spurred Jonah to break the silence. "Dude. That was gay."

"I know," Joe replied as he turned and reached toward the gate. "Why don't you get a haircut and have two eyes for a change?"

He tried to push the gate open, but it was rusted shut, another sign of their impending gloomy doom. Even the cosmos and the immutable laws of the universe were against our heroic duo! Iron seemed to oxidize faster in the humid alternate universe they had stepped non-vicariously into. 'WTF', they would have texted each other, but their cell phones both displayed 'NO SERVICE'.

To the right of the organically welded gate, Joe spotted a plastic intercom, which looked to have been purchased from 'The Beverly Hillbillies' estate sale. It had not withstood well the harsh heat and swampy atmosphere of dozens of Alabama summers, but still had buttons that looked like they could be pushed. Jonah glanced around hopefully, but Ellie May, Jethro, and Uncle Jed were nowhere to be found.

One button looked more important than the others, so Joe pushed it. A blue spark sizzled in a ring around it, as the dust that had collected over the years vaporized in an impotent, but unsettling, puff.

"Did it shock you?" Jonah asked.

"Yes and no. It surprised me, but it did not electrocute me. You think it worked?" The boys looked at each other and tried to remain strong. This trip was getting longer and stranger by the minute, and the Grateful Dead were nowhere to be found.

***

black 45 dog

Seconds passed, and the two grew more restless than scared. Finally, after repeated, frenzied depressions of the intercom button, an ancient female voice replied, "Yes?" It scared the bejeezus out of the boys, who were now balanced on their toenails like terrified felines.

"Grandma? It's me, Joe E."

"Excellent. We've been expecting you, son. I'll open the gate."

"Who's we?" thought Joe, although Jonah hadn't caught the conundrum. Granny was supposed to be alone and in need of care. Had they come all this way for nothing? Had she another caretaker? The walkway gate did not open, but the driveway gate creaked as it slid open from left to right. Joe was deep in terrified thought. Was this a cage they were walking into, to be tormented for eternity, or a sanctuary, where they could seek refuge from evil?

The boys walked across the grass and into the perimeter of the fortress, and the iron fence slammed shut violently behind them at three times the speed it had opened. Things were getting weirder by the second. The boys' attention shifted to the u-shaped, glistening cobblestone driveway they stood on and the dripping foliage and fog surrounding them.

"This shit is 'Fright Night'," said Jonah, startling Joe E.

"Everything's gonna be okay," Joe consoled. "*We're screwed*," he thought to himself as he uttered the words. The quarterback can never give up and can never show weakness, he reminded himself, although he had supreme doubts about the safety of their situation. He wasn't Joe Montana, after all. He was Joe Dirt.

They approached the giant, ornate wooden doors, which opened as they neared them. A corpse appeared in the expanding void with a gruesome, high-pitched, "Helloooo, boys!" The two teenagers almost jumped out of their jeans. Jonah did, in fact, leap out of his Spicoli slip-ons, but quickly sat down on his butt on the sidewalk to put them back on, after realizing what they had just encountered was just a little old lady, 'the Granny', not some Sam Raimi 'Evil Dead' character.

"Grandma, I'm Joe E. It's very nice to meet you."

Granny smiled warmly, opening her arms in a welcoming

black 46 dog

gesture. "I'm sorry we've never had the pleasure of meeting, son. I haven't left this house in twenty-odd years. I would have loved to have met you sooner, but your mother never brought you to visit me, as much as I begged. She said she was scared, but that was just an excuse, Joe E. I love you so much. You're going to be my knight in shining armor."

Granny was as sweet as Georgia peach cobbler. The boys lost their fear, excited to be on the good side of their perilous journey, home at last.

"Come in, boys. There's tuna fish sandwiches in the kitchen. I'm so glad to see the two of you. You've come to rescue me. How noble! I wish Grandpa Joseph was here." She dropped her head and looked as if she might start weeping.

"Grandpa Joseph is here in spirit, Granny," Joe consoled, cradling the miniature woman in his arms. "Don't have a stroke, Granny. Everything's going to be okay. Joe E. and Jonah are here. Everything's gonna be just fine."

"You're the spitting image of your uncle," the nonagenarian said as she regained composure and gazed needily into Joe's eyes. "You have to look after me. There are strange things afoot around here, and I can't face them on my own. Please take care of me. I'm old and alone. I can't defend myself."

"You can count on me, Granny. Me and Jonah, I mean." Joe turned toward his friend with an introductory sweep of his arm. "This is my best friend, Jonah. I don't think you knew he was coming, but, like I said, we're best friends, and we're partners in this vision quest." Jonah wondered what a little old lady needed to defend herself against, but smiled like a naive teenage girl at her first nude modeling gig.

"You'll need Jonah, you will," she said, sounding suspiciously like a Yoda. Joe's eyes glazed China-white as he contemplated relying on Jonah for the trio's mutual salvation – not a complete vote of confidence. He might rather have Serah if he was going into battle.

Jonah just smiled and tried to look pretty.

***

They entered the foyer, and Granny informed them their

black 47 dog

room was at the top of the stairs. She explained she was no longer physically able to make the trek to the second floor, but instructed the boys to sleep in Grandpa Joseph's study – a small room bordered on all sides with floor to ceiling, fully-stocked bookshelves.

"Fold-out cots are in the hall closet, along with blankets and pillows. I'm sorry – unless you want to carry me, I can't make it up the stairs," she said.

"That won't be necessary, Granny. We'll find our way," Joe E. reassured.

"I've moved into the guest room down here on the first floor," she replied. "I hear noises above me at night Joe E. – on the second floor. I'm scared of what's up there – and outside, too. Horrible sounds with no explanation. Take care of yourselves, boys, and don't forget to check on me. I can't escape by myself. I'm a helpless old lady. You're my savior, Joe E. – my Moses. I've been wandering this barren landscape for what seems like forty years. Lead me out of this desert."

Joe was bewildered by his grandmother's words. After the trip he had just taken and the circumstances he was now an integral part of, he was more than a little concerned. He kept a brave face until Granny and Jonah had both turned away. Then, he threw his head back, eyes wide, and silent-screamed at the ceiling, "God, help me get out of this alive!"

Granny excused herself to her bedroom, and Joe E. and Jonah rushed up the stairs and deposited their luggage in Grandpa Joseph's study, then bee-lined back down to the kitchen for the tuna fish sandwiches in the old fridge, which were excellent. Granny had been conscientious enough in her preparation to include both sweet and sour pickles in the tuna salad, which greatly pleased the boys. In addition, she had cut the sandwiches in quarters, which made them glide down easily, like sliders. She was a good Granny, and the boys were happy to have met her and greatly appreciated her delicious little sandwiches.

After they had devoured the contents of the oversized plate, they further explored the refrigerator and found it contained only the very dried-out partial carcass of a large salami, no doubt left long ago by Grandpa Joseph. They were famished from the long trip, like

black 48 dog

soldiers returning from the field, and had an almost insatiable appetite for all things protein and carbohydrate and sodium and sugar, but left the salami to its own devices.

"Let's check the pantry for more food," said Joe E. as he thrust open the heavy wooden door. The pantry was a large walk-in space, but it was too dark to see the contents. Joe stopped suddenly as he entered, feeling for the light switch, which caused Jonah to run into him, propelling Joe forward into the black hole. Just as Joe E.'s finger managed to find and flip the light switch to the 'on' position, his forehead met the hanging light bulb. It was like a comic strip character having an 'a-ha' moment – the light came on at the same instant his oily forehead clunked into it. The boys laughed at the coincidence, then eyed the mostly empty shelves – nothing but strands of garlic bulbs and some large jars of spicy German mustard.

"Well, at least we don't need to worry about vampires, I guess," said Jonah.

"Or do we?" asked Joe E. as he eyed the garlic bulbs with concern.

***

They made their way back to their room, which seemed to be an architect's afterthought. More than likely, it had been designed to be a Victorian sewing room but, since it had inadequate light, had been reassigned as some kind of isolation chamber, or more accurately, Grandpa Joseph's study. The room had no windows, and the total square footage did not exceed 80 square feet. They pushed the large antique desk into one corner to make room for their cots. The space was still cramped, in spite of this rearrangement.

"This house is huge," Jonah complained. "Surely, there are better rooms we could use as our sleeping quarters."

"Probably so," said Joe E. "But I think Granny put us in here for a reason." He inspected the walls around him, each of which was a built-in bookcase from floor to ceiling. One wall was gardening books. One wall was classic literature, and another was dedicated to all things Southern.

The last wall's books dealt with supernatural subjects and numbered in the hundreds. If Joe had known who Aleister Crowley, master student of the occult, was, he would have compared the two men's book collections, but Joe lacked the prior knowledge to make this connection, which was probably a good thing. He did think back to the garlic in the pantry and what Granny had said, though, and spoke authoritatively, "We may need to use the information in these books at some point. We may also need those links of garlic and that German mustard. Who knows?"

"Joe, what the hell did you get me into?" asked Jonah once again.

"I didn't get you into anything, bro. I'm going to nominate you to the 'Guinness Book of World Records' for 'person most sounding like a broken record'. We're in this together of our own Honda Accord, dude. Come on – be strong. All we have is each other, so don't make me do all the heavy lifting. I'm sure everything is gonna be fine. We'll buy some food tomorrow. Granny will give us some money."

CHAPTER EIGHT

The next morning, the boys awoke to the fresh, crisp, celery-green chlorophyll dawn that greets us all – be you a heroin addict, be you a teetotaler, be you a rabbi, be you a rabbit. Everything and everyone gets a fresh start each time El Sol rises over the horizon, and thank God, it comes every morning, whether we are deserving or not.

Mornings start small in nature, as long as no roosters are around. Butterflies warm their engines enough to flap wings and flutter into flight. Intricate, dew-covered, seemingly LSD-inspired spider webs sparkle in the first rays of the new rising sun. Little cold-blooded lizards get their batteries charged by the daylight as they prepare to forage for ants. The locusts start their beautiful music, taking over for the sleepy crickets that have chirped through the night. All these observations are even better without a throbbing hangover. Say the Serenity Prayer now, if you know what I'm talking about.

Vintage seniors, like Joe's grandmother, often wake not knowing where they are or what they did the previous evening. Alcoholics and the mentally ill often encounter the same situation. These unfortunate souls spend the first thirty minutes of their morning figuring out where they are and what they are now supposed to do. Who am I, where am I, where is my car, and where are my underwear, in other words. I hope you can't relate.

***

New starts and fresh mornings do wonders, each sunrise a second chance to get things right – probably the thousandth second chance, but who's counting? Were the previous twenty-four hours a tangled jumble of hodgepodge confusion and coincidence? With any luck, the next will be more enlightening.

The boys felt much better upon waking and were optimistic, having slept tranquilly in the eye of the supernatural storm. They had awoken feeling as if they had conquered demons merely by surviving their trip to this point, which was a big mistake – kind of like when George Bush gave a speech on a flight deck in front of a banner reading 'Mission Accomplished' a few years too early.

***

The boys ambled downstairs, having no sense of what time it was. They sank into the parlor couch and tried to figure out what to do next.

"We need to explore the grounds today, Jonah, and figure out what this place is all about," said Joe E., confident in the new day's light. "I bet there's some cool stuff to check out."

"We need to go to town and get some groceries first," Jonah replied. "Does your grandmother drive?"

"You know as much about her as I do, bro."

As if on cue, Granny emerged from her room. "Hello, boys, did you sleep well? I slept like a corpse," she said with a grackle cackle. "I'll soon be one."

"Granny, don't talk like that. You'll be dancing on me and Jonah's graves, the way you're going."

"Joe E., do you have any idea how ancient this little old lady is?"

"No, Granny."

"Let's just say I'm older than your mother and younger than the Grim Reaper. That old bastard has been trying to collar me for thirty years. I'm older than the dirt they'll throw on my coffin. You two can be pallbearers at my big kiss goodbye!" She was acting a little loopy – maybe from some medication she was taking. "Come into the kitchen with me, boys."

They followed her in, and she opened the oven door to pull a half-gallon of Heaven Hill vodka from the interior. Maybe it wasn't medication affecting her mood, after all. She reached in a cabinet and procured a giant glass. She clattered ice cubes into it from the refrigerator door's dispenser and proceeded to fill the vessel with the ethanol, emptying the big bottle in the process. She seemed to have forgotten the boys.

Her grandson spoke, startling the old woman. "Granny, we need to get some food. Can you give us some money to go to the store?"

"Of course, Joe E. Let me go to my purse, then you two can go to the variety store and purchase some provisions." She made her

black 52 dog

way back to her room and returned with a handful of bills, which she shoved into Joe's uncalloused hands, clutching them tightly as she did so. "Be strong, son, and make the right decisions." These strange warnings were starting to confound Joe.

The boy inspected the wad he held, dumbfounded. "Granny, this is Chinese money or something."

She looked down at the paper currency in his hands and said, "Oh no, that's Confederate money, sonny. I'm sorry. I withdrew from the wrong account." She took the bills back from him, left, and returned, this time handing him ten one-hundred dollar bills of modern money.

"You boys call that cab driver, Ophis, to pick you up. Go to town and buy whatever you need or want. Spend half on food to last the summer and have fun with the rest. I can't take it with me where I'm going."

Joe E. and Jonah glanced at each other, aghast.

"Are you sure, Granny?" asked Jonah. "That's a lot of money!"

"Consider it an advance payment on all you're going to do for me this summer. I've got lots of odd jobs and chores for you boys to do around the house. By the way, I like you, Jonah. I wish I could see your eyes through all that hair, though. Get yourself a nice haircut."

"Yes, Granny," replied Jonah as Joe E.'s eyes boggled. It was obvious the boy desperately needed a normal family dynamic. Joe had never seen him like this. Jonah's family was always screaming at each other.

***

The boys called the local taxi service, and the same driver who had delivered them the night before arrived about twenty minutes later.

"How you boys make out last night?" he axed. "Looks like y'all survived."

"We're fine. Why do you ask?" said Joe E. with stern confidence. "I think you know more about this place than you're letting on." He had realized he needed to be tough from here on out.

"People say da place be haunted," the cabbie said, averting

his eyes to avoid making eye contact with Joe. He felt guilty about how he had handled the previous night, abandoning the boys before they had made it inside. "Strange stuff done gone down up here on dis hill."

"Like what?" asked Jonah with previously unseen potency. It seemed as if the two boys had matured dramatically in just one night out of their comfort zones.

"Don't know much – happened over twenny years ago. Talk of demons and crazy clowns and stuff. Nothing happened up here lately, though, far as dis ol' man can tell."

"Is that all you know?" said Joe E. as he flashed a twenty.

"That's all I knows, boys, I promise. Jus' take care yo'selves. That's all the advice I can give y'all. And dat be da honest troof."

"Thanks," said Joe as he handed the driver the bill. "I think we're going to need you more after today, as we are not licensed to drive. Will you be available?"

"I'm the only cabbie in town, lil' brother. Keep tipping like dat, and I'll be yo personal chauffeur! I'll even drive tha hearsch at you boys' funeral." He quickly realized the joke he had made was inappropriate, given the circumstances. "Jus' kiddin', boys. Don't get me wrong. You gon' be fine as Beyonce."

Joe and Jonah looked at each other and smiled. This old black man was cool, Granny had lots of money, and the old Fleetwood they were riding in had air-conditioning and tinted windows. And, the sun was shining. They weren't scared. They were ready to rock. And shop. And then rock some more.

***

The boys spent the rest of the morning and most of the afternoon hopping from place to place with their driver, whose name they finally learned was Otis. They had called the old man 'Ophis' at least a dozen times, but he never once corrected them, until Jonah asked what kind of name Ophis was. When they grew hungry, they bought slabs of barbequed ribs at a soul food joint run by Otis' cousins, and the three of them ate on a concrete picnic table in a large park that had a river running through it. The boys were smiling so big, Otis told them they should buy some gold teeth with their money.

black 54 dog

The teenagers didn't speak while eating, as the ribs were Memphis-style, dry-rubbed manna from Heaven and were something they had never experienced, having not spent much time in the really deep, really dirty South – where the old black folks sit on wooden porches, and the old white folks sit in garages with the door open, both for some reason fascinated with the passers-by.

"My family been in dis town over a century," Otis told them. "The pit those ribs was cooked on ain't been cold in fitty years, no lie. You boys get in any trouble, you jus' call me, and I'll do my best to help. I ain't talkin' no law trouble, though. Mr. King, Jr. never walked through Stringtown. The law 'round here don't take kindly to black folks like us. I'm talkin' 'bout other types of trouble. They's been plenty 'round here. The spirits of killed slaves still shuffle the streets of Stringtown."

The boys laughed nervously. They had just become honorary members of the African-American population of Stringtown, and they were probably the two whitest kids around.

***

The trio spent the remainder of the afternoon buying a Unabomber-worthy hoard of groceries, along with a compact disc player, new earbuds, a used Playstation, and numerous games. They stopped at Radio Shack and bought walkie-talkies, so they could keep in touch at all times, in case any funny business went down. They even bought a walkie-talkie for Otis, so they could call him when they needed a cab ride or a rib delivery. After all, the boys' cell phones seemed to be of no use in this dead zone. They stopped at the package store, and Otis bought a couple half gallons of vodka for Granny, along with a carton of smokes. They returned to the house around six in the late afternoon or early evening, having had a fun day exploring their temporary hometown.

"You boys be real, real careful 'round here," Otis cautioned as he dropped them off. "And stay outta them woods. The ghosts of a hundred hanged slaves call that forest home. 'Member – you in Stringtown."

"Thanks," Joe E. replied. The sun was beginning to wither, and the day's fun seemed a trifle superficial after Otis' parting warning. Joe handed the old man another twenty and said, "Don't spend it all in one place."

The boys wrangled their bags and set them on the curb. Otis hit a button and rolled down his passenger window to speak to them before he left. "Y'all jus' calls me if you needs me," he said. "I'll be available. I bet I ain't had three fares a day lately. Damned recession." He laughed and began creeping away slowly. "You boys gon' be alright," he said through the car's window as he picked up speed. "I'll catch you lil' brothers on the flip-side. Peace out."

Joe smiled, then reached down and threaded his fingers through as many plastic bag handles as he could. "Let's get this stuff inside, Jonah, and hunker down for the night. I'm gonna kick your uncoordinated ass at Halo," he said without a care in the world or the Dirty South.

***

The dynamic duo spent the evening playing games and listening to old school Outkast through their still sanitary new earbuds. Otis had taken them to a cd-swap store run by one of his young cousins, who had recommended the boys purchase the album as part of their initiation to all things Southern.

The boys had no experience with rap, but they liked this thing called Outkast. They jumped around like wannabes, miming, "It's tha return of the gangsta, thanks ta ya old ass punk mutha-f***as. It's tha return." They listened to 'Da Art of Storytellin' and absorbed something new to them – and they were better for having done so. Their minds had officially been exfoliated and widely opened. Free your mind and your ass will follow, someone once said.

At one point, Jonah stood on his cot between songs and orated. "What are we here for, and what are we listening to? The promise is that we are on the path to enlightenment, and if you get the hump out your back, you'll see life in the form of a story rap. There's a fine line and we're on it. This Dirty South has a story to tell and that's liberation and baby I want it."

Jonah was very buzzed and was articulating one of the lost jive languages of Babel. Joe had never seen this side of his friend. Jonah had found something he related to more than the songs of the emo disaffected youth he typically championed.

"What the hell are you talking about?"

black 56 dog

"My genes are stained from the oil and the gasoline," Jonah said, still speaking in tongues. "From now on the only new music I will listen to will be Dirty Souf rap."

The Thunderbird fortified wine Otis had purchased for the boys had them supremely loopy, and they were having fun like the tipsy teenagers they were, although they would not feel at all well in the morning. The adjective 'fortified', when added to the noun 'wine', means the wine isn't strong enough, so it has had stronger alcohol added to make it more intoxicating. It was the first time Joe had drank alcohol, but he still murdered Jonah on Halo. They played on a little portable TV from the hall closet where they had found the cots. Granny slept through their obnoxious evening, oblivious to the second floor representing taking place above her – thanks, no doubt, to the anesthetic side effect of the fresh bottle of cheap vodka the boys had placed in the old oven.

***

The teenagers slept hard and woke late the next morning. Nothing unusual had happened during their second night, other than Joe E.'s explosive night biscuits, caused by excessive salami consumption. They were in a good mood, despite their massive headaches. They went downstairs and found Granny in the kitchen, making bacon, eggs, and toast. Her vodka glass sat on the counter next to the stove.

"Grab a plate boys," she said, smiling. "You need to eat a good breakfast. I've got lots of work for you today." The three ate heartily, and the boys were happy. The food and orange juice bandaged the boys' aching craniums, and Granny was in high spirits. The sun shone outside, and all was right in their world.

"First thing you need to do for me, boys," she said, "is work in the yard. Everything is overgrown, and I want you to start pruning back all the excessive growth, especially the kudzu. I'm going to wash these dishes and take a little nap."

"Yes, Granny," said Jonah. "Do you have any sunscreen? It's awful bright out there."

Joe E. was flabbergasted again.

***

Jonah and Joe E. worked hard all morning, focusing on the

black 57 dog

kudzu that flowed and growed over anything and everything in its path – up the power lines, over the wrought iron fence, over the little garden shed. They threw large chunks of the vine into the vacant lot next door and had made a pile the size of a mini-van by the time they got hungry for lunch. Having no means to tell time and not having worked outside long enough to have acquired the ability to estimate it, they had worked until almost two in the afternoon. They decided to let the pile of vines dry in the sun and burn it when convenient. The boys looked at each other with a satisfied smile and went in the house in search of sandwiches. Granny wasn't around, so they began preparing a lunch for themselves.

"No salami for you today, Joe E. My nose is still burning from last night," commanded Jonah.

In the middle of their lunch, Granny entered the kitchen, wearing different clothing than she had worn at breakfast. She had the omnipresent vodka glass in her hand, although it was now empty.

"Good morning, boys!" she exclaimed. She looked at them perplexedly. "Why are you boys eating sandwiches for breakfast? And why are you so sweaty? Have you been wrestling? Let me cook you some bacon and eggs. I've got a busy day planned for you."

She went to work, gathering the makings for a second hearty breakfast of the day. Apparently, she had taken her nap and woken up thinking it to be the next morning. No wonder she had lived so long. She lived two days in the time other people lived one.

After their second breakfast of the day, Granny gave the boys instructions for the work of their second workday of the day.

"Boys, today I want you to work on cleaning out the cellar. Nobody's been down there for going on thirty years. It's been locked shut for decades. I can't remember why."

Joe E. spoke. "Granny, we're tired from all the wrestling. Can we tackle that job tomorrow? We've got all summer to do chores. We need to have a little fun."

"Oh, you lazy boys need to play video games all day, huh? Well, alright," she said with a giggle. "Joe E., you remind me so much of your Uncle Ernie. He just loved the Pac-Man. I could never get him out of his room after I bought him that Akari."

"I didn't know I had an uncle, Granny."

black 58 dog

"Oh yes, you had an uncle, son – your mother's older brother. He was a good boy. I can't believe your mother never mentioned him to you. It seems as if she always tried to distance herself from the family," Granny sighed. "Your Uncle Ernie's room is next to Grandpa Joseph's study upstairs. I've kept it just as he left it. You two can go in and play the Pac-Man, but don't disturb anything. That room and a few pictures are all I have left of my precious son. And now my daughter, your mother, is gone too, Joe E.," she said with another sad exhale. "Will you boys at least wash these dishes for me? It's time for my nap. Have fun, you two, and stay out of trouble."

Granny filled her glass and trudged back to her room. She seemed very sad.

"Joe, your Granny is a crazy old alcoholic, but I like her," Jonah said in an awkward attempt to lighten the mood.

"Whatever gets her through the night," Joe E. replied. "She's old. She's paid her dues. She lost my uncle and my mom and now Grandpa Joseph. Maybe us being around will cheer her up. Let's do the best we can for her."

Joe began scrubbing dirty plates, then paused to gaze out the little kitchen window. He witnessed an idyllic scene, but also adventure and danger, and smiled. "I'm having fun, Jonah, are you?"

"I'm having a friggin' blast, Joe E.! I think I'm even growing a muscle after all that yard work. What's gonna happen next? Anything is possible."

"Who knows, brother? I bet it's gonna be something we remember for the rest of our lives! Do you miss Serah?"

"What do you think? Do you miss her?"

"Hell naw, my dirty Southern brother."

They both laughed the laugh only best friends can share, then set about cleaning and scrubbing until they had completed another task, feeling a rewarding sense of accomplishment as they put the dishes away.

***

The boys explored Ernie's old room with kid gloves, treating it as hallowed ground. Their initial wariness vanished, as the boys settled comfortably into the space vacated by another teenager decades ago. They felt at home for the first time since they had arrived.

They turned on Ernie's old television, and it worked. The old Atari 2600 was still attached, and the boys were happy to see that it was operational, as well. They reclined on the floor and smiled at each other.

Joe and Jonah played video games in their new little sanctuary for the rest of the day, relishing in vintage Donkey Kong, Asteroids, and Berzerk. They didn't bother to hook up the Playstation to Ernie's television. Having no clock and having lost the constant need to consult their dead zone cell phones, they played until late in the evening. Around midnight, they trekked to the pantry to find the stuff needed to make home-made nachos, which they ate in Ernie's little room while watching 'Caddyshack'. They loved Ernie's old bedroom, since it was comparable to Jonah's.

The movie had come from a collection of VCR tapes shelved along one wall, alphabetically organized. Ernie seemed to have preferred comedies. As always, Jonah chose the movie, selecting one he had viewed years ago with his mother, as he so often did. During 'Caddyshack', Jonah repeatedly punched Joe E. in the arm, yelling out, "I got alla dat one!"

Finally, Joe had enough. "I'm gonna find a golf club and tee off on you, buddy! I got all dat one," he aped. "That new muscle of yours is gonna get you in trouble, if you don't watch out!"

Joe was laughing, but Jonah picking on *him* was the wrong way around, and he wasn't used to it. "Hey, tough guy," he said. "Take on your sister if you think you're a badass, not me!"

"I'm going to take care of Serah when we get back, just you wait and see," Jonah answered.

"Sure, dude. I'm not holding my breath on 'dat one'."

***

After the nacho feast, they returned to Grandpa Joseph's library to bunk down for the night. Joe E. stayed up another hour, reading from one of his grandfather's books, while Jonah put his Volcom cap over his eyes and went swiftly to sleep.

CHAPTER NINE

The boys had breakfast with Granny the next morning, then set out to start work on the cellar, which was in the yard outside, not attached to the house. It was a cellar, after all, not a basement. It had a door that lifted up and open from its resting position flat on the ground – like opening a coffin buried up to its lid. Many cellars have concrete counter weights to help lift the heavy door, but Granny's did not.

Originally, the cellar had been multifunctional, used for both storing food and taking shelter during storms, but it had been locked and abandoned many years ago. Now it was grown over, hidden from view and forgotten.

The boys searched the yard until they found the door Granny had described, then cleared the kudzu and dirt away. After doing so, they saw a hole had been dug next to the door and filled with concrete, into which an upside-down iron 'u' had been anchored. Both ends of a short chain were permanently harbored in the u-bolt. The chain threaded through the cellar door's handle, shutting it indefinitely. Someone, long ago, wanted this door to be permanently closed.

The job was ugly, done in haste. Although rusted, the chain, the door handle, and the u-shaped anchor bolt still had enough strength to prevent the boys from opening the door. They searched the garden shed for bolt cutters or a hacksaw but found neither. They knew Granny was napping and didn't want to disturb her. They needed to get the door open, though, so they could explore the cellar. They were very curious about what they might find. Maybe the cellar was locked to guard some kind of treasure.

"Should we call Otis?" asked Jonah.

"I guess," Joe replied while wiping his brow and perusing the surroundings. He glanced at the decrepit house across the street from their compound. "Hold on. Let's go over to that house and ask if they have any tools we can borrow."

The boys walked across the road in the blaring sunlight and knocked on the door. No answer came for some time, so they began walking back down the little sidewalk to the street.

A cranky old masculine voice came belting through the door. Although almost to the street, the boys heard it clearly.

"Wadda you punks want?!?!"

They turned to see an old man's pinched face peering at them from the window next to the front door. They strode back up the walk to the little house.

"Sir," Joe E. spoke through the door. "We were wondering if you might have a pair of bolt cutters we could borrow. We're helping my grandmother across the street."

"You need bolt cutters to help her cross the street?"

"No, we're helping my grandmother *across* the street."

"You punks tryin' to break in and steal something?"

"No, sir, of course not. We're trying to open the cellar. We need to clean it."

The door opened and another ancient corpse-to-be stood before them, all of five feet tall and sickeningly thin. He wore a stained light green and yellow plaid shirt and old charcoal gray slacks, pulled up way too high.

"Why aren't you two in school?!" he screamed at them, jabbing a crooked index finger in each of their faces repeatedly.

"Sir, it's summer," Joe said with much frustration.

"Oughta have year-round school, dammit! Come with me to the shed. You two better be on the up and up."

Jonah and Joe strolled across the yard to the tiny building on the side of the house.

"What the hell are you doing?!" the old man railed. "Get offa my lawn! Use the sidewalk for hell's sake!"

The boys leaped back to the concrete like startled housecats and followed the oldster on the narrow sidewalk leading to his driveway and then to his tool shed. The three entered the sturdy little building, which seemed to hold every non-power tool ever fabricated. Mr. Cranky handed them a pair of bolt cutters with two and a half foot long handles. Bolt cutters use leverage, one of the six simple machines of the ancients, to magnify power input enough to cleave steel. That's why the handles were so long – to increase leverage and amplify power. Jonah could barely lift the unruly contraption, so he handed it to Joe E., who threw the tool over one of his strong shoulders like a lumberjack toting an ax.

"Leave the cutters on my porch when you're done with 'em. AND STAY OFF MY LAWN!!!" the old man crowed like a cantankerous rooster.

"Yes, sir," they replied. "Thank you, sir."

They were a little shaken by the interaction with Granny's neighbor, but everything they went through on this adventure seemed to be steeling them for some impending adversity – one that would come camouflaged by a rolling fog – a shroud of vapor which would conceal their adversaries. Events like this were essential in the maturation of these two young men – more than they could ever know.

***

"Man, Joe, everything that happens is so weird. This isn't anything like school."

"This is the real world, Jonah."

They alternated attempts at breaking the chain. One struggled, then the other, over and over again, until they decided to work together. This was another lesson learned – they would need to always work together to achieve their goals.

They each grabbed an arm of the tool and pushed at the other with all their power. They tried time and time again, invariably twisting against each others' force and spinning to the ground. They weren't going to give up, though. This wasn't the old Joe, and this wasn't the old Jonah.

Finally, Joe E. screamed a guttural yell to the heavens, having reached the limits of his composure.

"Yaaaahhhh!!! Give me those friggin' bolt cutters, Jonah!"

Joe took the tool in his hands and sized up one of the two links of chain attached to the anchor bolt. He breathed deep and found the patience to locate the perfect placement of the jaws on the steel, despite the shaking of his hands from over-exertion and low blood sugar. He brought the handles together in front of his chest with as much force as he could, like a strongman trying to bend an iron bar. He screamed at the top of his lungs, his body convulsing with the effort.

He failed but did not give up, deciding to change strategy. He

black 63 dog

turned his body to the bolt cutters, so both his hands were on one handle and the other handle was braced against his chest. Jonah watched in awe. Joe E.'s shoulder muscles were about to rip through his t-shirt like an Incredible Hulk. He pulled the two handles together against his body for interminable seconds, shaking and screaming, until the bolt cutter's two teeth came together with an uneventful clunk. The chain had been cut, and Joe laid on his back on the grass, panting like he had just run a marathon.

"Did I do it, Jonah?" he asked with eyes closed.

"We did it," Jonah said. He fell on his back next to his friend, his tiny lungs heaving sympathetically. "We did it, Joe E."

The two boys laid on the grass in the sun for some time. Their friendship was growing faster than the kudzu threatening to crawl over their bodies if they didn't get up soon. They both fell asleep in the hot sun until Joe E. woke an hour later.

He shook Jonah awake. "Let's take these bolt cutters back to the old man and grab some lunch. I feel like we've done a day's work already."

"I feel like we did two days' work," Jonah replied, rubbing his eyes. "We're going to look like Arnold Schwarzenegger by the end of the summer."

"One of us may. I can't speculate as to which one," Joe said with a hint of sarcasm.

They went inside after depositing the bolt cutters on the neighbor's porch very quietly. The oppressive heat gave them second thoughts about working any more. Jonah suggested they had done enough. It was three in the afternoon, so Joe agreed, and they called Otis for a delivery of mesquite-smoked chicken quarters, along with homemade slaw and green beans seasoned with garlic and bacon. The decided to eat on the screened-in back porch of the house, which would protect them from mosquitoes but still allow the breeze and the smell of the flora and fauna. Hard work made the boys appreciate their meals of late, and they looked forward to the next day's chore – they would clean out the cellar, starting as early as possible.

Otis was happy to see the two teenagers again as he arrived. He was becoming attached to his new pals and vice-versa. The boys were sitting on the curb as he pulled up.

black 64 dog

"Brought you some of Aunt Esther's homemade peach cobbler for dessert, boys. Best in the county," he said as he rolled down the window. The sun caught his gold front tooth with a bling. "Y'all deserve a good meal. I can't eat with y'all, though I wisht I could. I got's to take sister to her doctor 'pointment. I gots da only car in da family. You boys have a good supper and call me next time ya gets hongry! Keep the fire in ya bellies lit. Jonah, you gettin' a suntan in this Southern sunlight. I may mistake you for one of my relatives if you stick around here." Jonah blushed Raggedy Ann red.

Otis pushed a button, still in his driver's seat, and the trunk popped open, allowing the heavenly aroma of the picnic to escape. The boys walked to the rear of the vehicle to retrieve the boxes and bags of food.

"Got yo Granny some smokes and drank, too," Otis said, craning his neck out his window, looking back.

"Thanks Otis, you're a real lifesaver," Joe E. said as he walked forward and leaned into the open driver's window to pay the old man.

"Me thinks you be the lifesaver, young Joe. Thanks for tha tip. 'Preciate it! See ya next time, boys."

***

The appreciative teens ate, then went for a walk. They trekked the perimeter of Granny's compound, inspecting the fence to ensure it had no Achilles weakness. With the exception of one back corner, where four of the bars had been bent, the fence stood intact and strong, despite the surface oxidation of the iron to become iron oxide, i.e., rust.

They walkie-talkied Otis and told him the meal was delicious and that they needed a bit of welding done. Otis assured them he could do it and would be there the next morning. The boys hadn't been carrying the walkie-talkies much, but now realized their importance and resolved to carry them at all times. The units had clips on them, which the boys attached to their belts from then on.

Jonah played video games that evening, and Joe E. read from his grandfather's collection of books. They were relaxed and feeling warm and fuzzy, like they were staying in some grand hotel, having all their needs met like a lucky celebutante. They slept great and,

black 65 dog

upon waking, went down to scrounge up a breakfast or have one cooked for them by good ol' Granny, as per routine.

Granny wasn't around – it was before seven in the morning. The boys were losing their by-the-clock routines, starting to operate solely on their synchronized biorhythms. Joe grabbed a forty-year-old coffee cup from the cupboard and filled it with cold well water from the faucet. He gazed out at the rising sun and felt like a man for the first time. He looked over at Jonah, who was wearing an old frilly apron, scrambling eggs, and laughed.

"Jonah, we have work to do."

"I know. We'll get started right after breakfast. We can't work on empty stomachs. You need to eat Joe, eat!" Jonah said, imitating an Italian mother.

"I'm not talking about chores, friend. All these tips and warnings are adding up and telling me we have some big tasks in front of us. Not just physical ones – supernatural, too, maybe paranormal. I'm learning a lot from my grandpa's books. I hope it helps."

"I know, Joe. I've got the same feeling. We have to be strong, brother."

"Are you up to it?"

"That's a stupid question. The real question is are *you* up to the job, Joe. E.? I'm a rock. This morning I am born again. My head feels unlimited, my soul is the sky."

"Did you call Otis for inspiration, or what?"

"I gots da blues, Joe E. – dem ol' cozmic blues, and I knows whats I gots ta do today."

"What are you talking about?"

"I have no idea."

***

Otis arrived an hour later with an awkward trailer hitched to his Caddy, which carried an old welding outfit.

"Hello, boys. Heard from a lil' ol' ghetto bird last night y'all needs a patch job." He grabbed Jonah's leg, causing the boy to giggle uncontrollably. "Where the hole at?"

"My leg's fine, Otis," Jonah shrieked in a girlish voice. "We need a fence fix."

Otis smiled his combination gold tooth/gap tooth smile. "Where da problem ats?" he axed more seriously.

The trio walked around to the corner farthest from the house to assess the job.

"Boys, did your Granny tell you what caused this?" Otis said after studying the twisted metal. "Somethin' done stretched these bars out like a Goliath that wanted outta the penitentiary. What on earth coulda did this?"

"You got me, Otis," replied Joe. "I can't imagine anyone or anything strong enough to bend those iron bars."

"Musta been an overgrowed armadilla on the warpath," Otis said, attempting to make a joke, although he was deeply concerned.

"Are overgrowed armadillas the size of a human?" Jonah asked while stepping through the mangled bars.

"Jonah, boy. You ain't never been outta the city has you?"

Jonah looked at Otis. He didn't need to answer.

"It weren't no armadilla, son. I don't wanna know what caused this. Let's just fix it and hope the thing don't come 'round 'gin." The old black man's hands shook. "Lord help us all," he mumbled to himself. The little hairs on the back of Joe E.'s neck tingled electric. He sensed the fear in Otis.

***

They replaced the original hexagonal wrought-iron bars with generic rebar, since the damage was in an unseen back corner of the lot. The result was like a scar on the face of a pretty girl, but it got the job done. When they had completed the task and Otis had gone, the boys went to the cellar door they had cleared kudzu from the day before. They found it wide open, its top laying flat on the grass. They noticed a hole the size of a silver dollar by the handle, which hadn't been there before.

"What the hell?" said Joe E..

"Who opened it?" Jonah asked.

"I have no idea," Joe answered. "Look at that hole by the handle. Why is that there? That wasn't there before."

"What are you thinking?" Jonah asked. "Is that a bullet hole? Did something shoot its way out?"

"It's too big for a bullet, but I think something was in the cellar – something waiting for the chance to escape when we unlocked it," Joe shuddered. "Oh. My. God."

"Nothing could have lived in there for all those years."

"That's exactly what I was thinking, Jonah."

"It would have to be something from another dimension."

"That's exactly what I'm worried about, Jonah."

They ventured into the black void of the cellar until the rays of sunlight no longer supported their resolve. They were both shaking in fear, searching for an excuse to abort the exploratory mission.

"We need flashlights. Call Otis," Joe spoke. "Let's get top-side."

"The walkie-talkie is already in my hand," Jonah replied as they back-tracked up the stairs. "Otis, come in Otis." His voice trembled. "This be your homeboy, Jonah. We need flashlights and batteries, brother. Come in...."

"Let me take Ethel home, and I'm there, lil' bro. Give me an hour," came the reply.

The boys sat on the grass while they waited for Otis to return.

"Let's close the damn door so we can relax," Jonah said.

"I'll go one better." Joe walked to the garden shed and came back with a piece of left over rebar from the fence repair. He put one end through the door's handle and the other through the U-shaped anchor, bracing the door shut.

"That oughta keep anything that's in there in there. We don't just need flashlights, we need weapons, Jonah. Let's check out the garden tools."

They raided the shed's numerous cabinets and drawers, searching for things that could draw blood. Joe E. ended up choosing a little hand rake with four sharp tines he could use like 'The Wolverine' to furrow flesh. Jonah chose a small pitchfork, but he was too weak to use it with one hand effectively while holding a flashlight. It was something he could place between himself and danger, though, so it would suffice.

Finally, Otis arrived with flashlights, still in the package, and dozens of batteries.

black 68 dog

"Sorry, boys, but I gots to run like a son of a gun. I gots half my family to deliver to various locales. Good luck with whatever you tryin' to do."

"Thanks, Otis," the boys said in unison.

They returned to the cellar. Jonah removed the piece of rebar and prepared to pull the door open with a rope they had tied to the handle. Joe was at the ready for anything that might erupt from the darkness.

"Ready, Joe E.?"

"Ready, Jonah." Joe swiped the air with the little rake a few times. "Bring it on!" he shouted.

Jonah pulled the door open slowly. No tentacles or zombies emerged from below. They both sighed loudly with relief.

Flashlights and weapons in hand, they entered the tomb of the unknown, shoulder to shoulder, stepping down the creaky wooden steps side by side. Their flashlight beams waved wildly back and forth as they attempted to spot any danger.

They reached the bottom of the stairs and stood back to back, circling slowly. The room was puny – maybe ten feet by ten feet. They inspected under the stairs and were terrified by what they saw – a tunnel through the concrete wall and on into the dirt, big enough to accommodate a horse or large demon. It looked to have been roughly channeled through the foot-thick wall and black clay by hand.

The boys walked to the edge of the portal and attempted to see into it without actually putting their heads into the passageway. The light from their battery-powered torches was too weak to penetrate the darkness and was suffocated, rendered impotent.

"What do we do?" asked Jonah.

"What we don't do is go in there with these flashlights. If we lost each other anything could happen. Let's get the hell out of here and think this through."

The boys hurriedly tiptoed out of the cellar, fearing too much noise might awaken something that should definitely remain asleep. They closed the door and put the piece of rebar back in place. After what they had seen done to the fence, they both wondered if the iron bar would keep the door shut if it was assaulted from below by an unknown force. They went in the house to the kitchen to get something to drink. They were mentally exhausted.

"Good morning, you two!"

It was Granny, emerging from her latest day or night. They both jumped at her voice.

"My goodness, you boys are white as a sheet," she said. "Go sit in the parlor while I make you some breakfast."

The boys went to the other room and sat on the antique couch, which was magnificent to behold but terribly uncomfortable. Joe looked around the parlor for the first time and saw something he never would have expected.

"Look, Jonah," he said, pointing to a spot on the wall.

"What is it?"

"It's a cannonball, dude. Got to be from the Civil War. Holy crap – that is so cool!"

The wall did, in fact, contain a fist-sized cannonball souvenir from 'The War of Northern Aggression', as The South prefers to refer to it. The ball had been shot by troops under the guidance of Major General James H. Wilson, Union commander, and had been left in the plaster wall as a reminder of the deadliest war our nation has waged.

Joe walked across the room and turned on the little TV, which rested on an old sewing table, rabbit ears extending upward. He turned the channel changing knob, which loudly clicked to announce each new frequency. He saw nothing but snow until a weak signal appeared on channel six. Joe returned to the couch. The local news was in the middle of its broadcast.

"That's right – a unicorn," stated the talking head on the tiny screen. "There are numerous reports this morning of a white unicorn being spotted on the outskirts of town." The smug reporter smirked.

"That's a good one, Jerry," his female counterpart spoke. "I think someone may be playing a little joke on us with a horse, a fake horn, and some SuperGlue."

"You may be right, Janis. These Halloween pranks get started earlier every year. In other news – the goat murders continue. Farmer Ted Hemple lost twenty last night, which was, once again, a full moon. Due to the graphic nature of the slaughter, we are unable to show footage of the crime scene."

black 70 dog

"Horrifying," Janis replied. "And in other news, look at this cuddly little kitten and her ball of yarn."

"Too cute," said the anchorman. "If I wasn't allergic, I'd have a dozen of 'em."

The boys looked at each other. They thought about the hole in the cellar door and the unicorn sighting and started laughing uncontrollably.

"What are you loonies giggling about?" Granny said as she entered the parlor. "You two go through more mood swings than a menopausal old lady. Now go eat your breakfast and clean up the dishes for me. It's time for my nap." She had the vodka glass in her hand as she walked to her room. "Have a good day and let me know when you're ready for your next project. You two are so funny. I just love having you for company," she said as she opened her bedroom door. "You two are scrumptious!"

Joe and Jonah looked at each other after the door shut.

"Could this get any weirder, Joe?"

"God, I hope so," Joe replied with a hearty laugh. "Let's eat and check the forest for unicorns."

CHAPTER TEN

The boys' walkie-talkies crackled to life with a porcupine bristle of static. "Jonah, come in Jonah. This be Otis. Over."

"That was quick," said Joe. Jonah had paged Otis only seconds before. The boys were walking through the field behind the house on their way to the forest. The grass was tall and somewhat annoying to maneuver through, but a path was being forged. The dew from the humid morning soaked their ankle socks and Vans.

"Ten-four Otis, this be Jonah." Joe was beginning to feel a little left out. These two seemed bonded by blood – he felt like a chaperone on a prom date.

"Whaddup? Whatcha need?" Otis axed with a hint of alarm.

"We need stronger flashlights. Put them on Granny's account at the hardware store. Get four of the strongest they've got. We don't need them until tomorrow, so how 'bout you bring us some ribs about lunch time along with the lights?"

"How's Granny set for vodka and smokes?"

"I'd say she's got plenty," Jonah said. "But you better bring some more!"

"See y'all about noon tomorrow, then. Take care y'allselves in the meantime."

"Ten-four, Otis. Over and out."

The boys reached the outer edge of the pasture and walked into the forest. By the light of day they feared nothing, but they knew they didn't want to be here after sundown. Unlike what one might expect, the forest was not quiet and peaceful – it was deafening.

"What's that sound?" Jonah asked, his face drawn in irritation.

"Locusts," Joe answered. "Cicadas. They live under the ground for something like seventeen years, then crawl up out of the soil and shed their exoskeleton. Then, they have wings and look like little alien creatures and hang out in the treetops. They're calling to each other. Look," he said as he pulled a discarded cicada shell from the nearest tree. "This is one of their old skins."

"Whoa. Now, of all the things we've encountered so far, Joe, that is definitely the weirdest. Are you pullin' my leg?"

"Absolutely not. I used to gather up the shells by the dozens when I was little and play with them."

"Those bugs are loud as hell!" said Jonah as he covered his ears. "Them locust-thingies are freakin' deafening!"

Joe laughed. "You love that loud rock and roll, though, don't you? I would have thought you could handle a few locusts. I like the sound. It reminds me of my youth."

"You're still a youth, Joe E."

"No, I'm not. The days of my youth are long behind me."

They walked about half a block farther through the overgrown undergrowth until they emerged into a clearing approximately the size of a football field. The sun shone through the white, puffy clouds, giving the scene a pastoral glow. The grass should have been waist-high, but had somehow been naturally groomed into a verdant, ankle-high lawn.

"Wow," said Joe E. "I didn't expect this. I'm glad I brought the Nerf. Go long!"

The two played catch, or I should say, attempted to play catch in the lush green grass. Jonah's hands rarely met the foam football at the correct instant or angle. He was hit in the face many times – thankfully without injury. Joe caught passes between his legs and behind his back and did funky chicken touchdown dances.

When they could take no more of the brutal sun and humidity, the boys sat at the end of the clearing farthest from Granny's house.

Jonah was panting. "Joe, you may be good at football, but I'll kick your butt at Pac-Man!"

"There, there, boy. You don't have to make up for your inadequacies. Just face facts – I'm better than you at everything."

"Not at skateboarding or applying eyeliner."

"You got me there, Jonah. I doubt the two of us will be doing either after this summer."

After lounging for about fifteen minutes, the boys were rested and got up to begin their walk home. They shuffled across the clearing, kicking the football ahead of them. Jonah happened to look up, and what he saw shocked him.

black 73 dog

"Holy crap! Joe, look!"

The unicorn they had all but forgotten was racing toward them at top speed with its head lowered. It had a spiral, twisted black and white spike, at least two feet long, emerging from its forehead and was coming after them with all it had. Joe kept his composure as the beast grew closer, clutching the football for defense, never taking his eyes off the frothing animal charging toward them.

"I'm going to let it get close and blast it with the Nerf, then we'll leap away," he said to Jonah, his eyes locked onto the maniacal unicorn.

The beast was within twenty feet when Joe heaved the football at the animal's head with all his strength. The ball stuck on the end of the sharp horn, and the boys leaped to each side. Without slowing, the unicorn passed between the two teenagers, raced the rest of the way across the clearing, and entered the brush – and that was that.

The boys laid on the ground in stunned silence for some time, then started laughing and continued to do so for three or four long minutes. They got up without speaking a word to each other and began walking to the house. They were getting used to the insanity of this summer before their senior year of high school.

"Call your boy and tell him to bring us a new football when he comes tomorrow with the flashlights and ribs," Joe said.

***

The two of them made it back to the house without further incident and decided to play a best of seven series of each of Uncle Ernie's old Atari games. After getting skunked in the first four Pac-Man games, Joe got up from the floor in front of the television. As the loser, it was his duty to get them a drink before the next round.

"When I come back, the game will be Missile Command, and I will kick your scrawny, white butt, Jonah. I shall return with orange sodas."

***

Joe was scrounging in the refrigerator when he heard his walkie-talkie spring to life.

"Joe. Come in, Joe. Bring salami. Over." Joe flashed an irritated smile but did as requested.

black 74 dog

When he got back to the room, Jonah rose from the floor, and the two sat, one on each side of the twin bed, to eat their snack.

"Is that guy your uncle?" Jonah asked, motioning with a thick slice of salami to a picture on the little desk in the corner of the room.

"I guess. Remember – I never even knew I had an uncle before we got here."

Joe walked over to the desk and reached for the picture, pausing before touching it to wipe his hands on his shorts. Satisfied the grease had been removed, he picked up the picture to examine it more closely.

"He does look like me. Check out his cool dog." He handed the picture to Jonah.

"That's a Scottie. My sister wants one. They're regal little bastards. Cost a fortune."

"His nose looks extra long."

"Yeah, it looks just like yours. He was your uncle, after all."

Joe turned to his friend, a look of irritation on his face. "The dog, numbnuts – the dog's nose."

"Oh. Yeah, I guess it is about an inch longer than most terriers. I think that's how Scotties are supposed to look. That extra jaw length makes them bite harder. Must be why Serah wants one."

"I would have thought she would want a pit bull."

"She's the pit bull, Joe E. There can only be one alpha dog."

Joe returned the picture to its place on the desk, and the boys went back to their tournament, but Joe E.'s eyes were drawn back to the framed snapshot during every break in the action. His uncle looked so much like him. It was freaking him out.

They played late into the night – so late they didn't wake until eleven the following morning.

Joe lay in his cot for some time, eyes closed, thinking about his uncle, wondering what he was like. Finally, he rose. "Get up, Jonah," he said while rubbing his eyes. "Otis will be here soon. Let's shower up and get ready to explore the cellar."

Jonah's head and body were covered by blankets. After some hesitation, a muffled phrase forced its way through the covers. "I can't wait."

"Sounds like someone needs a little help waking up." Joe started a Vaudeville-worthy pantomime, swinging his arms back and forth like a little kid mustering the courage to jump off the high dive, threatening to pounce on his friend as he had so many times before.

Jonah rose suddenly, fully dressed. He had been playing possum. "Keep your filthy body away from me!" he screamed as he leaped from his cot and threw his pillow at Joe.

Thankfully, no meal of bacon and eggs waited for them in the kitchen. Granny must have been asleep. As good as her cooking was, they were tired of so many breakfasts and were even more tired of washing dishes. The boys had important things to do today and didn't need to be encumbered by KP duty.

They went to sit on the back porch to wait for Otis and continue waking up. The morning dew was burning off, and the sunlight sparkling off the backyard's foliage made their eyes squint. They became sleepy again.

Jonah reclined, cat-like, in one of the porch's comfortable lounge chairs. "I kinda like the sound of those locusts, too, Joe E."

"I love it," Joe replied as he leaned back in a wicker chair with his eyes closed.

Both boys fell back into sleep and were startled awake by Otis knocking at the rattle-trap screen door a short time later.

"Boys, wake up and smell 'dem ribs. Let's eat."

Jonah rose and flipped the hook and eye latch that secured the door.

"Otis, my brother, it's great ta sees ya," he said. Joe rolled his eyes but smiled, nonetheless. The ribs smelled wonderful.

The three ate together on the porch, staring through the screen at birds and dragonflies, not speaking.

When Joe was done, having cleaned the bones and sucked the spicy sauce from his fingers, he asked, "How ya been, Otis? You gettin' along okay?"

"Hell, I can't complain, son. Just another day in this little town I been livin' in forever. You boys are the most excitement I've had in years. How you two been gettin' on?"

"We're doing fine," Joe responded. "Were you able to get us some better flashlights?"

"Oh, yeah. They be what they search for coal miners with. They is strong! What you lookin' fo' in the dark, anyways?"

"We don't know. We're supposed to clean out the cellar, but after what we saw done to the fence we're a little concerned with what we might find."

Otis wiped his forehead with the white cloth he always carried. "Never knows what you gonna discover under all this kudzu. Maybe you gonna find a buried Confederate treasure. Keep you hopes up."

"Hope may be all we have," Jonah said.

"Hope is the *best* thing to have," Otis replied. "I been clinging to hope since I was you boys' age. I'm still clinging to hope."

"Here, Otis. Take this," Joe said as he extended a fistful of dollars. "It's only ten over the bill, but I have to make Granny's money last the summer. Is that enough for now?"

"Sho nuff," Otis said with a smile. "You bought me lunch, too, young'un. And that's exactly what I done been hopin' for – an extra ten-spot! Thank ya, thank ya, thank ya."

Joe and Jonah caught each others eye and smiled. They liked their new friend. "Did you remember the football?" Joe asked.

"Course I did. We don't never forget about football in Alabama. It's in the passenger seat of my hooptie."

They picked up the remnants of their lunch, and Otis left, taking the rib bones to feed his mutthound. He thanked them profusely for the ten dollar tip as he left, and the boys thanked Otis equally in return. Neither wanted the other side to feel taken advantage of. Everything was hunky dory, and they told each other to have a good day as they parted ways.

Otis settled in to the worn driver's seat of his taxi and rolled down the window to speak to the boys before driving away. "You have any type a problem in that cellar, you call me," Otis said. "I'll be back in a black flash."

***

The time for their second excursion into the cellar was at hand. The boys weren't particularly scared – they were ultra-wary of the unknown and hyper-aware of the unexpected, but not scared.

They had no idea what they would encounter, but they thought they could handle whatever confronted them – with the aid of a little improvised weaponry, that is.

Joe decided to duct-tape the plastic handles of two hand rakes to the top of each of his wrists, which would allow him to swipe at enemies, but also leave his hands free to grab and grapple. Similarly, they fastened the handle of Jonah's little wooden pitchfork to the boy's inner forearm. This would strengthen his grip on the weapon and also ensure it wouldn't be taken and used against him. They resembled a white trash Freddie Krueger mash-up of duct-tape and medieval garden armaments.

The boys opened the door in the same manner as before and descended into the old cellar. They walked around and under the stairs and prepared to enter the add-on chamber.

"You're going first, Joe E."

"As if I didn't know that, Jonah. Follow behind, but if something pops up in front of me, you better not block my way out."

They entered the narrow, dirt-walled hall. After about eight feet, it turned to the right, and after about five more feet, it opened up into an empty room about the size of the main cellar.

"Maybe this was the root cellar and the other part was the storm cellar," Joe wondered aloud.

"There's still more," Jonah said, pointing his flashlight to another passageway leaving this room. They entered this channel and came to a 'T' with halls leading both left and right. Joe led the two boys to the left.

"I think we're under the house," Joe said, although he was disoriented from the twists and turns of the cellar's subterranean corridors.

They came to the end of this hall. It wasn't actually the end, though. They discovered a hole about three feet square continuing on. Joe got down on his hands and knees and shone his light into the small chamber.

"Holy crap, Jonah!"

"What is it?"

Joe reached into the void and pulled out a large red shoe – a clown shoe, to be specific. He aimed his flashlight into it and let out a scream.

"Yaahh! There's foot bones in it!"

The boys got the heebie-jeebies and scuttled back the way they came until they were back at the main cellar, both hyperventilating.

"What the eff, Joe E.? A dead clown? You gotta be kidding me."

"Don't ask me, dude. I have no explanation. All I know is whatever that was has been down here for a long time."

"What do we do?"

"We explore the rest of the tunnels. Let's go back."

Summoning all their courage, the two walked back into the chamber of horrors. This time, they turned right at the 'T' and entered the largest room yet, which had no other halls or tombs leading from it. One wall had dozens of holes of varying size dug into the earth. Joe began shining his light into them, one by one.

"This must be where they kept the different vegetables and stuff," he said.

The first two holes he inspected were empty, but the third was filled with a substance not immediately identifiable. Joe tentatively reached in and pulled out a handful to examine. Jonah's spotlight showed them to be stringy, little dried up things, intertwined like tangled fishing line.

"They're worms," Jonah said. "Dried worms. A lot of them." Joe thrust them to the floor in alarm.

They found nothing else in any of the other small chambers. They went topside and braced the door shut with the rebar.

"Okay. We found a dead clown foot and a bunch of dried worms. What a day," said Jonah.

"We were almost gored by a unicorn yesterday," Joe reminded.

"What a summer, then, Joe E."

Jonah saw something out of the corner of his eye and did a double-take. "Look, the unicorn's over there in the trees," he said, attempting to act natural.

"His camouflage isn't too good, is it?"

"Nope. She sticks out like a sore thumb."

black 79 dog

"How do you know it's a she?" Joe asked.

"There's only one horn."

"Oh, okay. I get it. You're insane."

"She doesn't look mean," Jonah continued. "Maybe she was freaking out yesterday. I bet someone tried to catch her, and she thought we were trying to do the same. Let's walk toward her very slowly." Jonah was full of courage, having explored the scary cellar and come out alive.

They inched forward until they entered the line of trees, within feet of the mythical beast. They attempted to act like they hadn't even noticed the unicorn.

"We need to feed it, so it will get to know us," Joe whispered while pointing at a hawk flying over. He was trying to talk like a ventriloquist.

"I've got a bag of Skittles," Jonah replied in the same manner, gazing authentically in the direction of Joe's obfuscation. "Horses like sugar cubes, right? Let's see if she likes candy."

Jonah poured out a handful of the bright candies and extended them to the animal, who was obviously interested. She stuck her nose in Jonah's hand and enthusiastically ate them all. The unicorn became excited. She stamped her hooves and eyed the bag longingly, begging for more. Jonah fed her the remaining candies and said, "I bet she'd really like some cotton candy."

She seems smart," Joe E. said. "Let's try talking to her. Maybe she will understand."

"Do you like candy?" Joe asked loudly and slowly, pointing to the Skittles bag and enunciating like he was talking to a foreigner or a toddler. The unicorn nodded.

"Will you stay here if we bring you more?" The unicorn nodded again. She seemed to be smiling with her black unicorn lips.

The boys smiled at each other and, without a word, ran to the house. Jonah had a large stash of candy in their sleeping quarters. They grabbed Sweet-Tarts, a Snickers bar, and some Charms Pops, then rushed back to the unicorn. She was excited to see them return with more treats.

"Let's name her," Jonah suggested. "Got any ideas?"

"Well, her coat is snow white. How about Snow White?"

black 80 dog

"Too obvious. How 'bout Sugar?" Jonah countered. "Or Vanilla?"

"I think Sugar fits her," Joe said.

Jonah thought for a second. "Me, too. I like her. Maybe she'll let us ride her."

"Let's save that for another day. Remember what she was like when we saw her yesterday."

The boys explained to Sugar that she needed to keep out of sight, as unicorns were not something people were used to seeing in these parts. The animal listened attentively. Her eyes showed a strong intelligence. They told her they would watch for her to show up at the edge of the forest to be fed.

As strange as all this was, the boys didn't over-think or even attempt to understand. They had just befriended a mythological creature, but not a word was said about it between them, as unnatural as it was.

As the boys walked back to the house, Jonah spoke. "You know, if Sugar didn't have that horn she would fit in a lot better around here."

"Are you suggesting we cut it off with the bolt cutters?"

"Heck, no. I oughta camouflage it with some of that paint in the garden shed. It would make her look like a horse from a distance."

"Best idea you've had in quite some time, Jonah."

"Thanks, Joe E."

CHAPTER TEN AND ONE

The boys entered the grounds and walked to the cellar to make sure they had braced the entrance with the piece of rebar. They knew Sugar had busted open the door, but also knew they didn't fully understand the dangers lurking below. They had no idea what else might surface.

"Next time we go into the cellar, I'm taking that bar down with us, so nobody can lock us in," Joe E. said as they walked across the lawn to the house.

They went upstairs, but didn't want to spend more time in their sleeping quarters. Grandpa Joseph's room was boring – nothing to do but read, sleep, or listen to their iPods. They went to Uncle Ernie's room to hang out. By now, they felt comfortable there and had made the unspoken choice to use the study solely as sleeping quarters. Their recreational time in the house would be spent in Uncle Ernie's old lair.

They entered the little bedroom, and Jonah plopped down on the bed. "Pac-Man, Basketball, or Asteroids?"

"Your pick, Jonah." Joe was getting more curious about his uncle and slid one of the closet doors open. "Look at these old seventies clothes!" he said as he shuffled through the wardrobe. "Bell-bottoms and butterfly collars – Ernie was a pimp!"

"Try some of them on," Jonah said. "Looks like you're the same size as he was."

Joe put on some of the outrageous clothing, and the two played a game of the original Atari Basketball. The game's on-screen appearance was dated, to say the least. The players' legs were hilarious as they ran up and down the court. The boys loved playing these deconstructed games, mainly to laugh at the graphics, or the lack thereof. These games didn't rely on complex moves or cheat codes – it was pure one on one reflex and hand-eye coordination. The playing field was even, though Joe played much better than normal in his new retro togs.

"Jonah, you better put some of Ernie's clothes on if you want to compete with me. I'm a throwback, and I'm throwing down on

black 82 dog

you!"

Jonah cackled, jumped up and changed into some gear even more ridiculous than Joe's. They attempted a highly competitive match of Missile Command, but couldn't concentrate. They were laughing too much.

Suddenly, Granny's head popped in the door. She looked straight at Joe E. and scolded him. "Ernie, keep it down, for goodness sakes! I can hear you two laughing downstairs!" As soon as her words were gone, so was she.

The two teenagers looked at each other and shook their heads in amazement, grinning like 'The Joker'. Joe got up, shut the door, and turned to Jonah with a sheepish look. The boys laughed louder than ever.

"How'd she get up the stairs?" Joe E. shrieked. They were in hysterics of Donkey Kong confusion.

Finally, Joe became more serious and said, "I don't want to play Atari any more, Jonah. I'm laughing too hard, and I can't concentrate. Let's see what else ol' Ernie left behind." He opened the other side of the closet and gazed down on its contents. "Whoa, dude, there's a million records in here."

Jonah got up from the floor and stood beside his friend as they visually inventoried Uncle Ernie's massive album collection, which had to number in the hundreds. The disks were neatly kept, standing upright in milk crates, so as not to warp. They were still playable if the boys could find Ernie's old turntable.

Joe looked up to the shelf at the top of the closet and saw the record player.

"Do you know how to operate one of these things, Jonah?" he asked as he reached to bring the old contraption down to a spot at the end of the bed. The record player was covered with a soft, black protective sheath, which he carefully removed. The machine had a brushed silver finish, state of the art when Ernie bought it. The unit was labeled Technics SL-1200MK2.

"Sure. Piece of cake." Jonah's mother had occasionally listened to records.

Joe folded the ebony plasticine veil into a small square and slid it under the bed. The record player was in pristine condition, beyond mint. The stylus glowed from the gold it was plated with. Solid gold is too soft for things like record needles, so this one had a copper and silver alloy core to provide the structural integrity needed to withstand the effects of gravity and friction the needle would encounter with use. The gold plating was of the highest quality, designed to deliver the most accurate transfer of analog data from the record groove to the human ear with negligible distortion. There was no telling how Ernie had afforded the top of the line needle cartridge, but there it was, shining like the gold tooth in Otis' mouth.

The player was a model SL-1200, manufactured by Technics in 1972, and was state of the art, then and now. It was no worse for wear and looked as new as the day Granny bought it for Ernie.

"What do you think, Jonah?" Joe said as he lifted the Technics from the bed and placed it gently on the little desk next to the picture of Ernie. "Do you want to listen to some music while we play games?" He moved the photo of his uncle and the vicious looking black terrier to the windowsill, pausing to gaze deeply into it once more.

"Hell yeah, Joe E.," Jonah replied while flipping through the phonograph recordings. "There's some amazing records here. Put this one on." He handed Joe Pink Floyd's 'The Wall' album. "We don't need no education – track five." The song was an old favorite of Jonah's and spoke to his core beliefs.

They plugged the unit into the wall socket, and Jonah helped Joe touch the needle to the appropriate groove, but nothing happened. They heard a faint squeak emanating from the needle, but that was all. It was a high-pitched, sibilant whisper at the lower threshold of audible sound.

"What's the deal?" asked Joe.

"No speakers. There's no speakers attached. Look around. They have to be here somewhere."

They discovered four speakers stacked in the corner of the closet, all attached to nothing and yearning to find their connection like a junkie wandering downtown Seattle. The boys chose the two most impressive ones and extracted them from the stack. The thing about speakers is that old and outdated ones are never thrown out when the system is upgraded, since an emergency backup may be needed at any time. Smartly, they had chosen Ernie's upgrades and left the stock speakers in the closet.

The speakers' wires were wrapped around the boxes, so the boys unwound the tangles and attempted to match their male plugs to the female counterparts on the back of the record player.

Their effort was unsuccessful, since the Technics did not have the correct connection ports. "What's the deal?" asked Joe. "How can you play a record if you can't hook a speaker up? Is this a headphones only thing?" He was imagining this was some predecessor to the iPod.

Jonah was studying the setup intently and ignored his friend's question. He figured out the problem. "There's got to be an amplifier. This is just a record player. It has no power to drive the speakers. Look in the closet. It's got to be there."

On the shelf opposite where Joe had found the record player, they discovered the stereo amplifier. It was a Pioneer, and its face had numerous pre-digital dials with needles, all dormant and paralyzed to the left side like victims of Bell's palsy. The Pioneer had not been treasured like the Technics. It looked old and dated and worn-out. The boys didn't expect much as they hooked the speakers up to the amplifier's 'output' and the record player to its 'input'.

"Plug the amp in," Jonah ordered.

Joe E. did as instructed, and the speakers woke with a loud pop, sounding like an exploding Black Cat firecracker smothered by a pillow. Or, more accurately, sounding like the first muffled burp from a roadie test-firing a kick drum at a Rolling Stones concert on their 1972 tour. The dials on the amplifier shot to life and flared to the right before taking their starting positions at zero db.

"What now?" asked Joe.

"Pink Floyd. Give it Pink Floyd like before. Play it." Jonah spoke with the irritation of a doctor working with a greenhorn intern – like Han Solo ordering his pet Wookiee to floor the Millennium Falcon into hyperspace.

Slightly perturbed, Joe pulled the hard vinyl record from the sleeve it had been returned to and loaded it on the launching pad for liftoff. He glanced repeatedly from the track order on the back of the record to the track listing on the disk's label, attempting to do the

black 85 dog

right thing. His hands shook too bad to do much good. The intern was too nervous to make the first incision.

Jonah grabbed the cardboard square from him and muttered to himself as he reached for the stylus arm. "Let me do it."

He glanced at the amplifier, then the speakers, and dropped the needle to the still dormant record. Jonah turned the turntable's power on and the song started, but it sounded like The Chipmunks. Jonah toggled a switch from '45' to 'LP', and Pink Floyd rotated in the round, in concert in Ernie's bedroom just like decades before.

"Grab your joystick, Joe. You like the song?"

"Yeah, it's pretty good. I'm picking the next one, though. Is that okay, your crankiness?"

"Whatever you say," said Jonah as he laid back on Ernie's bed with closed eyes, forgetting about the game he had challenged his friend to play. "Whatever you say, Joe E."

The stereo rocked. And rolled. The only minor difference to a modern system was that there was no subwoofer, but that was for the best, since Granny was snoozing in her room below, and amplified bass waves surely would have disturbed her golden slumber. The song ended and the boys sprang to life in excitement.

"Hey, Jonah, let's put on a new set of Ernie's pimp clothes and pretend we're living in the past, in the time when the music came out – like we're hanging out with my Uncle Ernie."

"I'm starting to wonder about you, Joe E. I never would have pegged you for a guy that would want to play dress-up. I'm plenty happy with my outfit, Mr. International Male."

"Don't get your hopes up. Guyliner will not be involved, Jonah. Sorry."

Joe was already shuffling through the clothes, looking for a tie-dyed, satin dress shirt he had seen in the closet. He found it and held it against his body like a woman in a dress shop.

"Hey, I want that one!" said Jonah as he jumped up and snatched the shirt from his best buddy's hands.

"I thought you didn't want to play dress up, Jonah. Play nice!"

After the costume change, they prepared to operate the record player another time – now with four speakers attached. They

black 86 dog

had noticed a pair of unused, available orifices on the back of the Pioneer and had put one and one and one and one together to equal four attached, and hopefully working, speakers. Electricity bristled in the air, like a crowd waiting for a Metallica show to start. Ever notice how a roadie always comes out first and plays a few bars of a riff the crowd knows, and the fans go nuts in premature ejaculatory revelry? They do that on purpose – damned dirty roadies.

"Let's try this again – ON STEROIDS," Jonah said as he brought the needle down once more. Music poured out of the record player's quadrophonic speaker system, and it was beautiful. It swaddled the boys like a bubble wrap version of the Shroud of Turin. Joe had never heard music like this, and Jonah had never heard music sound as good as this. Everyone knows record players don't provide the benefit of time travel, but if they did, this one would have transported Joe and Jonah smack dab into the month of June in the year 1979.

They were anesthetized by the opus, 'Another Brick in the Wall', which they had chosen to play a second time, having been unsure of what other track they should listen to. In their near comatose state, neither had the wherewithal to change the record after the song ended, so the needle remained engaged, allowing the next song on the album, 'Mother', to cue after a four second break. This track was a haunting ode, which hypnotized them.

The boys sat in silent awe of the monumental work of art they were hearing for the first time. Their minds drifted to their absent moms, and they grew sentimental. As the final notes faded to black, they looked at each other out of the corners of their eyes. Both struggled to stifle tears.

"Dammit, Jonah! Play a happier song!" Joe begged, wiping his eyes with the back of his hand. "Yeah, I really feel like playing video games, now. What a bummer!"

"Sorry, bud," Jonah said as he thumbed through the cardboard skeletons of the elephant graveyard of 33 and 1/3 r.p.m. long players. "I don't know most of this stuff. We're going to have to explore Ernie's collection like Clark and Lewis."

"Lewis and Clark."

"Same thing. Here, let's try this one. I can't tell what it's called, it's just got symbols on the cover. It's Led Zeppelin, though, and they're supposed to be pretty good." He had selected Led 'Zeppelin IV', aka the 'Zoso' album, and was extracting the record from its sleeve. He placed the disk on the turntable and played song one, dipping a toe into the ocean he would swim in for the rest of his life.

Robert Plant shrieked his "Hey, hey mama!" intro and the band answered with the most awesome guitar riff the boys had ever heard, which startled them to attention.

"Wow! That's more like it, bro!" said Joe E., who was getting pumped up by the song like a UFC fighter preparing to enter the octagon. "Let's play some b-ball, boy! What's the name of that one?"

"'Black Dog'."

Joe looked at the picture in the window and then back at Jonah with a smile. Could this be some kind of sign? Probably. It seemed to be a positive, rather than ominous one, though, so he took little notice of it.

The boys played their most competitive game of Atari 2600 Basketball yet, timing their cross-over moves and pull-up jump shots with the brontosaurus stomp of John 'Bonzo' Bonham's squeaky kick drum pedal. They were headbanging and body-rocking to every call and response of the mighty Zep, in a world of their own.

They were time-traveling, just like you are right now. Everyone time travels forward as seconds pass from the future, through the present, and into the past, but Joe and Jonah were as close to actually traveling *back* in time as one can get. They hadn't even needed a DeLorean or a stupid old crazy professor. They had been transformed from modern teenagers into 1970's teens without trying, and were now in the glory days of the best decade in which to be between the ages of twelve and twenty. Their Atari 2600 Basketball game was brand new and very 'far out'. Their clothes were 'hip'. The music was 'right on'. It was an involuntary collision between the past and the natural instincts of 17-year-old boys, regardless of the year or decade. It all seemed absolutely natural, somewhat primeval, and lusciously carnal.

"Man, I wish we grew up in your uncle's time," Jonah said.

"Me, too, Jonah. Me, too. But we aren't living in the past. We can't be homesick for a home we have never known. We are in the here and now, and if we spend our time wishing to be someplace else we are going to be vulnerable."

***

They played their game through the first three songs of side one, but were unprepared for the final song of the album's first side, which was 'Stairway to Heaven', song four.

I'm telling you from experience – always watch out for song four. It might be 'Fade To Black' from Metallica's 'Ride The Lightning' album or 'Sanitarium' from 'Master of Puppets'. It might be 'Memory Motel' from The Stones' 'Black and Blue' record. It might be 'Walk This Way' from 'Toys in the Attic'. It could be 'Surprise! You're Dead!' by Faith No More. Hell, it could even be 'Thriller' by Wacko Jacko. Or it might just be 'Dazed and Confused' or 'Since I've Been Loving You' by the mighty Led Zeppelin. I could go on and on. Just heed my words – watch out for song fours. They're life changers. Don't be scared – learn from them.

In this case, song four was 'Stairway' – the most important song four and most played hard rock song of all time. Although both of the boys had heard it before, neither had listened closely. When the needle came to its repetitive clicking after the track had ended, they looked at each other like Watson and Crick upon discovering the double helix structure of DNA.

***

"Whoa, that was friggin' incredible," Jonah said.

"Beyond incredible. When did that come out? That blows away all the crap you listen to," Joe E. replied. "Does it have a date on it?" They were having a hard time believing such monumental works of music had not taken place on their watch.

Jonah picked up the album sleeve and searched for the copyright date. "1971. Can you believe that? I didn't know they had electric guitars in 1971! You're right, Joe. That blows away everything I have ever heard – period, the end."

"Start it over from the beginning," Joe said, still entranced. "It's going to be a long night."

"The beginning of the song or the beginning of the album?"

"'Black Dog', dude. Black freaking Dog! Aaaooooooo!!!" he

black 89 dog

howled at the moon outside the window like a crazed animal.

"Aaaaaoooooo!!" Jonah joined, sounding like a rabid chupacabra. They were losing their minds and returning to some sort of '2001: A Space Odyssey' monolithic and instinctual great ape 'dawn of man' primality – and they were having a blast doing so, wearing vintage, disco-era clothes. You should have seen it.

They played various games while listening to their newfound guidance system, until they could barely keep their four eyes open. 'Stairway to Heaven' had sealed their summer's fate, and they knew it. By the third listen, they were setting down their game controllers and meditating with eyes closed, on the verge of leaving their earthly vessels. This was not done consciously – they knew nothing about transcendental meditation. They stopped speaking. They had been granted the ability to communicate intricate feelings without words. They existed in synchronicity, thinking of all the coincidences the young summer had brought them, sensing they were arming themselves for some battle they would fight before the season's end.

They already had strong feelings about the forest surrounding their fragile domain, and 'Stairway to Heaven' seemed to hold the keys to understanding their fate. Hell, they had already befriended a unicorn – anything was possible. 'Stairway' sounded like the narrative of their journey, although neither of the boys could understand the symbolism in the lyrics. They were fascinated, though, and eager to learn more. The forest would play a key part in their saga, just like in the song. They were intrigued and terrified at the recognition of this fact.

Who was this lady in the song searching for her passage to paradise? Could it be Granny? It also talked about rings of smoke through the trees and the voices of those who stand looking. What are they looking at? Are they watching the house? Creepy. The piper's calling you to join him, the song said. Yikes!

The music stopped after their fourth listen to song four of 'Zeppelin IV', but it was fifteen minutes before the boys could move. Eventually, Jonah rose and selected a different album by a band called Rush. The sleeve had a strange picture of a naked man doing a ballet move on top of a human brain – heavy handed symbolism, perfect to ensnare the teenage mind. The record was called

'Hemispheres'. Jonah avoided song four and opted for the third, instead. The song he played was entitled, 'The Trees'. More messages from more supernatural guidance counselors beat on the boys' brains like peasants pummeling a pinata. If Jonah had played track four, he would have gotten 'La Villa Strangiato', aka 'The Strange House'. Jonah had flunked Spanish and had no awareness of Italian, so the foreign words had not been translated, and the song was not played. It was for the best. The boys needed to concentrate on the forest, not their house.

"Something is trying to warn us about the forest," Joe E. said. "I thought the cellar was what we need to watch out for, but I think the real danger lies in those trees."

"I couldn't be more confused," answered Jonah. Joe found it hard to take his friend's concerns seriously in his disco get-up. "We're friends with a freakin' unicorn and an old black taxi driver. Your grandma drinks gallons of vodka and eats breakfast two or three times a day. We dress up like pimps and play video games that look like they were programmed in Soviet Russia and chop kudzu all day. I don't know whether I'm here, there, or everywhere – I can't tell if I'm coming or going."

"I know what you mean, but I think you're over-thinking it. We're never going to understand what's happening to us. Well, I take that back. We'll probably understand *what* is happening at some point, but I don't think we'll ever understand *why*. Hell, I don't know. It may be as simple as what's good versus what's bad. We just need to 'go with the flow' like your surfer dad did. What are we gonna do, call the newspaper? We're on our own. I'm going back to my cot to study some of my grandfather's books. Care to join me?"

"I don't want to join you in your cot, but I'll take a look at your grandpa's books."

Joe studied like he never had before. It was new to him – he had aced all his public school tests with ease, without preparation. He grabbed volumes at random, with titles like, 'The History of The Vampyre', and immersed himself. He was amazed, both at what he learned and all he did not know. He would never again think himself smart enough to get by without cracking a book.

Joe felt his life was at stake – that he was in danger of being burned at the stake or of getting a wooden stake through the heart. The thought didn't scare him. It motivated him. From time to time, he looked up at his friend, who was struggling to understand the text he was reading. Joe smiled – Jonah had never cracked a book, either. They were both in the same boat – the same lifeboat. But, even if they were in imminent danger from some Poltergeist, they were still enjoying themselves and getting stronger every day.

They stayed up very late, studying for their impending offensive like General Dwight D. Eisenhower planning the D-Day invasion of Normandy Beach. All their free time could not be wasted playing trivial video games, they had realized. They didn't want to be flanked by some haunted Viet-Cong death squad wandering the forests of Alabama and end up decimated. They needed to police up their minds and study military history and the supernatural and prepare for the battle sure to come, even if they were dressed like a 'Saturday Night Fever' casting call.

They fell asleep at a very late or very early hour, depending on whether you are a glass half full or glass half empty person. They woke late – around 11:30. They showered and found Granny in the kitchen, doing what Granny did best. Today it was French Toast, which was a nice change. They volunteered to wash the dishes and asked the old Southern dame what she wanted them to do next. The answer – clean out the old barn behind the house.

The boys took it to be a barn, at least, since Granny had referred to it as such. It was actually a carriage house – a remnant of the Victorian era. Basically, it was a garage for the horse-drawn means of transportation used before the advent of the internal combustion engine and the vehicles subsequently produced by the Ford company. It was a large rectangular wooden building with swinging doors on each side to facilitate the coming and going of horse-drawn coaches – a relic from the past rarely mentioned in the present, having been forgotten by a society in love with the automobile.

Granny's carriage house was quite big and had stables along one side to nurture the beasts of burden that provided the literal horsepower to motivate land-based travel in the pre-automotive era. It had a second level, used to store the hay needed to fuel the tenants of the stables. This upper level had a large open square without safety rails in the middle of its floor, to facilitate the transfer of hay up or down. The bales were stored on the second level and thrown down through the opening as needed. The second floor was accessible only by climbing a ladder up through the hole – the carriage house had no stairs and, of course, no escalator to Heaven.

***

After the antique dishes had been cleaned and carefully put away, Joe and Jonah went to the old, decrepit barn – the last element of the property still unexplored. They found its old doors had been locked and chained shut in a style similar to the cellar. Someone or something had long ago viewed these two spaces as dangerous to enter, or conversely, didn't want something to get out.

They had another pleasant encounter with the old man across the street in order to borrow the bolt cutters again, but were careful this time not to walk on his precious lawn. He came to the door clutching a little white miniature poodle that looked older than him, at least in dog years. The animal was shaking in his arms, but the boys couldn't really tell if it was the poodle quivering or the old guy holding it. Regardless, they walked away with the borrowed tool and the knowledge that they were hoodlums and should be on a chain gang.

Since the metal was rusted, they had little difficulty breaking the chains this time and returned the cutters back to the geriatric's front porch.

The old barn hadn't been used in countless years but remained structurally sound, due to its solid, slave state construction. It was not scary for the boys to explore in the daylight after both sets of doors were opened wide – just dirty and cluttered, like everything else they tried to clean up around the old mansion.

They found nothing unusual on the first floor of the carriage house – some petrified horse crap and hay, pitchforks, brooms, bridles, a couple whips, and an old wagon wheel. A rickety wooden ladder rested along one wall. They propped it up and climbed through the hole in the middle of the carriage house's upper floor. A substantial amount of hay in large piles remained on the second level.

"We need to remove this old hay. It's a fire hazard," said Joe E.

"It's been here forever, Joe, and nothing's burned down yet. Maybe this whole barn should go up in flames, anyway. It gives me the creeps."

"I guess you're right, Jonah. There are more important things for us to put our efforts into. Let's check things out, though, while we're here."

Joe and Jonah walked the perimeter of the room and made an odd discovery behind the largest pile of hay.

"Look, Jonah, there's a set of clothes back here," Joe said as he picked up a long-sleeved, white cotton shirt that looked to be very old. It was shredded, as were the short black pants and navy blue overcoat they found with it.

"They look like pirate clothes, Joe," said Jonah.

"Yeah, right off Jack Sparrow. I'm not even going to venture an explanation."

They finished exploring the carriage house and found nothing else which confused or distressed them. It was stifling in the barn, and they were sweaty and exhausted from the oven-temperature heat. It was now well into the afternoon, thanks to their late start, and the boys had wilted.

They decided it had been a while since they had seen good ol' Otis, so they walkie-talkied him, and he arrived within the hour with some smoked ham sandwiches, cole slaw, and potato salad.

"What you boys been up to today?" Otis axed as the three ate leisurely on the back porch.

"Just cleaning up the old barn," said Joe.

"Well, why don't you boys let me inspect whatcha done and see if it be up to snuff?"

The three finished their picnic and walked to the building together. Their shadows were growing longer as the evening fell around them. As they approached, Otis walked slower.

"Boys, that ain't no barn, that be a carriage house. That's where the slaves used to care for the beasts of burden. I don't particularly like such places. Sometimes the slaves even had to live in the stables with da hosses."

black 94 dog

"We already checked it out, Otis," said Jonah. "There's nothing in there to be scared of."

"I'll be the judge of that, boys."

They entered the unlocked doors, and Otis took a long look around. "See that whip," he said. "That weren't jus' for hosses, I bet."

The boys gulped audibly. All of a sudden, the place seemed really creepy – almost worse than the cellar.

"We found those clothes on the second level," Jonah said, pointing to the pile on the floor. "They're pirate clothes. Arggh!"

"Boys, them ain't pirate clothes," Otis said, holding the old shirt gently in his calloused hands. "Dem's slave clothes, and it don't look like nothin' good happened to the boy wearin' dis outfit. I gots to get outta dis place. Please excuse me, y'all."

Otis began walking extremely fast to his cab, calling out behind him as he went. "Boys, you gots ta be careful 'round this place. I be gettin' some very strange vibes, and I'm thinkin' yo Granny's place might jus' be haunted! I'd stay outta that cellar and outta that carriage house, too, if you knows what's good for ya! Call me if you need me, but remember that I do not like this place, and I don't wanna be 'round here." The boys had not seen this side of their friend since he had abandoned them on the curb the night they arrived.

"Okay. Sorry. Drive careful, Otis," Jonah called out. He turned to Joe with puppy dog eyes and an extended lower lip.

"Let him go," Joe said. "This is our fight, not his. We're gonna get to the bottom of this and right the wrongs that have happened here. I give my word."

Jonah turned away from his best friend in a vain attempt to keep Joe from seeing the tears welling in his eyes, thinking he would be made fun of. Joe reached out and pulled Jonah tight to him in an awkward hug. He looked up at the immense sky and locked eyes with God.

CHAPTER TEN AND TWO

Joe and Jonah somberly returned to Ernie's room, but weren't in the mood to play video games. Otis' reaction had scared the bejeezus out of them. After sitting in silence for a half hour, Jonah plugged the Pac-Man cartridge into the Atari and began mindlessly playing a game in single player mode. Joe stood, staring out the window at the carriage house below, the picture of his Uncle Ernie and the black dog in his hand.

After a period of deep thought, Joe went to the closet and found the Led Zeppelin album. He sensed they needed to hear the song again. He started 'Stairway to Heaven' with the volume low and returned to the window.

As he listened, he spoke to Jonah. "Tomorrow we're getting Otis to take us to the library to use the internet. I'm gonna do a little research on Led Zeppelin and this 'Zoso' record."

"Whatever you say, Joe E."

Jonah walkie-talkied Otis with the request, and the old man said no problem, as long as he didn't have to go anywhere near the carriage house.

***

Otis picked up the boys the next morning and dropped them off at the local library, which had three computers for the public to use. It took a bit of persuading to convince the librarian to let them use one, since they had no library card and no evidence of being residents. They finally convinced her they were visiting for the summer and needed to do research on a paper due the next fall. The librarian was impressed by their initiative and praised them for being good students, which caused Jonah to blush sunburn pink. Joe did all the talking. They had long ago figured out it was always best for the more clean cut of them to speak to authority.

Their first search, 'Led Zeppelin', guided them to the band's Wikipedia entry. It was straightforward enough and enlightening, as far as just how successful the band had been during the seventies. Seeing the band line-up, Joe clicked on 'Jimmy Page'. Scrolling down the guitarist's Wiki page, they learned Mr. Page was a devotee

black 96 dog

of the English occultist, Aleister Crowley, and that 'Led Zeppelin IV', aka the 'Zoso' album, was heavily influenced by his studies of the dark side of the supernatural. That was the album containing 'Black Dog' and 'Stairway to Heaven', so it made perfect sense.

"We're getting warm, Jonah," Joe whispered.

"Creepy," whispered Jonah.

"Don't worry. We're arming ourselves with this information. We aren't getting scared, we're getting informed."

Intrigued, they searched 'Led Zeppelin IV' and found out the album had been voted 66th on Rolling Stone's list of the 500 greatest albums of all time – how appropriate.

"It probably would have been number one on the list of the top 666 albums of all time," Jonah said.

"Right?" replied Joe.

Joe learned that the album's artwork featured a depiction of 'the Hermit' from the tarot deck, another ominous sign. He also read that if this picture was held up to a mirror, the reflection would show the image of a black dog.

"WHOA!" said Joe E. upon reading that. "That black dog of Ernie's has something to do with all this. I can feel it."

"Yeah," Jonah said softly, although he wasn't paying attention. He was zoning out, staring at a kid's display on the wall – 'A,B,C's and 1,2,3's'. His eyes were glassy. No matter – Joe was focused enough for both of them.

The next search of 'Stairway to Heaven' brought even more enlightenment. The song had been channeled to Robert Plant and Jimmy Page, Zep's frontmen, in toto, instantaneously, which was just plain weird. On top of this, Joe learned that if the record was played backwards, Satanic messages were audible. This phenomenon was called 'backmasking'.

Jonah didn't take much notice, but this backmasking thing caught Joe E.'s attention, bigtime. Joe researched the concept while Jonah daydreamed. Supposedly, the classic rockers of the seventies and early eighties had been able to lace their songs with imperceptible hidden messages that couldn't be heard, but could be subconsciously understood and obeyed. The only way these backmasked messages could be deciphered was by playing the

black 97 dog

record backwards. It seemed to Joe to be a bit of a conspiracy theory, but until he tested the concept, he chose to reserve judgment.

Joe grabbed a piece of scratch paper and scrawled the backwards message that appears on 'Stairway to Heaven', then pocketed it.

Having done their due diligence, Joe paged Otis for the return trip. He arrived promptly with a gold-tooth smile plastered on his face. It made him feel good to be of service.

"Y'all need to make any more stops?" he axed as the boys made themselves comfortable in the plush interior of his Lincoln Cadillac. "Mister Otis be at your service. I'm free all afternoon."

"Thanks, but no, Otis," Joe E. said. "I'm anxious to get home and get to the bottom of all this insanity at my Granny's."

"I hope you do, and I wish you would, Joey. (He thought Joe E.'s name was Joey, like so many others.) I want y'all to be able to enjoy yo' summer without having to deal with things you had no ideal you were gettin' into. There may be a poltergoose you gotta kill up there on tha hill," he said, followed by a hearty laugh. The boys were glad to see him in a better frame of mind than the night before.

"Thanks," the boys said in unison, once again. They spoke simultaneously more and more lately, like twins, but they weren't yelling "jinx" every time it happened. In fact, they hardly noticed it anymore.

When they arrived, the sun still had an hour or so before dusk would set upon the haunted mansion, and Joe had unfinished business to attend to before the sunlight exited stage left.

"Jonah, we're going to the clearing in the forest to throw the Nerf until dark, then we're walking home through the trees together. That's right – I am not scared and neither are you! Don't speak, brother. Trust me. We are doing this for a reason."

They went to the inexplicable void in the forest – the place where the lush grass never grew higher than their shoe tops without the chore of mowing. They frolicked around like the doofus 17-year-olds they were, pretending they were playing human Atari 2600 Football, which was not at all successful in the modern, physical interpretation of the sport. By that, I mean they were restricting their movements to those made in the old video game – not fluid and very

black 98 dog

unnatural. It was like mixing 'the robot' dance with football. They had fun, though, which seemed to be all that mattered and all Joe had wanted for himself and his friend. It was their summer, and he wasn't backing down.

As the sun set, the boys sat in the far end of the clearing, watching the beautiful orange and red rays of the daily natural phenomenon that goes unappreciated by most people. In the early days of color television, a multi-colored screen signed off each night. Sunsets have been under-appreciated ever since.

Unexpectedly, something snorted behind them, which startled them from their hippie interlude. They turned their heads in horror, expecting a monster, but saw only Sugar, smiling sweetly at them like a double-dip ice cream cone with sprinkles on top. She approached without fear and lovingly nuzzled their necks, which tickled the boys and made them giggle. Jonah raided his pockets and fed the precocious animal a Twix and a full sleeve of Sweet-Tarts, which she especially enjoyed, crunching loudly as each one was offered to her mouth. She had glossy black lips, which framed her huge, happy smile. They were all smiling, in fact. Joe had been right to initiate a return to the forest.

"I'm gonna ride her, Joe E.," Jonah said with as much conviction as Seabiscuit's hobbled jockey.

"Be careful, dude. She's a little wild. I doubt she's ever had a human on her back. You're light as a feather, though, so she probably won't mind too much."

At the mention of the prospect, Sugar bent her front legs in a curtsy, allowing Jonah to grab her long white mane and mount her, in the most innocent meaning of the term. She rose and thrashed her head back at him, throwing the coarse long hair on the back of her neck into Jonah's face in an act of unbridled enthusiasm.

"She wants you to hold onto her mane," Joe volunteered.

"Oh," said Jonah. "I thought she wanted me to condition her hair with some of that mane and tail treatment."

"A smart-ass on a unicorn – what next?" Joe laughed.

Jonah grabbed the mane-reins, and the two set off like a Ricochet Rabbit, instantly and absolutely flying in the growing darkness. It was difficult for Joe E. to see if Sugar's feet were

black 99 dog

contacting the turf. She seemed to be gliding like a bewitched hovercraft on a sugar high. Jonah was hooping and hollering as they circled the open field at an impossible speed, as if it was Sugar's own little private racetrack and he was Sugar's own little private jockey. He had a terrified look on his face most of the time, though, like a kid riding his first real roller coaster.

Eventually, the mare slowed to a stop and curtsied again, dropping Jonah off next to Joe E. Jonah was visibly shaking. Not in fear – he was trembling like someone who has just base jumped off the bridge over Victoria Falls. Tears of joy streamed down his cheeks. If he had applied his guyliner that day, it would have been staining his socks at the moment. In fact, not only had Jonah not applied guyliner since leaving home, he would never do so again.

"Let's put Sugar in the carriage house," he said. The boy was wild-eyed, his hair finally removed from his eyes. His unkempt locks were, in fact, stuck angling straight back, which struck Joe E. as hilarious. Joe needed a laugh and was happy to have one at his friend's expense.

"The wind made my eyes water," Jonah said, not realizing that Joe wasn't mocking him for his tears, but was instead laughing at his new up-do.

"Sure. Okay. Yeah, the wind. Good idea, though, Jonah. Let's put Sugar in the carriage house for the night. You look like you've been riding 'bitch' on the back of a Harley for 500 miles. Your eyes are so wide you look like Igor from that 'Young Frankenstein' movie we watched. I think I found your new nickname, IGOR!"

Jonah rotated his hunched shoulders toward Joe and hissed like a vampire seeing light for the first and last time. He was playing along, and it was funny.

"You're going to scare Sugar," Joe said as he laughed the child-like giggle of the uncorrupted innocent.

By this time, it was fully dark. The three strolled warily down the path through the forest, their heads on a swivel. They exited the trees, walked through the field behind the house, and reached the front gate. Sugar didn't much like the prospect of entering the property, but did so at the encouragement of her friends. The boys led her around the house, opened the doors to the barn, and led her into one of the old stalls, thinking she would be happy and secure in this safe haven. Sugar was nervous, but the boys attributed it to her lack of ever having been confined.

"Don't worry, sweetie," Jonah told her. "We can see your new house from our window, and we'll make sure nothing happens to you." Sugar was anxious, but complied obediently, trusting her new friends.

After leaving the unicorn in the comfortable stall, the boys tied the barn doors shut with some old hemp rope from inside. The old cord was not suitable for much more than appearance, but they saw no need for heavy security.

"Think she'll be okay for the night?" asked Jonah with the utmost concern.

"She's as safe as we are," answered Joe E. "Probably safer. She knows how to defend herself. You don't."

***

Our heroes tiptoed upstairs to Grandpa Joseph's study and de-briefed silently to themselves. Joe, of course, was piecing pieces of puzzles together like a TV detective – part 'Rockford Files', part 'MacGyver', part 'MacGruber'. Jonah was still glowing like a newly crowned homecoming queen, having ridden his pet unicorn through double rainbows and summer showers of bubble-bath glitter.

The boys took turns bathing and met up in Uncle Ernie's room, per usual. They were still very awake and were feeling more confident than scared, for once.

"Jonah, what did you glean from what we researched at the library?"

"Well, I guess that Led Zeppelin band was supposedly evil, even though all the teenagers who listened to them were having the time of their lives. Actually, they seemed nice. Maybe they just got caught up in something bigger than them, just like us."

"The teenage fans or the band?"

"All of them."

"That's pretty much what I got, but did you catch that part about that backmasking thing?"

"Backmasking? What's that? Trick or treating with the mask on the back of your head and walking up to the door backwards?

Trick or treat is the question. The answer is TRICK!"

"Not even close, you weirdo. Backmasking is when you play a record backwards and hear secret messages the band put in the song. Supposedly, these guys had the ability to write a song both forward and backward, with equal and opposite meanings in both directions. I guess the fun and games were on the regular side, and they hid the bad stuff on the reverse version of the song."

"Could they really do that? It sounds impossible."

"Well, let's test it," said Joe. "I'm gonna try to say the alphabet backwards. Or should I say, backwards alphabet the say to try gonna I'm."

Jonah looked at him and half-cocked his head like a confused dog. "Oh, I get it," he said after a moment. "That's hard!"

Joe started the trial and made it only a few letters before he messed up. "Well, I think it takes practice. It has to take a lot of practice. Nobody could do that simultaneously with music and make it be coherent, do you think?"

"The human mind is capable of anything," Jonah responded. "And the stuff beyond the human mind is infinite. Just ask Sugar."

"True. That definitely puts it in perspective. Anything is possible, and we'll do a lot better from here on if we suspend our preconceived beliefs of the laws of the world. On top of that, we must add to our world-view what we learn from my grandfather's library."

"That's funny," Jonah said. "I learned exactly that from one of those old books. It said that most people deny the possibility of the paranormal, so when they see something they are unfamiliar with, they just pretend it doesn't exist."

"That's a form of denial. Absolutely anything is possible, Jonah. No matter how implausible."

"What's that mean?"

"No matter how unlikely, you doofus."

"Everything is unlikely around here," Jonah said. "But that's what keeps happening."

"Exactly! That's the oxymoron."

"First it's doofus, and now it's moron. I'm not stupid, Joe, and I'd really appreciate it if you would stop with the name-calling!"

Joe tilted his head slyly, looked at Jonah, and smiled. "Just get a good night's rest, bro. You know you're my best bud, you little brainiac. Tomorrow is going to be a big day, mark my words. We're arming ourselves for battle, and we don't want an Achilles weakness. Everything must be planned. Surprises could be deadly."

"I'm with you, master."

"Thanks, Igor."

The two laughed and prepared for bed. Their sleep would be fitful and fraught with strange dreams and visions. In spite of these nocturnal anomalies, they slept so soundly they did not hear the sounds of unicorn shrieks and the carriage house's doors being broken open by poor, tormented, innocent Sugar.

UNLUCKY CHAPTER TEN AND THREE

Jonah woke with a start at the crack of dawn, although the boys' sleeping quarters had no windows to allow the first rays of the new rising sun to enter and wake him. His intuition had shaken him with the terror of a Mayan whose sleeping family is being attacked by a black panther. Jonah opened his eyes, placed himself in his surroundings, and bolted upright, screaming at Joe.

"Wake up, Joe! Wake up! Sugar's in trouble!" Jonah hastily pulled on his t-shirt and threw clothes on top of his friend's still supine body. He tore out of the room at a gallop with Joe chasing behind. Jonah had made it through basic training and was now ready for a firefight. In fact, he was literally growling as he ran to protect his precious unicorn friend.

They reached the carriage house and found the doors had been busted open violently. The weak rope they had bound the doors shut with was broken, almost turned to dust at the stress points. Upon entering, they found Sugar's stall empty.

"Dude, look at this," said Joe as he examined the breached exit. "There's hoof marks imprinted deep into these doors. She donkey-kicked her way out. I'm surprised she didn't split the wood!"

"What is happening?" Jonah cried. Tears streamed down his cheeks once again. These were tears of anger, though – the first tears of this type Jonah had ever shed. "Joe, Joe, Joe. What is going on here?!" he wailed in abject frustration with clenched fists.

"Stop crying, brother, and let not your heart be troubled. The war has started. BRING IT ON!!!!!" Joe screamed to the sky, nearly foaming at the mouth with fury. He grabbed a pitchfork, climbed like a spider up the ladder to the second floor, and bayoneted every pile of hay violently, like an American soldier fighting for his life on the island of Iwo Jima. Finding nothing, he slowly descended the ladder to the first floor, attempting to gather his thoughts and harness his blind anger.

Joe calmed himself, realizing a general doesn't destroy his quarters every time a man is lost in battle. He needed to internalize the pain and attempt to cope with it years later, long after the war had been won or lost, post-traumatic stress be damned.

"Don't worry, Jonah," he said. "I told you today was important, and this just makes it even more so. Sugar is fine, she just wanted out – I'm sure of it. She got spooked. She isn't used to being corralled, that's all. We'll find her." Joe grabbed his friend and hugged him sympathetically. "Try not to worry, Jonah. I'm not going to let anything happen to any of us. You can take that to the bank. Let's eat some breakfast, then we'll take some candy into the forest and find Sugar. She's fine – I guarantee it. I'm getting royally pissed-off, though! What next?"

They ate hastily and entered the forest with determination. They called and called as they trudged through the foliage, but Sugar did not appear. Jonah grew despondent through the expedition, and the two were finally near exhaustion. The heat and humidity had long since soaked them to the bone, and they didn't want to get lost, God forbid.

Joe stopped, lifting the front of his t-shirt to wipe his face. "Let's go back and shower and hang out in Ernie's room for the rest of the afternoon. We're liable to get heat stroke if we keep this up. I need to work on my research. Don't worry – Sugar is okay," Joe said with the strength of a platoon commander.

"Umkay," Jonah replied with his head down. The poor boy was in bad shape, but Joe wasn't going to let this setback rule the day or undermine his friend's previously growing assertiveness.

***

Back at home, the boys had showered and were eating finger foods in Ernie's room. "Education and preparation are the keys to our success, my dear boy," Joe orated, pacing the small space at the foot of Ernie's bed. "Let's examine the evidence." At this, he produced the tattered, spiral-bound notebook he had been taking notes in for the past few days.

"Okay, there seems to have been some shady, and probably criminal, goings on here, involving slaves during the Civil War era. To me, that seems to be the logical basis for any kind of haunting we may be dealing with. We didn't do anything, and Granny didn't do anything, and the house doesn't seem to be possessed, but wronged spirits may be roaming the property, seeking retribution before they can be at peace. It's almost like a disturbed Indian burial ground, I think."

"Next, I have to believe something about a black dog is important. I'm basing that on how many times the black dog has come up since we've been here. It was the title of the first song on that Led Zeppelin album we played – not to mention, my Uncle Ernie had a black dog, and its friggin' eyes seem to be staring at me when I look at that picture. Maybe I'm crazy or imagining it, but it's weird, dude!"

"Okay," Jonah managed to mumble through his state of shock.

"It's all coming together, right?" begged Joe.

"Kinda, I guess."

"Okay. Jonah, get that Led Zeppelin record. I want to see if something I discovered at the library is true."

Jonah obediently fetched the record. "What now?"

"See that picture of the old man climbing the mountain? It's called 'The Hermit', and it's from tarot cards."

"I've got it," said Jonah. "Now what?"

"Hold it up to the mirror, and tell me what you see."

Jonah did as instructed and gazed for some time at the reflection of the artwork. "I see the face of a black dog."

"Exactly. That's what my research said you would see. Now we have to play the song backwards," Joe said.

Jonah handed the record to Joe, who loaded it onto the player. "Let's play it forward first, all the way to the last note. We need to get a feel for the speed of the revolutions. Watch how fast the label turns. Once the song gets to the end, we'll try to duplicate the speed in reverse, from end to beginning. We have to think backwards."

They played the song until it ended, then flipped the toggle on the record player to 'stop'. The needle was still in the groove. Joe placed his fingers on the disk, took a deep breath, and began to rotate it in the opposite direction at approximately the same speed.

"Listen for some kind of message, Jonah. There has to be a clue here," he said.

The process proceeded through two-thirds of the song with

no indication anything supernatural had occurred. Joe struggled to duplicate the correct speed in reverse. The boys listened attentively, but heard no secret messages, just Tower of Babel gibberish. As Joe reached the end, which was really the beginning of the song, they were feeling let down at the lack of revelation.

"It didn't work," said Joe.

"Look out the window," Jonah countered. When they started the reverse version of the song the sun was shining, but the sky was now charcoal grey, and a storm was brewing. The wind whipped wildly, throwing leaves against the little window of Ernie's room. A lightning bolt cracked, touching down in the field behind the house. The boys were temporarily blinded, then deafened by the subsequent thunder clap.

Joe stared out the window, attempting to survey the back yard and the carriage house, but saw nothing out of the ordinary. Rain was coming down now.

"Let's check the barn," he said.

Armed with their garden implements of terror, the boys braved the elements as they ran to the carriage house, but found nothing had changed since their last visit. They returned to Ernie's room and sat next to each other on the little bed, wet and battered.

"Something happened, but I don't know what," said Joe.

"Do you think it was bad or good?"

"It can't be any worse, can it? Something happened – that's all I know. Maybe we can get to the bottom of it in the morning. Find a different record – something positive. And play it forward, not backward, for God's sake," Joe said with a jaded laugh. "We've done all we can today. I'm gonna make you my little Pac-Man bitch, now, Jonah." They laughed and pretended everything would be okay in the morning.

The teenagers stayed up until two, matching random combinations of records and video games, trying not to worry. They discovered the Electric Light Orchestra and were awe-inspired at the complexity of their orchestral pop songs. Alice Cooper preached to them from his bloody bully pulpit. The Kinks provided 'Waterloo Sunset', which produced edge of the eye, sentimental tears, quickly wiped away. Queen spilled out 'You're My Best Friend' amid wide, affectionate smiles and youthful thoughts of gratitude. Linda Ronstadt channeled Warren Zevon's 'Poor, Poor Pitiful Me' to their yearning eardrums. Jefferson Starship assured them 'Miracles' were possible, then told them to 'Count On Me'. God bless the musicians of the seventies and the songs they produced. They have consoled many in their time of need.

The boys were just dipping their toes in the water, but every song spoke to them and replenished their straying souls. They didn't need manna from Heaven – they had plenty of food in the pantry downstairs. What they needed was food for the soul – and they were discovering sacred hymns which gave them the spiritual nourishment they craved. Joe was using his notebook to record the names and album data of these motivational songs, so they could find them easily when they needed to hear the melodies and messages they carried. He had titled a page, 'Inspiration', and was listing the songs that provided it in neat order.

The next morning the boys woke with purpose, smelling bacon and eggs. It had been a couple days since they had interacted with Granny, so they bounded downstairs and into the kitchen like terriers seeking treats. The old matriarch was diligently toiling over numerous pots and pans. She turned as the boys entered and smiled.

"Boys, I'm specially preparing grits and red-eye gravy for you today, to go with your bacon, eggs, and biscuits. I've slept so peacefully since you came – I want to reward you. Everything seems to have returned to normal. I can't thank you enough."

Joe and Jonah locked eyes and smiled dubiously at each other.

"Granny, I told you we were going to take care of you," said Joe. "Why don't you let me finish the cooking?"

"I'll hear nothing of it," she replied, somewhat curtly. "You boys have worked so hard. I'm making you a grand breakfast to show my appreciation. You'll do the dishes, of course, but this morning you will feast like the noble young princes you are." She started singing a song as she cooked – "*All things shall pass. All things shall pass away.*"

"Granny, what song is that?" Joe asked.

"I don't know, son. I heard it coming from your uncle's room many years ago, and it came back to me today. Don't you like it?"

"It's a beautiful song, Granny," he replied. "Do you know who sang it?"

"One of those crickets or beetles he used to listen to and worship so much. I thought it was so much noise until he was gone. That's when I realized those songs he played were beautiful to him. And that's when they became beautiful to me. I hear you boys listening to them at night, as well."

"Are they too loud, Granny?" asked Jonah.

"No, son. You play them as loud as you want. You both are so sweet, just like my little Ernie."

"Granny, what happened to Uncle Ernie?" Joe asked.

"He went away."

"Where did he go?" asked Jonah.

"I wish I knew, son. One day he was just gone. It was not long before Christmas in the year 1983." She turned away, and her gaze fell to a point on the kitchen floor. "He left me without saying goodbye." She started to cry, which brought both of the boys to the edge of their young emotional boundaries. "Boys, please don't leave me without saying goodbye."

"Granny, we would never, ever do that to you," Joe said. "Let me fill your glass. Let us finish the cooking. We'll wash the dishes and put them away. Why don't you just rest today and let me try to figure out what's been going on around here? Uncle Ernie may be gone, but his spirit is still here. I can feel it."

"God bless you, son. I'm old – very old. Don't concern yourself with me. My life is over. This summer isn't about me – it's about you and Jonah. There's something here you have to discover for yourselves. Something that might bring me the peace that passeth understanding I need before I pass away. I pray for you every day. Please pray for me, son. I love you boys."

"Jonah and I love you, too, Granny. We'll figure out what's happening. Don't worry."

"Godspeed, boys," she mumbled as she left the kitchen with tears in her eyes and a full glass of chilled vodka in her hand.

"I feel sorry for your Granny, Joe," Jonah said after she had gone. "Why do you think she stays in that little room all the time?"

"She's scared. I think all these things that have happened here have traumatized her, and she is seeking sanctuary. I bet she sits in there looking at pictures of Ernie and Grandpa and stuff."

"I bet you're right. Maybe after we get to the bottom of things, she'll come out and enjoy her own house for a change."

"That's what I'm hoping for, Jonah."

***

As they washed and dried the old dishes, Joe told Jonah of the plan he had for their day's activities. First, they would explore the grounds and try to ascertain if anything unusual had happened as a result of their 'Black Dog' backmasking experiment. Next, they would contact Otis and ask him if he would be available the following day to take Granny to visit Grandpa Joseph in the nursing home. Then, they would search for Sugar, armed with candies of all types. Finally, the boys would sort the records in Ernie's collection, seeking clues and dating them to see if they could tell when Ernie had disappeared. Jonah thought the plan was perfect. He was becoming a great number-two man, Joe's Spock to his own Captain Kirk.

Having put the dishware in the old cabinets, the boys summoned all the resolution in their bodies, as they again prepared to check the carriage house for any change that might have resulted from their backmasking experiment. They felt strong enough in their will to enter unarmed.

They pulled open the two doors and charged into the old building, searching every corner and crevice for evidence of change. Finding nothing different than before, they climbed the ladder and found nothing unusual on the second level. They were at once relieved and disappointed. They were ready for the battle, but the battle wasn't ready for them. Whatever they were fighting was playing cat and mouse, trying to lull the boys into inattentiveness, at which point the attack would come like a blitzkrieg.

Joe was thinking like a five-star general by this point, thanks to many hours watching 'The History Channel'. He was preparing for a battle of attrition and guarding his flanks, mentally planning ambushes at strategic points around the property and in the forest.

Having searched the carriage house, Joe walkie-talkied Otis

and asked him to arrive at the house the next morning about eleven. He told the old man they wanted to take Granny to call on Grandpa Joseph at the nursing home for an hour or so, then have a nice barbecue lunch together. Otis was agreeable, as usual. He told Joe his Grandpa Joseph was a great man and suggested they take him a plate of brisket. He assured the boy he would be on time and would act as the consummate chauffeur and chaperone.

"Otis, my friend, are you busy at the moment?" Joe asked. "We need something as soon as possible."

"What be that?" Otis axed. "You jus' name it."

"This sounds weird, but we need a lot of candy. A crap-load of candy."

"Halloween's months away, son. Don't tell me you done went through all that good food we bought."

"I can't explain, Otis. Just bring us about ten of the biggest bags of Skittles you can get. Anything like that will work – M&M's, Reese's Pieces, stuff like that. In fact, buy thirty dollars worth, and I'll give you two twenties upon delivery."

"I'll be there within the hour," came the reply. "The Candyman shall cometh."

Forty minutes later Otis screeched to a halt at the front gate, where Joe E. and Jonah sat on the curb waiting.

"I ain't gonna axe what all these sweets be for. Just remember to brush yo teef," he said. "I'll be here tomorrow like you want. Until then – stay cool, little men."

"Thanks, buddy," Joe said as he packed the candy into the backpack he had retrieved from upstairs while waiting for the delivery. Otis left as fast as he had come, and Jonah asked Joe what the plan was for the re-connection with Sugar.

"Jonah, I think Sugar feels we betrayed her. Think about it – we penned her up and something terrible seems to have happened and terrified her. She probably thinks we set her up. After all, she's a simple animal in a new world she's unfamiliar with. One time, I had a new dog when I was a kid that ran away on the first night we had her. She was scared, too – rightfully so – and she bolted. We spotted her around the farm the next day and lured her back with slices of bologna. She ended up living with us for twelve years. Her name was

CoCo Chanel No. Heinz 57. That's what we're going to do with Sugar." Joe smiled with satisfaction at the memory. "We're going to lure her back with food."

They walked into the woods until they reached the clearing where they had encountered Sugar two times before. Joe opened the backpack and handed two large bags of Skittles to his friend.

"Spread these around the clearing and throw them as far as you can into the trees. Pretend you're Johnny Appleseed planting a future candy apple crop. We need to lure Sugar back and tell her we didn't mean to scare her."

Jonah did as instructed while Joe did the same on the other side of the open space. After doling out numerous bags of candy in this manner, the boys sat in the middle of the field and laid down to recuperate from the summer heat and humidity, which was relentless and draining, as usual.

"Joe, why is this clearing devoid of kudzu, while a block away kudzu is trying to overtake everything on your grandmother's property?"

"Good question. You tell me, Jonah. What's your theory?"

"Maybe the kudzu is trying to cover up the bad, but allows the good to remain uncovered."

"You answered your own question. Seems to me you're right, too. You're smarter than you give yourself credit."

"Thanks," Jonah said, smiling. "That means a lot, coming from you."

"I never said you were stupid, Jonah. You wouldn't be here with me if you were."

CHAPTER TEN AND FOUR

The two best friends lazed in the sunlight, hoping Sugar would make her appearance. I would have said they were lazing on a Sunday afternoon like the awesome Queen song from 'A Night at the Opera', but there was no telling what day it was. The boys had stopped keeping track of such trivial things as days of the week and dates of the month. It was all they could do to keep track of hours of the day, and they did that by the position of the sun in the sky and the shadows it cast when it encountered the house or the trees surrounding it. Time had little meaning to them, other than they didn't want to be out after dark if it could be avoided. All they were aware of was that right now was the middle of the afternoon – that was all.

***

The boys noticed a kettle of vultures had gathered, circling above them. They laughed as they realized the birds thought they were seeing a couple corpses laying on the grass below. As the winged consumers of carrion circled above them, Joe and Jonah became drowsy from the hot sun and the hypnotic rotation of the airborne scavengers.

Soon, the two sleep-deprived teenagers were slumbering, having a simultaneous dream of a beautiful translucent princess wandering through the here and there of the tissue paper time-line of life. It was an exquisite fantasy, and the boys both smiled as they slept. One instant this maiden was an apparition and the next she seemed to be tangible reality, as in all the finest dreams.

This enchanted lady was not visiting to satisfy some masturbatory urge like the chick from 'Weird Science'. She had a purpose beyond looking like a sexy, hot mess. She had been sent from above.

As the boys slept, the apparition of the woman raced around the perimeter of the grass field, peering into the forest as if she was searching for something threatening in the trees. She glided along without taking steps, the hem of her gauze skirt never revealing her feet – she was hovering. She looked like an Elven princess from 'The

black 113 dog

Lord of the Rings' – all soft focus with an opaque, porcelain complexion. She was very concerned with something that seemed dangerous in the forest and was unwilling to venture into the trees.

Jesus walked upon water and this seraph walked upon air. She had no wings, but was no less angelic, despite this lack of Biblical accoutrement, than the Archangel Gabriel. She was also, quite possibly, simply the result of the chemical interaction of an excess of Skittles and Sweet-Tarts reacting in two teenagers' minds.

She raced back and forth from one side of the clearing to the other, so fast she was a blur. She was frantic, trying to find what she was looking for. She wasn't looking for something, actually – she was *looking out for something*. Something all around them.

She moved to a place above Joe, floating horizontally over him, her radiant face inches from his. She wanted to speak, but lacked the ability to verbalize her warning. She wished to scream, so she could wake the boys from their supernatural slumber, but she could not. Communication, for her, consisted of mutual thought interaction and intuition, not crude human verbalization. She was like an actress in a silent movie trying to make her first 'talkie' and things weren't going at all well.

With a start, the heavenly lady heard a sound which altered her course of action. There were smoky fires and loud cackles of laughter to the east, and she turned toward them in terror. Archaic pagan songs from the distant past drifted to her on the wind, and she was terrified by the sound of the symphony of destruction.

Still unable to wake the boys, she raced to a point at the edge of the clearing where the disturbing sounds seemed to originate. Although the boys had never noticed it, there was a small opening in the trees, the entrance to an ancient path. The maiden looked back at Joe and Jonah, her face racked by distress. She was searching for answers to unspoken questions and was visibly distraught by the dilemma. Reaching some conclusion as to what to do next, she charged down the corridor through the gauntlet of trees. After a hundred yards, the path cleaved into two trails. She was unsure of which to take. She froze for a time, suspended above the path in peaceful, contemplative beauty. Her eyes drifted shut as the melody from the woods enchanted her with its siren song.

black 114 dog

Suddenly, she woke with a start and an organic body pulse, like Jimi Hendrix's Stratocaster being plugged into a Marshall stack with a loud crack. She knew she had been tricked. She had been sent to protect the two teenagers and had been baited away from them by a song she couldn't resist. The wind began to blow violently as she twisted in confusion. Leaves hit her as she turned and raced back the way she had come. The path was gone now. The trees had returned to their natural state, via xylem and phloem muscle memory, and the trail had disappeared. She fought through the rough branches and sticky vines, which attempted to entangle her and keep her from accomplishing her mission.

She reached the grass of the little field and hesitated. She sensed danger and turned to see that the forest she had just emerged from was now engulfed in fire. Dry wood crackled, and creatures of the forest screamed through the flames, locusts being burned alive.

In an instant, she was again suspended inches above Joe and Jonah, now in a frantic state of hopeless terror. She glared down at them in frustration, then anxiously scanned all around, sensing danger everywhere. She was a spirit of motherly love and was desperate to save these two children.

The heroine raised her determined face to a tornado of wind descending from above, which swirled smoke and debris furiously around the three of them. Still the boys slept, unaware of the danger rotating around them like great whites. A light snaked down through the center of the whirlwind like a trail of gasoline lit by an arsonist's match. It started as a thin pencil line, helixing from the sky above, but swiftly transformed into a spell-blinding strobe of dragon's breath. The maiden shielded her face from the red cyclone with one arm, then looked toward the hot light and thrust into it, willing to sacrifice herself. She lifted from the ground and accelerated toward the pulsing glow with abandon and absolute conviction. She was climbing the stairway to Heaven.

Upon meeting her path's resolution in the sky overhead, she exploded in a firework beyond anything the boys would see on any July 4th, and she did so with a loud bang directly over their dozing heads. The sky was an eclipse of charcoal blackness, until the sunflower aerials of her soul burst open and descended in comet trails like falling stars, pulled toward the earth by God's gravity.

***

The boys had been visited by their guardian angel....

***

Hearing the thunder crack of the explosion overhead, the boys started awake with a jerk, seeing tracers from the streaming pyrotechnic as they adjusted the focus of their eyes. A rain of ash fluttered down into the clearing. They were bewildered and clutched at each other in fear. Daylight was returning, but they were blinded by the ugly mixture of confusion, ash, and concussion. A swarm of wasps stinging them awake would have been preferable.

The smoke of the forest fire drifted into their position, obscuring the boys like a squad of American soldiers lost in the fog of a forbidden, out-of-bounds Cambodian jungle. Joe and Jonah were coughing hard and had no foxholes to take shelter in. The forest was blazing furiously. If you have seen video of the people in the streets near Ground Zero immediately after the terrorist attacks of September 11th, you can imagine what the boys were experiencing. It wasn't a white-out and it wasn't a black-out. It was both.

"What's happening?" screamed Jonah.

"I don't know! The forest is burning up! If we stay here we'll be okay! Drop to the ground and cover your head!"

Jonah did as Joe instructed, and the two pushed their faces into the sod and breathed through the thick grass, which filtered out most of the particulate. The humidity in the heavy air kept the smoke from rising as fast as it would in a dry climate, so it lay on the boys like wet London fog for long minutes.

After what seemed like an eternity, the fire smoldered out, still smoking black and heavy. The green, moist kudzu had snuffed out the rushing flames. What had burned so readily were the dry, dead trees that had been strangled and suffocated by the vines long ago. The healthy kudzu had won out, as usual – even fire couldn't stop it. The boys felt lucky their lives had not been snuffed out, but they wanted to know who or what had started the blaze. They were angry and confused. Where was Smokey the Bear when they needed him? Probably burned alive with Bambi, Rocky, and Bullwinkle in the enchanted forest.

black 116 dog

As the smoke thinned, the boys rose to their feet and tried to grasp the situation at hand. Their eyes burned, and they coughed like three-pack-a-day smokers with emphysema. Jonah rubbed his bangs into his eyes for relief until he finally found himself able to pry open his formerly glamorous eyelids. What he saw before him was absolute, artistic beauty, like a painting on the cover of a vintage Yes album. Sugar had returned and stood majestically in front of the charred, smoldering wasteland to the east. She smiled – revealing multi-colored Skittles stuck in her teeth.

"Joe, Sugar came back!" Jonah yelled. He ran to the animal and hugged her neck with love.

"I told you it would work!" Joe E. screamed through the tears of joy in his eyes he would later blame on the smoke exposure. He sprinted to the magnificent unicorn and hugged her neck from the opposite side of Jonah. "We love you, Sugar," Joe whispered. "Don't ever leave us again."

The reunion was a godsend, and the boys took some time in regaining their composure. They embraced Sugar like a long-lost friend, and she nuzzled them in return with equal and opposite love. She had seen and heard many things in the forest that had startled and worried her. Like the lady in the vision, though, she was unable to articulate these thoughts verbally. Everyone involved in this was in their own private Idaho, and the connections between each other were spider web thin, but strong when wound together, like the orange cables on the Golden Gate Bridge.

Eventually, they finished their love-in, and the boys turned to examine the blackened remnants left behind by the flash fire, which had consumed an area about the size of the natural clearing. The smoking skeletons of the charred trees made the forest look like a barren, post-apocalyptic planet from a science fiction movie.

"What could have started that fire, Joe?"

"Who cares?" Joe answered, attempting to be nonchalant. "I'm tired of trying to figure out why everything happens. We're just going to have to deal with it and move forward, nothing more. My plan worked and Sugar is back, and that's that! Who cares how the fire started?! Maybe we don't even want to know."

Secretly, Joe knew something or someone had attempted to

black 117 dog

exterminate them, but he was relieved the assassination attempt had failed. They had survived the first ambush. He didn't want to worry Jonah and undermine the boy's growing confidence.

"Damn right, bro," Jonah said with a beaming smile. "That is that! End of story!"

Sugar whinnied like a happy unicorn and almost knocked Jonah down with a unicorn love-nudge. Joe got a good laugh out of that, but was also a little jealous of the show of affection. He smiled for a second, then grew serious again.

***

The boys spoke intimately with Sugar and reassured her they had meant her no harm when they had penned her in the carriage house. Being unable to speak, she was, of course, powerless to inform them of her fears that long, dark night and could not explain to the boys why she had barged out of the barn.

Jonah and Joe E. were sure they had made the mistakes, though, and felt they owed an explanation and an apology to Sugar. They were at peace with the unicorn after their confession. She was hugged repeatedly, fed more candy, and sent back into the forest to the west of the clearing. They did not want to pen her in the carriage house again. She seemed able to survive by her wits. Joe told her never to go to the east side of the clearing. He had a very bad feeling about that area. They all did.

As Sugar neared the trees, she glanced back longingly at her friends before entering the stand. She didn't want to be alone, but continued onward into the congregation of oaks and cedar, cherry and pine. She was scared, but strong.

"Joe, What do you think happened to all the locusts in those trees that burned? I don't hear a thing. They were so loud before."

"They must have burned alive."

"That arsonist bastard. I hope whoever started that fire hangs until dead."

"They will. He will. Whatever. If we can find out who or what started that fire, they will absolutely pay, Jonah. Mark my words."

***

The boys walked slowly home without speaking. As they

black 118 dog

passed through the iron gate, Joe finally spoke. "We've done everything I wanted to do today, except for the project in Uncle Ernie's room. Are you up for it, Jonah? We need to date and catalog the entire record collection. I understand if you're not up to it."

"Bring it on, bro. I want to get the upper hand on all this unexplainable stuff and drag it out into the Alabama sun, so we can get a good look at it." Jonah was determined like a weekend warrior, which means he was now almost as strong as a volunteer United States National Guard soldier, which is very strong, indeed.

Joe smiled at his friend. Jonah was steeled for war, and Joe was in charge of the battle. The two of them were in the midst of supernatural war games, and it was time to turn the record over to side 'B', flip the script, and go on the offensive. Was this a terrorist threat on American soil? No. Was this a threat of another type on American soil? Yes. Were they fighting Islamic Jihad? No. Were the boys heroic, nonetheless? Yes.

"You're turning into a soldier, Jonah," Joe said. "I always took you for a medic, but I think you're ready to fight. Show me your war face!"

"GRROWWWWRRRRRR!!!!!!"

"Hell, yeah!" Joe exclaimed. "You're an animal!"

The boys screamed in unison at the top of their lungs until they were dizzy, then went in the house.

CHAPTER TEN AND FIVE

The boys returned to the little bedroom and began the task of cataloging Ernie's massive record collection. They worked efficiently – Jonah called out the necessary information, and Joe diligently recorded the details in his trusty notebook. He made a heading for each group with the band's name, which he underlined. Below that, he listed each album from the artist, along with the date of copyright. In addition, the boys examined the track listing of the albums, searching for songs that might be relevant to their situation. When they saw an intriguing title, they listened to the song. This slowed the process, but Joe was nothing, if not thorough, in his methodology.

They uncovered records with eerie titles like 'Welcome to My Nightmare' and 'We Sold Our Soul For Rock-n-Roll', 'Highway to Hell' and 'Their Satanic Majesties Request'. They explored songs with titles like 'Running With The Devil' and 'Heaven and Hell' and 'Sympathy for the Devil'. Band names like Black Sabbath and the creepy covers of some of the classic rock albums gave the boys the heebie-jeebies. This was rock and roll with themes they had never encountered. Their era of music dealt with subjects like Green Day odes to masturbation and Nickleback and Creed throwaway white trashola crapola.

They even found a double album by a guy called George Harrison, titled 'All Things Must Pass', with a song of the same name. The boys listened to the track and heard what Granny had been singing in the kitchen. Sad, but enlightening. The song was almost like something slaves might have sung to maintain their faith and spirit while they toiled in the cotton fields. Almost.

The work continued until near daybreak, at which point they were less than a third of the way through the record collection. They hadn't expected to complete the task in one night, but it was going much slower than expected, since they stopped frequently to listen to non-scary songs with intriguing titles like 'Space Oddity' and 'Rocket Man'. Some of these songs were listened to over and over, the boys laying on the floor in a meditative state, contemplating what they heard.

An hour before dawn the boys dropped the needle on a record that featured a half-man/half-dog on its cover, 'Diamond Dogs' by David Bowie. Within seconds, the boys were bolt upright and fully awake, as the howl of a manimal ripped open the album's first track. They listened to the entire record, thoughts racing through their minds like the chaos of a Mumbai intersection. They couldn't make sense of a bit of it. References to Nietzsche, Cassius Clay, and Big Brother were outside their frame of reference, and they had no computer to do research.

They were intrigued, nonetheless, and the album would become a favorite of both of theirs in the future. They were mentally exhausted by the end of the second side, having been hypnotized by 'Chant of the Ever Circling Skeletal Family'.

"That song is a Nirvana mosh," Jonah said deliriously, his viddy orbs nearly rolling back in his gulliver.

"Suuure, bro. Let's call it a night and get a few hours rest," Joe said. "Otis will be here at eleven. We'll take Granny to see Grandpa Joseph and pick up where we left off when we get back."

Jonah did not respond. He had fallen asleep on the floor with a Marvin Gaye album in his hand.

***

Joe left his sleeping friend where he lay and returned to his cot to catch some needed shuteye. He woke a couple hours later and took a shower before waking Jonah to do the same. Joe was wide awake, despite the short nap he had taken, and was champing at the bit, ready to discover what the day would bring. As Jonah showered, Joe rapped on Granny's door and informed her of the surprise they had planned for her. She was happy – more than happy, in fact. She was elated and dressed for the excursion like she was going to the Kentucky Derby, with hat, white gloves, and all.

Otis arrived on time and acted as a chauffeur, rather than a simple taxi driver. He was familiar with Joe's grandmother from his childhood long ago. She had been one of the most well-to-do Southern belles in Alabama, quite ravishing to behold. Otis greeted Granny respectfully and escorted her on his arm slowly, step by step, from the gate to the Towncar. Joe sat next to Granny inside the car, holding her hand lovingly. Jonah sat in the front seat next to Otis, struggling to stay awake and alert.

They drove leisurely to the nursing home, where Grandpa Joseph lived in his hazy shade of winter. Granny was happy to be out on the town. She smiled sweetly as she gazed from side to side at all the changes the town had undergone since the last time she had seen it.

Upon seeing her husband, Granny lit up like a Houston debutante at a social function and proceeded to flirt sentimentally with him, remembering the days of their future past. Grandpa Joseph sat in silence with a glazed look and a slight smile on his face, as Granny reminisced story after story. He said nothing in response, but understood, nonetheless. He had long since forgotten these details of their courtship, but hearing her talk about them brought synapses to pathways in his brain that had long ago become dormant. Wanting to leave them to their own devices, Otis and the boys retired to the courtyard to catch up on things.

"Well, how things been goin'?" axed Otis. "You ain't walkie-talkied me much, so I suspect you been handlin' your bidness, but how things really been?"

"Complicated," answered Joe. "Like a riddle that needs to be solved. But that's just what we're doing, Otis. I can't really explain, and I'm not gonna complain."

"Complaining never got nobody nowheres," Otis replied. "And explaining be yo privilege. You jus' gots to hold on. And be strong."

"That's exactly what that Outkast album we bought when you took us to that CD shop said," exclaimed Jonah with unbridled enthusiasm. "That's what we're doing!"

"That's all you gots ta do. It's simple. Joe, you told me you be looking for answers in the past. Remember, they's knowledge in the present, as well. Uncovering the ol' days may call up things that might jus' be better off stayin' buried, 'specially 'round Stringtown, but I ain't gon' tell y'all what to do. You boys be getting stronger and smarter every day. You turnin' from boys to men, jus' like that R&B group sister loves so much."

After the visit, Otis drove them to the barbeque joint, and they all ate happily and heartily. Otis had remembered to bring a

black 122 dog

carry-out brisket dinner for Grandpa that morning, but the others had not eaten, so they were famished. Following lunch, they stopped for vodka and cigarettes to re-supply Granny's pantry, then returned home.

Granny was glowing, the happiest the boys had seen her. There were no mysterious, dire warnings from her for the time being, only smiles. In fact, she had barely spoken since seeing her husband. Her eyes were far away – attending distant wedding ceremonies, Thanksgiving dinners, and cotillions decades ago. Joe had his arm around her the entire trip home, and her withered hand gripped his with surprising strength. They spoke no words, but family is family, and blood is thicker than you know what, and, to quote Forrest Gump, "That's all I have to say about that."

They arrived home, and Otis drove away smiling. Granny shuffled to her room, still radiant, and the boys went upstairs to Ernie's room to get back to work. They waded back into their project, but took many more breaks to listen to songs than they had the day before. Things didn't seem so urgent after their enjoyable excursion. There was an ebb and flow crimson tide happening within their Alabama summer. Traumatic events, like attempted arson murder in the forest, spurred them to immediate action, but days like this one told them there was no hurry and that they were in little danger. There was a struggle between urgency and complacency taking place in their work, but the job was getting done on their terms, which was what needed to happen.

The work was slow. It was not a task to be rushed. In addition to the aforementioned details they were recording, the boys had decided to organize the albums in alphabetical order, which would make them easy to reference when needed. Their methods were old-school, pre-internet, but the records were also pre-internet, so it made sense. Even Al Gore would agree, if he wasn't so busy telling people how to live their lives.

They found themselves returning time and time again to pockets of the collection that held the most meaning to them. They needed to absorb certain tracks more than others, in order to completely understand the significance of the most important song lyrics. Sometimes they just liked the melody, though. There were no rules.

They were attempting to absorb the massive entirety of 'Classic Rock' and all it encompassed, but had no prior knowledge of the data they were inputting into their cerebral computers. They were starting from scratch, but over and over they were inspired, scared, or amazed by the songs they selected, seemingly at random, to examine in detail.

For example, they didn't know who or what a Jethro Tull was, but they decided to listen to a song called 'Aqualung' and were mesmerized. They initially thought the song was about Aquaman, but found out it was actually about a London bum with terrible hygiene who liked to watch little girls at play, as their frilly panties peeked from under short skirts. They had no point of reference for subject matter like this, but they understood it, nonetheless.

They were listening more intently to these songs than to any they had heard in their short lives. They memorized words as they soaked up melodies, using to the fullest advantage the Commodore 64 between their ears. This was not a scenario they were used to. It was not one bleating earbud parked in a left ear and concealed by a swoop of hair while a teacher droned on and on about a math test in an underachieving all-American high school. This was intent examination of aural art, not unlike a Louvre patron studying the Mona Lisa.

***

Hell, I'll say it. They were interpreting three-minute outbursts of Rorschach expression equal to the Mona Lisa in the loose, unapologetic, modern definition of what is called 'art' – a definition that includes rock and roll. Sure, I love the Mona Lisa, but I'm not as intrigued by her enigmatic smile as I am by the notes Jimmy Page played on 'Ten Years Gone' or 'Stairway to Heaven'. Those songs have inspired, influenced, and intoxicated way more people in the modern era than an antiquated portrait of a less than average looking Italian gal, no matter how mysterious and intriguing her sly smile. How many commuters do you see on the subway listening to Paganini on their iPod and reading Goethe on their iPad?

That makes me feel dirty – like I just uttered a few racial slurs. You see, I am somewhat well educated, as far as art in the classic sense, and will surely regret these bold statements when they make their way to print – but I'm sure the readers of a book like this will understand the point I'm trying to make. Art is in the eye of the beholder, just like beauty. Bowie was a paranoid coke addict, drawing pentagrams on the window blinds and singing about aliens – and he made some of the best music of all of the times.

It's a pointless argument, I admit. It's like arguing whether the modern Patriots are better than the old-school Packers. Who knows? One thing I do know – a dead calf suspended in an aquarium full of piss isn't art. It's a waste of good veal.

***

Point of fact about modern art versus classic art – I tried to read 'Robinson Crusoe' the other day for old times' sake. Yes, I read when I have time away from my various skullduggery. I got bored and confused by the end of the first chapter. The story was as foggy as an early morning in the vineyards of SoCal, where so many grapes hope to stake their claim to fame as a drop of Boone's Farm Strawberry Hill.

Surprisingly, 'Robinson Crusoe' was one of my favorite books as an early teen. In retrospect, I can't believe I was adept enough at reading comprehension to decipher the literary curly-cues that permeate the book.

There can be no argument whether the story has stood the test of time, as there are numerous modern adaptations of it, but trying to re-read the novel was comparable to removing a deep splinter. Layers and layers of superficial skin blocked what was being sought – the meaning of each sentence. No wonder the library card said the book had not been checked out in five years.

I've never seen so many run-on sentences in my life. Modern editors would commit ceremonial seppuku if they were forced to read this style of prose all the live long day. In fact, after a few pages of it I was in want of a snow shovel, and, since I had none, gave up on the reading of the manuscript, deciding, instead, to partake of a dram of rum from a small cup I had long-laboured to carve from the stem of a bamboo plant, did just that, then proceeded to pass out in my drunken and inebriated state on the shore of the beach and did, thus, *incur a sunburn which made me now darker by some increment even than my trusty servant, Friday, who had, during my absence, ventured into the verdant growth in search of, and with the intent of, killing a wild boar, although hunting too many would surely doom us to a life without our primary source of meat, which could not be supplanted by the few eggs we might gather from the sea-going birds nesting in the upper tier of the desert island's volcanic peak, not to mention we would have great difficulty traversing the dramatically elevating, jagged, black, volcanic terrain leading to the delicate nests holding the soft-boned, unborn offspring of those noble fowl.*

Reader, you can breathe now. How'd you like that sentence-slash-paragraph? How 'bout a few hundred pages of that? Wanna grab a beer and listen to Zeppelin? I thought so. Let's be friends. From now on you can call me Ishmael, and I'll call you Friday. Or you can call me Ray, or you can call me Jay, or you can call me Ray Jay, or you can call me RJ. Just don't call me Johnson! And if you understand that reference you can call yourself 'old'. YouTube it, youngsters. You're going to be Googling and YouTubing half the stuff in this book, if we're lucky. That sounds obscene, but that's where we're at nowadays. If I said I was gonna 'Google' and 'YouTube' somebody twenty years ago, I would have gotten slapped or shot! At least you have the internets, and Al Gore has blessed you with the ability to instantaneously search out the meanings to all these obscure references I drop with excruciating ease. I should be sprinkling internet ads among the paragraphs, for God's sake!

At this point, I would like to introduce you to the subjects of what I hope will be your next internet searches. First – a guy called Charles Bukowski, who used to throw up when he woke up and had a hard time holding a job. Google away and consider the similarities and common symptoms of bleeding ulcers and alcoholism and failed relationships that so many famous writers have in common. After Bukowski you need to research William S. Burroughs and Hunter S. Thompson. Why do these writers who tell stories of drug abuse and manic, nomadic life insist on using their middle initial? I'm going to recommend to the writer of this book that he use his middle initial from this point forward and be christened an alcoholic, drunken, tragic poet and successful novelist. Then you can bash him in the

black 126 dog

head with a champagne bottle and launch him into the surf. Hopefully, Friday will find him bobbing in the waves and row him to 'Celebrity Rehab Island'.

***

According to scientific study, music speaks to people and invokes emotion more deeply than any medium, other than smell. Think about it. You could be stranded on a desert island, just like Robinson Crusoe, and sing a favorite song to yourself and become inspired and motivated to build a raft that will float you to freedom and prosperity, just like the most famous of Cuban refugees, Tony Montana. Would thinking about a painting or a movie or a television show, or even a smell, inspire you to do that? I think not. I don't care how funny 'Seinfeld' or 'Cheers' or 'MASH' were – they aren't going to save your life. They will not sustain you through a prison sentence. Did the slaves recite comedy sketches while they toiled in the cotton fields? Or did they sing holy spirituals that inspired them and later inspired a group of Brits going by the name of Led Zeppelin who, in turn, inspired me to write this book? Listen to 'In My Time of Dying' and email me if you think my theory is wrong. My spam filter is set on 'destroy', so good luck getting through.

I'm beleaguering the point, but strand yourself for a year or two on a desert island like ol' Robbie Crusoe if you think I'm wrong, and let me know what sustains you, doubter. Strand yourself on a dessert island if you want to gain a lot of weight, obese American. (Spelling geek joke. Sorry.) Hell, go work a few twelve-hour overnight shifts on an assembly line and tell me what gets you through the night, as the air pistons blast your psyche into sweet, green, oblivion-flavored Jell-O. I don't need you to answer my query – this is all rhetorical. I have lived the examples I propose. I already know what sustains a person through a long shift in a manufacturing plant or being utterly alone, shipwrecked. Thoughts of true love, thoughts of dogs and family, and the melodies and poetic words of a millionaire-waltzing, buck-toothed gentleman named Freddie Mercury, who died tragically before his time, are what's gonna make you a survivor. Spirituality is a great addition to these, as well.

Low art, like rock-n-roll, relates to people like us and is easily interpreted, while high art takes opera glasses to see clearly.

And who among us owns opera glasses? Beer goggles, maybe, but opera glasses, no. I rest my case. And the fat lady hasn't even begun warming up. She's still at the dessert table of the buffet loading up on MoonPies.

***

The boys enjoyed themselves immensely during their rock and roll education. The only thing that could have made it better would have been if Uncle Ernie could have personally guided them through this discovery process. Uncles are great for stuff like that. Big brothers often work, too. Hell, even a cool teacher can do wonders for an open-minded kid searching for artistic enlightenment.

In these internet days, all it takes is a website name scrawled across the palm of a hand at school to start the process of digital archeology. Then, 3:30 arrives, and the kid races home to YouTube and Google what the cool substitute teacher told him about. The trail of discovery is inflamed in a manic digital scavenger hunt. One clue leads to another, via the text comments below an awesome video or some link to another link. Next thing you know, the Temple of the Dog has been discovered without even getting any dirt under the fingernails. Grunge Nirvana has been achieved and nobody had to commit shotgun suicide to do it.

Let me provide a theoretical example. Say a kid and his best friend like an Audioslave song, so they search 'Audioslave'. A link comes up in their search, which references the band Soundgarden. Chris Cornell, Audioslave's lead singer, used to sing for Soundgarden, so that's something likely to happen. They click on the link and listen to 'Black Hole Sun' and like it. Next, they discover that Soundgarden played a song in the movie 'Singles'. They illegally download the movie and watch it. This exposes them to another band called Alice in Chains, so they research them. They learn that Alice's lead singer, Layne Staley, died as the result of a terrible drug habit. They search 'Seattle drug overdose' and read the story of Andrew Wood, the lead singer of Mother Love Bone and one-time roommate of Chris Cornell. Andrew Wood OD'd the night before Love Bone's album was to come out, after too much partying at the band's album release party. How tragic is that? The boys YouTube Mother Love Bone and like what they hear. Next, they discover that members of

black 128 dog

Soundgarden and surviving members of Mother Love Bone gathered shortly after Andrew's death to record an album in his honor. That band and their album are called 'Temple of the Dog', and the music they made is some of the most emotional you will ever hear. You still with me?

The chain reaction continues. During the fifteen days of recording the 'Temple of the Dog' album, an unknown singer by the name of Eddie Vedder flew to the Jet City from San Diego to audition for a new band called Pearl Jam, which was rising from the ashes of Mother Love Bone. Eddie provided counter-point vocals on a few tracks of the 'Temple of the Dog' album and became the lead singer of Pearl Jam. And the rest is history.

God – those last couple paragraphs could have come from 'Robinson Crusoe: The Grunge Days'. Hopefully, I've clearly illustrated the simple process of connecting digital dots to discover things that can be life-changing. Jonah and Joe were doing the same thing, although with little help from the information superhighway. They were doing it like Uncle Ernie did – one song at a time.

***

The two boys had endured their fair share of stripping away the kudzu from their psyches this young summer, exposing their super-egos to intense sunlight and extensive examination. They had paid their mental and physical dues. They were learning more about life than they had ever known existed, relishing every second of every 33 and 1/3 revolutions per minute.

In case you don't know – a full-length record rotates 33.33 times every minute. If you want to listen to a single on a record player, you have to flip the toggle to 45 revolutions per minute, and you might have to put an adapter in the record's hole to accommodate the spindle. I'm saying all this because I'm getting sick of telling you to Google everything I mention. I don't own stock in the company, after all.

***

At one point in the exploratory process, Jonah asked a question of his compatriot. "Joe E., do you think anything happened when we played 'Black Dog' backwards?"

"Something happened, Jonah, but I don't know what."

black 129 dog

"Well, let's play another song backwards. Maybe something more obvious will happen. Let's backmask 'Stairway to Heaven'."

"NO!" Joe screamed, shocking his friend. "Didn't you see what that song says backwards when we were at the library?"

"No. I guess I wasn't paying attention. What did we find out?"

"Don't ever backmask that song, Jonah. That's what we found out. I wrote down what it says when played in reverse." Joe grabbed his backpack and fished for the scrap of paper he had scribbled on at the library. He found the paper and unfolded it with shaking hands. "This is what the song says backwards."

"Oh, here's to my sweet Satan,
The one whose path would make you sad,
Whose power is Satan,
He will give those with him 666,
There was a little tool shed where he made us suffer,
Sad Satan."

"Do you still want to play it backwards, Jonah?"

"Hell, no, but c'mon, Joe. A tool shed?"

"The carriage house is the tool shed."

"My God, you may be right."

"You still want to backmask it, Jonah?"

"It's not worth the risk. It could be true, you know."

"That's right, it could be true. Let's go to the carriage house and check it out again. Something had to have happened when we played 'Black Dog' backwards."

"Okay, I guess," Jonah answered.

***

They stopped at the front doors of the carriage house – the ones they could see from Ernie's bedroom window. They swung them wide and inspected the premises like CSI investigators, combing every inch for clues. Jonah went to the back doors, which faced the forest. Looking down at the dirt just inside this entrance, he made a startling and terrible discovery – footprints leading from the doors to the stall where Sugar had been.

black 130 dog

"Oh, God," he said loudly. "Look, Joe!"

Joe raced over and gazed at the ground in astonishment. What he saw terrified him – footprints that looked to be from a very large dog. These tracks were much larger than any known dog's, though, and at times it looked as if the animal was walking upright. In turn, the prints sometimes turned into a four on the floor pattern like those from a normal representative of the Canidae family. The tracks led to the stall where Sugar had been, then to the center of the building, turning back into sets of upright prints near the ladder, where the animal, no doubt, had made its way upstairs. Joe couldn't believe they had missed the tracks on their prior inspection, but they had been looking for actual beings, not concentrating on fingerprints or footprints.

"Holy crap," whispered Jonah. "That thing could be up there right now! What could have made those prints, Joe E.?"

"A dog. It had to be a large dog."

"Walking on two legs?"

Jonah was right. The prints clearly indicated the path of an animal walking on two legs at times. In addition, they had to have been made by an animal weighing at least two hundred pounds. The nails were over two inches long and curved like a scythe, by the appearance of the indention they had left in the soft dirt of the carriage house floor.

"We gotta get outta this place, Jonah," Joe whispered. "It's too late for this. We'll check these prints out more tomorrow. Maybe a coyote got in here." Joe was swiftly retreating toward the doors. "C'mon, dude. Let's get the eff outta here!"

Jonah needed no further encouragement. He almost ran up his friend's calf muscles on the way out. They slammed the doors shut without bothering to tie them and ran around the house to safety.

As they passed the cellar, still braced shut with rebar, they heard something that stopped them in their tracks. An animal was howling/barking/growling from the underside of the cellar door. The two boys stopped and looked at each other in terror.

"Dude, that thing is down there!" Jonah screamed.

"What thing?"

"The thing that scared Sugar! Holy crap! Don't let it out, for

black 131 dog

God's sake!"

"How could it have been in the carriage house if it's locked in the cellar, Jonah?"

"How can anything be anywhere? Nothing makes any sense here, Joe!" Jonah clutched his head and sat down in the grass. "I don't know what's going on. I just don't know...."

"I'm letting it out, Jonah."

"Don't do it! Let it die down there!" Jonah shrieked.

"I can't do that," Joe said as he reached to slide the iron bar from its braces. He mustered his will and thrust the door open, which took all the strength and determination he had left.

Nothing happened. Jonah looked through cracks in his fingers as Joe stood like a cage fighter ready to meet his opponent, but nothing happened.

"I'm going in," said Joe. "I read about those guys in Vietnam who went into the tunnels, and that's what I'm gonna do. This is war, dude!"

He charged down the steps, now familiar to him, but encountered nothing with bitey teeth.

Two or three minutes passed. Jonah was almost catatonic from the ordeal, but watched the entrance. He had managed to get to his feet and had a large stick ready to clock whatever emerged from the cellar, if it was not Joe.

Suddenly, Jonah heard barking from the cellar and readied himself for the beast to emerge. He waited for agonizing seconds, yet was met with no opposition or explanation. The suspense was getting the best of his goat. Finally, he stuck his head into the door's opening and yelled to his friend.

"Joe E., are you there?"

"Of course I'm here. I'll be up in a sec."

Half a minute later, Joe the Conqueror emerged from the void, clutching a black canine with a long snout. The animal was a Scottish terrier and appeared to be docile, although wary of the situation, judging by its darting eyes and uncomfortable state of being.

"That dog looks exactly like your uncle's black dog from the picture."

black 132 dog

"It doesn't just look like the dog. It is the dog," Joe answered. "Playing 'Black Dog' backwards conjured it. We have the black dog!"

"Is it evil?" Jonah screamed.

"Is Sugar evil?" Joe answered before kissing Black Dog's cold, wet nose. "Is you evil?" he asked the animal in baby talk while rubbing the top of her head.

They raced into the house and upstairs with the dog, although they knew not what to do with it. She was filthy – covered with the funk of forty thousand years and in dire need of a dip. The stench in the small space of Uncle Ernie's room was overwhelming. The animal's fur was saturated with some sort of Ghostbusters-style ectoplasm substance, which reeked like landfill runoff, aka leachate, the most vile substance known to modern man. The animal might have been White Dog, as dirty as she was.

"Joe. We have got to bathe that dog – NOW," Jonah stated with authority. They did just that – four times. Cleaning the bathtub afterward proved to be an even more arduous chore.

Pondering where to house the still black, but now clean terrier, they decided to clear a place in Ernie's closet for the little canine to bed down. She was calm and endured all they put her through without complaint, but was by no means excited or affectionate during the process. She was no nervous, trembling Chihuahua, lunging at their faces with tongue licks of inane affection. She seemed to be intelligent and independent, able to understand and logically consider everything the boys said and did, just like Sugar. Apparently, these supernatural animals had greater intelligence than normal four-legged, earthly creatures. Joe bedded the little canine among the Puma sneakers on the floor of the closet and shut the sliding doors closed for the night.

"This is just like 'E.T.', said Jonah. "Remember how Elliot kept E.T. in the closet with the stuffed animals?"

Joe laughed. "Right? E.T. was camouflaged by the toys, and Black Dog laying down in the closet is invisible, too. Nice observation. Let's call it a night and hit the cots, buddy. I hope she'll sleep there until morning without barking and howling and waking Granny."

"Granny's heard so much barking and howling from us, she'll

just think we're up playing video games," Jonah said.

"You're probably right. I'm beat, man. Let's hit the rack. It's been a helluva day."

"You can howl that again, Joe E."

CHAPTER TEN AND SIX

The following morning the boys raced to see if Black Dog had been contained and content for the night. They opened the closet door to find the dog whining in pain, rubbing her snout on the carpet and the closet wall.

Joe bent down and reached for the animal's long muzzle and was snapped at violently. He recoiled, regrouped, and reached in again – this time more slowly – and Black Dog let him examine her. He grasped the animal's face and squared it to his. He saw one long canine tooth on one side and none on the other. He hesitantly lifted the dog's black lip on the short side and saw her fang had been broken off. She was in pain, as every panting breath she took flowed over the exposed nerve. Unlike a typical dog, her fangs, at least by judging from the remaining one and the picture on the desk, protruded to the extent that they were visible at all times. Most dogs only show their canine teeth when they growl, but Black Dog was different. The constant appearance of her little daggers wasn't overtly threatening, but if she got mad at you it would not be pretty.

"Dude, I think she broke her tooth trying to get out of the cellar," said Joe.

"Poor thing," said Jonah. "Let's call Otis and get her to a vet."

"Only thing we can do, I guess."

They walkie-talkied their friend, and he arrived promptly. He transmissioned to them when he arrived at the gate, and the boys hustled Black Dog out to the taxi. They didn't want to be discovered and questioned by Granny.

"Where'd you get that animal?" Otis asked with a 'what now' expression on his face.

"She's a stray, and she's hurt," Joe answered. "Her tooth is broken. We need to get her to a veterinarian."

"You say she needs a new toof? Vets don't do dat. Dentists do dat."

"Well, we have to do something," Joe said. "She's in pain."

"I know exactly whats to do. Get in the back, boys, but keep

Miss Thang from relieving herself on the tuck and roll."

"Don't you mean 'Miss Fang'?" asked Jonah.

Otis smiled and shook his head. "Boys, I don't know what to think about y'all. You lucky you my friends."

Otis sped the suffering animal to get help. Joe and Jonah stroked the dog's beautiful fur to console her. Black Dog was so coal black that her eyes were hard to see, even if she was looking directly at the boys. When she had gazed up at them from the closet that morning, it scared both of them, since she appeared to be eyeless in the dim light.

"Where we goin', Otis?" asked Jonah.

"You see dis?" the old black man said, baring his teeth in the rear view mirror and pointing at his gold tooth.

"Yeah," Jonah answered.

"We goin' to the man who put dis gold toof in my grill. He'll fix up the dog. She gonna get a gold toof jus' like ol' Otis!"

Joe said, "Otis, that's gonna be too expensive. Can he make a new tooth for her out of silver?"

"Sho nuff. He an artist."

***

They arrived at a little shop a few blocks away from downtown Stringtown. They walked in and saw it was a combination barbershop/grill shop. The barber/dental jeweler, Big Earl, was finishing up a hi-top fade on some dude who hadn't left the eighties in hairstyle or dress – straight out of the glory days of Kid 'n Play. At least he sported a traditional pencil eraser-style fade, not a 'Gumby', dammit! The patron gave them a strange glance as he paid Big Earl and left the shop in ketchup-colored parachute pants. In his hammer-time world, Otis and his gang were the oddballs, not him.

Big Earl inspected the four of them and said, "C'mon, Otis, I don't cut dog hair, even if the thang do be black. You know better than that!"

Otis smiled. "Big E, this dog needs a new toof, not a fade. Show the man, boys."

Joe was holding Black Dog, so Jonah carefully slid back the animal's lip to expose the broken canine tooth.

"How you 'spect me to work on a dog? It gon' be bitin' at

black 136 dog

me!" Earl stated.

"Dunno," said Otis. "Ain't ya gots nothing to knock her out with? Maybe we can use some Thunderbird or Boone's Farm. They's a store round the corner. Don't know how we gon' make her drink, though. That drank be foul."

Big Earl smiled. "I know whats ta do. You boys got a hundy on ya?"

"I'll give you $120 if you can fix her tooth," said Joe E.

Big Earl rolled his eyes as if irritated, which he wasn't. "Bring the beast to the back room. Follow me." He grabbed a grape-flavored Phillies Blunt from a box on the counter, and they all walked to the rear of the shop.

Earl handed a set of keys to Jonah, his index and thumb holding a selected one. "Boy, do me a solid and locks tha front door."

"You gots it my bruva," Jonah replied.

The 'what you talkin' about, Willis' double take Big Earl did was priceless, but Jonah did not notice, as he was already on his way to the front of the shop.

The barber looked at Joe skeptically, attempting to discern whether he was being pranked or punk'd, but the boy's serious demeanor squelched the thought. The big man shook his head slightly and chuckled as he sat down at the table and removed the plastic cover from the Blunt.

Earl cut down the length of the cigar with a razor-knife and removed the tobacco, adding what smelled like very strong marijuana in its place. He re-rolled the Blunt, licked its wrapper and lit it, taking a few long drags with his eyes closed. Joe wondered if a dentist getting blasted before a procedure was the best of ideas.

"Put the animal on the table," Earl said.

Joe did so and Black Dog stiffened in fear. Earl stroked the frightened animal a few times and said in a Barry White voice, "Relax, little girl. Earl ain't gon' hurt ya." He took a long drag from the cigar and lifted Black Dog's ear delicately. He blew the lungful of smoke into the animal's ear canal. It tickled Black Dog, and she shook her head. Earl laughed and repeated the process in the other ear, then back and forth four or five more times. Jonah, Joe E., and Otis looked at each other disbelievingly, wondering if this was going

black 137 dog

to work. They were all getting an hellacious contact high and stifling giggles. Black Dog was beyond docile at this point, her soft little black eyelids at half mast.

The barber grabbed a piece of hard wax and a pocket knife and whittled a model of the prosthetic tooth, checking the fit numerous times against the nub in Black Dog's mouth.

"Does the animal need a full grill?" he axed. "I can do that for three hundy. Hell, I can put diamonds in it and er'thang if you got money."

"Just do the one tooth in silver, please," said Joe. "Will it be strong enough like that?"

"I ain't just doing the tip, son. It's gonna have a sleeve over the rest of the tooth, and I'm gonna glue it on with Gorilla Snot. It ain't goin' nowheres." Black Dog didn't seem to mind, much less notice, what was being done to her in her hydroponic-induced stupor.

Earl mixed up some plaster in a small plastic vessel, which looked to be from a pudding cup. He let the plaster partially harden for a few minutes, then pushed the carving into it. Once the plaster had fully hardened, he turned the cup upside down and brought a little butane-fueled torch to the wax, which melted and dripped out, leaving a void.

He had created a crude mold, which he poured molten silver into. After letting the metal cool and harden, he cracked away the plaster and checked the fit of the apparatus on Black Dog's fang. He glued the silver piece to the stump, then wrapped the remaining stalk of the tooth and the upper part of the prosthetic in layers of silver foil. Using the torch on the lowest setting, he delicately welded the whole thing together without burning the animal, which was amazing to behold. He was an artist, just as Otis had declared.

Upon finishing, Earl beamed with pride as he inspected his work.

"This dog be pimpin!" he exclaimed. "Dirty Souf big pimpin!" All of them laughed at this.

Joe held Black Dog's face to his to inspect the work. The animal was still groggy, but was regaining consciousness slowly.

"The silver tooth's longer than the other one," he said. "I'm not criticizing, I'm just sayin'."

"I done that on purpose, boy," said Big Earl. "If you gonna be a pimp, you gots ta represent. Black Dog be representin' to tha fullest!"

"It looks great," said Joe. He reached in his pocket and handed Earl four twenties and a fifty. "You did a great job. Thank you!"

"Don't you two boys need a gold tooth, like your friend, Otis?" Big Earl axed. "You be pimpin' like Black Dog when you strut out my door."

"Can we, Joe?" asked Jonah like a dog begging for a biscuit. If the boy had been born with a tail, it would have been wagging furiously.

"Maybe next time, boy," Joe said, tousling Jonah's mane as if petting a sheep dog. "You do need a haircut, though. I do, too. How 'bout we get a little trim, Big E, and come back later for our gold teefs?"

"Let's do this," Big Earl replied in his deep, kind voice.

Joe was first in the chair and Earl gave him a nice haircut. Jonah was extremely wary, more so than even Black Dog had been, but followed his friend into the chair and received a haircut like he hadn't had since early childhood. His eyes were no longer obscured, and his ears were uncovered for the first time in ten years.

Joe E. asked Earl how much they owed him for the white boy haircuts, but the huge man assured him they were even. Jonah thought Joe and Earl were screaming at each other, but realized he could hear infinitely more clearly, since his hair no longer muffled every sound. He couldn't wait to listen to a full-strength version of 'Stairway to Heaven'.

The boys and Otis thanked Big Earl and left the shop happily, as the big man settled into the barber chair to nap until the arrival of his next customer. The chronic he had smoked had anesthetized him, as well. It had been a long time since he had a day like this in his little barbershop, and he was content.

"Told ya I'd get that dog fixed up," said Otis as he drove the three of them home. "That be the bess lookin' dang mutt in tha county! Sho nuff!"

The old black man looked in the rear view mirror of his taxi and saw three smiling faces beaming back at him, one of which had vicious looking canine teeth with a touch of silver bling.

"Tarnation, that Black Dog be lookin' fine," he said. "She needs her a new collar and a medallion!"

"How much do you think I should spend on that?" asked Joe.

"I think that lil' girl be the most important four-legged friend you ever gonna have. That's fo' sho'! She be worth whatever you can spare."

"You really think so?" Jonah asked.

"That little miss thang be very special, y'all. You keep her by yo' side up there at Granny's place. Y'all boys need some protection. She likes you two, I can tell, and she ain't gon' wander off. Keep her close by y'all at all times. She be you boys' protector!"

Black Dog smiled a wide, loopy smile, and Otis caught her glimpse in his rear-view mirror and smiled in return, their precious metal grins reflecting to each other like sister satellites beaming invisible messages back and forth.

CHAPTER TEN AND SEVEN

It was late afternoon, and the boys had no chores to do, so they decided to hang out in Ernie's room with their recuperating pet and finish cataloging the albums. The culmination of the job was in sight, and they felt confident it would be finished by the evening's end.

As they worked, Jonah posed a question to his best friend. "So, you think when we play a song backwards the thing in the song transports into the cellar?"

"Dunno. It seems like that, but who knows? What if something comes through somewhere else? I don't want to take any chances. We need to be really careful. We could make a mistake and bring through something evil. For example, I don't think we should backmask that Judas Priest song, 'The Ripper', we listened to. We might bring through Jack the Ripper for God's sakes! Think about what would happen if we brought that bastard to Stringtown."

"Not good, Joe. Worst. Idea. Ever."

"And don't forget what we learned about the backward message on 'Stairway to Heaven'. We may love the song, but I think the clues in that one come from the forward version. Why don't we take a break and listen to it again?"

"I'm the dee-jay. I play what I'm requested to play," Jonah said as he got up to put on the record.

When the song ended, Jonah spoke. "You know Joe, we need to feed Sugar. It's been a while since we saw her. Let's go into the forest before it gets dark."

"Alright by me."

They tucked Black Dog into the closet. She was more than happy to return to her isolation chamber for a nap, after the procedure that had been performed upon her. The boys left the house with a large bag of M&M's and walked into the trees where they usually entered. They followed the path to the clearing, calling out to Sugar all the way, but saw no sign of the shy unicorn.

They walked into the clearing from the south and took a left, leaving the open space and entering the forest on the west side. This was uncharted territory, and they were nervous. The east side was still burned-out, but was being quickly covered by the mile-a-minute growth of the kudzu vines.

The boys had never been this far into the forest. The locusts crowed loudly, as usual, which can cause confusion, since the noise can make it difficult to concentrate. Many people new to a Southern forest become disoriented and eventually lost, due to the loud calling of the locusts in the trees. The boys walked slower and called out to Sugar even louder, trying to be heard over the noise of the insects.

"Look, there she is!" Jonah screamed, tugging at his friend's arm. "She's drinking from that creek over there."

At this, Sugar looked up at the boys with the typical expression of a relieved unicorn. They ran to where she stood and shoved the open bag of candy to her muzzle. She was famished and ate the entire contents in less than a minute, although she ended up with a wad of chocolate in her mouth that she chewed like cud for some time before swallowing. The babbling water was peaceful, and the boys stroked Sugar's ivory fur and long white mane as she nuzzled them in return. Everything seemed hunky dory – until the trees suddenly grew quiet. Without warning or reason, the locusts had stopped their cacophonous symphony. The silence was deafening and as creepy as a naked grandfather. A bird's song drifted to the three of them through the silence. It was a tune the boys knew, but didn't place immediately.

"What's that mockingbird singing, Jonah? I know that song."

"I know it, too, Joe E.," said Jonah, staring ahead vacantly like a blonde trying to remember her Social Security number. "It's 'Stairway to Heaven'." His face was white. "I can name that tune in three words. Oh. My. God."

"Stay calm, Jonah. I don't think we're in danger. It's a clue. Let's go back to the house and listen to the song again. We're gonna get to the bottom of those lyrics."

Jonah shook his newly shorn head in disbelief. "Okay," he said. He turned to Sugar. "Are you gonna be okay, girl?"

The animal nodded, and the boys said their goodbyes and ran through the forest back to the house. They half expected something weird had happened while they were gone, so they checked the barn and the cellar, but found no differences. They ran upstairs and flung the bedroom door open without a thought.

"I'll put the record on OH MY GOD," Joseph screamed as he took his first step into the room.

A shock wave hit the boys like a pair of 'SS' lightning bolts. The smell of death permeated the little room like the 'Zyklon B' the bastard Nazis pumped into the crowded showers of the concentration camps. At least those poor Jews smelled the signature almond smell of cyanide with their last breaths. Whatever Hiroshima smelled like a week after the atomic bomb drop was what Joe and Jonah were now inhaling. Joe grabbed the plastic trash can by the desk, and both boys began vomiting into it, their heads side by side.

"WHAT IS IT????" screamed Jonah. There was no need to scream, but the boys felt like they were in an F-5 tornado.

"I DON'T KNOW!!!!"

Joe scanned the room to identify the source of the debilitating odor. He ran to the far side of the bed and saw a simple dog turd on the floor. It was no more than four inches long, but might as well have been a glowing chunk of Plutonium. He bent over and grabbed it with his bare hand, retching like a rock star going through withdrawals.

"Open the window, Jonah!" he shrieked. Jonah did as instructed, and Joe threw the death log over the back fence into the adjacent field. Without another word, he raced to the bathroom down the hall to wash his hands with scalding water until they almost blistered.

Jonah stumbled to the bathroom door behind him. "What was that?" he panted.

"That was a turd from Black Dog. I think she's evil." Joe's eyes were watering like the bloody tears of a dying angel.

The boys returned to the room, which had aired out, thanks to the open window.

"Where is she?" Joe said. "I'll strangle her myself if I have to." He looked under the bed and found nothing, then remembered he had placed the dog in the closet hours ago. He walked over and, ever so slowly, slid the partially open door wide. Black Dog was curled nose to tail like a little grub worm and couldn't have been more peaceful if she was sleeping on a nun's lap.

black 143 dog

Joe reached down with the intent to grab Black Dog, race downstairs, and fling her back into the cellar. Suddenly, the little minx woke up, yawned, and looked up at her master with the love of a thousand Valentine's Day cards. "Daddy, you're home! I love you so much!" she would have said if she could talk.

Joe broke into a smile. "We need to walk her more often, Jonah."

He scooped up his little black friend and kissed her softly on her ribs, her pink skin peaking through the soft black fur of her underside.

"Yeah. And maybe we should buy some gas masks in case she has another accident, Joe. Should I call Otis?"

***

The boys regained their composure after the nasty episode and got back to the business at hand. "We need to listen to 'Stairway' again, Jonah," Joe said. "Really close."

"I know, I know. Let's do this thing. Do we need to take notes?"

"No. We need to absorb this stuff. It's osmotic."

"Like I know what the hell that means, Joe."

"Just rest your little head and meditate. You'll know what you need to know when you know it."

"Sounds simple enough. Wake me when we're done."

***

By now, they should have had the lyrics to the song memorized, but they had been exposed to so much new information over the course of the summer that their brains were rebelling from overload. It was almost as bad as Mr. Thompson's Chemistry class in the second semester. Almost.

They started the record, and the tune played along peacefully and melodically through the intro and the first verse, but the words they encountered in the second stanza brought the boys to their feet with pacing anxiety. They did figure eights around each other in the small space at the foot of the bed as they listened.

The ballad's second verse said there was a songbird singing in a tree by a brook.

"Holy crap, Jonah."

black 144 dog

"HOLY CRAP, JOE!"

"The mockingbird was the songbird. She was singing 'Stairway to Heaven' by the creek. By the brook!" Jonah screamed like a Jethro realizing his wife is his sister.

"It's a good sign," Joe mumbled. "It's got to be. It isn't a bad omen. It can't be! It's a positive sign, telling us we're on the right track, Jonah. We have to stay optimistic. After all, we have Sugar and Black Dog here to help us. Dammit, I want to kick some ass! I'm tired of this crap!"

"I'm sick of being scared, Joe E.," Jonah said.

"Me too, dude. Me friggin' too!" Joe punched his left hand with his right hand with a loud smack. "We're going to get to the bottom of this if it kills us!"

"That's what I'm afraid of, Joe!" Jonah wailed, falling face-first onto the bed. "Why are we here?!" he screamed into the pillow.

Joe sat on the bed next to his friend and placed his hand caringly on Jonah's back. "I give you my word, Jonah. I'm not going to let anything happen to us. Be strong. Hold on and be strong, like Otis said. We shall overcome. We need to get back to work. We may not have much time."

Three hours later the spiral notebook was full, the classic rock logbook complete. The boys were exhausted, so they put Black Dog in the closet and went to Grandpa Joseph's study, where they fell into the deepest sleep of their young lives. Jonah slept without dreams, but Joe was tortured by scenarios from his wildest imagination. In one dream, he was possessed by evil and performed acts that Anton LaVey, the High Priest of the Church of Satan, would be ashamed of. In another, he was Aleister Crowley, chairing a meeting of 'The Order of the Golden Dawn'. In yet another, he was the Biblical Moses, leading God's Hebrew children out of Egypt. Joe E., the teenage prophet, tossed and turned like the turbulent waves of the Red Sea in his little sweat-soaked cot.

Joe woke from his pseudo-sleep at dawn. He was terrified by these visions and determined to find answers, so he rushed to his uncle's room without waking Jonah. He peered into Black Dog's little haven and saw she was asleep, then closed the closet door quietly. He sat on the bed and searched his mind for answers. There were so many questions. He meditated for a full hour – asking for answers and waiting for a response from the great beyond.

Suddenly, he lifted his face from his hands and began searching the room in wild-eyed abandon. He looked below the bed and found nothing. He eyed the desk and yanked the drawers out and threw them on the floor, searching the meager contents and finding nil, even looking on the bottoms of the drawers.

He fell down to the shag carpet and slid under the desk like a mechanic rolling a creeper under a broken down Caprice Classic. Surveying the underbelly of the desk, he saw something unusual. Below the main writing deck was a modification that drew his attention. Part of a cigar box had been taped to the underside of the desk like a hidden inbox. He reached into it and pulled out a small book. He had found his uncle's diary.

The little book was locked, as many diaries are, but Joe easily broke the worn vinyl strap holding it shut. He sat on the bed and began reading the entries, starting at page one, dated, 'November 12th, 1980'.

He saw nothing of note for years, the entries typically spaced out by two or three days, sometimes skipping for a month or more. The passages documented the mundane activities of an introverted teenager, but became much more interesting around the month of October in the year 1983. Joe noticed the entries started being accompanied by various symbols, some of which he recognized from the 'Zeppelin IV' album, along with others he could not identify. They looked ominous, though. He knew that.

October 31, 1983:

I'm not too old to rock n roll, but I think the age of 13 is at least a year too old for trick n treat. Guess I'll sneak a smoke and hang out in my bedroom with Robert Plant and Jimmy Page. ZOSO forever!!!!

November 7, 1983:

Boredom. Nothing to say that ain't been said before. Thank heaven for Eddie Van Halen.

November 24, 1983:

Thanksgiving is here and I don't feel much to be thankful for. Well, I take that back. I'm thankful for my records and my turntable.

I wish my parents could understand me. I don't even like turkey dammit! Some holiday...

November 26, 1983:

The preacher said that heavy metal records had hidden backwards messages on them. A boy from school told me you could hear them if you played records backwards. I tried it with my sister's 'Send in the Clowns' 45 and 'Waiting for the Worms' by Pink Floyd. I didn't hear shit. Maybe those songs don't work. They aren't heavy metal. Maybe that's why I didn't hear nothing. There was a bunch of lightning tonight.

November 30, 1983:

Was working in the yard for mom and heard something down in the cellar. Must have been a coyote or raccoon, but it scared me. It sounded big. I chained the door shut. I'll get it out when it's dead.

December 10, 1983:

I'm gonna try that backmasking thing on the record I bought today. It's by the craziest guy in rock-n-roll, Ozzy Osbourne. The album is called 'Bark at the Moon'. I'm going to play the first song in reverse and see if I can hear any messages. Wish me luck!

December 11, 1983:

Something weird seems to have happened last night. Something busted out of the barn, but there should have been nothing in there. I checked it out and saw weird footprints and they scared me so I just ran back inside. I think I may have done something terrible.

December 15, 1983:

Something very bad is happening here. Last night I heard strange howling and it was no coyote. I'm terrified that I have caused something evil to happen by playing 'Bark at the Moon' backwards. I think I conjured a wolf or maybe even a werewolf. Tomorrow I'm going to spend the night in the barn with a shotgun and kill it before anybody finds out what I've done. I destroyed the record. I wish I never bought it. If somebody finds this in the future, please heed my advice and don't do what I have done. Only evil can come of it.

***

That was his uncle's last entry. Joe shook with fear, finally understanding what he faced. The werewolf was still around, probably living in the forest. That's what had scared Sugar out of the carriage house and left the weird tracks. The werewolf had set the forest on fire, too, trying to kill the boys as they slept. He would try to kill them again. He would never stop. Joe was certain of it.

Joe ran to wake Jonah. Jonah reacted by pulling his sheet over his head. Joe went back to Ernie's room. He picked up the spiral notebook and went through every page, scanning the release dates of each record they had listed. Everything seemed to be from the 1970's until he came across a 1980, then a 1982. Finally, he saw two 1983's, but he was certain of one thing without doing any internet research. 'Bark at the Moon' was the last record his Uncle Ernie ever bought. (He was right – the album was released on the 10th day of December in 1983.)

Turning to the crates of records, Joe was compelled to confirm one more thing. He fingered through the albums like a record collector at a swap meet, until he found 'Bark at the Moon'. He took a deep breath and looked inside the sleeve. Just as he suspected – the platter was not there. The diary had told the truth. Uncle Ernie had destroyed the record. So had it been written, so had it been done.

Joe's mind raced like a junkie in need of a fix with only two dollars in his pocket. He sat on the bed staring straight ahead, seeing nothing but swirling kaleidoscopic images of confusion and fear. He still held the cardboard record sleeve as the reality of the situation crashed down upon him, as if 'The Wall' was being torn down and falling on his head. In exasperation, he turned around, slammed the record sleeve onto the bed, and began punching it with all he had. He was crying and, basically, losing it. Jonah walked in and watched in silence until the fit was finished. Joe crumpled, his exhausted body falling onto the disfigured piece of cardboard, sobbing.

Jonah sat down next to him and placed his hand on his friend's quivering back, like Joe had done to him the day before. "You figured it out, didn't ya, Joe?"

Joe E. turned and gazed through his human thunderstorm, locking eyes with his worried friend. "We're in trouble, Jonah. We're in big trouble. There's a werewolf in the forest, and he wants to kill us."

The boys sat without speaking for a few moments. Thoughts spun through their minds like whirling wheels of fortune, the pointer clacking staccato cracks through the choices. 'We're doomed', 'fight back', 'protect Granny', 'we're screwed', 'save Sugar and Black Dog', 'go home'. These were their choices, and the clicker continued round and round, sounding like an angry hammer attacking nails, the strikes reverberating through their heads like the beats of a tell-tale heart. Finally, the wheel slowed to a crawl, and the pointer hung on the imminent final nail for what seemed like an eon. The next space read, 'certain doom', but the pointer could not hurdle the nail. It sank back into the previous space, which read 'fight or die'.

"We're not giving up," said Joe. He wiped tears from his eyes and regathered his momentarily lost strength. Joe was embarrassed at his loss of composure. He resolved that it would be the last time he reacted in such a manner, and it was.

"You're right. We can't," replied Jonah. "If we give up, we're dead. Doomed."

"The werewolf got my uncle, and I'm not going to let Ernie's death go unavenged, Jonah. We're going to fight back and kill that furry a-hole."

"Let's kick some wookiee ass." At this, Jonah let out a terrible imitation of a Chewbacca call.

"We have got to be calm and plan this," Joe said, ignoring the lame Star Wars joke. "If we descend into chaos, we're dead. We need to lay in ambush and trap the werewolf somehow. We have to control our fear and use his rage to undermine him. He's going to come after us with all he's got. We're gonna lure him into our snare. It's gonna be just like trapping rabbits down on the farm."

"Did those rabbits want to rip your throat out, Joe? And don't you mean it's going to be just like killing womp rats in your T-16 on Tatooine?"

"Thinking like that isn't helping, you jerk," Joe replied. "Nice reference, though, Jabba. You've watched 'Star Wars' way too many times. Why don't you take Black Dog out to pee and let me think for a minute."

Jonah picked up the dog and walked to the door. As he

black 149 dog

reached for the knob, Joe spoke.

"BE CAREFUL."

***

Jonah returned safely, carrying the dog, and found Joe on the floor of Ernie's room, records strewn about him. The answers were in those circular pieces of plastic, and Joe knew it.

"Joe, Granny's making breakfast again. I think we should make an appearance," Jonah said.

"Jeez. How many dozen eggs did we buy?" Joe said with a chuckle. "Let's go see how the old dame's doing. Don't mention Wolfie or Black Dog, and act naturally, if that's possible. We need to put on a brave front."

They went downstairs and repeated the morning meal scenario for the umpteenth time, but this time pocketed food for their little black dog, Black Dog.

"You boys are eating twice as much as you usually do," Granny said. "All those chores I've been giving you have resulted in very healthy appetites. And just look at Jonah's muscle. He'll be getting all the girls at school next year. Oh, and I love your haircuts!"

"Thanks. We love your cooking, Granny," said Jonah with an Eddie Haskell smirk. "We'll be happy to do the dishes, as well, Granny. We love you, and thanks again for cooking us an exquisite breakfast and complimenting my new look."

"You two are such a godsend in these trying times. Be careful with the dishes, boys," she said as she picked up her vodka on ice. "They're antiques – fine china."

"That lady is a saint," said Joe as the old family matriarch left the room, the swinging kitchen door clacking back and forth like another wheel of fortune searching for its resolution.

"She's the patron saint of scrambled eggs and vodka," said Jonah. "We can't let anything happen to her. And I mean that with all seriouosity."

"I think I know what you mean, bro. I'll let you choose, today – do we research in Grandpa Joseph's study or do internet research at the library? It's your choice."

"Definitely upstairs. My pockets are full of bacon. Let's go feed your dog."

They did the dishes yet again and ran up the stairs to feed their supernatural hound. Black Dog didn't eat like normal animals, with chew and swallow, and such. Black Dog consumed food without masticating, inhaling spears of bacon like mortal humans inhale the smell of cooking bacon. She was ravenous and seemed able to dislocate her jaw like an anaconda to download the maximum amount of food in the shortest time. She was an animal.

"I think she's still got the munchies," laughed Jonah. "Have you ever seen anything eat like that?"

"Nope. If she eats like this all the time, we'll need to go on another shopping trip. Hey, Jonah – that's a great idea. We need groceries, and we need to go to the lumber yard for some wooden stakes. We need more candy for Sugar, too. Call your boy."

Jonah paged Otis, who arrived shortly after. The trio stocked up on necessities, fortifying for a possible siege like the one on Khe Sanh. Otis knew better than to ask what these strange supplies were for and why there was such an urgent need for them. He could see by the seriousity of their demeanor that this was business, not pleasure. The dookie was fixin' to hit a very large fan, and the outcome would not be pretty for those on the wrong side of the whirling blades.

Upon returning, the boys stowed the groceries in the pantry and checked on Black Dog, who seemed to be perfectly happy to sleep the day away in Ernie's closet. No doubt, that had been the place of many naps she had taken in the days long ago with her previous master.

If one could have read the little terrier's mind like some dog whisperer, one would have understood that the little Scottie thought Joe E. was, in fact, Ernie, so she was completely at ease. She didn't have a clue who this other dude, Jonah, was, but she was putting up with him.

CHAPTER TEN AND EIGHT

The boys walked to the carriage house, Joe carrying the wooden stakes and Jonah holding two shovels. It was time to set the first trap. As they opened wide the swinging front doors, Joe spoke. "We're gonna dig a pit inside the back doors and line it with stakes. Then, we'll lure the werewolf into the barn and wound or kill it."

"Let's do it, bruva," Jonah said. "Let's do this thang!"

They shoveled what they hoped would end up being a grave for the lycanthrope. A rough outline of the trap had been scratched in the dirt with a stick before they began digging. The pit was narrow at the point inside the swinging doors, where something would enter, and fanned out as it vectored into the interior.

"The deeper we can make it, the more damage it will do," Joe instructed, although they met the limit of their capabilities a mere three feet down. "This will have to do," Joe panted. At that depth, the rocks were so pervasive it became impossible to dig deeper.

The boys set the stakes in the clay-infused gumbo earth and covered the trap with woven kudzu vines. They spread hay over the makeshift netting to disguise it. Darkness would also help in that regard. The trap was easily seen in daylight, but would be invisible at night, no matter what the cycle of the moon and the light it provided to the lycanthrope's enhanced sense of sight. The trap was primitive, but they hoped the werewolf would barge into the barn in a rage and meet his doom.

They tied the back door shut with some worthless old hemp rope, making it appear they were attempting to deny entry.

Joe E. had trapped coyotes and other animals with his father growing up, the pelts of which they sold. The entire concept of trapping seems barbaric to most, but until you have lived all the lives of all the men on this earth, judgment should be reserved. One must also consider that things men do in times of great need are many times reconsidered and abandoned in times of plenty.

Joe and his father used many tactics to lure animals to their death. They had even left a tape recorder beside traps, which played the sound a rabbit in distress makes – best described as the

black 152 dog

soundtrack to a torture session of Thumper being water-boarded. It was not pleasant and could be heard for miles on a calm night. Coyotes will venture untold distances if they hear such Bugs Bunny caterwauling. Combine that with a piece of inviting sardine resting on a hair-trigger (hare-trigger for the sharp-witted) in an iron claw, and you will find a trapped varmint in the morning. That is, if the animal hasn't gnawed off its own leg to escape. (Now you know the meaning of the phrase 'coyote ugly', so you won't have to watch the terrible movie.)

Gruesome it is, but that's what some humans do to feed their pink little babies. Possums and other four-legged creatures often eat their young, rather than attempting to feed them. That pretty much validates the argument for the country boy or mountain man that traps or hunts to feed his young'uns. There are no further statements, your honor. I rest my case.

***

The boys were filthy after digging the pitfall trap, so they returned to the house for a hot shower. They spent the evening in Ernie's room, playing records and spazzing out on old Atari games. They hadn't spent five minutes watching television in a month and hadn't even noticed. They were smarter and stronger as a result.

You might be surprised that they were having fun, even with the knowledge a killer Wolfman was stalking them, but the way they saw it, they had known they were being stalked for some time. Now they knew what they were up against. That knowledge had given them some relief. Knowing who or what you are fighting is better than dealing with the possibilities a frightened imagination will conjure. Just ask a little kid that is scared of monsters without cute names like Frankenstein or Dracula – monsters that bite the heads off children and have eighty eyes, a million teeth, horns, and fins. A runaway imagination will always come up with something way worse than the actual dust bunnies living under the bed.

The boys slept in peace that night, although this time Black Dog was snuggled up next to her master in his little cot. Way too crowded, of course, but neither complained.

The next day found them sleeping in much later than usual. It was the last good night of sleep they would have for a long time.

CHAPTER TEN AND NINE

The boys walked Black Dog when they woke. The little terrier needed no leash or urging to go this way or that, like most dogs. She was always three feet or less from Joe E., guarding him like an obedient sentinel. Sugar would have performed the same duty for Jonah if she were allowed to.

The boys made sandwiches and ate, then went upstairs, but knew not what to do. They were caught up on their chores, so they tried to think up more traps to use in their fight with Wolfie, but were unsuccessful. In their hearts, they knew the battle would take place face to face, and no quarter would be given by either side. 'No mas' would not be accepted, as no prisoners would be taken.

Joe decided they should spend the day in Ernie's room, studying songs from the record collection and searching Grandpa Joseph's books for relevant information. He was even considering playing more songs backwards – ones he thought might bring them some aid.

He told Jonah of this and was met with panic, but he assured his friend it would only be done if they were sure of the outcome. They would need to be thorough and contemplative in yet another journey through Ernie's collection. There was no question they needed help, but they couldn't make the same mistake Ernie had. Blue Oyster Cult's '(Don't Fear) The Reaper' didn't seem like something they should play, needless to say.

"Let's find some innocent hippie song to play backwards first, as a control," Jonah suggested. "We gotta figure out how this thing works."

Joe sat bolt upright as if he had been tased. He grabbed Ernie's diary and read the November 26, 1983, entry again. His uncle had played 'Send in the Clowns' backwards.

"Oh my God, Jonah, look! Ernie backmasked this 'Send in the Clowns' song. Remember what we found in the cellar? He said something was down there, but he thought it was a raccoon. That was a clown trying to escape, and we found part of the body. Holy crap! And, it says he played 'Waiting for the Worms'. Remember all those dried up worms we found?"

"That's awesome, Joe! Let's find a song about weed. We'll have a whole cellar full!"

Joe gave his friend a hateful look. "You doofus. I don't want you smoking anything while that werewolf is around. Stay sharp and focused! My God, man!"

"I guess you're right. But we could play 'Money' by Pink Floyd, couldn't we?"

"Maybe after we kill the werewolf. For now, we have to put all our thoughts and energy into battling the mangy demon lurking in the forest."

"Yes, Joe. You're right. I'm sorry."

"This is serious, Jonah."

Jonah lowered his head like a scolded dog. "I know. I'm sorry."

"It's okay, bro. We'll have the time of our lives if we kill this bastard, and we'll have one helluva story to tell afterward. Let's do this."

"I'm focused like a laser beam. A *laser*," Jonah said with a Doctor Evil voice.

"You can't be serious, can you?" Joe E. asked with an irritated smile.

"Don't worry, Joe, I'm with you. I'm just trying to lighten the seriousity of the situation."

"Why do you keep saying seriousity all of a sudden?"

"I've always said it. I think I got it from Otis."

***

The boys hovered over the record player.

"Okay, let's do this. Can you get the right speed?"

"I think so." With this, Jonah started the record at approximately 33 1/3 reverse revolutions per minute. He had to use two hands to overcome the record player's obtrusive arm, which challenged his awkward coordination. He had tried to hurdle it with one hand, but the speed dragged each time his fingers left the disc, so he had to develop a two-handed technique, which kept the platter rotating at a more uniform rate.

They were using the ultimate hippie song, 'San Francisco (Be

Sure to Wear Flowers in Your Hair)' by Scott McKenzie, as a control. Every valid scientific experiment must follow the guidelines of the scientific method, and every experiment must have a control as a basis for comparison. This had been hammered into their brains by Mr. Thompson, God love him.

They felt this would be as safe a song to try as any, but were worried they might transport leagues of smelly hippies from the Summer of Love through, rather than flowers. Although capable of mass destruction, (just ask the people that cleaned up after Woodstock) Joe and Jonah knew any hippies they brought through would surely be peaceful and relatively harmless.

The process came to its resolution without any lightning strikes or other dramatics. The boys looked at each other with a deep mutual sigh and walked slowly from the room, then down the stairs, Black Dog trailing obediently behind. There was no excitement, only resignation.

Joe and Jonah checked the carriage house first and found nothing, then walked to the cellar and pulled the piece of rebar away. With another deep breath, they flung the door open.

The smell from the cellar blasted them like nothing they had ever encountered. It was so strong, they both leaned back and shielded their faces, as if observing a nuclear test explosion at close range.

I know what you're thinking – dozens of stinking, unwashed, beatnik bohemians were clamoring to escape the cellar. Thankfully, this was not the case.

Jonah composed himself first and began to laugh. He leaned over the hole to get a better look into the formerly dank cellar. "Oh my God, Joe, look!" he said as he surfed down the cellar steps on his heels.

Joe stepped forward and peered into the underground space his friend had disappeared into. He started laughing like an elated Burning Man attendee. The cellar was filled to the brim with flowers of every type, every smell, every color, every everything. He did a cannonball into the hole and never hit bottom. He found himself suspended and floating on daffodils, orchids, roses, and a hundred other species. Black Dog landed on him in short order. The boys swam in the blooms like a couple three-year-olds in a ball pit at a McDonald's Plus. The sheer magnitude of odor made it difficult to breathe, but the fragrance of the mixture was so intoxicating it was hard to complain. They inhaled deeply in their excited state, and every bloom they crushed increased the floral aroma's concentration. They were in no danger of suffocation, but were in some danger of intoxication, since many of the flowers were of the genus *Cannabis* and the species *Sativa*.

Joe navigated through the mess like a Vietnam War soldier fighting through elephant grass and called out, "Jonah, where are you?"

"I'm under the stairs," came the muffled reply.

"Come back out. Meet me at the top." Joe grabbed Black Dog and ascended the steps, now slippery from the oil of crushed blooms. He sat on the grass and breathed the fresh air to some relief. The space above the cellar's opening appeared wavy from the exiting fumes, like the horizon above the hot blacktop of a Texas highway. Black Dog sat next to him, catching her breath and smiling her toothsome grin.

"Man," Jonah exclaimed as his head popped through the opening. "This is a trip!"

"You can say that again, buddy! Okay, I think I have it figured out. Ernie said in his diary the werewolf came through into the carriage house, right? Everything we know of that has come through into the cellar has been harmless, but the Wolfman came through into the carriage house. I think bad things use the barn as their doorway into our world and good things use the cellar. Does that make sense to you?"

"Makes sense," said Jonah. "What do we do now?"

"Let's get some trash bags and clean up. We can't let all those flowers rot down there. Rotting flowers smell far worse than weeds."

"The chores never stop around here, do they?" complained Jonah.

"Would you rather be picking up werewolf poop?"

"Nah. Guess not."

They went to the garden shed and retrieved a full box of large capacity leaf and lawn bags, which they began filling with a scoop shovel. After topping off eight bags, they reached the entrance to the tunnel under the stairs, which also overflowed with blossoms. Before continuing, they took a break up top and drank an ice-cold Coke in the glinting sun, taking long, tall swigs like actors in a commercial. When they finished their drinks, they returned to the spot below the stairs to start excavating the corridor. Suddenly, a grunting noise came from somewhere deep in the shaft. Something was alive down there with them.

"Holy crap, the werewolf!" said Jonah. "Let's get out of here!"

The boys raced up the stairs, slammed the door, and put the rebar back in place. They sprinted to the carriage house to retrieve two pitchforks and returned to the cellar door, panting. A week or two ago, they would have been taking refuge in the house under their cots, but things were different now. The boys were different now.

"Oh my God, where's Black Dog?" asked Joe E. in a panic. He looked all around, then sprinted to search the carriage house, checked the garden shed, and returned to where Jonah still stood, trembling with fear and determination.

"She's still in there, Jonah. We've got to go in and get our dog."

The boys threw open the heavy door. The elation of their past excursion into the florid cellar was long since gone. They crept slowly down and found Black Dog under the stairs, frozen on point, staring mesmerized into the underground corridor like a knee-high statue carved from a large chunk of obsidian. Her teeth were bared, but she did not growl, instinctively knowing that silence was her ally.

"He's in there," Joe said. "We're gonna wait for him to come out and stab him as he comes through the doorway. Let's kill this mutt and get this nightmare over with."

They waited in silence for countless minutes, pitchforks at the ready. Finally, they heard the sound of something creeping down the tunnel toward them on all fours. Its breathing was labored and heavy.

"Get ready," Joe whispered. Black Dog took a step forward and froze on point again. She wagged her tail in anticipation and bared her formidable fangs. She was in her element and wanted to protect her master and his friend from any danger, no matter how grotesque.

An upright figure burst through the flower blooms, sending colorful tracers in every direction.

"Whoa, dude. This is heavy, man!"

The beast could speak!

It was no werewolf, thank God. It was a freaknik flower child. Black Dog rushed in and attached herself to his leg with a loud crunch. The hippie screamed in pain and confusion. He was lucky – he had only been pierced by Black Dog's two canines, rather than the ten tines of pitchfork fury aimed at his vital organs.

"Who are you?" screamed Joe E. as he pulled Black Dog from the time-traveling throwback's leg.

"I'm Hairy Larry, dude. Man, get that hound from Hell away from me! What happened, man? I was in Frisco ten minutes ago. Did you guys dose me or what? Are you the Merry Pranksters?"

"Larry, I'm sorry to inform you that you are now in Stringtown, Alabama, and it is the year 2009. You've been transported forty years into the future," said Joe E. "Welcome to now."

"Whoa. You dosed me good, man," Hairy Larry said with a laugh. "Was that Owsley or what? Far out! I don't even remember drinking the Kool-Aid!"

***

The boys explained to Hairy Larry they had given him no mind-altering substances, then led the dippy dropout to the garden shed and told him to wait there. He was as obedient as Black Dog in his confused state and did as instructed.

Joe and Jonah went to the house to get some dried meat and bottles of water to send the sad sack off with. They talked on the way and decided Hairy Larry would not be a beneficial ally in their battle with Wolfie. He was Mother Nature's son, no doubt, but that was about it. In fact, his outrageous body odor would surely lead the monster to their position. They decided to send him off into the New South, forty years after his last anti-war protest, and let him fend for himself.

They packed his provisions in one of Jonah's many

black 159 dog

backpacks, led Larry to the gate, and sent the poor hippie on his way. He beelined toward the old man's house across the street, no doubt to beg for food and shelter. Hopefully, he would not attempt to squat on the property, for that would mean certain buckshot.

"That's not a good idea, Larry," Jonah yelled. "Keep walking, dude. You'll be okay. Good luck! Don't camp in the forest!"

Sure, it was harsh treatment, but desperate times call for desperate measures, and the boys could take no chances. They had no way to send Larry back to 1969 in San Francisco, so their only option was to set him free to survive on his wits, if he had any left after his epic drug usage. Heck, he might even be able to start an ice cream company and make millions, they told themselves to ease their guilt. Hairy Larry stumbled down the yellow brick road toward Stringtown, singing a song the boys didn't recognize. The song was 'Friend of the Devil' by the Grateful Dead, but that probably means nothing. The track wasn't released until 1970, but Hairy Larry must have been present at the early songwriting sessions that produced the classic.

***

The teenagers hauled the remaining flowers from the cellar and put the trash bags by the curb, to be carted away by the luckiest garbage men ever to smoke a spliff. That would be the best smelling garbage truck of all time after the driver pressed the 'crush' button.

This experiment had consumed the day, so the boys ate dinner and started their normal evening ritual. They hadn't seen Granny in some time, so before they started their first Atari game, Joe went downstairs and stuck his head in her room hesitantly. He saw nothing in the coal mine blackness, but heard her snoring, so everything seemed to be fine. The more she slept at this point, the better. Things were getting weirder by the minute, and they didn't want Granny to have to deal with the circumstances. The poor woman had been through enough.

They attempted their usual routine of video games and salami and cheese cracker snacks, which they now simply called 'platter'. 'Platter' was whatever they consumed during their evening sessions, ranging from Cheez-Whiz on French bread to sardines and Louisiana hot sauce on Ritz crackers. They prepared these nosh sessions in the kitchen and brought them upstairs on a huge serving plate, hence the name they had coined for their nightly ritual. They interrupted their game play and classic rock session that night with multiple interludes of platter consumption, discussions of their situation, and attempts at decision making.

They wanted to lure Wolfie into the pit trap in the carriage house, but couldn't figure out what to use for bait. They were also struggling to determine which, if any, allies could be summoned from the bowels of classic rock. They were simultaneously heartened and concerned by the hippie song experiment from earlier that day. Pangs of guilt struck them as they snacked on kippered beef – they worried about the plight of Hairy Larry, but what else could they have done? Lives were at stake, and they couldn't afford to support a drug-addled weirdo in the habit of leeching a living from the teat of society, while they battled the Antichrist.

Joe settled into his cot that night and petted his ebony-colored terrier until they both fell asleep. His slumber was fitful, as usual – tortured with all the decisions he needed to make. He woke with the dawn. Jonah was sleeping peacefully, and Joe was happy for that. He knew this epic battle was his burden to bear and that Jonah was his Barney Fife, willing to die for him in the ultimate supporting role, but not one to lead the fight against the forces of evil. Joe was the project manager on this job, whether he had applied for it or not. He was the night manager at Hell's 7-11, and Jonah was his mop-boy. Blue Raspberry Slushee clean up at the drink station, please.

CHAPTER TWENTY

Joe went to his deceased uncle's room and searched for the record he had been thinking of through the restless night. It was early in the morning, and his thousand yard stare didn't work well for this clerical function. His eyes wanted to gaze, rather than focus, and his mind had a cotton gauze blanketing it. His brain overwhelmed and his office skills dulled, Joe felt like a zombie administrative assistant. He found the record he searched for and took a long look at its cover, which depicted a black and white image of a blimp bursting into flames like some post-Wright brothers Icarus/Hindenburg tragedy, ready to plummet to earth at terminal velocity like a lead balloon. 'Oh, the humanity!'

In the purple haze of five a.m., Joe didn't notice the cardboard sleeve did not match the vinyl disk contained within it. The record he pulled out was labeled 'Led Zeppelin II', not 'Led Zeppelin'. The two LP's had switched jackets, but Joe E. had intuitively known where to find the song he searched for. Decades ago, his uncle misfiled 'Led Zeppelin II' in the 'Led Zeppelin' sleeve, and Joe had mentally made the same mistake in reverse, which wasn't really a mistake. It was the right thing to do – kismet in Kashmir.

Joe had decided to try an alternate approach to what had previously been attempted in his crusade. He wasn't going to attempt to call through a person or thing this time. He wanted to call through a message.

Having listened to the song 'Ramble On' during one of their listening sessions, Joe had landed on the possibility of willing the beast to move along and disappear without a fight. The song's lyrics spoke of leaving when the summer ends. Joe wanted to place this idea in the Wolfman's feeble brain. There seemed to be no obvious physical entity mentioned in the lyrics that would be pulled through by playing the song backwards. The song's words were conceptual – about the idea of leaving on an extended vacation. It seemed safe.

Joe E. hoped playing the song in reverse would somehow influence the werewolf to ramble on and disappear, to terrorize some different teenagers in a different place. This theory was born of hopelessness and a selfish hopefulness to avoid a fatal fight. They were not Spartans, after all. They were teenagers. In addition, 'Ramble On' was not a song four, which seemed to disarm any alarm. It was song three of the second side, which is now called song seven on the CD.

Joe felt overwhelming anxiety at the possibility of pawning his problem onto other people, but saving the lives of Granny and Jonah and their supernatural superfriends took precedent over imploding somebody else's solitude. It was selfish, and Joe was riddled with guilt at the thought of succeeding, but maybe another person or different people would be better equipped to kill a werewolf, he reasoned. It was a moral dilemma, just like the Hairy Larry situation, but General Joe had to think of the greater good. Lives might have to be sacrificed to achieve the desired result. Joe had learned that – not from studying Patton or Alexander the Great, but from viewing the movie, '300', and listening to Iron Maiden songs. Three hundred Spartans sacrificed their lives to inspire the unification of the city-states of Greece to defeat the Persian army. They died for the greater good. Sometimes sacrifices have to be made.

Joe had also seen the Clint Eastwood movie, 'Dirty Harry'. He wanted to kill the werewolf like Harry killed liquor store robbing San Francisco punks. "Do you feel lucky, Wolfie? Well, do ya, mutt?" He shook this fantasy from his mind. He wasn't Clint Eastwood, and this wasn't a movie. The world is a harsh and unforgiving place, and Joe had no .44 caliber Smith and Wesson Model 29 AutoMag loaded with silver bullets. Joe had only his cunning wit and a grandmother and a friend and a unicorn and a taxi driver and a terrier, all of which he needed to protect from harm. That was the microcosm. In the macrocosm, he had even more on his shoulders. The weight of the world pushed down hard, and he was no Charles Atlas. In addition to those close to him, Joe wanted to protect the village of Stringtown and the whole of mankind. He wanted to do that more than anything, but he felt as weak as a plant in a pot. He needed water and a fertilizer spike – a steroid boost to the xylem and phloem running up and down his jellyfish spine.

black 163 dog

That description freely mixes man and plant and vertebrates and invertebrates and is biologically incorrect, like 'The Thing' from the John Carpenter movie. Joe was battling just that, though – a 'thing' which mixed species, an unholy mutant. And to destroy a mutant, Joe had to think like a mutant. Or in this case, a 'muttant' – a Heinz 57 from Hell.

Mustering his resolve, Joe E. played the track backwards, praying it would reverse their situation as the record revolved in retrograde. His nemesis had a weak mind controlled by primitive instinct, just like Jonah's little sister. Joe hoped to outsmart the beast, rather than fight it physically, just like he did with Serah.

The sun rose as he performed the operation. It was tedious, since the song was very long. At the culmination, he looked out the window to see if any black clouds had snuck up on the red and orange horizon. Nothing seemed to have happened, but he would not know the result of his actions until he inspected the cellar and the carriage house. He left the room and descended the stairs to the parlor. He mustered his will and opened the huge front door, leaving the sanctuary of the house to inspect the cellar alone. He trusted his instincts and entered unarmed. He found nothing in the cellar or its catacombs.

Walking to the carriage house, Joe expected the worst as he remembered his theory about good and evil and their respective portals into Stringtown, Alabama. He unlashed the rope on the front doors and entered cautiously. He heard nothing, but sensed he was not alone in the barn. He smelled something he had never encountered, even in his days of slopping pigs and skinning animals back on the farm. The stench was overpowering, and it did not come from millions of flower blooms or Black Dog turds. Joe felt threatened and wished he was armed, but did not turn back. "I am armed," he thought to himself. "Who needs a weapon when I've got the strength of these biceps and triceps and tendons and ligaments."

As he reached the center of the building, he saw something had fallen into the trap. He knew this because the kudzu net no longer covered the hole. Joe walked to the edge of the pit, and what he saw made him very sad.

Something had come through the portal as the result of

black 164 dog

playing the song backwards and had fallen through the vacant space in the second floor into the pit of spikes. Joe E. visually examined the dead, impaled corpse of the fallen angel/demon. He became frightened and ran upstairs to listen to the song forward, to seek clues to the identity of this misshapen creature. This time, he woke his friend to help him figure out what had happened.

Having described what he found dead in the pit, Joe asked Jonah to listen to 'Ramble On' with him to figure out what had happened. At the culmination of the song Jonah spoke. "Joe, it's obvious. You pulled Gollum through. Haven't you seen 'The Lord Of The Rings'?"

"No."

"Holy crap, Joe. You are one naive hobbit. You killed Gollum!"

"What's Gollum?" Joe asked with his head down. He was ashamed. He had killed whatever Gollum was and felt sorry for the creature, whether good or evil or a combination of both.

"Gollum is a creature from 'The Lord of the Rings' that was transformed from good to evil, due to his lust for the Ring of Power. Now you've killed him, Joe."

"How do you kill a fictional character?"

"I don't know, but you did it. I want to see what he looks like. What color was the blood?"

The teens ran to the barn with Black Dog trailing closely, as usual. She was a natural born heeler. They raced to the edge of the pit, ignoring the smell, and gazed upon the formerly tortured and now deceased little Gollum. Black Dog sniffed deeply the monster's body odor. Gollum's musk was a new smell to the little terrier, and it was like Chanel No. 5 to the scent receptors within her moist black nose.

"What are we gonna do with him?" Jonah asked.

"I don't know, but he's already riper than a black banana, and the hot afternoon is only going to make things worse. Let's go up to the bedroom and cool off and brainstorm this thing."

They entered the house to the smell of frying bacon. "Here we go again, Jonah," said Joe as he walked toward the kitchen. "Run upstairs, Black Dog. We'll bring you some food." The little Scottie raced up the stairs obediently on her short, muscular legs.

"Hello, Granny," Jonah said as he entered the kitchen. "Well, well, what a surprise to see you cooking breakfast. What a pleasant surprise, indeed! We're famished!" He had really gotten into the Eddie Haskell routine with Granny. In turn, he was a black man around Otis. The kid was an emo chameleon, for God's sakes.

"Growing boys are always hungry!"

When they finished eating, the old matriarch asked the boys to search the street for roadkill and walk the grounds to see if a coyote had dragged up something rotten. She could smell the Gollum in the house, even over the smell of the bacon. She filled her glass and retired to her room, leaving the boys to do the dishes, as per routine.

This gave Joe and Jonah time to mull over the situation while their hands pruned in the dishwater, as they performed the menial task of washing and drying the dishes yet again. Performing this task over and over was truly a blessing for them. It required just enough concentration to ensure that the plates would not be broken, but allowed them enough headspace to think about what was happening in the world around them. Granny knew what she was doing.

Jonah lifted a glass to inspect it in the bright light coming through the kitchen window. "We could call Otis. He could put the Gollum in his trunk and take it and dump him somewhere."

Joe reached out to take the glass from Jonah, cradling it in a dish towel. "He'd never get another fare the way that thing stinks. And where do you expect him to take it – the BBQ shack? Yum! Supper time!"

"The way they cook, he'd probably taste great by the time they got done smoking him. I'd eat it – gotta be better than school food."

"I'll pass!" Joe E. laughed. Somehow, they still retained their sense of humor, although the jokes had grown decidedly more morbid.

"I've got it!" Joe shouted. "He looks kinda like E.T., right? Stringtown is going to have their first alien crash site. Call Otis and tell him we need a buttload of aluminum foil and any spare car parts he can scrounge. Go ahead and tell him what happened. He's the only

black 166 dog

person we can trust. He needs to know what we're up to, in case he doesn't want to be a part of it."

Jonah picked the walkie-talkie from its holder on his belt and did as commanded. The story Jonah told Otis alarmed him, but he had known a strange call would come from the boys at some point in this weird and wonderful summer. Nothing came as a surprise to any of them any more.

Joe and Jonah went upstairs to their cots and tried to escape what was happening to them. They didn't sleep, just laid in the darkness, talking about their senior year to come and the girls they wanted to ask out if they made it home alive. They had constructed new self-esteem already and, quite possibly, also developed the courage to ask out the girls they fantasized about.

Finally, their walkie-talkies came to life with the message that Otis had arrived with the goods and was waiting out front.

They walked down to meet him at the curb and look over the items he had been able to locate that might assist them in this devious plan. Otis opened his trunk, which held a conglomeration of goods worthy of a hoarder's table at a flea market. Bicycle parts, pieces of lawnmower, loose bolts and other fittings, and a bunch of other metal crap filled the trunk – enough to lower the vehicle's rear end considerably. His back seat held forty packages of heavy-duty aluminum foil with which to tie the sculpture together.

"Do you boys know how they looked at me at the grocery store when I bought all that foil?" Otis said. "I told them we was havin' a family reunion and was barbequing a herd of goats. Lordy!"

Joe went to the garden shed and returned with a wheelbarrow, which they shoveled the items into from the car's enormous trunk.

"They's a clearing over thataway," Otis said, pointing in the opposite direction from the space in the forest familiar to the boys. "I thinks that be the best place to do this thang. If y'all don't need nothing else, I gots to be ramblin' on. Good luck with tha endeavor and may God forgive us all. I pray my maker don't count me as an accessory to a murder, be it human or otherwise."

Otis sped off, and the boys wheeled the parts to the shed and spread them out for a better look.

"We need to hodge-podge these together like they came from the violent crash of an alien vessel into the earth," Joe said.

After an hour trying to force various pieces together, Jonah was frustrated. "Joe, we're going to make some kind of saucer out of foil and scatter these parts around it – that's all we can do. Let the conspiracy theorists put the pieces together for us."

"I guess you're right," Joe said. "I pray to God it works."

"Me too. I think it will. And I don't think God wants any part of this, Joe. Don't you be blasphemin', boy!"

They repeatedly pushed the wheelbarrow to the clearing Otis had guided them to, until they had transported the necessary elements of their ruse to the 'crash site'. Next, they molded the aluminum foil into a small, crumpled saucer shape, complete with a little booster seat in the middle. They worked hastily and haphazardly at the crime scene – like a desperate crime of passion murderer realizing he has stabbed his cheating girlfriend to death in an uncontrollable fit of rage. The result was sloppy, but they needed to finish before the growing stink of the rotting Gollum caused the involuntary manslaughter to be discovered by the authorities. Surely, Wolfie had one helluva sense of smell, too, and might decide to investigate.

Finally, they decided they had done all they could. They returned to the carriage house and loaded Señor Stinky into his wheelbarrow hearse. The smell was so bad that the boys pulled the wheelbarrow backwards, which allowed some of the stench to trail behind them. Black Dog chose to follow the makeshift meat wagon with her nose in the air, snorting up as much of Gollum's stink as possible while they walked.

They reached the location of the mock crash site for the final time and gave Gollum an impromptu funeral. It was the least they could do.

"God," Joe spoke. "Forgive us for the involuntary manslaughter of this beautiful creature made in your image. May he forever feast in Valhalla and leave his earthly vessel among sad wretches like me and Jonah. Please lift his soul from the wretched corpse that lays before us and carry it to Heaven."

With this, the boys delicately lifted poor, dead Gollum from

black 168 dog

the wheelbarrow and placed him in the molded aluminum seat in the middle of the 'space ship'.

"He looks cute," Jonah said. "We should take a picture for the internets."

"Don't worry, buddy," Joe said. "He's gonna be all over the internets when somebody finds him. Wait and see."

The two teens walked home slowly and dejectedly, then rinsed out the wheelbarrow in the yard. They weren't proud of what they had done. After all, they weren't 'Goodfellas' laughing on the way home from a little midnight dig in the desert. They were formerly innocent teenagers.

"Jonah, what have we been reduced to? Crackheads have better morals than us!"

"We have been condensed to the core of ourselves, like Marines in basic training, Joe. It's not something that can be helped. We are simply reacting to events as they unfold. We have no control. Our psyches have been stripped and made to parade nude in front of the student body. Now it's time to get dressed and rebuild ourselves on a stronger framework."

"Wow," Joe said. "You might need to be the leader from now on."

"We both know that's your job," Jonah replied. "Thanks, though."

"You're welcome. And you're right, Jonah. We need to do less reacting and start playing a more proactive role in our destiny. We need to create our reality. I'm sick of being a puppet to outside forces!" He took a deep breath and gritted his teeth in determination. "WE ARE SPARTA!!!" The boy had possibly watched too many movies, but inspiration is valuable, no matter where it is found. Somewhere deep in the forest, the werewolf was shaken from his slumber in the damp cave he called home. He was not happy at being awakened.

"Hey, Wolfman! We're not scared of you!!!!" Joe screamed at the top of his lungs.

The Wolfman bared his teeth.

"C'mon, Jonah. Yell it with me."

"Hey, Wolfman!!" they screamed together. "We're not afraid

black 169 dog

of you!"

"Who's afraid of the big, bad wolf?!" Jonah screamed. Black Dog howled.

The Wolfman was not amused at being roused from his sleep by this nonsense. He slashed the wall of the cave he took shelter in, leaving four deep trenches in the earth, imbedding dark soil under the nails of his right paw. It was almost dark, and he would exact revenge soon. It had been days since his last kill, and he thirsted for fresh blood. He had spied on Sugar for two nights and learned her habits. Tonight he would kill her and feast on her chewy, cherry-flavored Sweet-Tart heart.

Jonah's conscience tweeted a message to him at that very moment.

"We've got to find Sugar," he told Joe. "Right now. She's in danger. I can sense it!"

"Let's do this," his friend replied.

They dumped the wheelbarrow next to the garden shed and sprinted like Usain Bolt to their normal clearing in the woods. They rumbled through the jungle like manimals, slashing vines and tree limbs to the side with wild swipes as they traversed the fauna gauntlet. Upon reaching the clearing, they bounced from boundary to boundary like pinballs, yelling for the unicorn all the while. Black Dog followed whichever of them she got a bead on, yelping and jumping in the air, trying to catch the grasshoppers that flushed from the grass.

Sugar came charging out of the forest to them. She was not seeking protection from the boys or out to reunite with them like a lost mutt being picked up at a shelter. She was looking for a fight. She knew the boys were taking an unnecessary risk being so loud and confrontational. She snorted and padded the ground with her right fore hoof, like a bull preparing to gore an ignorant Pamplona tourist. Her actions were appropriate. She had smelled the Wolfman spying on her the last couple nights and had feigned ignorance, as dangerous as that was. She was smarter than him and was ready for a fight.

The boys sensed Sugar's seriousity and rushed her back to Granny's property and down into the cellar for the night. The steps were difficult for her to negotiate, but this was the best place to shelter her. They knew the Wolfman would expect her to be in the carriage house. Joe had realized they had something going for them – they were smarter than their nemesis. They re-staged the pitfall trap that had worked so well on Gollum and went upstairs to watch the hellhound get spiked to death from Ernie's bedroom window. Joe was possibly growing a tad bit over-confident.

The moon was full that night, and the boys watched the barn from their perch on the second floor until early in the morning, but eventually fell asleep leaning on each other. They did not see the scrungy frame of the brown and black, vicious Chewbacca lookalike cut the rope at the back door of the carriage house with a three inch fingernail. They did not see the creature creep into the stable and fall into the trap. They didn't hear him cry out in pain as one of the spikes pierced his leg.

The werewolf tore out of the pit, slashing everything around him in his rage, splintering every piece of rotten wood his ragged claws encountered. The Wolfman raged against the machine like a Tasmanian suicide bomber. He had a tick in his left ear, too, which really pissed him off. He let out a black howl that slashed the nighttime like a box cutter through a Picasso masterpiece.

The boys were asleep, but Black Dog was not. "AAAAAAOOOOOOUUUUU," she wailed in response to the Wolfman's cry. The boys moved a little, but were so tired and deeply asleep that even this did not rouse them from their golden slumber.

The Wolfman regained his composure and re-covered the trap with the woven kudzu. He didn't want the boys to know they had struck the first blow. He left the barn and shut the doors behind him.

***

The morning came, and the light through the window woke Joe E. He didn't realize he had fallen asleep. He believed he had watched the barn all night and thought nothing had happened.

Joe gazed out at the sunrise, which God had painted with reds and oranges of hues not included in even the 64-count Crayola big box with the sharpener in the side. Joe was deliriously groggy as he searched for consciousness in this new day. This was good, created by a good God. This sky was something even the most hateful evil could not undo. The Big Guy in the Sky would shake his Etch-A-Sketch and start fresh in a little less than twenty-four hours, though, to repaint his morning stream of consciousness. Joe knew he was on the right side of this moment in history and took heart and inspiration from the beautiful watercolor before him. He rubbed his eyes and yawned and stared into the big sky for half an hour.

Eventually, his bladder prodded him to rise to his feet. He delicately moved from his spot as Jonah's pillow, picked his friend up, and laid him on Uncle Ernie's little bed. These early morning interludes were becoming a habit for Joe. He used them for daily reflection. The weight of the world may have been on his shoulders, but Joe grew stronger each day as a result of this solitary introspection. Religion hadn't been deeply instilled in Joe, but he found himself praying more and more. He didn't know how to say traditional, formal prayers. He simply went over things in his mind and stated his desire to do what was right. His mental resolve grew with each of these meditations, like the muscles of a high school football player after a weight lifting session. Joe E. was doing spiritual bench presses, and the results were evident in a different place, far from his biceps and quads and abs.

Joe sat next to his friend on the bed and contemplated the sunrise for another fifteen minutes. This was not the time to hurry, even though he needed to pee. He thought to himself that he needed to start drinking coffee, as it might aid contemplation. He got up and opened the closet door to see his little Scottie sleeping the slumber of the angels. She was kicking her feet and trying to bark in her sleep. She was dreaming. Her mouth didn't open, so the resulting muffled yelps sounded like a newborn puppy trying to find its mother. Joe smiled like a proud father.

He reached down and picked up little Black Dog. After kissing her numerous times, Joe threw her on his drowsing friend, startling the boy awake with a scream. He hadn't lost the joy of harassing Jonah, no matter how much he was growing to love him like a brother.

"What the?" shrieked Jonah as he sprang to his feet beside the bed. "Why do you continue to terrorize me! I thought the Wolfman had me! We need to cut Black Dog's toenails!"

"You were drooling on my uncle's pillow, you slob. Since you're awake, though, let me tell you what I've come up with."

"I can't wait," said Joe's exasperated companion.

"We need to go into town to the record store and get a copy of the 'Bark at the Moon' album."

"Brilliant idea, Joe. Let's play it backwards and call up a good white werewolf to battle the evil black werewolf in the forest. They'll kill each other over territory, right?" There was a subtle hint of sarcasm in his voice.

"No. That's not a bad idea, though. That's why you're my number two man. Actually, I think we need to hear the song to understand our enemy."

"Yeah, yeah. I'll go with you. As long as we pick up some barbeque while we're out."

"I thought you were a vegetarian."

"Funny."

***

The boys walkie-talkied their homeboy, Otis, and he was there by mid-morning. When they arrived at the used CD store, they informed the shop-keep of their desire.

"Whoa, wodey. That gon' be a tough one. I deal in tha Dirty Souf, ya dig? Gangsta rap – ain't got no Ozzy."

"How long will it take to order it?" asked Joe E.

"I can have the CD here in three days, bro."

"We need the record. A CD won't work," Joe said.

"Thass a problem," the shop-keep replied as he scrolled down the list of available records from his internet record supplier. From time to time, he ordered records for local DJ's to spin, so he knew what he was doing. "That rekkid be outta print. I'ma have to find it on EBay or sumpin. Let me make a call to my homie in Needville, first. He hustles stuff like dat. He a white boy. He still crunk, tho."

The proprietor made the call to his friend, who ran a more traditional vintage vinyl shop in the neighboring town. He confirmed that his associate did, indeed, have a copy.

"Home Slice sez he gots it. It'll take about three, fo' days ta get it by tha mail. Post office be slow round here."

black 173 dog

"Otis, can you take us to pick it up?" Joe asked.

"Sho nuff. Line it up," Otis said to the record dealer, who was still on the phone with his friend. "We gots a twenny fo ya for hookin' us up, right Joe?"

Five minutes later the trio were leaving Stringtown on their latest mission. Two hours after that, they were on their way home with the classic vinyl in hand. The boys sat in the back seat, staring at the album cover. It gave them the creeps.

They reached the house, and Otis was granted a twenty dollar bonus for his assistance. The record had cost sixty bucks with all the finder's fees. Joe was reaching the end of the money Granny had granted him, but this was not the time to be frugal. Otis drove away, smiling his gold tooth grin, and the boys walked slowly upstairs to learn what they could from the song that had brought this all about.

***

"This is it," said Joe as he prepared to drop the needle in the record's first groove. He took a deep breath and let gravity do its work.

The boys sat in silence, listening to the track for the first time. To the teenagers that reveled in it in the early eighties, it was fantasy, but to Joe and Jonah it was four minutes and seventeen seconds of harrowing, harsh, threatening reality.

"They buried him. He's back from the dead to avenge his death," Jonah said.

"Yeah, you're right," Joe responded. "That's pretty clear. He's not happy, to say the least. I bet he ate that clown we found. I think there's one major difference between this 'Bark at the Moon' werewolf and traditional ones, though."

"What's that?"

"He's a werewolf in the song, so he was a werewolf when my uncle pulled him through. Therein lies the major difference to the typical lycanthrope – he was already transformed when he was transported through by my uncle. I don't think he changes back to human form with the cycle of the moon."

"Lycanthrope?" Jonah asked. "Isn't that some kinda flower?"

"A lycanthrope is a werewolf, Jonah – a shapeshifter."

"Oh, okay. So you're saying he is a werewolf all the time, whether there's a full moon or not."

"Exactly. He's a tortured wolfen soul, day and night, regardless of the cycle of earth's natural satellite. I don't think he wants to come out in the light, though. I think all werewolves are uncomfortable in sunlight."

"That gives us the opportunity to kill him every night," Jonah said.

"Or he has the opportunity to kill *us* every night, Jonah."

"My glass is half full, bro. Just like Granny's."

Joe laughed. "I like the way you think. I'm a little worried, though."

"You think I'm not, Joe? I have confidence in our leadership. I believe it will sustain us."

"Are you talking about Black Dog?"

"I'm talking about you, Joe E. You know that."

"I don't need any more pressure on me, Jonah."

"It's not pressure, doofus. It's a vote of confidence."

"Thanks...."

CHAPTER TWENTY AND ONE

Joe had been formulating the skeleton of a plan since the Hairy Larry experiment/incident. He was thinking seriously about pulling through some characters and other things, via backmasking, that might be allies in the epic battle surely to come. He didn't think he and Jonah and Black Dog and Sugar could kill the werewolf without help. He was loosely forming a battle strategy, which would involve ambush and trickery and would take additional numbers.

Although still in the embryonic stage, I can provide a scenario that illustrates Joe's rough draft. Let me paint the scene. Imagine a lost, wealthy, white frat boy in a drunken Mardi Gras fog. He's a pledge and is being hazed by the initiated members. He has been blindfolded and dropped off in an unknown location with orders to find his way back to their hotel. He strips off the blindfold as they squeal away, tires smoking. Thankfully, he is not naked.

The pledge unknowingly stumbles across the boundary of the 1403 apartment units of the Magnolia Projects of New Orleans. He senses danger, like a mouse being watched by an elephant. (Elephants hate mice.) Disoriented, he walks farther into the perimeter. Whitey glimpses a gangbanger in his peripheral vision and walks faster. Up ahead, a baby gangsta steps out of a stairwell. The pledge veers away and two more pop up, loitering at a rusted playground, eyeballing him like crocodiles waiting for a baby zebra to take a drink. The freshman is in too deep with nowhere to turn. He breaks into a sprint, only to be met by a group of thirteen and fourteen-year-old's bent on taking what is his, including, possibly, his life. It's not going to turn out well.

Joe E. had a similar scenario in mind for the werewolf – an elaborate trap composed of misdirection, confusion, intimidation, and, ultimately, DEATH. (Reader – my frat boy example isn't born of racism. The same tactics are used by Cajun rednecks stalking a wild boar through a swamp. My writing is post-racial.)

Joe worked on his plan while he slept. It was amazing that the boys could sleep at all, with the knowledge they were being stalked by the Wolfman. Each night when they turned off the light in the study they entered a near comatose state, and each morning they woke like the people in the 'Alien' movies, as if they had been in a hyperbaric sleep chamber for the last eight hours.

The boys were asleep now. Jonah did not dream, but Joe's sleep was fitful, as usual. The image of the werewolf from the album cover was burned in his mind and terrorized his subconscious. The beast raced through his dreams – an entity Joe could not see, but one he could sense. There were shadows and sounds all around him in these nightmares, but he could only hide, shaking and crying, his hand over his own mouth to muffle the sound of his fear. He was too terrified to confront the werewolf, even in his imagination.

Between nightmares, Joe also thought about another plan. Not the plan I described earlier – that would be easily mapped out like a Halloween haunted house, but with much shorter lines at the entrance. He was coming to the conclusion that he needed allies and would have to use Uncle Ernie's records to get them. After all, Granny couldn't help, and Otis didn't have the spine for it. Jonah would fight with him, but Joe didn't know what kind of fight the boy would muster against the strength of an otherworldly demon.

Nothing in the choosing of their compatriots would be obvious, just like the Hairy Larry incident. The supernatural was unpredictable, but by now Joe had an inkling of what might be thrown at him. He had played a song about flowers and been granted an obnoxious hippie as a by-product. He had played a song with the message to 'ramble on' and been handed a dead Gollum. Every song had a little shank in the ribs tickle to it. Joe knew rushing his decisions could be deadly.

Joe needed to analyze the lyrics in great depth and trust his instincts before he backmasked a song, for once and for all, never to be reversed – unless he was willing to murder whatever came through the portal or set it free into an alien world. The werewolf was lucky by comparison – he operated solely on instinct and was without conscience. This would be a battle of primitive, animal survival of the fittest, versus intellectual superiority and the morality that accompanies such knowledge. A rattlesnake doesn't feel guilt after biting the soft leg of a three-year-old child, and a three-year-old child doesn't feel guilt after biting his father's leg while daddy is taking a nap. The father feels no remorse after chopping the snake's head off, but feels terrible after yelling at the son who has just taken a chunk out of his calf. Conscience has many angles.

Guilt and consequences would accompany any misstep Joe made, and they would haunt him for the rest of his life. In other words, the werewolf had a leg up (That's a bad joke, and I'm sorry.) from the beginning of this chess match. The Wolfman was ignorant, and the phrase 'ignorance is bliss' absolves the sins committed by those with low intelligence. The wolf had no morals and was incapable of remorse, but Joe was the opposite. If Joe killed something he did not eat, he would feel very guilty. Joe came to this concept while dove hunting when he was thirteen. He told his father he felt bad after killing a dove, but his dad assured him it was okay, since they would eat it. Joe thought about what his father had told him and said, "Dad, I don't think we should trap animals, since we don't eat them." They never trapped again. (This tenet would not be honored by Joe in regard to the werewolf, though. Joe E. had no desire to try barbequed lycanthrope, no matter how succulent it might be.)

***

Joe woke with the dawn as he would for the rest of his life, glad to be away from the nightmares. He went to Ernie's room and began studying the notebook for possible soldiers he could command in the army he was preparing to summon.

After inspecting the list with all the scrutiny he could muster, he saw few options. After all, he wasn't familiar with most of the songs, and he didn't have the internet available for immediate research, which was good and right. This was an analog battle started in 1983, not a digital game. The consequences would be physical, and real blood would flow when damage was inflicted – ANALOG. Hit points would not be deducted, health meters would be meaningless, and blood would not be represented in pixelated Pantone – DIGITAL.

He considered each artist and whether they, or their name, appeared to be, even superficially, evil, like Ozzy Osbourne was when he recorded 'Bark at the Moon'. Most of the records didn't seem constitutionally wicked, so the majority passed through this initial weeding out. He also considered the titles of these artist's albums and their songs. Tons of rock songs are based in the deception of the double entendre, so this stage was fraught with danger. The back cover of the Rush album, 'Moving Pictures', even featured the rare triple entendre. Joe felt like he was walking through a minefield without a metal detector. What appeared bad could be good and vice versa.

During this vetting process, Joe became more confused than resolute in what he needed to do next. Most of the titles seemed to be arbitrary, and he knew not what to eliminate. After all, 'Black Dog' suggested the hounds of Hell, but had produced the impossibly loyal Scottie-dog, now his closest companion other than Jonah. Joe didn't know if 'Freebird' was a passenger pigeon, a dodo, or a raptor that would gouge out his eyes with razor-sharp talons.

He had very little to go on, since he was by no means an expert on classic rock. He needed Uncle Ernie to help him, but wanted no part in resurrecting the ghostly specter of his familial predecessor. In fact, Joe *had* discovered a song called 'Uncle Ernie' by the Who. Would the song conjure a zombified version of Ernie or a loving uncle to guide him? The question had haunted Joe E. from the minute he dictated the title to Jonah days before. He even had a dream/nightmare in which he played the song backwards and conjured up a half-decomposed evil zombie Ernie, and it was no 'Weekend at Bernie's/Ernie's' summer fluff matinee. Joe E. needed guidance but had only instinct – not much different from the werewolf.

His short list of possible allies consisted of Aqualung, the Iron Man, The Who's Tommy character, and Maxwell from The Beatles song, 'Maxwell's Silver Hammer'. Let us now examine these options in further detail, just as Joe did.

Jethro Tull's Aqualung character seemed to be sympathetic to the cause. The guy was a gutter-dwelling homeless man, down on his luck and beaten into submission by society, but had not been reduced to taking the lives of the innocent, ala Jack tha Rippa. Aqualung's primary attribute appeared to be knowing how to cope with the most harsh of circumstances. He had seen it all in the gutters and dungeons of London and survived. If he could co-exist in the shadow of Big Ben with Jack the Ripper, he might not be scared of Wolfie. He might even want to rid the world of the woolly bully, since he lived in a city that had been terrorized by history's most famous serial killer. Joe didn't know it, but Aqualung had been questioned about the murders numerous times by Scotland Yard detectives and harbored a deep hatred for the Ripper.

Joe was a benevolent person and held a compassionate view of the homeless Aqualungs he saw in modern life. He didn't immediately label them as worthless trash, like most Americans do. He gave them the benefit of the doubt. In his mind, they were probably either mentally ill or had fallen on hard times, one or two missteps shy of what we call 'success'. Joe's dad had once hired a man down on his luck to work on the farm, and he turned out to be the most loyal employee one could ever wish for. Joe thought Aqualung might be a similar case. He resolved to play the record backward when the time was right. Aqualung needed a second chance, and Joe was willing to give it to him.

Next, Joe E. considered Black Sabbath's 'Iron Man'. He was very hesitant about working with any song a band by the name of Black Sabbath had produced. After all, their lead singer was Ozzy Osbourne, the man who wrote and sang 'Bark At The Moon', the song behind this whole terrible ordeal. But – Joe also intrinsically understood the binary nature of man, even without having read Herman Hesse's 'Steppenwolf'. He sensed that not all Ozzy had done was evil. Joe didn't know it, but he understood the duality of man – every human is both a sinner and a saint.

Joe listened to 'Iron Man' countless times and concluded the man of steel was innately good, but prone to react unpredictably in stressful situations, kind of like Frankenstein when frightened by fire. Iron Man was powerful and made of metal – the Wolfman's claws and teeth would be ineffective against him. Unless Wolfie understood magnetism and could use it to his benefit, Iron Man seemed like a good bet. Joe was worried about a myriad of other details, though. How big was the creature? Would his joints need to be oiled? Did he have an 'off' switch? Joe decided he would wait.

Next, Joe E. listened to The Who. This was a little different, since the whole 'Tommy' album was a character study. Realizing this,

Joe chose not to listen to just one song. He rightly felt the need to absorb the entire 'Tommy' album, comprised of four sides of music on two records – a double album. He didn't know what drew him to this record, but he knew better than to question his instincts.

It took Joe days to understand 'Tommy'. The decision regarding Aqualung had come quickly, but the second the needle hit side one of 'Tommy', Joe entered another world, stuck like a skipping record. He was like a mad scientist on the verge of a monumental discovery, rarely leaving the bedroom to eat or go to the bathroom. He was possessed, or better stated, obsessed, and his only companion was Black Dog, who sat patiently on Ernie's bed, watching Joe pace the floor. Frequently, he grabbed the notebook and scratched frenzied notes into it, mumbling to himself.

Jonah sensed that Joe needed space, so he spent his time during this period practicing riding Sugar bareback. He delivered food to Joe and Black Dog at the appropriate times, then disappeared. Joe listened to the four sides of 'Tommy' in their entirety over fifty times, back to back to back to back. It became an inspiration to him through this thorough examination. Joe was transfixed by the story of this Christ analogy who was both deaf and blind, but could still be a pinball wizard on the Bally table. That's the type of person he was looking for, Joe concluded. Basically, he needed Jesus – or in this case, Jesus Christ Skywalker.

Tommy reminded Joe E. of Luke in the first Star Wars movie. Joe mentally dwelled on the scene on Han Solo's freighter when Luke was blindfolded and playing light saber laser tag with the little floating drone, learning to 'use the force'. It was a painful game, but it trained Luke to become a Jedi Knight. The scene was an apt simile to Tommy and the pinball machine he high-scored without the sense of sight and without a tilt.

Joe spent three days in Ernie's room with the shade drawn, just 'being', absorbing information. If you could have seen the process, you would have thought he looked like the post-traumatic stress disorder Martin Sheen in the intro of 'Apocalypse Now'. He just 'was', like a lost statue of Buddha being slowly covered by vines in a Vietnamese forest. He was just 'being', like a crocodile basking in the sun. He was 'in the now', like a hummingbird sucking syrup. It was meditation. And concentration. And deliberation. And defenestration. And Yoko Ono was nowhere around to screw things up, thank God and Buddha and Buddah Records.

***

The decision to call through the hippie-Christ, Tommy, was still clouded in uncertainty, even after seventy-two hours of meditation on the subject. On the surface, Tommy seemed to be just another hippie, no different than Hairy Larry, but Tommy was not that at all, Joe came to realize. Tommy was pious and had an aura around him that seemed to ensure he would, at the least, not be a detriment to Joe and Jonah's cause. More than likely, he would determine their success or failure if he was summoned from vinyl – a big 'if', to be sure. Joe was not sure enough to do it. He would wait and see what happened with Aqualung.

The 'Jesus Christ Superstar' soundtrack was also in the record collection, and Joe listened to it numerous times as well, but ultimately felt that attempting to resurrect Jesus, Himself, might be a bit over-reaching and would surely open numerous big cans of large worms. Joe was too prudent to even consider the possibilities. Judas might be called through and make some deal with Wolfie for thirty dog biscuits and undermine the entire operation.

The title of The Beatles track, 'Maxwell's Silver Hammer', intrigued Joe E. He imagined a dude with a big silver sledge obliterating Wolfie with a mighty blow to the chest. He was excited to listen to the song – he thought a silver hammer might work just as well as a silver bullet.

Joe was severely disappointed after hearing the track. It seemed to be the story of a maniacal psychopath bent on smashing in the heads of all those around him. Joe was surprised the peace-loving Beatles had produced such a violent work.

He discovered another intriguing Beatles song on the 'White Album', called 'The Continuing Story of Bungalow Bill'. It was about a bumbling tiger hunter who rode an elephant. Joe saw some potential in Bill, but the song seemed to portray the hunter as capable of accidentally causing a lot of damage. Joe nixed Bungalow Bill, as well. The Beatles weren't being much help. He didn't think the werewolf would settle their differences over a 'We Can Work It Out' singalong around a kudzu campfire, either.

The decision had been made. Aqualung, Tommy, and Iron Man had competed nobly for the title of homecoming king, but Aqualung was the victor. The other two would have to wait until next season.

***

Joe also became aware of numerous titles among the records that would work in the Wolfman's favor, if the beast ever gained access to the record player – songs like 'Running with the Devil'. Joe took note of these and resolved to detach the record player's removable needle cartridge any time the boys weren't using the machine. Overkill, perhaps, but things were getting serious, and no precaution was too extreme. He also imagined calling Aqualung through and then having the derelict drunkenly resurrect the 'Werewolves of London'. The record collection was extensive, and the possibilities were innumerable, for both good and bad.

Joe E. recognized that his uncle's possessed record needle had to be controlled like 'The Book of the Dead' or the Ark of the Covenant. If it fell into the wrong hands it could mean oblivion to all that was good. Joe was the only one who understood the Death Star potential of this machine, and he knew he had to wield absolute authority over its use. He decided to carry the needle cartridge in an empty ibuprofen bottle when not using it, padding it on all sides with cotton balls. He deposited the little vessel in his right front pocket and soon acquired the habit of touching that pocket over and over, like a nervous tourist checking his wallet, amid a mob of locals making their way into a soccer match or a bullfight.

***

On the fourth morning of his isolation, Joe rose at sunrise and was ready. He cued up the Aqualung song and backmasked it, to put it bluntly. His mind had been made up, and there was no conjecture left in the boy. Ten minutes later, he was staring down at the bearded, smelly subject of the song from the entrance of the cellar, pitchfork in hand.

"Aye, me brother," Aqualung spoke as he ascended the steps. He talked like a pirate. He was drab and grey, as if in black and white, rather than Technicolor. He carried a large presence, for he

black 183 dog

was bundled and bustled with innumerable layers of clothing. "And to what do I owe this? And whereabouts are we situated at the present? I must have tipped one too many pints last night, as I know not where I be. I'm deeply sorry to have trespassed your underground vault for the night's sanctuary, me friend. Might ye direct me to the nearest pub or tavern? And with that I'll be on me way."

"There's no bars nearby and you aren't trespassing. I brought you here. Don't worry, mister – I'll give you vodka if you help me. Help us, I mean," Joe said with all the courage he could generate.

"I've heard of the spirit vodka. Fetch me a taste, lad, and I shall be happy to listen to your proposition. Egad, London be more elevated in temperature than I remember!" Aqualung wiped alcohol-laced sweat from his grimy brow with his forearm.

Joe did as asked, having brought a large glass of the spirit with him. He also had a shot glass to slowly distribute the hard stuff to Aqualung in exchange for his assistance. He dipped into the large vessel, normally used for sweet tea, and handed a dram of the Russian liquor to the Aqualung.

"What be it ye need assistance with?" the derelict asked warily after his first dose. "Aye, that burns. In a good way, mind ye. I mean no criticism, to be sure. I would no sooner speak ill of a gift of drink as I would spit on a fine lady."

"Don't be so wary, Mr. Lung. I'm not out to harm you. I'm not the police or Scotland Yard."

"What utter relief I do feel at that revelation, me boy! My interactions with authority have been, shall we say, excruciating. I thought ye were going to question me once again, in regard to the unfortunate murders of those ill-fated ladies of the night."

"No. I'm not attempting to prosecute you," Joe said with a stern look. "This is no indictment. I know you had nothing to do with that."

"Rightfully so, young inspector. I should not be indicted, for I have done no harm."

"I know that."

"I am no Ripper. I am a simple drunkard. That is my only crime and harms none, other than meself. I enjoy a tip of the wrist, sometimes to over-indulgence. For that, I apologize. But, I assure you, I have taken no sadistic liberties with the wayward ladies of the night."

"I know you aren't Jack the Ripper, okay? Let's move on. What about your affection for young girls? Do you appreciate them in an unsavory manner? Have you committed crimes against them?"

"I'm simply an observer of their behavior, lad. That is all. Does an uncle eyeing his niece at play receive such scrutiny? I am childless. Barren," Aqualung said with a dramatic sigh. "What I would give to have a little girl."

"What!?" Joe exclaimed.

"That didn't come out right, lad. I am utterly alone and childless. Watching children at play brings happiness to this old sod. Am I supposed to watch rats crawl the alleys to experience pleasure? Why must everyone yell 'fire' if I sit on a park bench and glance in the direction of the joyous voices of kids at play?"

"So you aren't a pedophile."

"I know not the meaning of the term, but I assure you I am not. Wait!! Are you asking if I practice paedophilia erotica?" Aqualung said with revelation. "I assure you again, I do not! I am an alcoholic, that is all, and I pray some glorious day a group of people will band together anonymously to support one another in the recovery from this affliction."

"Okay, Aqualung. Welcome to Alabama. My name is Joe. I'm sorry to be so accusing. I have to be very cautious."

"Why dost thou call me this name – Awkwelung? I am not known by such moniker. My name be Collin James."

"I'm sorry, Mr. James. Just consider it a nickname – a shortcut."

"Well, if you must," Mr. James said.

"I'm glad to hear your explanation of the indiscretions you have been accused of, Collin. In Alabama you are innocent and exonerated of any crime. You have to help me, though."

"You seem a might young to be a constable or judge. I feel as if there is some catch, of which I know nought at the present."

"Another dram?" Joe asked with a Cheshire smile. "Make yourself at home, as much as you can."

"An undercurrent of some sort is at hand," Aqualung

black 185 dog

responded as he took the ration of liquor from Joe's hand. "What can I help you with, guvna?" he said with a sly grin Jack Nicholson would be proud of. "Me thinks not that your strange white shoes need a shine."

"They're called sneakers – Air Jordans."

"Seems the buckles have fallen from them," Aqualung replied. "Be they worn?"

Joe laughed and filled Aqualung's shot glass.

***

The two sat for some time on the ledge of the cellar, as Joe briefed the classic rock character to their situation. Aqualung enjoyed many more shots of vodka and especially liked Granny's Marlboro Reds. After an hour or so, the smelly man appeared to wilt.

"Are you feeling ill?" asked the boy.

"The intensity of sunlight here is not something I'm acclimated to," said Aqualung. "I'm from the gloom of bloody London. May we venture into your castle for further discourse? How do you endure this glare?"

"You get used to it," Joe answered. "Okay. Let's go upstairs. I've got a song I need to play for you. It's about you, in fact."

"Ahh. You have minstrels in the castle who sing of my exploits. Just like those of noble King Arthur."

"Not quite, buddy. Songs have been written about you that are, shall we say, unflattering. I just need to know first – can I trust you?"

"Ye can, lad, if ye have more of this vodka and these 'red' small cigars. What realm of Queen and Country dost thou serve in this Alabama, may I ask? Be we in Ireland or the Land of Scots? The black terrier at your side suggests the latter."

"You are in America."

"By that, do you mean I have been somehow transported to a post-revolutionary colonial territory, in which my Queen has been deposed and is not in rule of?"

Joe laughed. "By that, I mean a descendant of your Queen still stands as a figurehead in your native land. She holds only symbolic power. She wears wool skirt-suits and has a son with horrible, crooked teeth. Fear not, though. The country you now find

black 186 dog

yourself in is free. You will not be arrested for providing for yourself by desperate means. Lots of people do it. You just need a cardboard sign, and people will give you money. You have committed no crime, if what you say is the truth. And, just so you know, I believe you."

"...And truthfully," Joe continued, "your indiscretions, if any, are beside the point, Mr. Lung. I'm asking for your help with no debt or forced allegiance to any godhead or symbolically empowered old lady with a jeweled crown and scepter. I'm humbly asking for your help. I am by no means attempting to entrap or prosecute you. Things here are much different than the situation you were transported from. The standard of living is markedly improved, but the circumstances are no less dire."

"It looks as such," Aqualung said with a chuckle, looking like a nasty cross between Keef Richards and Jack Sparrow. "Are you saying you need help from a lunger like me, yeah? Hard to believe, matey," he said with a deep, tubercular laugh. "Got another smoke? Tell me the whole of it."

By this time, Jonah had crept up and was eyeing Aqualung with much disdain and distrust. After all – the man was no Sugar. A horse, er, unicorn, kept a cleaner stable than him. Jonah misinterpreted him to be another Hairy Larry.

"Jonah," Joe said, turning to his friend. "Will you get me another pack of ciggies from the pantry?"

"Whatever you say, Joe E.," he responded as he turned toward the house, still mean-mugging Aqualung. He didn't like any of this one bit.

Jonah returned and handed the fags to Joe, ignoring Aqualung's hand, which was outstretched to him in addicted anticipation.

"Be these small cigars enchanted by some chemical or magic to make me do thy bidding?" Aqualung asked.

"Just smoke the damned things," said Jonah. "Joe, how is this dude going to help us?" Jonah turned toward Joe, shielding his nostrils from the stench of the vagabond Aqualung. "What the eff is he going to help us with, Joe?"

"Boy, you don't want to know what I've seen," replied the old man before Joe could answer. He flashed blackened, broken shards

black 187 dog

of teeth. "I should be asking why you're here with me. My name is Collin James. Will you introduce me to your comrade, Mr. Joe? I'm rather used to receiving a negative reaction from the public, so I will ignore this boy's behaviour and simply request a civil introduction."

"Jonah, this is Mr. Collin James, the Aqualung. Mr. James, this is my best friend, Jonah."

"Pleasure to meet your acquaintance, Sir Jonah," Aqualung said with the nobility of a gentleman.

"Okay," said Jonah. "Well, are you on our side or not?"

"At the present I see no reason to oppose you. Settle your fears, son, and let not your heart be troubled."

Jonah smiled begrudgingly and reached out his hand halfheartedly to shake that of the strange man. Aqualung grasped the limp offering and held it firmly and honestly. "I'm at your service, me boy," he said, gazing directly into Jonah's formerly hair-covered eyes.

"I'm sorry," Jonah said. "But if you betray Joe, I'll murder you. I've done it before." Joe was aghast, but impressed.

"I have no intentions of doing that, young Jonah. My goodness, what threats! I know not why you've called me here, but I feel compelled to assist you in your cause. That is all I can promise. I'll do me best, but I do not deserve to be threatened!"

"That's all we ask, your best," said Jonah. "I apologize. I'm sorry for threatening you. You wanna meet my unicorn? Her name is Sugar."

"It would be my privilege, lad. Where be this eunuch with the horn?"

***

With that, the three left for the forest with Black Dog leading the way. The experiment seemed to have worked as Joe had desired. Aqualung was not evil, just misunderstood. At least Joe hoped that was the case. Aqualung was acclimating to the Alabama sun already. He was in jovial spirits, happy to be out of overcast London and elated to have been introduced to the alcoholic's best friend, vodka. What a sight they were, skipping together through the tall grass in the hot sun with Black Dog in front, barking excitedly.

***

black 188 dog

Sugar didn't mind Aqualung one bit. She ate the candy he fed her without hesitation, although he took the liberty of eating most of it. He had never been wealthy enough to afford the confections of the London sweet shops he passed on his daily rounds. Sugar seemed to be a great judge of character, and Joe E. took heart in her acceptance of Aqualung.

After some time, the mutual adoration society felt they had lingered too long and said their goodbyes to the unicorn. Sugar walked into the stand of trees, and the humans and Black Dog returned to the house. It was dusk when they arrived.

"Okay, Mr. James," Joe said. "This is my grandmother's house, her castle. We need to keep you out of sight, so as not to alarm her. I'll see if the coast is clear, then we'll sneak you upstairs, get you bathed, feed you, and find a place for you to sleep."

"Well, lad. Hmmm." Aqualung said, looking uncomfortable. "I tend to feel a touch of imprisonment indoors. There's a right nice hedge over there, where I would feel much more at home and your Granny shall never encounter me. And, as for bathing – I have something of an aversion to that, as well. I have a few peculiarities, you see. Might ye bring me a kebab or a bit of shepherd's pie and see me in the morrow?"

"Okay. That might work out well, actually. Don't be offended, but I must ask that you stay out of sight for the time being. If anyone sees you, they might call the authorities," said Joe.

"You know I desire no part of that," replied Aqualung. "I shan't be seen, I assure you. I am adept at concealing myself. Might I have a bit of vodka, to temper the cold night?"

"Sure. That's perfect. I'll send Jonah out with your provisions, and I'll see you tomorrow. Sleep well, and thanks, Collin. Really, thanks."

The boys went inside and made sandwiches. Joe went upstairs with his and Black Dog's plates to do more research, and Jonah returned to the large shrub in the front yard to have his meal with his latest crazy friend. Jonah knew Joe needed some space, so he lingered in conversation with the wizened Briton for over an hour.

By the end of their dinner together, Jonah had been won over by Aqualung's medieval charm and was enamored with the latest victim of their backmasking shenanigans. Victim – it's a strong word, but it was the one that kept encroaching into Joe's, and now, Jonah's brains. Both boys were fighting the feelings of guilt attached to those they involved in their cause. It was understandable – Joe and Jonah were coming from a world in which you didn't do a thing without getting a signed permission slip prior. They were now seeing that life doesn't pause to contemplate questions like, "Is this safe?" and, "Is somebody going to get killed by a werewolf?"

The answer to guilty questions like these was easy – they were victims, too. The boys had not volunteered to fight the werewolf, either. None of them – Joe, Jonah, Granny, Aqualung, Otis, Sugar, and Black Dog – had signed up for this. Recognition of this justified the boys' backmasking actions. They were all in the right place at the wrong time – drafted to fight, like the boys that lived and died in the Vietnam War. The fight was good vs. evil, enough said. If your number gets called, you have to show up and go to war. The boys couldn't dodge this draft and neither could the others.

INTERMISSION: "And Now A Word From Our Narrator"

Movies are what normal people that don't do drugs use to escape mundane reality. We stand in line and pay an absurd price for a ticket, then pay five bucks for a Coke that costs the theater a dime, then munch six-dollar popcorn that costs the theater a nickel. On top of that, the corn is popped in unhealthy coconut oil and slathered in imitation butter, which potentially robs decades of life from an avid movie-goer. Then, we sit in the dark and whisper snarky comments to each other about how crappy the previews are – "Who would pay good money to watch that horse-faced slut play a prostitute turned princess?" And that makes us happy.

Drug habits are cheaper than this, we at some point realize, so we go to bargain matinees starting at two on a Saturday afternoon, so we can afford to watch people we identify with battle aliens and giant spiders and vampires. It's okay to talk during the previews, but during the feature you'd better shut up and have your cell phone on 'stun', or face the wrath of somebody older than twenty who remembers you don't answer a call at the movies or talk loud in a library.

Then, when the movie's over, we file out in orderly fashion, leaving trash on the floor, rather than throw it in the huge waste bin conveniently placed by the exit. We stop for a pee, then get blinded by the sun's nuclear fusion blast as we exit fantasy land. And that's when it happens.

That's when the most primal and vital of the many feelings in the movie-going experience occurs. Throwing open the exit door and getting shocked and awed by the drastic contrast from the dark, whispering, refrigerator interior of the theater to the asphalt, heat, and glare of the movie's parking lot is akin to the experience a baby goes through at birth. This is made all the more dramatic if you live in a place where it gets blisteringly hot in the summer – places where people go see expensive movies they've never heard of, just to spend a couple hours in the air conditioning.

***

black 191 dog

If you want some cheap amusement and can't afford to actually go to a movie, loiter by the exit door of a theater sometime and listen to every single person that walks out comment. First, they'll remark how bright it is, it's too hot, too cold, the movie sucked, or the movie was great. Everyone's a critic.

The best movies leave you feeling like you are entering an alien world as you hit the theater's parking lot. Think about that. You are returning to reality, not the opposite, but good movies flip the script. When a movie convinces you what is onscreen is real and your true life on earth is the foreign concept... wow! Powerful stuff. You've been convinced life on Pandora with the nine-foot tall blue aliens is real and feel as if you are traversing an alien landscape as you make your way from the movie theater to your Nissan. You have been brainwashed or hypnotized, at least for a couple hours – engrossed in some other world so genuine and sincere it has made you forget the circumstances of your true existence. Please re-read the first sentence of this chapter now.

***

We funnel out of the theater like people who have just ridden the latest bad-ass roller coaster at Six Flags, although we don't have to go through a gift shop on the way to the exit, to get suckered into buying a tank-top we'll never wear, emblazoned with the words, 'I Survived Sasquatch'. Likewise, I'm sure lots of members of the 'Adventurer's Club' have 'I Climbed Mt. Everest, thanks to the assistance of a Sherpa guide, and all I got was this lousy T-Shirt' versions of the same in their walk-in closets. Conquest, whether it is riding the most brutal roller-coaster, watching the scariest movie, killing the African beast, or climbing the tallest mountain, breeds narcissism and is done for validation of the ego. Gift shops realize this – people want to brag after conquering a threat to their survival and are willing to pay thirty bucks to do it. Noble is the man who conquers without the need for reward. They should have sold shirts on the way out of the first screenings of 'The Exorcist', reading 'I Survived Linda Blair'. They would have sold a ton.

I will further elaborate my point from the previous paragraph, though it will garner me few friends. Why does the Great White Hunter need to stuff the Polar Bear he shot and display it in

black 192 dog

his great room? Like a real-life Bungalow Bill, the big game hunter was undoubtedly led to his kill by a guide, and surely paid the state of Alaska an outrageous fee to take down this stately and intelligent beast, just to be a trophy in his castle. How is that an accomplishment? I assure you, every man with a head mount of a hippo or rhino or lion king in his study has a small you-know-what (brain – get your head out of the gutter) and a large ego and feels the need to prove himself at 300 yards with the aid of a large scope and a small tribe of natives or Eskimos willing to carry his massive kill back to civilization, in exchange for a Snickers bar and a carton of Marlboro Reds.

This begs the question – 'Does something have to be physically experienced to really be 'experienced'?' I mean, can't you watch 'Moby Dick' and come close enough to what it's like to harpoon an albino Sperm Whale? Or, are you so ego-driven and wealthy that you will pay someone to take you out on their whaling vessel, so you can truly understand this feeling? Do your weak arms have to lug a spear at the real-life Mocha Dick, only to have the boat overturned by his violent tail, then drown? I'll stick to a movie and my over-priced popcorn, thank you – coconut oil and all.

***

One other thing can create this phenomenon of pure, unfettered escapism – good music. Not Muzak piped in through Wal-Mart speakers, drifting down upon shoppers like the deadly dew of Nazi death-chambers. Not outrageous bass blasting from the death-rattling trunk of a rusty Cadillac driven by a societal parasite gang member next to you at a red light. Don't glare his way. Just let it be. Karma will out, just like truth and murder.

Put on a pair of headphones – the old kind, like musicians use in the studio. They are known in the biz as 'cans' – earbuds on steroids. Lay down on your back on the carpet and close your eyes and lose yourself in the music you love. You'll discover so much you never heard before, even on songs you have listened to thousands of times. Listen to the Rolling Stones play 'Angie', and you'll hear Mick Jagger's 'ghost vocal' guide track hollering with unrestrained emotion in the background at 2:18 and 2:55.

You'll hear the static blast of overdrive on the second chord of the first song on 'Led Zeppelin I'. You'll hear Jimmy Page count in track seven of 'Zeppelin III'. You'll hear John Bonham's squeaking kick pedal on the studio version of 'Since I've Been Loving You'. 'Black Country Woman' on side two of 'Physical Graffiti' even has an airplane flying over. Awesome! Leave it in the mix. During the chariot race in 'Ben Hur', a plane flies by in the background, which is awesome in exactly the same way. Dig up the Beatles Anthology and listen to Paul McCartney's exultant scream before 'Sergeant Pepper's Reprise' takes flight. I could go on, but you get the idea, and you've got plenty of things to discover for yourself, on your own – unfettered human joy and enthusiasm.

The examples I just listed are, technically, 'errors', yet they are so wonderful – because they are human! Think of how boring baseball would be without errors – the Yankees would win every game. If Led Zeppelin and The Beatles never made a mistake, why would a person like you or me even attempt to write a song? See how it works? Errors are there for a reason.

Not one thing created by man is free from error, no matter how awesome an accomplishment it may be, for to err is human. The Mona Lisa is flawed, as is the Eiffel Tower, as is 'Sgt. Pepper's', as is your lawn. Lou Reed and Bob Dylan can't sing very well, which makes them all the more human and vital. Nothing is perfect. You've heard the phrase a million times, but do you understand it? Reverse the nouns and see the philosophical truth. Perfect is nothing. The only thing that is perfect is nothing.

Now take it a step further and interject some spaces into some key words for even deeper understanding of this concept. No_thing is perfect and every_thing is beautifully imperfect, which is exactly why mankind's accomplishments are so amazing, so human, so real, and so awe-inspiring – created by people so similar to us in their humanity that they cut their own ear off and mailed it to a prostitute, like Van Gogh, or put a shotgun in their mouth and mailed it in, like Kurt Cobain. It's as obvious as the mole on Marilyn Monroe's otherwise perfect face.

Also, our humanity compels us to find beauty and inspiration in even the saddest of songs and the most tragic of circumstances – amen to that.

black 194 dog

I know that went off the rails about two-thirds of the way through, but we're riding the stream of consciousness roller coaster. Shirts are for sale in the gift shop on the way out.

CHAPTER WOLFMAN

The werewolf Ozzy wrote a song about appears to be the villain in this book. This should be obvious by now. If not – you really need to work on your reading comprehension. The thing is – he is not an evil sociopath by choice. He is a victim of circumstance, just like a kid murdered by a school shooter.

The werewolf Ozzy wrote about had a name, Charles Humboldt, and he never meant to be the tormentor of two teenagers' souls. He was a simple accountant, accounting coins and watching for wheat pennies, until he was attacked shortly after leaving the local library with a 'Book of Lists'. He had perused the volume in the bibliotheca and been amused by its accounts of 'Most Flatulent Beans', and such. Soybeans were at the top of the list, if you're wondering. The book was printed in 1975, so the data may have since changed. I feel sorry for the researchers on that study.

The library was open late on Tuesday nights, and it was getting dark when he left. The moon was full. Charles hurried to his Pacer, expecting nothing beyond a Big Mac and an order of fries to culminate his evening. His mind wandered to Mexico – he was a dreamer. He had never been there, but frequently admired the tourism brochures of Acapulco and Cozumel. He was saving to go on a vacation, but had nobody to send a postcard home to. He fantasized about meeting a sexy Latina on the beach and marrying her on a whim. Charles was a hopeless romantic and also the ultimate Lone Wolf, although he had no letterman's jacket proclaiming him as such.

***

Lenny from 'The Laverne and Shirley Show' had that jacket, but Charles did not. Lenny wasn't an athlete, so how did he get that 'Lone Wolf' letterman's jacket, anyway? What did he letter in? Shoot, he was a high school dropout, for Pete's sakes.

Hellooooo. Could it be more obvious? Lenny was a werewolf. That's the subject of another book, though, so I shall move forward without further examination of this disturbing revelation. And don't get me started on Squiggy, who was a vampire. This isn't a 'DaVinci Code' type of book.

***

Charles had no letterman's jacket, as I said. All Charles had was his 'Book of Lists' and a coupon for a free order of fries with the purchase of a Big Mac. He was absentmindedly preoccupied walking to his car, thinking about 'special sauce' and the flavor of exotic Mexican girls.

The accountant fumbled with his keys the way people in horror movies fumble with their keys when they are trying to escape a chainsaw murderer. Charles wasn't being pursued by an insane mental ward escapee, though. He was just clumsy. He mumbled expletives to himself as he attempted to find the right male key to fit in the car door's female lock, to put it in sexy-time terms. Like I said, he was a loner. He watched porn by himself, and this was what it had reduced his sick thoughts to. Opening a car door aroused him. He was a closet perv. He had even toyed with the idea of getting a job at the YMCA in order to be near teenage girls, but had decided that accounting paid much more, and he was saving for that Mexico vacation, after all.

He finally found the right key and got the door open. He sat in the worn seat and started the car. The Pacer's engine roared like an awakening lioness. 'RRROOOWWRR'. It was an animal. More of a possum than a lioness, really, but I'm trying to set a scene here.

Charles did his best to harness the power of his vehicle. He suddenly changed his mind on the Big Mac, instead choosing to drive his car to a little 1950's throwback chicken shack called 'Dodo's Drive-In' to get a milkshake and three chicken wings.

He ordered and attempted to drive around the building to the pick-up window. The turn was so sharp, he had to back and forth his Pacer like he was parallel parking to successfully negotiate the curve. Charles was upset by this. Many people get upset easily when behind the wheel of a vehicle, and Charles was no different. He growled with impotent road rage. Finally, he reached the pick-up window without further damaging his paint job, which was already scratched to hell.

"Why don't you straighten out that curve!" he yelled at the teenage girl who appeared at the window wearing an apron covered with flour.

black 197 dog

"What curve?" she asked with just a sprinkle of attitude like kids sometimes do.

"The curve to the pick-up window!" Charles responded.

"You want the wings or not, mister?!"

"Yes, please. I'm sorry. I just want to make the suggestion you do something about that hairpin curly turn."

"Suggestion noted, sir. Please pull forward and enjoy your Dodo's!"

Charles rolled up his window, ensuring the smell of fried chicken would not escape his vehicle. People with nice cars don't pick up food at drive-in windows, because they don't want to smell hamburger or chicken nuggets the next morning when they drive to work. Charles no longer worried about this. He liked to uncover new smells emanating from his seats when he entered his vehicle. It was an adventure. He was the Lone Wolf, after all, and wolves, like dogs, like to smell strange odors. He should have gotten a part-time job at a used car lot, sucking the farts out of car seats with a Shop-Vac. That's an old joke we used to tell in high school, and I've been waiting this whole book to use it. I may have written the whole book just to use it.

Charles smiled, since he had thought of the same joke. He pulled away happily. The girl leaned out the pick-up window, holding Charles' milkshake, but it was too late. Charles was so distracted by the smell of the chicken wings, he had completely forgotten about the vanilla shake.

He drove to a nearby convenience store to buy a Lone Star beer to enjoy with his yardbird. Beer and chicken made him happy. All he needed was a couple Wet-Naps, and his night was complete. Luckily, the brown paper bag from Dodo's included two of them. The chicken was greasy, and Dodo knew it and didn't care. Dodo provided alcohol-soaked napkins, though, so all was well.

Charles felt wonderful as he purchased his beer. He was having a splendid evening. The girl behind the counter slid a brown paper bag onto the can to help battle the effects of the South's extreme humidity. An old black man with milky eyes lurked outside the front door asking people for change. He made Charles uncomfortable. He made everyone uncomfortable. Charles hustled to his car with his head down, attempting to avoid eye contact.

"Say, can I have some of your purple berries?" said the homeless man, as Charles again fumbled for his keys. The man's name was Kick-Dirt, and everybody in town knew who he was. If you want to be a local celebrity, just start walking the streets, ranting and raving. More people will know your name than that of the guy who delivers the local news on TV.

"What are you talking about?" asked Charles with profound irritation.

"You's a meat eater, huh? I smell them wangs."

"Who doesn't eat meat? This is Texas! What do you want, Kick-Dirt?"

The derelict looked at Charles and bared his teeth like a dog. If there would have been a movie camera on the scene, it would have zoomed in on Kick-Dirt's teeth. The camera then would have wowed in and out to suggest something scary. A film-maker would do this to insinuate something terrifying was about to happen, or 'fixin' to happen if you speak Texan. You've seen this camera move on 'Tales From The Darkside' and 'Creepshow' and 'The Twilight Zone'. Something scary was definitely about to happen.

"Cold day for July, dontcha thinks?" the homeless man uttered next. He looked at Charles, and Charles looked back at him, and the drifter smiled the widest smile Charles had ever seen. The cracks between Kick-Dirt's teeth were filled with what Charles thought was dirt, but Charles was colorblind and couldn't tell dark brown from dark red. The man's teeth were caked with coagulated blood, but Charles had no way to know, being colorblind and all.

Charles didn't know what was in Kick-Dirt's teeth, but he wouldn't have cared, regardless. He was hungry for the wings of fried chickens, and he was thirsty for his beer. He was lonely, too, but that could be drowned out by playing 'Stairway to Heaven' very loud on his car stereo, which is exactly what he did. Led Zeppelin can cure everything, which Charles and I strongly believe.

He drove three blocks to the entrance of the huge park his town was known for. It was pitch black. Pitch is black, because pitch has an absence of color. Charles was colorblind, like I said, so it made no difference to him. Charles liked to say to himself that he

black 199 dog

lived in a 'colorless world of truth'.

He crept into the park as slow as his Pacer would go. He put on his sunglasses, even though it was pitch black. Pitch is black, but viewing it through sunglasses takes it from simple innate and inbred Anglo-Saxon racism to absolute moral disgust. He felt totally cool wearing his convenience store knock-off Ray-Bans at night, driving through the park. He had done this hundreds of times before, so he knew the long and winding road and maneuvered it without thought. The Guadalupe River flowed near him. He could not hear or see it in the darkness, but when he rolled the window down he could smell the brown water. It was a force of nature, just like him.

Charles finally decided which concrete picnic table and bench he would sup at and parked. He walked to the table and chose to sit on it, rather than the bench. He saw no other lights in the park, but sensed movement around him. "The gays," he thought to himself. "Hopefully harmless." The gays in parks at night are comparable to zombies in Hollywood flicks, although they are not searching for brains.

He opened the brown paper bag and took the white, waxed cardboard box from it and opened its origami lock. The smell of the freshly-cooked wings burst forth upon the wind.

Charles ate the first piece of chicken, then opened his beer with some difficulty due to the slick, greasy coating on his fingertips. He was enjoying himself immensely. He was used to being alone and took much satisfaction from simple pleasures. He finished the wings and the tasteless roll that accompanied them, then lit a Doral cigarette. He was frugal, being an accountant and all, and required no expensive designer Marlboro product for his gratification. He didn't even really smoke, but a beer and some fried chicken seemed to warrant a 'digestive' to supplement his meal and aid the stomach's purpose and function.

He sat on the table and felt a presence approach him in the dark. He peered into the blackness and saw a lone figure nearing him. The park's overhead lights had long ago been shot into impotence via bb's. Charles could see the silhouette of a human figure but could not make out its facial features.

"Hey, dude," the form spoke.

black 200 dog

"Yeah," said Charles, trying to be imposing, which didn't suit his nature.

"Hey, dude," again.

"Yeah. What?" asked Charles, perturbed.

"Whatcha doin'?"

"Smoking a cigarette. Why? You want one, or what?"

"No. Hey, dude," the mystery man said a third time. This time the angle of his head looked to a point behind Charles.

Charles turned to see another person had walked up behind him, and this was the person the first figure was speaking to with his last greeting.

Charles was surrounded. These weren't zombies. Worse, they were the type of gay males that prowl parks after dark. (Hey – be gay if that's your thing. I'm just telling the story of what happened.)

"Okay," Charles said to both of them. "I'm not gay. I don't know if you guys are, and there's nothing wrong with that, but I don't want anything to do with what goes on in this park after dark. I'm just trying to smoke my cigarette and finish my beer before I go home. You guys can just go off into the bushes and do your thing and leave me the hell out of it."

At this, the two figures walked away from Charles and more than likely had an unsafe sexual encounter which won't be mentioned in further detail. Ever notice that parks close at 10:00 p.m.? Now you know why.

Charles rolled his eyes and lit another cigarette. He didn't smoke in the car and was so disturbed by this interaction that he had decided on a rare second cigarette before heading home – big mistake. Charles sat on the table and leaned back to look at the stars as he blew out the smoke of his final fag. He gazed upward at the full moon.

A creature in the darkness got a whiff of fried chicken bones on the wind and crept stealthily toward Charles. This creature had excellent night vision and watched the Lone Wolf lolling on the table, delaying the trip to the solitary isolation of his little apartment.

The creature was a werewolf, of course, and raced at his helpless victim like a killer whale charging from the depths to impact a baby seal. Charles didn't have a chance in Hell. He saw the

black 201 dog

werewolf galloping on all fours toward him at the last possible second and froze. The beast leaped and tackled helpless Charles, knocking him from the table onto his back on the hard ground. Now, the werewolf was on top of his victim. Kick-Dirt lunged into Charles' body and ripped out his throat with a fatal bite.

The back story of Charles has now been told. Of course, Charles became a lycanthrope and 'Bark at the Moon' was the song written about him by a guy who bit the head off a bat. Poor Charles – he didn't want to kill and maim everything in his future. But, sadly, he did just that.

CHAPTER TWENTY AND TWO

The summer in Stringtown, Alabama, was in full bloom now. Everything seemed fine and perfectly normal to its citizens. The first day of school was only twenty-five days away, and the boys would be leaving a week before that. They were short-timers, like men in the Vietnam War counting down the final days of their tour of duty. The boys could easily hunker down inside the perimeter and wait out the siege, return to the world, and resume life as usual. That's what most people would have done.

Joe and Jonah's minds were in flux, as if their nerves had been plugged into a 220 volt outlet after seventeen years of 110. They were doubting the mission, questioning the nobility of the cause. After all – they could leave, return home, and pretend they had never known of the existence of the werewolf. Granny was old. She didn't really matter much. Sugar could surely fend for herself. Aqualung would probably get locked up by the local law enforcement and labeled as crazy. The boys could smuggle Black Dog home or just leave her on the curb as they boarded the Greyhound. Next summer nobody would remember they had ever been to Stringtown – except Otis, but what would he do about it? He didn't even like being around Granny's house. They could just ignore it all, pretend they'd never known of the werewolf, and nobody would be the wiser.

Both of the boys had thoughts like this. Relief did not accompany these ideas – dirty green guilt did. It was strange – the boys were spending less time on the Atari since they had called Aqualung through, but were instead just sitting in Ernie's room, staring into space and thinking. Sometimes they played music, but the songs reminded them of what was happening, so they mostly just sat there in silence. They were thinking all the time, though. Not thinking like a mathematician trying to solve a complex calculus problem – thinking like two confused teenagers. Not processing in any organized way, just meditating and hoping enlightenment would somehow find its way through their soft skulls. This went on for two days. They didn't even make it outside to check on poor, confused

black 203 dog

Aqualung. They were seduced by the temptress, Denial.

The third day after the arrival of Aqualung happened like any other day, but Joe woke up pissed off – at himself. His mind raced with an out of control inner dialogue. "Dammit, Joe, face reality. Kill that supernatural son of a bitch. Do it for Granny. Do it for Stringtown and Otis. Do it for... DO IT FOR YOURSELF, YOU COWARD!!!"

He shook his friend to wake him.

"It's time to do this, Jonah."

Jonah wasn't asleep. He was laying on his cot with his eyes closed, thinking similar thoughts.

"I know Joe. It's time."

Black Dog yelped a strange bark that, if translated, meant, "It's about time, master. I'm ready!" She had been in a virtual coma for the past couple days, sleepwalking between numerous cozy nooks and napping positions. She had conserved her strength, but now she was awake and alert, bouncing around, anxious to venture out again, yipping and yapping and making sounds dogs usually don't make.

The boys went downstairs. They were determined and every step was deliberate.

"Jonah, go start breakfast," ordered Joe. "I'll get Aqualung."

He walked outside and strolled behind the hedge that concealed the Jethro Tullian derelict. Chicken bones, fish bones, and crumpled magazines lay scattered on the ground around the snoring pauper. Joe picked up one of the periodicals and saw it was some strange version of pornography, called 'Ye Olde Ladies'. It featured senior citizens doing things not possible prior to the formulation and distribution of Viagra. "What the hell?" he thought to himself.

He pushed Aqualung with his foot, attempting to guide the man to consciousness. After multiple, increasingly more violent nudges, the man finally snorted awake, standing up achingly. Joe could smell that Aqualung was well past the 'sell by' date and was sourly ripe.

"Ah, yes, Master Joe. Where hast thou been?" Collin said, rubbing his dark eyes.

"I've been busy. What is all this stuff?"

black 204 dog

Collin looked at the detritus around his feet. "Yes, well these things, they be the remnants of my daily sustenance. Seems you boys have forgotten about poor old Collin James, forcing me to forage for my own survival."

"Where did you forage, may I ask?"

"There be a large bin, back of the dwelling 'cross the way," said Aqualung, pointing in the direction of the old man's house across the street. Joe shook his head as he pieced it all together.

"Come inside, Collin. We're going to have a nice breakfast together."

"Wonderful, lad. Splendid!" Aqualung exclaimed, brushing dirt and leaves from his heavy wool clothing.

"I'm sorry I was gone so long, Collin."

"No worries, matey. Me knew you'd return when you were good and ready."

They entered the kitchen to see Jonah with rolling pin in hand, working over some dough. A pot of oil was heating on the stove.

"Whatcha makin'?" asked Joe. "Donuts?"

"Sort of, but not quite. I'm making beignets – French fritters. I'm sick of bacon and eggs."

"Wow. I'm impressed. Where'd you learn to make those?"

"Family and Consumer Sciences class – the only class I ever got an 'A' in."

Joe stuck out his bottom lip, tilted his head, and nodded. "Home Ec, huh? Hell, maybe you'll become a chef someday, Jonah."

"I dunno. Prob'ly end up a dishwasher."

"Well," Joe said. "Whatever makes you happy. I'll cook some bacon and eggs for Mr. James and Granny and Black Dog. They might like some, in addition to the... whatchamajigs."

"Ben-yays," said Jonah like an actor on Sesame Street over-enunciating for the three and under crowd.

Granny came bounding through the swinging door, humming a tune. "Well, hello boys!! I can't remember the last time I've seen you. I thought you might have skedaddled back home without kissing me goodbye!"

Joe rushed over to hug the sweet little lady. "Granny, we

would never do that. You know we love you too much! We've just been a little busy, that's all. We're working on something... a project!"

"We're working on a project," Jonah echoed.

"That's right me lady, a project," Collin piped in with enthusiasm.

Granny turned to Aqualung and let out a startled, "Ooooh!"

"I'm so sorry Granny. We didn't mean to scare you," Joe said. "This is Collin James. He's a friend of ours. Uhh... he's a gardener. He's going to be giving us a hand getting the grounds in shape."

"Pleased to make your acquaintance, madame. I beseech your forgiveness for startling you," Aqualung said.

"Oh, it's quite alright, Mr. James. Pleased to make your acquaintance, I'm sure."

Collin pulled out a chair and ushered Granny into it. For a gutter bum, he was quite charming.

Joe began cracking eggs into a large bowl as Aqualung sat down across from Granny, smiling with genuine warmth through brown teeth.

"We're making a special breakfast, Granny," said Joe. "Jonah's making French fritters and everything. We're kind of celebrating, I guess. It's probably going to be our last breakfast with you for a while, what with our project and all."

"Are you boys making a fort in the forest?" Granny asked.

"Something like that," Joe answered. "Don't worry about us. You may hear us coming and going at odd times, but that's just because it's so darn hot. We may be out at night more than usual."

"I understand, Joe E. This humidity is truly terrible. You're young men, but I know I can trust you to stay out of trouble. Oooohh!" she yelped again like she'd been goosed.

She whipped back the table cloth to see Black Dog smiling up at her. The pup had grown tired of not being introduced and had pushed her cold wet nose into the old lady's leg, startling her.

"Well...," Granny said, looking like she was in a trance. "I don't believe it."

Joe rushed over and picked up his terrier. "Granny, I found this little girl. Her name is Black Dog. Do you like her?"

"She is an exquisite animal. Give her to me!" She took Black

Dog from Joe and kissed the animal's cheek. Black Dog wagged her tail and made strange whimpering sounds. They remembered each other. Granny looked at Joe, then at Black Dog, then back at Joe. She closed her eyes and tilted her head back. "Thank you, Jesus," she mouthed.

CHAPTER TWENTY AND THREE

Granny had returned to her room, and the four others were full from the great meal and happy. They walked to the clearing in the forest to throw the foam football. The simple things in life now provided them with the most joy. By now, Jonah had become skilled enough to catch most of Joe's spirals with his hands, rather than his face. Aqualung sat at the edge of the clearing, smoking cigarettes and talking to himself in what sounded like Shakespearean sonnets, petting Black Dog. Sugar was making her way through the forest toward them, but was yet to be seen by the boys.

"What do you think we should do, Jonah?" asked Joe as he threw the ball to his best man. They moved close together so they could talk, still tossing the ball back and forth.

"Whatcha mean?"

"Do you wanna fight this fight or let it blow over and go home?"

"It's not going to blow over, Joe E."

"I know, but we can let somebody else do it. We're just teenagers. We didn't ask for this."

"Teenagers fought World War II," Jonah countered.

"They volunteered, though. We didn't."

Jonah caught the ball and examined it for damage as he talked. "Did they really volunteer, Joe? Or did they understand it was their duty?"

Jonah threw an errant pass over his friend's head that made Joe E. turn and run after it. It was a throw the boy couldn't have made a month before, but he had become much stronger lately. Joe jogged to pick it up and saw Sugar emerge from the forest's boundary within feet of the ball.

"Dammit," he said with a smile. Joe was undergoing a crisis of conscience and confidence. He wanted life to give him an excuse not to proceed, but his daily horoscope was not agreeing with what he thought were his desires.

He walked over to Sugar and placed his head next to hers. He felt an overwhelming strength pulse through his body as he nuzzled her jaw. It immediately changed him. His resolve became rock-solid. He never once questioned his duty from this point forward.

He looked up at the sky and said loudly and firmly, "Huddle up," and walked to the center of the clearing. "Jonah, get Otis on the horn."

They gathered at the center of the field – Sugar and Black Dog, Jonah, Aqualung, and Joe.

"What be up, fellas?" Otis axed through the speakers on the boys walkie-talkies.

Joe picked up his handset from his waist, depressed the button, and spoke, "Otis, listen. I've got something to say. Please hear me out."

"Ten-fo, Joe. Ten-fo."

"Okay, everyone," Joe continued. "Jonah, keep the 'talk' button on your handset engaged, so Otis can hear what I have to say."

"You got it, bro."

Joe spoke loudly. "We've got a situation on our hands – something I never would have believed possible a short time ago. This town, including us, is being terrorized by a werewolf. My uncle caused this to happen many years ago, but he didn't mean it. It was purely accidental, but it is actual, and we have to deal with it. This is not a movie or some computer game – the wolf is as real as we are. We have to do something about him, or he will continue ending lives of the innocent and wrecking the lives of the survivors."

Joe looked at Sugar. Her giant, soft eyes met his. She conveyed so much intelligence and understanding without the ability to speak. "Sugar, you are truly the most beautiful creature I've ever seen. I will not allow you to be harmed." The unicorn purred quietly in response. She understood.

Joe turned to Jonah and extended a hand toward his best friend, who grasped it in response. "Brother, you are strong now. You are a man. I will not allow you to be harmed, but you must pledge the same to me." They exchanged a firm handshake – their first as men.

"I do, Joe. Forever." The two hugged. Things were different now. This was not like a father scooping up his crying toddler. They

black 209 dog

hugged as men do, like a father hugs his son upon returning from war. They were equals.

Joe E. fixed his eyes upon little Black Dog, who returned his gaze with a loving look. A tear ran down his tan cheek, which he quickly wiped away. The dog stood at attention like a little soldier. She was strong. "Black Dog, we're soulmates. I'm never going to leave you. And I will never allow anyone or anything to ever cause you pain." Black Dog barked twice in response, the effort lifting her front legs off the ground.

"Collin," he said, reaching his hand out to the Aqualung. This was not like the handshake he had exchanged with Jonah. His palm was down. It was a gesture of holding hands, rather than shaking them. "You are a great man, whether anyone else thinks so or not. I *know* you are. You are my ally in this fight, and I'm counting on you." Collin James grasped Joe's hand and squeezed it as his eyes met those of the boy. It was like the 'Dead Zone'. Joe felt all the hurt and anguish and fear this poor man had experienced and still held within him. That multitude of feelings, which all added up to pain, rushed into Joe and nearly overwhelmed him. They both fought back tears like respectable men do at a funeral – with quiet dignity. So many words passed between their grasp – nothing needed to be said verbally. They understood each other. They had known one another for a precious few days, but that didn't matter. They were soulmates, too. They all were.

Joe reached to his hip and brought his hand-set to his mouth. "Otis, you are a very noble man. I wish you were here right now, so I could look you in the eye. I hope I have not brought any harm to you, your family, or your town. I apologize if I have – and I will respect your decision, whether you choose to help us or not."

He released the talk button to gather his thoughts before continuing. "Otis, we're all in this together. None of us has asked to be here, but here is exactly where we all are. It is what it is. Call it fate. Call it destiny. Call it duty. Are you willing to help us fight this werewolf?"

"I'm with ya, son. Stringtown and its people done been terrorized long enough. You this town's savior, Joe. Jus' let me know what you needs me ta do."

"Thanks, Otis. I knew I could count on you." Joe returned his handset to its place on his hip, seeing Jonah was holding his out like a microphone to capture Joe's words, and continued. "There is something evil here – and probably watching us right now. In fact, I hope that is the case. That evil is the Wolfman, a creature so enraged he lusts to tear out the throats of all who are good – all of us. Alone, we will lose the battle. The werewolf is too strong. If he catches any one of us without the others, he will murder that individual, bathe in the blood, and wallow in the intestines he rips from the gut. He will devour the heart and imbibe the soul."

"What does that tell us? It tells us we must be a team. If we do not band together to fight this unholiest of demons, we will be eaten alive. Our enemy is the arch-demon. He is the molesting priest, the bribed politician, the raping soldier of fortune. He is anti-Christ. He has no capacity or want to determine what is right and what is wrong. He is without morality and feels no guilt. He is an instinct-driven sociopath, bent on hanging our corpses from the trees, as talismans to ward off those who would avenge our deaths. Physically, he is infinitely more powerful than any one of us. We are solitary uselessness. Alone, we will be ripped asunder like unwanted vegetation, like kudzu, as if our souls are devoid of consciousness. We will die as individuals."

Joe paused to gather himself. He was silent for a full minute before he spoke again.

"But we can survive as a team!" he screamed. "We can survive if we stand together in battle, willing to do whatever it takes to defeat this evil invading what should be our peaceful existence. If we do not succeed in this fight, we can, at the very least, die the death of the valiant, the failed hero – knowing we have given all we could, which is our life. Our life, not our lives. Together we have a life, alone we have lives. Lives that will be lost. Lost and forgotten. Forever."

Joe dropped his head. The others were silent, trying to digest this spontaneous, life or death pep talk.

An abrasive cry ripped the silence like a rake being dragged across sheet metal. Not a plaintive cry – an angry bellow – not purely man, not purely animal. The pep talk had affected the eavesdropping werewolf to the point of visceral anger. Until now, both sides had simply been aware of the presence of one another, like kids in junior high staring across a barren dance floor, girls on one side, boys on the other, both unwilling to act. Now things were going to get interactive in an extreme way, like popping the top on a hot, shaken-up energy drink.

"Git home!" Otis yelled over the intercom. Frantic honking came from the direction of Granny's manor. He was parked out front.

"Let's go, Joe!" screamed Jonah at the group. "Come on, Sugar!"

The five of them lit out toward the house like flushed jackrabbits, as the sun seemed to base-jump from the heavens.

The humans were slow – Sugar and Black Dog ran circles around them, stopping from time to time both in front and back to scan for the Wolfman, inspired by Joe's words to act as guardians and place themselves between the humans and the inhumane evil.

"He's after us!" Jonah screamed as they rushed through the field that broke the space between the forest and the house.

"Take to the barn, lads," Aqualung directed.

Joe yelled into the handset to Otis, who was honking his horn in front of the house in an attempt to guide them home. "Otis, go to the barn and get ready to lash the doors behind us!"

They made it to the carriage house, not having seen the werewolf, but sensing the violent presence of the beast pursuing them. The Wolfman remained strategically out of sight. He could easily have run the group down, but for some reason chose not to. Possibly, he did not take them seriously, or he might have realized he was outnumbered. The troop raced into the barn and scrambled to find rope to lash shut the doors. The back doors were still open slightly from when the Wolfman had fallen into the pit trap, but the boys weren't even aware that had happened.

And there they sat in silence, trying to muffle their heavy breathing for what seemed like hours. The first moments after the chase found them frantically scrambling to fasten the doors shut with found rope, while those not involved in that task made ready with hastily-scrounged weapons, expecting the lycanthrope to burst through at any second. After tying together the door handles, they huddled in the center of the space, not wanting to be near either set of doors, or even the walls, for that matter. Sugar and Black Dog did not have to be told to be silent.

Time went by and their defenses lulled. They did not know the werewolf had been circling the barn on all fours the duration, hoping they would think him gone and make the fatal mistake of emerging from their Alabama Alamo. He was an animal, but he was a smart animal.

Suddenly, the walls and doors of the barn sprung to life as they were clawed furiously from the outside, from what seemed to be all directions at the same time. The group's patience had lasted longer than the beast's.

It seemed the Wolfman would burst through any second, but he was smart enough to know doing so would result in injury, if not his death. He was acting on instinct, but it was a supernatural instinct. He was no turtle, trying to live through the crossing of a busy road, dependent upon dumb luck. He was something from another world, trying to guarantee his survival.

The group cowered back to back in the center of the barn, expecting the attack to breech the fortress. Finally, the assault on the structure ceased amid deep-throated otherworldly growling, which could not be produced by any natural creature made by God. The sounds of the Wolfman were more disturbing than those of a vomiting teenage girl being exorcised.

The werewolf let out a demonic howl, to which Black Dog responded with one of her own. She could no longer contain her hatred for the ugly, matted beast. Together, the two sounded like a freight train bound for Hell. The duet ended abruptly, and the wolf was silent. But was he gone?

Hours passed. Joe had taken note of how long the Wolfman had waited the first time and didn't want to exit before light. Eventually, the sun brought forth the dawn, and Joe felt safe enough to utter, "Open the doors."

The command was carried out in an ever so tentative manner. There was no sign of their nemesis. Joe looked at Black Dog and Sugar, who had been comforting each other through the night, and ordered, "Stay here and rest." Sugar walked into a stall, trailed by the

black 213 dog

terrier, and the two of them laid down together, at peace for the moment.

The humans, armed with pitchforks, stalked outside to inspect the dirty work of the werewolf. They were dumbfounded upon seeing the damage the beast had wrought. All walls and doors of the exterior of the building had been scarred deeply, from about a foot off the ground to about eight feet high, with a myriad of ugly slashes made by the Wolfman's formidable claws.

They were speechless as they inspected the damage.

Finally, Jonah spoke. "If he wanted in, he could have gotten in."

"That, the beast did not want," Aqualung countered. "He knew a pitchfork might find his soft throat or belly."

"He be sending a message," Otis added. "And I gets it loud and clear."

Joe ran his hands across the deep gouges in the old wood. "He thinks he's smart, but we're smarter. Let's get some rest."

They called Sugar out and led her down into the cellar, which was no easy task. Large, hooved animals and home-made wooden stairs don't do well together, but it was the only way they could keep her safe. She didn't complain – she knew it had to be done. The others returned to the surface and put a new length of chain and lock on the door, replacing what they had removed at the beginning of the summer. The rebar they had been using to brace the door shut could easily be removed by the werewolf, and the humans were far too wary to make a simple tactical error, such as that.

"Collin, you're not sleeping outside any more. The war has begun, and it isn't safe. Granny knows about you. From now on, you sleep in my grandfather's study with Jonah. I'll sleep in Ernie's bed. Otis, how are you doing?" Joe asked.

"I be a-ight. Be better when I gets away from dis place. Got a couple fares today, then I gon' lay low. You look like you plannin' some thang. Is you?

"I am."

"Well, it better be good, son. We up against some freaky-deaky. Call me if you need me. You know my name. Look up the number." Otis walked to his cab, which had sustained no damage, and drove away.

The three men and Black Dog walked up to the front door and reacted in horror at what they saw. A four foot tall upside down cross had been scraped into the door by the evil one's claws.

"Bastard," Jonah said as he propped his pitchfork against the left door and swung open the right one they used as their entrance.

Aqualung leaped forward and threw his body against the door to close it, pushing Jonah to the side. "Don't go in, boy! The demon may be inside!"

"My God! Granny!" screamed Joe as he charged into the house with pitchfork blazing. He ran to the old lady's bedroom and found her sleeping, snoring loudly. He walked back to the foyer to meet the other two.

"He hasn't been in here."

"How do you know, Joe?" asked Jonah. "He might be waiting upstairs for us."

"Smell. There's no smell. I guarantee you that bastard stinks like a Texas feedlot. We need to start using our animal instincts if we're gonna kill him. Jonah and Collin, will you find something for us to eat? I need to talk to Granny."

Joe walked into the old woman's bedroom and placed his hand on her shoulder. "Granny, it's Joe E. Wake up."

Granny opened one eye, then the other. "What's the matter, son? What's wrong?"

"Everything's wrong, but it's okay, Granny. I need to tell you the truth about what's happening around here. There's something bad, something evil, in the forest, and I'm worried about your safety."

"Is it the thing that howls at night? I've heard it for years, and it scares me so."

"Yes, it is that thing. It isn't human, Granny, and I'm going to do my best to kill it. I think it took Ernie from you. Try not to worry. Jonah and I can take care of ourselves, but I don't think you should be here right now. I want to take you to the rest home."

"Joe, no! Not yet!"

"I don't mean forever, Granny. Just for now. It isn't safe for you to be here. It should just be for a week or so. You can spend time with Grandpa Joseph."

black 215 dog

"Okay," she said. "I understand. I'll go to the old folks' home, but I want you to check in with me every day and let me know you're okay. Promise me you will. I can't have anything happen to you. You're my son, Joe E."

Joe called Otis back to the house, and they drove Granny to the facility. Although still without sleep, Otis was happy to assist, since it was a duty unrelated to killing or being killed by a werewolf. Jonah stayed at the house to sleep. When they arrived, Joe talked to the administrator and assured him all fees would be paid in a timely manner. He didn't let the nature of the situation be known. That would have created a village panic. Joe fabricated a quick story about Granny's house being remodeled as a surprise for her upcoming birthday and assured the man it would be good for Granny and Grandpa to spend some extra time together, since they were recently separated. The administrator knew the prestigious history of Joe's grandparents and the fortune they were rumored to have and informed Joe the couple would be treated like Southern royalty.

Joe rode in the passenger seat of the cab on the way back to the house. He didn't look well, and Otis noticed it. "Boy, I knows you gots the weight of the world on ya, but you gots to try gettin' some sleep, or you ain't gonna be no good to nothin' or nobody."

"I know, Otis," Joe said, struggling to keep his eyes open. "I'm going to bed when we get back. I'll holler at you tomorrow."

"Make sho' and lock the front door," Otis said.

***

Joe entered the house, locked the doors behind him, and allowed his exhausted frame to lean against the cool interior side of the entrance for a minute or two, enjoying the conditioned air of the fortress. Feeling somewhat rejuvenated, he trudged to the stairs and ascended, hearing the snoring of Jonah and Collin halfway up. Forgetting his vow to sleep in Ernie's bed, he opened the door to Grandpa Joseph's study and made his way to his cot, stepping over Aqualung, who lay on the floor. Joe E. immediately fell into one of the deepest slumbers of his life. His sleep was without nightmares.

CHAPTER TWENTY AND FOUR

The three humans, each the only sons of their mothers, slept the rest of the day and through the night without dreams. It was as if the sandman of the apocalypse had passed over and anointed every first born male in Stringtown, Alabama, with an opium sprinkle, ushering them into a sleep deeper than the Gulf of Mexico.

CHAPTER TWENTY AND FIVE

Joe struggled to consciousness, drifting in and out like a wave in the Gulf of Mexico, unable to kick-start his heart. After an hour of this, he started awake as if by blitzkrieg, knowing something bad had happened. He was groggy from the long sleep and thought immediately of Granny. The events of the previous day came back to him, and he realized she was safe, having been delivered to the old folks' home. He laid still for a moment in the darkness, scared to move, allowing his eyes to adjust to the absence of light in the room. He could hear Jonah and Collin slumbering. He rose slowly upright, hearing breathing at the door. He froze, willing his eyes to see detail normally seen only with the aid of night vision goggles. He saw Black Dog at the door, on point. Her eyes turned to meet his in disturbing infrared. She looked at the doorknob and then back at him, accompanied by a worried whine.

Joe tiptoed to the door and opened it to the hall. The smell bothering Black Dog hit him like a ton of rotting head cheese. It was the smell of the werewolf.

Joe dropped to his knees and crawled the few feet of the hall to the entrance of his uncle's room. The door was slightly ajar, unlatched. Joe pushed it open a little further and peered inside, seeing the room only partially. Nothing seemed out of kilter. Mustering his will, he elbowed the door fully open. It brushed across the orange shag carpet as it revealed the room.

Joe sensed the werewolf was not there and rose to his feet, entering with the authority of ownership.

Joe saw the window had been broken and entered. The remains of a storm that had passed through in the night sent swirling breezes through the room, causing the old curtains to flutter. He scanned the bedroom and pursed his lips in defiant rage. The record player sat on the floor, its power cord plugged into the wall. "I've got the needle," Joe E. thought to himself in panic. He reached to his pocket to check for the ibuprofen bottle holding the precious and all-powerful record needle. It was in its place. He breathed a sigh of relief.

black 218 dog

Joe was confused and worried. He flung open the closet doors, but saw nothing out of place. He turned and bent over the record player to examine it. He felt reassured, knowing he had the needle in his pocket, and playing records, either forward or backward, was impossible.

Recognition of what had happened hit the young man like a kidney punch. A record rested on the player's rubber platform. Joe lifted it and held it to the light streaming through the ripped window, like an elementary school student watching a solar eclipse through a piece of cardboard with a hole in it.

Light shone through the grooves at random and intermittent intervals. Things weren't making sense. He had the needle in his pocket, yet something had apparently burned a hole through the soul of this record.

Joe looked at the label and gasped as he read it – Black Sabbath, 'Paranoid'. The first track had been damaged. Joe referenced the label and saw the title of the song – 'War Pigs'. Still confused, but slowly realizing what had happened, he again looked the room over. A sickening feeling mauled his gut as he saw the edge of another album protruding from under the bed. He walked over, lifted the bedspread and saw more records had been hastily stashed underneath.

Joe reached under the bed and pulled albums into the light, attempting to evaluate what had taken place. Exasperated, he let out a sigh, then lowered his head with eyes closed. His mind was churning like the innards of a grandfather clock. He opened his eyes and saw the orange shag carpet, but noticed something had changed. Another clue from the crime scene hit his searching eyes, bringing with it complete understanding of what had taken place in Ernie's room while he slept.

The old carpet had been snagged around the record player and the foot of the bed where the records had been stashed. Long orange worms of yarn had been pulled from the backing.

Joe didn't have to think long to understand what had happened – it was painfully obvious. The werewolf's claws had become tangled in the old shag carpeting while he did his dirty deeds. "Okay," Joe thought to himself. "It was the werewolf. Big surprise. But how did he play the records?"

The answer struck him like a hit from an unfiltered Lucky Strike. He hunched his shoulders in despair, then threw his head back, eyes closed, silently pleading to the heavens, hoping against hope he was wrong, but knowing he was right. "What now?" he thought.

Joe didn't want to believe what his mind was screaming at him. The werewolf had played the records with his corrupt, overgrown toenail, backmasking them in an attempt to build an army to destroy all that was wholesome and good in Stringtown, Alabama.

Joe's hands trembled as he examined the maimed vinyl disks. He wanted to know all that had taken place. 'Iron Man' by Black Sabbath had been played, as had 'The Battle of Evermore' by Led Zeppelin and 'The Ripper' by Judas Priest. And even 'Werewolves of London' by the late, great Warren Zevon.

"Oh my God. We're in trouble," he mumbled.

Black Dog uttered a plaintive whine in agreement.

Joe walked to the window and gazed down at the barn, hoping he would see the doors still tied shut.

The doors were flung wide, of course. Joe closed his eyes and sighed loudly. Black Dog barked over and over, like a screen door batting against an abandoned house in a cheap horror movie.

CHAPTER TWENTY AND SIX

The boys were at the library an hour later, researching song lyrics. They started with 'War Pigs' and discovered that as a result of the werewolf's actions, they could expect to encounter demonic generals, witches, sorcerers, and any number of other things mentioned in the song – even Satan.

'The Ripper' was obviously about Jack the Ripper, but the song's lyrics gave the boys a good lesson on his tactics – he liked to sneak up on his victims from behind, preferably in a dimly lit area.

'Werewolves of London' conjured images of well-dressed, lycanthropic Brits with stereotypically crooked fangs, impeccable tailored clothes, and a weakness for strong cocktails and Chinese take-out.

Joe didn't need to study 'Iron Man'. He had already formed a hypothesis regarding the man of steel, which stated that Iron Man only acted in the wrong when he was scared, like a Frankenstein when startled by fire. At least that's what Joe E. hoped.

The boys spent a full hour researching Led Zeppelin's 'The Battle of Evermore', another song Jimmy Page and Robert Plant claimed was written 'instantly', as they alleged 'Stairway to Heaven' to have been. If true, that declaration brought with it many questions. Namely – were these songs delivered to these striking young British lads by Satan, himself, through some vehicle of the occult? Jimmy Page was heavily enchanted with Aleister Crowley, the early face and preeminent voice of occult magick in Britain around the turn of the 20th century. Page even lived in the devotee of Satan's former house.

Regardless, 'The Battle of Evermore' was an epic – a true Beowulfian saga. It seemed to be based upon the battle at the culmination of 'The Lord of the Rings'. Jonah had seen the movie dozens of times, so he understood many of the song's references and explained them to Joe, just like he had about the Gollum. The cast of characters included the Prince of Peace, the Queen of Light, a Dark Lord, the angels of Avalon, and the black, faceless ring wraiths on their steeds of the apocalypse. College courses should study this

black 221 dog

song. The boys' heads swam with the imagery of it. On top of all this, the song also spoke of the 'Dragon of Darkness'.

Before leaving the library, Joe printed a copy of the song's lyrics. He felt he understood the other songs well enough, but this one would take intense studying to decipher. He folded the piece of paper over and over until it was very small, then stuffed it into the ibuprofen bottle beside the enchanted record needle, which he put in his right front pocket.

'The Battle of Evermore' was incredibly complex and not easily understood. It was like the 'Book of Revelations' set to music – some things were literal and some things symbolic. Joe needed to figure out who the characters in the song really were. Was the Prince of Peace Jesus? He had no idea who the Queen of Light could be. Jonah said the Dark Lord was surely the necromancer, 'Sauron', from Tolkien's books, but Joe thought him to be Satan. The ring wraiths were the unsympathetic judge and jury of all they crossed. He could only hope the Dragon of Darkness was a symbol of some sort. If not, it surely wouldn't be an agent of good.

In addition to all these questionable characters, the song told of an epic battle, just like the one Joe E. knew was coming. He thought about the title – 'The Battle of Evermore'. That meant the battle for forever. His head was spinning like a whirling Dervish tweaking on meth and smoking Adderall through a crack pipe made from a broken-off car antenna.

Otis dropped the boys off, and they walked around to the back of the house. Joe looked up to the bedroom window and saw that Aqualung was on watch as he had been told to be, with Black Dog cradled in one arm, also watching vigilantly.

Joe gave Collin a subdued wave as he and Jonah walked to the carriage house. If this was a modern horror movie, weird theremin music would be playing, and you would be whispering to yourself, "Don't go in there, you idiot!" But this was not a modern horror movie – the main difference being Joe had realized something while analyzing the songs the werewolf had chosen to backmask. 'War Pigs' and 'Evermore' held the major clue – there was going to be an epic battle. They would not be ambushed and killed while inspecting the carriage house or doing something tangential like that.

At least that's what Joe hoped. He knew he could be fatally wrong, but he also knew now, more than ever, he had to trust his instincts. He was confident enough in his sixth sense not to arm himself.

As they approached the open doors of the carriage house, they saw the ground, softened by the night's rain, had been trampled on a path which led from the barn to the back corner of the wrought-iron fence where they had made the repair. Apparently, a number of beings, both animal and human or mixtures of both, had scaled the fence and trekked into the forest. It brought no surprise. It had been expected. The boys didn't get emotional and weepy about it. They were well past that type of childish behavior.

The carriage house was empty, so the boys shut the doors and went to the cellar to check on Sugar.

The lock and chain were undisturbed, so they opened the door without fear and descended to check on the lonely unicorn. She was there, safe and sound, although agitated, until she was fed M&M's, which placated her like a PMS'ing woman in need of a chocolate bar.

Seeing no safe alternative, the boys knew they must again lock poor Sugar in the cellar for her own safety.

Jonah looked deeply into Sugar's sad eyes and was affected emotionally. "Joe, let's lock Black Dog up with Sugar to keep her company."

Black Dog yapped a single sharp bark. She looked at Joe with a steadfast expression and shook her head from side to side. She understood everything they said, and her tail was not wagging. She did not want to leave the side of her master, which her doggy body language clearly conveyed.

"You may get dog-bit if we do that," Joe said. "Why don't you stay with Sugar for an hour while I go upstairs to think."

"Okay," Jonah replied. Sugar whinnied like a happy unicorn often does.

***

Joe sat on Ernie's bed with the battered old notebook in hand. He wasn't studying the notes about the classic rock songs. He was sketching battle plans and booby traps in the few remaining blank pages left in the ledger. Black Dog had gone into the closet to sleep.

black 223 dog

After deducing and documenting a trap with above-average potential, Joe looked at the gaping window and decided he must protect his war manual the same way he guarded the record needle. This inspired another thought, as thoughts often do, and he brought the notebook to his knee to record another idea. In doing so, he dropped the nub of a pencil he was writing with, and it fell to the carpet, bounced, and rolled under the bed.

"Dammit!"

Joe looked down at the orange shag carpeting but didn't see the fugitive writing instrument.

"Dammit, again," he said as he fell to his knees in search of the stray Dixon Ticonderoga #2.

He searched the shag and saw nothing but the twisted yarn of the old carpet, which looked like orange gummy worms. Having no other instrument to write with, Joe laid down beside the bed and lifted the hem of the bedspread to peer underneath. The pencil was orange, like the carpet, so he squinted for a glimpse of the graphite tip. The eraser had long since been decimated. Seeing nothing, he slid under the bed chest-down, trying to make himself flat, like a mechanic working on a low-rider with a hydraulic leak.

Snaking his way under the low clearance of the bed, Joe saw the little pencil remnant near the aft leg of the twin-sized bed frame. He smiled and extracted his left arm from below his body and extended it like the claw in the arcade game where you try to grab a stuffed animal. As he reached out, he saw something strange on the leg of the bed's frame.

"WTF," Joe thought to himself. Although he had been placed in circumstances that surely warranted an F-bomb or two, he still felt uncomfortable using the word, even in his mind. WTF to him meant "What the freak?"

This mental exclamation was the result of what he saw just above the pencil nub. Something was taped to the leg of the old bed. He reached as far as he could, but it was still out of arm's length. Rather than crawling farther under the bed, Joe got up and walked around to uproot whatever it was from the other side, forgetting the stray pencil for the moment.

He ran his hand up the leg of the bed frame until he

black 224 dog

encountered the protrusion, then used his fingernails to pry up a corner of the tape that anchored it. All this was done by feel, similar to the activities on a spacewalk. He extracted something and brought it from under the bed into the light. It was an old piece of lined paper, taken from the very notebook Joe had been writing in. It had been folded six times on itself to make it as small as possible.

Joe held the paper in his hand for a moment and said a silent prayer before unfolding it. His prayer was that it would not reveal more trouble. When he had unfolded it, he sat down on the bed to read the contents, which were handwritten in faded pencil. It was dated at the top, '1983'.

"To whoever finds this, fear for your life," it began. "My name is Ernie and I've done a terrible thing, probably worse than murder. I have done this terrible thing purely by accident through my stupidity. The preacher at church said heavy metal records were evil and had secret messages. My friend said to play the record backwards to hear them. I tried it and couldn't hear anything. I should never have done it, but I was stupid and curious so I did it."

"I think the preacher was right, because something happened when I played records backwards. I immediately noticed that something was here that wasn't here before. I don't really know what it is, but I think its a werewolf and maybe even some other stuff. I know things like that aren't supposed to be real, but I really think they are. I have heard noises since I played the records backwards that aren't natural. And I heard the farmers are losing animals like crazy."

"I don't know what else to do but try to kill the werewolf. I've seen movies about it. I'm going to use a stake and try to stab it to death. I waited for it in the barn last night. I had a shotgun, but I fell asleep and I didn't kill him. I don't think a gun will work anyway. I have to use the stake."

"If you are reading this it means that I was killed by the wolf. I probably deserved it. I'm sorry for bringing evil to Stringtown. I didn't know what I was doing, I swear. I don't really know what to say, except I'm sorry and I wish I had never been born."

"I am rightfully dead."

Ernie

black 225 dog

Joe stood by the bed holding the paper, tears welling in his eyes, his lips quivering. He felt his uncle's pain and guilt and understood. Joe had made mistakes backmasking records, too, after all.

"God damn it!" he screamed as his trembling hands tore the letter apart. "What did you do, Uncle Ernie?! Why did you do this to us?!!!"

Seconds later, Jonah thrust the bedroom door open and grabbed Joe, who was sitting on the bed with his head down. Joe didn't lift his head as Jonah pulled their bodies together roughly.

"Dammit, Joe, you scared the hell out of me! I heard you screaming when I was coming up the stairs. What's wrong? Is everything worse?"

Joe lifted his head to lock eyes with Jonah. The glossy tracks of tears marked his face. He was gritting his teeth, his lips pulled back like a cornered dog, sucking air loudly.

"We've gotta kill this friggin' werewolf, Jonah."

CHAPTER TWENTY AND SEVEN

The boys were struggling through the installation of bars on the broken window of Ernie's room. Due to more pressing concerns and the height of the window, they had chosen to install the bars on the inside for the time being. Otis had delivered them, and the boys were hastily screwing them into the window's frame. If you have ever driven through an inner city neighborhood, you have seen these bars on the windows of little houses that little people live in – people that have paid for years on mortgages and can't afford to evacuate when a hurricane of crime blows their way.

The boys covered the opening with clear plastic from the garden shed before attaching the iron bars. The make-shift window pane was held in place by silver-gray duct tape.

As they finished the project, Jonah saw something at the edge of the forest. It was a human figure, staring toward the house. "Look at that," he said. Whatever he was seeing was hard to focus on through the heavy plastic.

Joe saw it, too, and said, "Look at those clothes."

"Hippie clothes," Jonah replied.

Joe's forehead wrinkled as he thought, attempting to understand. "It's that Harry Larry dude. We need to warn him not to hang around the forest."

Hairy Larry looked directly at the window, as if he could see the boys looking down at him.

Joe and Jonah walked downstairs, through the front gate, and around the perimeter of the fence, until they reached the field behind the house.

"Why doesn't he walk this way?" Jonah asked. "Surely, he can see us. He's staring right at us. Idiot."

The boys made it to within fifty feet of the stupid hippie, who stood motionless with his hands clasped casually behind his back.

"He doesn't have a care in the world," Jonah continued. "He has no idea he could be lunch meat at any minute. Dude, his beard is seriously outta control."

The boys were within thirty feet when Joe gave Jonah the safety arm, like a mom does to a kid in the passenger seat when a car pulls out in front of their mini-van.

"Stop!" he whispered.

The boys froze and locked eyes with the hairy hippie. The throwback smiled a closed-lip grin and tilted his head to the side, like dogs do when you talk to them.

Suddenly, he bared his teeth – his fangs. He brought an arm around from his back and gave the air a vicious swipe, revealing claws that would make Freddy Krueger cringe.

"It's the Wolfman," Joe yelled. "RUN!!"

The Wolfman brought his claws up above his head, like Ozzy Osbourne calling for a concert crowd to scream. He let out a roar. This was no howl from a 50's matinee. It sounded like every black metal singer in Norway throat singing in unison.

Black Dog awoke and rammed the closet door with her little head, knocking it from its guide and causing it to fall to the floor. She ran down to the front door, but found it shut. She paused for a quick second to think, then raced back to Ernie's room. She had decided to jump out the broken window, not knowing the boys had placed bars on it. She charged up the stairs and through Ernie's door, launching herself toward the window as she entered.

Already in midair, she saw the new bars and attempted to change her direction, which was physically impossible. She managed to turn sideways in her flight and slammed violently into the steel rods, falling to the floor in shock. She had fractured the ribs on one side of her body, but they had not punctured her lung.

The boys had lit out for home at top speed. They reached the fence in seconds and rounded the corner before pausing to look back in the direction from which they had come. The werewolf was still there, standing nonchalantly, the smile still on his rotten face. With a sudden movement, which startled the boys, he dropped to all fours and was into the forest and out of sight, as if he had never been there.

"He thinks he's invincible," Joe said.

"I'm wondering if he just might be," Jonah said. "Did you see those fangs? And where'd he get the clothes?"

"Uncle Ernie's closet."

black 228 dog

CHAPTER TWENTY AND EIGHT

If this was a movie, it would be time for a montage. You know – a song accompanied by scenes of the boys doing a bunch of things in preparation for battle – some song like 'Eye of the Tiger' with images of the young men preparing traps, and such. They do that in movies to move the story forward in an entertaining way. So let's pretend that's what has happened. While you're at it, pretend the song was 'Run Like Hell' by Pink Floyd and pretend the images on the screen were of the boys chopping down trees and high-fiving each other, Sugar whinnying, and Black Dog licking Aqualung's bearded face.

***

The boys now stood at the edge of the clearing, shovels in hand.

"Another one done, boys. Be it the last?" Aqualung asked as he closed the old notebook. Black Dog was on sentry duty a few feet from Joe, not looking at the humans she guarded. She had become very serious since her accident. Joe had noticed a change in her demeanor, but he was completely unaware of her physical condition, since she had not allowed him to know she was in excruciating pain.

Wiping his brow with the back of a gloved hand, Joe said, "We've done everything I can think of, Collin. Jonah, call Otis and see if the ribs are on the way."

Jonah did so and was happy to hear Otis's answer – he'd be there in fifteen minutes.

***

The little black dog was in severe pain, but she was determined like only a terrier can be. Ever heard the phrase 'tenacious as a terrier'? It's true. Terriers can focus better than the kids we are currently trying to educate in our schools. Funny thing is – terriers have all kinds of ADHD, too. The Jack Russell terrier is the living definition of hyperactivity disorder. A Jack Russell will fetch a tennis ball until his lungs explode and his master is in need of rotator cuff surgery from the repeated throwing motion.

I offer a perfect example – a true story, no less. A bull terrier named 'Jacko' once killed 1000 rats in less than 100 minutes. That's

6 seconds per rat. These dogs aren't just hyperactive – they have OCD, and they are obsessed and compulsed to the max! Thankfully, in old Victorian England, when they reveled in such displays like Jacko's, there was a successful rat-catcher named Jack Black who supplied the rodents for such gaming and gambling. I'm not lying. I do my research better than '60 Minutes'.

***

Thirty minutes later, the group sat in the grass around the cellar, chomping on the flesh of smoked pigs, thankfully not of the 'war' variety. Multiple styrofoam containers sat on the cellar door, quickly being emptied of their mesquite-imbued contents. There were no side dishes today, only meat.

"These ribs are delicious, y'all," said Aqualung, as he broke a bone in half to suck its marrow. He was adapting to the ways of the modern Southern man adeptly. Black Dog loudly crunched on the latest bone thrown her way. Sugar was happily chewing away at her feedbag, which was filled with Skittles and Reese's Pieces, her favorites.

"How's Granny doing, Otis?" Joe E. asked. "Has she enjoyed your food deliveries?"

"She be fine as can be. Her and Grandpa been enjoying their picnics under the shade tree, drinking sweet tea. She ain't even asked for no vodka."

"Thanks, bro," Joe said. "You know I appreciate it."

"Say no more," Otis said. "I value being of service. I likes yo' Granny. Always have."

Joe smiled at the thought of Granny so happy she didn't need to numb herself with demon alcohol. Maybe she just drank in the lonely house because of the situation she was in, he thought. Maybe losing Ernie and then Grandpa, while living in fear of the werewolf, was just too much for her to handle at this stage in her life. Without knowing it, Joe had added another brick in the wall of his determination to do what had to be done.

The group ate without further conversation until they had decimated the sizeable feast. They gathered up the trash, placed it in a large bag, then washed their hands in the warm outpouring of a garden hose that had been baking in the hot sun. Finally, the hot water they had cleansed their hands with turned cool, and the group took turns satiating their thirst. Afterward, they stood in a circle around the cellar door, waiting for something to be said by someone. They all knew who was going to share – who they all needed to share.

Finally, Joe spoke. "We all know what's coming next, guys."

Subconsciously, Joe tapped into the greatest sports pep talk of all time, given by Coach Herb Brooks. It inspired the U.S. Hockey Team to beat the Russians in 1980 – the biggest underdog win in the history of modern sports. Nobody recorded the pep talk, but it was re-enacted in a Disney movie, and Joe had unintentionally memorized it, for he had seen it countless times. He wasn't a plagiarist, and he wasn't a pugilist, but Joe had a big fight ahead of him, so he simply tapped into the pool of knowledge in his young brain, reaching deep inside himself to find some way to motivate his team. It was all he could do, and it was all that needed to be done.

Joe gazed directly into the nuclear sun above him, temporarily blinding himself. Purely by accident, he had used the same technique implemented countless times by the nervous lead singers of a thousand bands – stare into the stage lights, and the crowd is gone. There's a song by Led Zeppelin that perfectly illustrates this phenomenon. It's called 'In The Light', and it opens the second CD of the album 'Physical Graffiti'. (It is vitally important that you, the reader, so invested in this story, now seek out 'In The Light' and immerse yourself, if you do not know the song. You can stop reading this book and light your barbeque pit with the pages for all I care. It is far more important for you to discover the songs on that album than it is for me to be strolling down a red carpet at the Hollywood premier of the movie, 'Black Dog'. I mean that with all my heart.)

Still blinded and unable to see the others, Joe spoke quietly, as if he was talking to himself. He had switched into right-brain mode – the source of creative thought and the gateway to the stream of his consciousness.

"Great moments in humanity come from the most difficult of circumstances," he said. He spoke in a whisper. The others leaned toward him, eager to hear what Joe felt important enough to enunciate.

"That's what we have here, men – opportunity. We didn't ask for it, but we must answer the call and fulfill our duty. If we fought the werewolf and his army a hundred times, they might win ninety-nine, but not this one. Not this time. In this fight we are the greatest band of brothers the world has ever known. And we will strike him down, because we can!"

Joe had raised his voice, but now spoke softly again. "You were born to be werewolf slayers. You were born to be here, today and tonight! A night we will take back and reclaim for humanity. No longer will the innocent and helpless be victimized by this tyrant! I'm freakin' tired of being terrified of the big, bad werewolf. The werewolf's time is over! Screw him!! This is our time! We will drag him out of the forest, kill him, and take back the night!"

"Hands in!" screamed Jonah as he extended his fist above the cellar door. Muscles, veins, and tendons rippled his formerly atrophied arm. The others stepped in and placed their hands on his. Black Dog stood on the door of the cellar, directly beneath the paws of the humans, barking her head off. Sugar paced around them, high-stepping.

Joe looked from face to face and saw strength in each. "There are two paths for us to choose from, men – the stairway to Heaven or the highway to Hell! No Quarter on three. One! Two!! Three!!!"

"NO QUARTER!!!!" they yelled in unison.

Sugar reared up, her front legs kicking like possessed Rockettes. She let out a neigh that sounded more like the roar of a mountain lion than her usual whinny.

They had the eye of the unicorn.

CHAPTER TWENTY AND NINE

"Okay, Joe," Jonah said. "Tell me again what the hell we're doing tonight? You want Chinese food all of the sudden? I thought we were going wolf hunting."

"Just call Otis and ask him to bring some cheap Chinese take-out for our dinner and enough extra to feed a couple guests. Aren't you tired of barbeque and bacon and eggs?"

"You're losin' it, champ," Jonah said as he reached for his handset.

Jonah spoke some sentences to Otis across invisible airwaves, crackling with life, then asked, "Joe, are we gonna need chopsticks?"

Joe E.'s eyes lit up. "Definitely. A lot of them."

***

You probably think the stress has gotten the best of the boy, but you would be very wrong in that assumption. Joe was, in fact, rising to his optimum performance under great pressure. That's what the best athletes and rock bands do. Ever thought of how difficult it would be to quarterback a team in the Super Bowl? Or how nerve-wracking it would be to perform music during the half-time? That's why old fogies like Brett Favre and The Stones do those things. They may have wrinkles, but they also have chin straps and guitar cords older than the guys in Green Day. In other words, they have experience.

***

The boys ate the Chinese food, although they couldn't identify the meat in it. When Otis was told it should be cheap, he apparently knew exactly where to go. Aqualung especially enjoyed it, though.

"My mouth is so coated with grease, I can't even taste the food," Jonah said. "It's sliding down my throat before I can finish chewing it."

"Spoiled, ye be," scolded Aqualung.

Joe laughed. "Just eat it. We'll have a good breakfast in the morning after our hunt."

black 233 dog

"I hope we live that long. And what exactly does that 'no quarter' thing we said at the cellar mean?" Jonah asked.

Aqualung answered violently, almost before the words had left Jonah's lips. "We shall take no prisoners! Any who oppose us will meet their death!"

"It's the only way," Joe added. "It's also the title of an awesome Led Zeppelin song."

***

After dinner, Joe and Aqualung went to the garden shed, and Jonah went to the cellar to check on Sugar. Jonah spent only a short time with his unicorn before he went topside. He suddenly felt like an outsider, not understanding exactly what the plan was and his role in it, if any. Joe had become so introverted during his scheming. Jonah felt like Joe no longer needed him, or possibly, he had been replaced by Black Dog and Aqualung. Nothing could have been further from the truth. Black Dog and Aqualung knew even less than Jonah. They were simply more willing to follow without question, having blind faith and absolute trust in General Joe.

Jonah walked into the shed to see Aqualung holding a heavy plastic bag with numerous warnings and poison labels on it, pouring its contents into a five-gallon bucket partially filled with water. Joe was stirring the concoction slowly with a handful of chopsticks. "That's enough, Collin," he said.

"Joe, are you losing it, or what?" Jonah exclaimed. "Do I need to take over leadership here?"

"Shut up," Joe reprimanded. Immediately, he felt remorse. "I'm sorry, Jonah. Sorry, bro."

"It's okay. May I ask what you are doing, though?"

"We're mixing up a little batch of werewolf killer. Collin, show Jonah the contents on the pesticide label."

Aqualung dragged the bag to a place in front of Jonah. Jonah read down the list, trying to mentally pronounce the chemicals, his lips moving as he did so. He might as well have been trying to read Egyptian hieroglyphics.

"See anything special?" Joe asked.

"Sodium iodide?" It was the first compound on the list he could confidently pronounce.

black 234 dog

"Nope. Farther down – silver nitrate, chemical formula AgNO3. Remember Mr. Thompson's class? It's what turned your hands black when you spilled it on yourself."

"That took forever to go away."

"Yeah. That was hilarious. But – do you get what I'm driving at?"

"Hmm. Silver nitrate. Werewolves. Yeah," Jonah said. "You want to turn them black. A practical joke to make them feel stupid. Gonna make them harder to see in the dark, though."

Joe laughed. "C'mon, Jonah. Think again. What kills werewolves?"

"Wooden stakes?"

"That's vampires, bro."

"Ahh," he said as he finally understood. "I'm an idiot."

"You should have paid closer attention in Chemistry class," Joe said. "Silver kills werewolves, Collin, in case you didn't know."

Joe stood up and fished something from his pocket. He flipped it like a coin to Jonah, who caught it instinctively. He opened his hand and saw a tiny metal hoop in his palm.

"That's one of Granny's silver rings," Joe said. "Go to the cellar and put it on Sugar's horn. Jam it down tight, so it won't come off when she skewers the werewolf."

Jonah smiled, finally understanding, finally feeling included, and left the garden shed to do as General Joe had instructed, belching a spicy heartburn burp from the 'General Joe's' chicken he had consumed an hour before as he turned to go.

When the door had closed, Aqualung said, "Master Joseph, remind me to thank young Jonah for the stinky belch he has cast upon us."

***

After depositing the ring on Sugar's horn, Jonah locked the cellar and went back to the garden shed, but found his friends were gone. He sniffed and made an awful face, not realizing he was smelling his own burp. He went to the carriage house and found Joe and Aqualung setting up a card table in the center of the building. As he walked toward them, Joe unfolded a white tablecloth and spread it over the little table, like a waiter in Hell's dining room.

black 235 dog

"Jonah," Joe yelled to him without looking up. "Will you get some plates, napkins, and silverware?"

"I shall retrieve the Chinese food," Aqualung volunteered.

Jonah and Aqualung went to the house together, returned with the bait, and laid out a decent looking place setting on the table. While they were doing that, Joe slid the woven cover that concealed the pitfall trap to the side and entered the hole. He went to work, replacing the trap's punji teeth with dozens of the laced chopsticks, which he jammed into the dirt with their black, silver nitrate-soaked tips pointing upward. When he had finished, he and Jonah dragged the cover back into position and threw a little hay on it to further conceal it.

Joe spooned the General Joe's chicken onto the plates, and they chained shut the doors on the front side of the barn, ensuring that whatever entered would come in through the entrance leading to the pit.

Finally, Jonah could no longer hold his tongue. "Joe, why are we trying to lure the werewolf with Chinese takeout? Am I missing something? Is he Asian?"

"Just wait and see if it works, bro. It will be easier for me to explain in the morning. I wish we had fortune cookies – Confucius say, 'You rousy worves breave rast breff tonight'."

"Let's go get a good night's sleep," Joe continued. "Hell, let's play a few games on the Atari. I'm not tired."

"Whatever you say," Jonah said, still perplexed.

"Might I play, as well?" Aqualung asked.

"You get the loser between me and Jonah," Joe answered with a smile.

Aqualung beamed. "I love it here in Alabama. We three shall be together hence forth!"

Joe and Jonah stole a glance at each other and shared a dubious grin. Aqualung might be harder to get rid of in the long run than the werewolf, but that was okay.

***

Upstairs, the three had fun playing games and listening to Jethro Tull at the request of Mr. Collin James, who related to the band on every level. It was as if Jethro Tull made music, albeit with electric instruments, which could have been heard in the pubs of London a hundred and ten years before, in a time when Collin James was an ambitious young man yet to know hardship. The Jethro Tull songs inspired Collin, so much he beat both Joe and Jonah at Pac-Man, despite holding a joystick in his grubby hands for the first time.

Black Dog was exhausted, her body fighting to re-knit her broken little ribs, and slept deeply in the closet until Joe lifted her gently and carried her to Grandpa Joseph's room for the night. She moaned as he carried her, so he placed her underneath his cot, instead of cuddling with her like he usually did. Joe had forgotten his pledge to sleep in Ernie's bed, since Aqualung preferred to sleep on the floor. It worked out for the best – Joe didn't feel right sleeping in his uncle's bed. It felt like he was taking Ernie's place, which might not be the best of karma.

The next morning Jonah woke with a sense of urgency. He heard Collin snoring on the floor, cradling Black Dog. He reached over to Joe's cot and felt for his friend, but did not find him. He wasn't overly alarmed, but he was slightly annoyed that he knew not where his best friend was. He then noticed the smell of frying bacon and smiled, shaking his head. He went downstairs to the kitchen and pushed open the swinging door.

Joe was inside, multi-tasking like a good chemist, mentally tallying times and temperatures as he bopped from pan to pot. Sugar stood in the pantry with her head protruding into the kitchen, as if it was a stable.

"Good morning, sleepyhead," Joe called out in a sing-song voice without looking at his friend. "Would you mind waking Collin and Black Dog for breakfast, buddy?" Joe started singing 'It's Getting Better All The Time' by The Beatles. Jonah liked that song. He smiled, went upstairs humming the tune, and returned with a rejuvenated Aqualung and a sore, stretchy Scottish Terrier.

Joe finally turned to acknowledge the others, smiling broadly. "You guys ready to celebrate the first victory in this war?" He had an apron on and his hands on his hips, and the others couldn't help but be at ease.

As if on cue, Otis poked his head into the kitchen. "Smells good, Joe, jus' like ya promised. Good times! Dine-o-mite, we gonna

black 237 dog

dine good tonight!"

Aqualung giggled like a schoolgirl. Having slept multiple times inside a beautiful house, supping upon the finest dishes Southern cooking could offer, he was giddy. "This be a sweet home, this Alabama!" he exclaimed.

Otis laughed heartily at this. "You right, Mr. James. This be sweet home Alabama." Aqualung laughed again, smiling so big that his eyes were forced nearly shut, and gave Otis an aggressive, medieval high-five like he had seen Joe and Jonah do. These were truly the best of times and the worst of times, just like the Styx song.

***

After a leisurely meal, Joe rose from his seat and spoke in the cultivated speech of the genteel. "Gentlemen and ladies, have y'all quite finished? Had you enough to sustain you for a spell? I hope it was not the awfullest meal y'all ever et." The Deep South was really influencing all of them.

The others nodded – they were as full as blood-gorged ticks and curious to hear what Joe had to tell them.

"Some of y'all may not know the werewolf recently broke into the house – specifically, my deceased uncle's room. Although I have the record needle in my pocket at all times, the vermin was able to McGyver the record player and played a handful of songs backwards, using his crusty fingernail." At this, Joe held up a three-inch piece of werewolf toenail he had found tangled in Uncle Ernie's shag carpet. The others gasped.

"Otis, you haven't been told this, but when a record is played in reverse in my uncle's old room, the subject of the song is called to reality, into the cellar or the carriage house. I know it's hard to believe, but, trust me, it is as true as the gold tooth in your mouth."

Otis was speechless and scared, his mouth agape. Joe stepped forward, cloth napkin in hand, and delicately placed it under the old man's chin and gently jacked his jaw back up to its closed position, wiping a drop of spittle from the corner of Otis' mouth after doing so.

"What I'm getting at is, the werewolf selected songs by choice – ones he thought could help him. I can't explain how he had the knowledge to choose them, but it definitely wasn't blind luck.

black 238 dog

But, through my careful analysis of the songs, I am prepared to defend against them. It is I who have the upper hand. And it is he who has the lower paw."

"Damned right, General Joe!" Aqualung burst forth.

"If I may continue," Joe said. "One of the songs our enemy played was a little ditty called 'Werewolves of London' by one Warren Zevon." The others reacted in horror.

"I know what you must be thinking – we are now overrun with more werewolves. That *is* the case, I must admit. But these werewolves are dissimilar to our nemesis, Wolfie. They are dandies, likely sporting ruffled sleeves and, quite possibly, frilly panties."

At this, Aqualung sprayed orange juice from his mouth in the direction of Black Dog, who jumped away like a startled feline. She didn't see any humor in the situation and gave Aqualung an unappreciative look, her tender ribs barking angrily at her from the sudden movement.

Joe ignored the exchange, stifling a smile. "The most important thing I learned about them, though, is this...."

"What?!" Jonah demanded after waiting what he thought was more than enough time for dramatic effect.

"Sorry, Jonah. I was distracted. What I learned through my analysis of the song is that these Werewolves of London absolutely love Chinese food. Lads, follow me to the carriage house. Let's check the trap!"

They practically skipped out of the mansion, but grew serious as they neared the barn. Overconfidence looked to be the Achilles weakness of both sides, fatal hubris. Joe realized this and the rest of the group matched his sober demeanor.

They crept the last few feet and checked the chained doors of the front entrance, finding them intact. They walked around the building, hugging the exterior wall of the structure, and saw the rear entry had been breached, according to plan.

"Stay here," Joe commanded. He sidled along the back wall and crept into the dark interior. He was being a tad bold, Jonah thought. Perhaps, Joe was overly convinced his battle plan had succeeded.

The others waited in silence until Joe said loudly from

inside, "Come inside, y'all."

Black Dog charged forward and jumped into the pit, landing on a pile of vintage clothing. Luckily, the chopsticks had been carried forward with the momentum of the wolfmen's bodies and now laid flat. Joe stood at the edge of the trap, in front of the untouched table setting, resolute as a statue of Lenin. "IT WORKED!" he proclaimed.

Otis, Aqualung, and Jonah stepped forward, seeing no bodies in the dugout, confused.

"I ain't seein' none of them dandy werewolves," Otis said.

"Look," Joe replied. He bent over the trap and began extracting clothing from it, pulling shirts off the punji sticks and from the teeth of Black Dog. "They fell into the trap and were killed, sent back to oblivion where they came from!"

Jonah laughed and joined his friend in the excavation process. "Lay them out so we can see how many we killed!"

They laid out three sets of fancy-boy outfits and stood around them, marveling at the detail the tailors of London had stitched into the clothing of the Werewolves of London.

"Wow. Getta load of that craftsmanship," Jonah said. "It's a shame for these outfits to go to waste. We should sell them on Ebay."

"Them wolf-boys be garbed finer than a Tuscaloosa hooker," Otis said.

"Wonder if we got all of them?" Jonah asked.

"Good question," Joe replied. "I know we didn't get the Wolfman, but I'm not sure how many Werewolves of London there are. The song didn't say. There could be more."

CHAPTER THIRTY

Otis returned to his duties as the resident cabbie of Stringtown, although he was almost immediately interrupted with an odd request to go shopping at the hobby store for the boys. He no longer questioned such interruptions while driving Miss Daisy. He simply placed the boys' request on the roster of pick-ups and deliveries and tended to his clients' needs in the order in which he received them. Unless it was an emergency, the boys were treated no different than any other fare. It wasn't meant as an affront to the needs of the boys – they understood the situation. Otis had to make his living, and the community depended on him.

Otis had delivered the requested items and gone back on the grind. It was now late in the afternoon of the same day the boys had discovered the remains of the trio of Werewolves of London who had walked down the wrong red carpet.

Joe and Jonah stood before Aqualung as he applied the paint Otis had delivered. Collin was finger-painting improvised camouflage on their faces, attempting to conceal them and simultaneously make them look like wolfmen from a distance. The boys were wearing the pierced clothes of two of the deceased Werewolves of London. The holes in the clothing were small and not noticeable, having been made by formerly harmless chopsticks. They were preparing to embark on a reconnaissance mission, in search of those they had yet to kill – those wanting nothing more than to kill them. They were noticeably more tense than they had ever been in their young lives.

"Ye be sure of this, laddies?" asked Aqualung with great concern. "Surely, another trap would be sufficient. I did not eat the entirety of the remaining Chinese food, after all."

"I don't think they'll bite on that lure again," said Joe.

"We need to take the fight to them," Jonah said as he straightened his frilled collar in the mirror on Ernie's door. He was in his element, primping like he used to in the old mirror at his mom's mobile home, so long ago. "Right, General Joe? And Collin, please don't call us ladies again."

black 241 dog

Aqualung cocked his head like a confused dog. Joe looked at Jonah and growled threateningly.

"Don't do that. You're scaring me, Joe."

"Good," said Joe E. as he reached to pet Black Dog, who was lying on the bed. She eyed him with concern but allowed him to touch her. "What time is it?"

Aqualung, having no sense of modern time-keeping replied. "The sun has fallen."

"Close enough. It's time. Lock and load," Joe replied.

"Joe, how do we lock and load with no weapons?"

"Jonah, do you really think I'd go out into the forest defenseless?" He reached to the desk drawer and pulled it open. "Take your pick."

"Butter knives? C'mon Joe!"

"*Silver* butter knives. Believe, Jonah. Think of the damage we did with simple, harmless chopsticks! You gotta believe!"

"Okay, I believe," Jonah sighed.

"Does not sound a bit like it," Aqualung said.

"I BELIEVE," Jonah said. He meant it, too.

***

Joe and Jonah left the house, shutting the door softly behind them. Joe had explained to Jonah the meaning and purpose of reconnaissance, which was to probe the area occupied by the enemy and gather information. Their actions needed to be carried out with the utmost caution and silence. They were not seeking a fight, just the opposite – they wanted to creep into the Wolfman's back yard, peer into his windows, and return home safely. They were not out to engage or enrage the enemy.

***

The boys wanted to accomplish this reconnaissance mission without being detected, of course. The reason they were wearing the clothing of the vanquished Werewolves of London was to give them the opportunity to infiltrate the ranks of the enemy, or allow them the chance to escape if they were detected. For cinematic reference, one can recall Indiana Jones knocking out a Nazi and stealing his uniform, or perhaps Luke Skywalker and Han Solo subduing and adopting the armored uniforms of Death Star stormtroopers. They do it in the movies all the time – it's nothing new.

***

The boys crouched as they crossed the field behind Granny's house. They were not taking their mission lightly. It was life or death. They had agreed not to speak unless absolutely necessary, and then it would be done only in the slightest whisper. The werewolves roaming the forest surely had hearing far superior even to that of the domesticated canine.

Aqualung looked down through the plastic window at the boys, but could see only bad watercolor abstracts through the opaque veil. Black Dog would not allow herself to be held, for her ribs ached badly. She bolted from Collin's grasp and was under the bed, whimpering loudly with worry, only her nose exposed from under the edge of the bedspread. Aqualung spoke to her. "I feel the same, little lass, but we must be strong and ready should our assistance be required." Collin looked at his newly purchased walkie-talkie laying on the desk and hoped he understood how to work it.

He picked up the handset and thought to himself, trying to remember his instructions. He said aloud, "Two clicks between us means we are alright." He depressed the talk button two times and waited. Within seconds he heard two clicks respond to him over his speaker. He looked at Black Dog. "See love, they are fine as red wine – for the moment, at least."

***

The boys made it to the forest, and their confidence was replaced by fear. They moved as one, practically on top of each other. Stealth is a skill every soldier is educated in, but it was being learned on the fly by the boys. As with everything else, instinct had taken over for intellectualism. They low-crawled and took cover behind every structure they came across. They weren't stupid. This was the means to survival. They were in over their heads, like a novice swimmer being carried away by a rip current, but they did not panic. Their experiences thus far had made them understand composure was key to their survival.

The boys were in the forest, but were not on their usual path to the clearing. Joe was the point man and understood the need to avoid their comfort zones to prevent being ambushed. They were about fifty yards into the stand of trees when he suddenly stopped. He dropped to the ground, landing flat on his belly. Jonah landed in the same position directly on top of him, which forced a grunting sound from Joe. Both of the boys held their breath, hoping the noise was not as loud as they thought it was. Canine yipping sounds came from every direction.

The boys' heads were so close together they could communicate through the quietest of whispers.

"Sorry, dude," Jonah said almost inaudibly.

"It's okay. Sit tight and observe."

Minutes passed.

"I think it's coyotes," Joe finally said in the faintest whisper.

"I can't tell," Jonah answered. "Let's backtrack."

The boys crawled back in the direction they had come from, but unknowingly circled farther east, due to the effect of dominant right hand, versus insubordinate left hand, and the sinister path left hands always lead to.

They were now even deeper in the forest, feeling like untethered astronauts. They were swimmers lost at sea in the middle of the night, sensing the sharks circling the water around them.

They laid motionless again. Their clothes were now so soiled, infiltrating the Werewolves of London would be impossible.

"How long have we been out?" asked Jonah.

"Feels like a week," Joe answered. It had been two hours.

The walkie-talkies on the boys' hips clicked twice, sounding like sonic booms. Joe grabbed his handset and depressed the button, whispering into it, "No more situation reports. Over and out."

Back at the house, Aqualung slammed his handset down on the desk, sure he had gotten the boys killed. "Oh my goodness!" he said as he glanced at Black Dog, who had fallen asleep. An agonizing look of worry came to his face, and he brought his hands up slowly to cover it. He had never felt so helpless and alone. He thought of the vodka in the pantry downstairs and stood up to retrieve some. It was the only thing which could relieve his stress. He strode toward the door and left the room.

***

Out in the forest, Joe and Jonah became more acclimated to

the darkness and mobilized again, although they were crawling only a foot or two at a time, then making observations, then moving again. Disturbing sounds were all around them. Jonah realized this was what Sugar had gone through every night in the forest. He understood how scared she must have been. An intense, almost debilitating tsunami of guilt washed over him, but he pulled himself together, knowing she was safe in the cellar. He resolved to never again put sweet Sugar through such torture. He didn't know his unicorn friend was in severe anxiety at that very moment, stamping around the cellar, sensing Jonah's desperation through telepathic means, which could not be explained by real science or pseudo-science or Uri Geller.

The boys found themselves at the edge of a clearing, confused. Had they somehow traversed the forest back to their usual haven by subconscious means, like a broken GPS? Their night vision was good at this point, since there seemed to be too many stars in the sky this night.

"It's not our clearing," Joe whispered to his friend. "This is where we dumped Gollum. I can see sparkles of foil in the grass."

Jonah's eyes struggled to focus. Finally, he said, "I can see them, too."

As the words left his lips, the clearing boiled to life. Long-toothed beasts raced into the space and began circling like a Slayer mosh pit in front of the boys.

"Werewolves!" Jonah whispered, then corrected himself. "No – German Shepherds. Wild dogs! Dingos! Hyenas!"

"Those are coyotes," Joe replied. "It's a pack of coyotes. They're goin' nuts."

"They look scared."

Jonah was right – the coyotes were terrified. Mothers grabbed the napes of their offspring and brought them to the center of the writhing mass, milk-swollen teats swinging as they moved. The older males bit at the hind legs of the females, urging them to go faster. The young males circled the outskirts of the hurricane's eye in a fury, biting at each other in misdirected, testosterone-fueled aggression. The sound of the pack would never be forgotten by the boys – it was a hyper-emotional mixture of fear, bloodlust, anxiety,

black 245 dog

confusion, and agitation. It didn't frighten the boys – it brought an overwhelming feeling of pity.

In an instant, the pack grew silent and hunkered down. The females and their pups were in the center of the circle, the males guarding them like sphinxes. Instinct instructed the coyotes to be hushed, and the group of them were, for a very short time.

Like a bolt of lightning, the situation came alive in a spontaneous riot. The male coyotes sprang to attention, waving their heads back and forth like downed power lines, flailing with ecstatic energy. The hair on their backs stood at attention, and their formidable fangs were on full display, as they rotated like an ever-circling skeletal family. They were deeply worried, very threatened, and full of fear. That fear turned them into the most vicious animals they could ever be.

A tornado of hate and evil stormed into the situation with the power of an F5 tornado. Werewolves, of the London ilk, supposed 'dandies', ripped into the coyote pack from multiple directions, decimating the familial group in minutes. The episode was heartbreaking for the boys to witness. The Werewolves of London showed no mercy to the females and their unweaned offspring, slaying them all in an orgy of violence.

Joe and Jonah observed the tragic episode in paralyzed fear. When the last throat had been ripped out, the Werewolves of London rose to walk again on their hind legs. They casually strolled into the forest at the far side of the clearing, picking their teeth with manicured nails and shaking their heads in dismay as they inspected the blood stains on their formerly fine clothing.

As much as the boys wanted to kill the dogs of war retreating before them, Joe and Jonah wisely chose to make their way quietly back through the forest toward home, almost too scared to breathe. When they reached the front door of the house, they were as relieved as plane crash survivors touching terra firma at the bottom of an inflatable slide. They stood together on the porch for a time, gazing at the upside-down cross on the doors. They were exhausted and covered with mud and grass stains, but alive and not defeated.

"Go to Hell, werewolves," Jonah said as he pushed the door open.

Upon entering, they heard sounds of anguish coming from the kitchen, which they recognized as Aqualung. They walked across the parlor room and opened the kitchen door tentatively. Collin's head was face down on the table, but upon hearing the creak of the door he looked up. He saw the two boys standing before him, their clothes caked with black dirt, their painted faces cracked and peeling away – warriors having returned from the brutality of the frontline.

"Oh my lads, praise be to the King of Kings! I have yet to see a more beautiful sight! Me boys have returned from battle! I thought ye surely perished!" Tears streamed down his face as he rose to embrace the boys.

Joe and Jonah were too weak to hug him in return. Their heads slumped onto the derelict's shoulders, one on each side. Collin helped them to seats at the table, sat them down, and poured three shots of vodka in a line in front of him. He gripped the outer glasses and slid them at forty-five degree angles to his left and right, to points in front of the young men. "Talk to me lads! Tell me what you've seen."

The boys drank the aliquots. They weren't used to the burning in their throats, but it seemed to inform them they had made it home. Joe reached up to his forehead and peeled off his acrylic paint mask in one piece and laid it on the table. It stared back, looking like one of the doomed minions facing the sausage grinder in Pink Floyd's 'The Wall' movie.

Recognizing the same thing, Jonah said in a militant voice, "If you don't eat your meat, you can't have any pudding!"

Joe laughed, reached over, and pulled off his friend's mask, then laid it next to the first one. "They look like pudding skins," he said.

Aqualung looked at the boys like they were insane, thinking the boys were suffering from shell shock. They hadn't lost their minds, but they were delirious. He filled their glasses again, followed by his. "Let's turn in lads. 'Tis been a long night. Maybe you'll tell me what you've seen in the morning."

"Collin!" Joe said loudly, coming back to life as if waking from hypnosis. "We will not hide from what we have seen tonight. No quarter!"

black 247 dog

CHAPTER THIRTY AND ONE

"I'm sure I saw six of them," Joe said as he bit off a piece of bacon. "I counted them when they were walking away."

"Seemed like a lot more than that," Jonah said.

"I know, but only six."

"*Only* six?" Aqualung said. "Seems a fit and formidable number to me."

"You should have seen them, Collin," Joe said. "We're lucky there's not more. They were like piranhas."

As with so many other references, Collin did not know what a piranha was. He understood vaguely what it implied, though, so he wiped the puzzled look from his face without asking for explanation. "What did they look like?" he asked.

"They were lanky, slender, and hairy. Kinda like hipsters," Jonah answered.

"Hipsters are wimps, though," Joe replied. "Those bastards were death on two legs. Death on four legs, too, for that matter."

"And they were regally garbed?" asked Aqualung.

Joe took a bite of scrambled egg and thought for a moment. "Well, they were when old Wolfie conjured them, but right now you'd win a fashion contest with them, Collin. Their clothes are caked with dried blood."

"They can't be too joyous of that," Aqualung said. "Might we lure and trap them in some way with the temptation of new apparel?"

Jonah's eyes lit up. "Yeah! We could put some racks of clothes in the shed and put up a few estate sale signs at the edge of the forest to lure them in. It could work!"

"Stop," Joe said. "I'm sorry, but you guys aren't taking this seriously enough. We witnessed mass destruction last night. This isn't a movie. What we saw could never be shown on a screen for mass consumption – it was no 'Twilight'. I can't believe we pulled off that Chinese food bit. We have to move past these 'punk'd'-type ideas. We're not making a YouTube video. Those bloodsuckers were ultra-violent."

"Butter knives ain't gonna cut it," Jonah said. "You're right.

black 248 dog

We've gotta cut them to shreds."

"Tell me about it," replied Joe.

CHAPTER THIRTY AND TWO

The day of the fight was nigh, and Joe was stressed out. They all were, but Joe was showing the signs of post traumatic stress disorder, even before the final battle still before them.

It had been two days since the reconnaissance mission, and Joe had been bunkered up in his uncle's old bedroom since, playing records both forward and backward. He had instructed Jonah and Aqualung to allow him this personal time without interruption, even for food. He told them to prepare themselves for the final battle in whatever way they needed, nothing more.

In response to the order, Jonah and Collin had engaged in regimented training with Sugar, instructing her from the ground, as well as from upon her back. They practiced exercises in which she performed rescue maneuvers at a gallop, extraditing one or both of the humans on the fly. She was ordered to lower her head and joust imaginary foes in front of her, carrying Jonah and Aqualung all the while. The ironic thing about all this was that she was already well prepared for the battle, unlike the humans that instructed her. A unicorn doesn't survive to be 783 years old, like Sugar, without battle skills. She had been through more than enough transitions of power to understand the ways and means of the battlefield.

***

It was time. Six degrees of separation were about to meet like a pile-up on the highway. The day felt different than any in the boys forty day tenure in Stringtown. The humidity was off the chart. Vultures circled over the clearing in droves, sensing the bloodbath to come, like dogs aware of impending earthquakes. The sun was blinding, glinting off the dew-soaked kudzu leaves as if they were faceted diamonds. Looking at the forest, one could see a myriad of psychedelic spider webs weaving together every tree into a single interlinked organism, like the tendons and veins and connective tissue in the human body, visible due to the miracle of condensation. In an hour the moisture would burn off the webs, and they would again become invisible filaments, unseen, but present.

It was nine in the morning, and the good guys were in the

black 250 dog

carriage house discussing strategy. They had eaten a nourishing breakfast, possibly their last. Joe was holding court, drawing in the dirt with a stick. From time to time he would ask Jonah and Aqualung if they understood. If the answer was no, he would brush the dirt with an old broom, as if he was erasing an Etch-A-Sketch, and start over, showing no sign of frustration. If the answer was yes, he would look into their eyes until he was satisfied their answer was truthful.

At half past twelve, General Joe was done. Strangely enough, he commanded an order of sleep. They would reconvene at eight that evening. It was the heart of the summer, and the dog days were long and draining. Joe knew rest was the sensible thing at this point. Sugar was even brought into the parlor room, to relax in the air-conditioning and prepare for the events ahead of her.

***

At eight the men met in the barn, as planned. Joe recounted the loose battle plans, worrying he would not be able to dictate the fight, and chaos would reign, dooming the humans. He gave no indication of these doubts to his team.

After finishing, Joe asked Jonah to place Sugar in a stall and go over her orders with her. Jonah led her away, talking softly to the unicorn about what she was expected to do. While his friend did this, Joe talked to Otis over the walkie-talkie, pacing nervously, but talking calmly and resolutely. When he had finished, he met Jonah and Aqualung at the center of the barn.

"Okay, let's do a mic-check. Spread out." After the three had moved to different corners of the barn, Joe spoke into his handset. "Com-check. Copy? Otis, come in for com-check."

The other three said "yes" and each performed the same process, until they were sure that the four of them were communicating unhindered. A flash of terror crossed Joe's mind as he realized the original walkie-talkies were still operating on their first set of batteries. He said a silent prayer to himself, asking God to energize them. He felt at peace after doing so.

Joe E. spoke over their intercom after they had finished the com-check. "Otis, we will be leaving this position at dusk. Are you clear on your instructions?"

black 251 dog

Otis answered after a short pause, "I'm ready men. God be with y'all."

"He is," Joe E. answered. "Over and out."

Otis did not respond, but simply clicked his handset two times, their code for 'yes'. He couldn't speak. He was sitting in the park in his taxi, parked under a shade tree. Tears ran down his cheeks as he prayed that he had not said goodbye to his friends for the last time. He picked up the worn Bible from the passenger seat and brought it up against his forehead as he leaned forward to pray some more.

In the last few minutes before leaving the sanctuary, Joe asked Aqualung to talk with him privately. They walked to a corner of the barn while Jonah went to commune one last time with his unicorn. During all this, Black Dog sat silently in the middle of the space, frozen. She was thinking about so many things – all she had seen and experienced over the last twenty-five years. She wanted vengeance, but did not want to lose control of her emotions like she had the last time she had met the Wolfman. She was running through situations that might occur and visualizing how she would react. She was ready to be a warrior and ready to die doing so. She wanted more than anything to exact revenge on the werewolf, but her primary objective was to protect Joe E., her master.

Joe walked to a corner of the building with Collin. "You know you don't have to do this, right?"

Aqualung gave Joe a sideways look, as if to say, "Child, please." Joe smiled.

"Okay," Joe said. "I appreciate your loyalty and commitment. Just promise me you'll stick to the plan. You're not to be on the front line. Your mission is to bait the enemy and act as the clean-up man. You have your weapon, correct?"

"You can count on me, young Joseph," Collin said as he pulled the silver dagger from his breast pocket. It was a letter opener, but was so overly qualified for that task one might as well have shot letters open with a pistol. "They will neither discern me from a hedge or the grim reaper. I understand my duty," Aqualung stated with conviction.

**

The sun dropped faster than a LeBron airball and dusk was upon them. The moon was full.

"It's time," Joe said.

Joe, Jonah, and Aqualung walked to Sugar and rubbed her black nose for good luck, then exited through the swinging doors closest to the house, leaving them open behind them. The days of chained entrances were no longer.

The three men and Black Dog walked slowly across the field to the forest, being ultra-observant, but seeing nothing out of the ordinary. They entered the trees and low-crawled to the edge of the clearing that had once been their playground, but would now be their battlefield. They found the foxholes they had dug during the montage and laid down softly into them, pulling the covers of hand-woven scrub over their bodies for concealment. Black Dog joined Joe in his burrow. Her ribs still ached, but she knew better than to yelp in pain. She snuggled against his body in the tight quarters and went dormant, conserving her energy for the battle.

They waited for what seemed an eternity. The sun was now in its grave, but the night was bright, regardless. A full moon hovered above, and all the stars in the sky seemed to have grouped over the little clearing. Don't misunderstand – it was dark, but once their eyes adjusted, they could see clearly as they peered from their trenches.

Without warning, Joe rose from his pit and threw the foxhole cover aside, caring no longer about silence or camouflage. Jonah and Collin remained in their places. He brushed himself off and walked calmly into the west side of the clearing, homemade spear in hand, Black Dog at his side. He made his way to the center of that end of the clearing and waited. Black Dog positioned herself in front of him like a fullback waiting to level a blitzing linebacker.

Nothing happened for a time. Finally, Joe yelled at the top of his lungs, "Bring it on, Wolfie!! It's go time – now or never!!" The challenge echoed through the silent forest.

On cue, the werewolf stalked from the trees into the opposite end of the clearing, walking on two feet, wearing no hippie clothes. The beast was pure hatred, muscles flexing in spasms of fast-twitch anticipation under his matted fur. The army he had conjured walked forward from the forest and assembled to his left and right, slightly behind him. Joe took count of the opposition. He tallied a couple dozen mega-boar War Pigs, muddy scum dripping from their tusks, intermingled with the six remaining Werewolves of London, who seemed to be amused at the threat before them. Out of the brush dragged another creature, hunched and bedraggled. Joe sized him up as best he could, squinting in an attempt to see better. Suddenly, Joe's world cracked. It was Aqualung! He was a traitor!

For the first time, Joe showed weakness as he let out a whimper, not wanting what his eyes saw before him to be true. Had Collin been a spy the whole time, a mole? Joe craned his neck forward to see more clearly through the darkness and realized it was, in fact, Jack the Ripper in the rotten flesh, not the Aqualung. Joe had forgotten for a moment what songs the werewolf had backmasked and what enemies he might face. A wave of relief and guilt washed over him. He realized now why Collin had been harassed so many times by the detectives of Scotland Yard, as the resemblance was uncanny.

Joe and the werewolf stared at each other like antagonists in a Clint Eastwood spaghetti western. All that was missing was an Ennio Morricone score.

"You will be killed today!" Joe yelled to the Wolfman. His words weren't a howl of fury – they were more like how he would yell to his little sister that dinner would be ready in ten minutes. "I will send you back to Hell, from where you came!"

The werewolf did not appreciate this. He lifted his arms to the sky, his claws snapping into fight mode like those of an agitated feline. He let out a howl, which sounded like a cackle of hyenas being mowed down by a Land Rover.

The hairs on the nape of Joe's neck stiffened electrically. He looked down and saw Black Dog's were doing the same, straight down her backbone. She stood at attention, four on the floor, ready for the command to attack. She was whimpering – not in fear, but in anticipation. She had no concept of fear and never had. Fear is what urges beings to protect their own lives. Bravery was what she felt, which urges beings to give up their lives for others. She was ready to end her life – more than willing to do so, if it was to protect Joe E.

Summoned by the werewolf's howl, a rancid beast the size of

a Volkswagen van, scaled with maroon-colored keratin armor plates, rose from the forest behind the enemy line. Joe's eyes became wide circles as he assessed this new terror. It was a dragon, the 'Dragon of Darkness', subpoenaed into being from the lyrics of Led Zeppelin's 'The Battle of Evermore'. Joe was paralyzed and unable to flee as the abomination stretched its wings and flapped them slowly, hovering over the enemy line. It let out a spew of sulfur fire over the battlefield, charring many of the swirling vultures. The deceased birds dropped into the clearing with sickening thuds, like suicide jumpers. The air was filled with the acrid stench of burned feathers and the cries of the wounded carrion consumers. Joe wondered if the beast had a weakness. He had no way of knowing scores of ticks from the forest had crawled between the dragon's scales and were gorging themselves on his evil blood that very moment. Everything has a weakness.

A burst of light split the sky behind Joe with a sonic boom. It was the Queen of Light, the boys' guardian angel, making her second appearance of the summer, shooting down from the heavens toward the dragon at nearly the speed of light. The dragon reacted, blasting fire at her, but she was too fast. She circled around the firedrake and came from behind it over its left shoulder toward Joe. She did not fear the beast. She swooped down to the boy and hovered before him, face to face. Still unable to talk, she mouthed words to Joe, "You are the Prince of Peace." Joe E. read her lips and understood.

The Queen of Light rose to a place a hundred yards over the battlefield and became a luminescent spirit of white light, white heat, which made the werewolves and the boars and the Ripper uncomfortable, since none of them liked to be without the cover of darkness.

Confusion blanketed both sides. The battle should have started, but so much was happening and potentially waiting to be unleashed, all parties were understandably hesitant.

Without warning, Joe felt something large descend from the sky behind him. Thinking it to be another dragon, he hit the deck, shielding Black Dog.

As it passed over, Joe saw it was a shirtless hippie with curly blonde hair on a hang-glider. It was Tommy! Joe had backmasked the

black 255 dog

record that morning but had not seen any indication the pseudo-saint had entered the fray. In case you're wondering, Tommy preferred the conveyance of the hang-glider, as seen in the movie named eponymously after him.

Tommy was not your average hippie, Joe quickly deduced. He had twin machine guns mounted to the crossbar of the glider and was on a direct course for the dragon. Joe thought this was going to be a bad trip for Tommy, until something unexpected happened. A blast of light emitted from the disco ball that was the Queen of Light, striking the delicate corneas of the dragon, which still hovered over the werewolf. The beam was a laser, strongly resembling one from a Led Zeppelin laser light show. It traced rapidly back and forth across the dragon's face, like a child scribbling out something in a drawing.

The dragon shrieked in blinded pain and anger, shaking its head and burping fireballs in all directions.

The Queen of Light had stunned the dragon with an alley-oop assist to Tommy's kamikaze mission. Tommy let out his famous war cry, captured on tape only once, on the song 'Won't Get Fooled Again'. "YEEEAAAAAHHHHHH!!!!!!!" He steered a course for the dragon's heart, guns blazing with barrels glowing red, delivering a telegraph message of deadly dots and dashes. He made a strafing run and coasted over the wounded beast's right wing, got caught in the turbulence from the flapping appendage, and lost control, only to regain it and somehow swoop into a loop-de-loop rivaled only by Donald Trump's hair.

He was on a path to meet the beast head on another time. The dragon vomited a ball of blue fire at Tommy, and the nylon covering of the glider burst into flames. Losing control, Tommy peppered the dragon with .50 caliber slugs from his twin Tommy guns as he descended. The lizard had met its match and attempted evasive action. One of its wings was barely attached, and the dragon veered sideways as a result, crashing to its death fifty feet from the clearing. Tommy trailed off like a falling star and landed a dozen yards to the right of the dying dragon.

The warriors at opposite ends of the battlefield decided it was time for the foot soldiers to go at it. The Wolfman was stunned the dragon had not won the war for him, but remained confident of victory. He turned his back to Joe and faced his minions. At the same instant, the Queen of Light dropped to a point mere feet over Joe's head and poured laser light into the opposing forces in a display that eclipsed any Pink Floyd concert. The werewolf called for the boars to charge, but the spooked War Pigs scattered in all directions, dazed and confused by the light show.

The Werewolves of London were stronger of will. They strode toward Joe and Black Dog, confident they could vanquish a simple human teenager and his little terrier with ease. They broke into a trot but were distracted by the Aqualung, who popped up in a newly open space at the side of the clearing, yelling. "Hey, limey bastards, come have a go at The Aqualung!" It was the first time he had referred to himself as such.

Four of the pack veered toward Collin, who hesitated strategically, then ran back into the forest. The Werewolves of London were anxious for the first kill, thirsty for blood, and over-extended themselves in their haste. They charged to the spot where Collin had challenged them and were snagged at the feet, their upper bodies propelled into the ground by inertia. They cushioned their impact with their front claws and became more ensnared. Their limbs yanked in vain, attempting to free themselves.

The Werewolves of London were caught by their overgrown toenails in a simple trap – a steel mesh obscured by leaves – not much different in theory to flypaper. The actions of the good guys during the montage were proving to be quite effective.

Jonah emerged in the corner of the clearing, his walkie-talkie handset at his mouth. "NOW OTIS!!" he yelled.

A car motor roared to life and headlights illuminated twenty yards deeper in the forest, shining on the trapped werewolves.

The Werewolves of London that were tacked to the ground were blinded like deer in the headlights, helpless to free themselves. The old taxi's bald tires spun in the wet grass, but caught hold and propelled the vehicle toward the enemy. "Woo-hoo, y'all!" Otis whooped as he rammed the enemy combatants. The bodies colliding with and then flying over the vehicle destroyed the grill, dented the hood, and shattered the windshield. One of the Werewolves of London's upper body entered the cab, protruding into the passenger

black 257 dog

seat area. The beast was still conscious and swiped at Otis, which caused the old man to slam on the brakes.

The cab skidded into the clearing and came to a circling, sliding stop. Otis jumped from the vehicle and raced to the critically injured Werewolves of London to put them out of their misery with a silver-nitrate soaked chopstick to the throat. "God bless your soul," he said before each morbid thrust. The stricken Werewolves morphed into confused, struggling men after a few seconds, then seemed to realize all that had happened to them, and were at peace as they drew their final breaths, leaving only their finely-tailored clothing on the dew-soaked grass as an earthly reminder of their presence in Stringtown, Alabama.

After dispatching the fallen, Otis turned and walked back to his taxi, shaking his head as he surveyed the damage his precious vehicle had sustained. He still had one Werewolf of London to dispatch – the one laying across the hood with his upper torso intruding into the car's cabin. Although immobilized by the steel and glass that gripped him, this Werewolf of London was still alive and cursed Otis with all he had. Otis was pissed off, seeing his prized vehicle in ruins. He raised a pair of chopsticks over his head with both hands. "God damn you to Hell!" he said, plunging the sticks into the back of the lycanthrope. Seeing his victim materialize into human form, flopping in the broken glass, Otis had a change of heart. "Lord, send this man's soul to Heaven," he whispered. He reached out to comfort the anonymous Brit, but the body vanished inches from his touch.

Sugar emerged from the forest at full speed, ridden by Tommy, the hang glider crash survivor, which shocked Otis from his eulogy. They charged directly at him, and he let out a yell, "It's me, Otis!" He thought they had mistaken him for the enemy, but they were instead targeting a London Werewolf creeping up behind the old man. Otis leaned against the car, attempting to make himself thin.

Sugar knew what she was doing, of course. She had seen the Werewolf of London the second she entered the clearing. She lowered her head and met the abomination with full force, impaling him on her deadly horn and killing him instantly, thanks to the silver ring she wore. Then, she had a corpse riding on her head and could

black 258 dog

not see. She shook wildly, bucking Tommy from her back in the process, but could not disengage the dead combatant. Finally, the werewolf to man to spirit process ran its course, and Sugar was left only with the remnants of the Victorian clothing draped over her, still stabbed through by her horn. She was still unable to see, so she laid down in the grass, hoping for the best. Tommy took off at a sprint into the forest, yelling like a maniac, intent on who knows what, and was never seen again. Jonah ran to his unicorn and pulled the veil from the animal's wicked spike.

The final Werewolf of London stalked toward Joe, furious that the rest of his pack had been liquidated. He roared threateningly, attempting to intimidate the teenager. He was unlike the others – much stronger, much meaner.

The Wolfman was still on the loose. He cared not that his troops had been decimated. They had kept him alive to this point. He had his own agenda and viewed his allies as disposable heroes. At this moment, he was skulking along the perimeter of the clearing, unseen, attempting to flank Joe as the last Werewolf of London engaged the boy. Jack the Ripper was nowhere to be seen, having taken to his usual methods, as well. The War Pigs had proven to be only a nuisance. The disgusted Wolfman had exterminated many of them with fatal swipes as they ran past him in the chaos.

Joe stood his ground as the lone Werewolf of London ranged up, stopped just feet from him, then backed out of reach of Joe's spear.

"You think you can toy with me?" Joe said. "You will not be long in Stringtown." Joe raised his spear to chunk it at the enemy before him, but stopped suddenly, having smelled something he recognized. The Wolfman was behind him to his left. Jonah raced in to help his friend.

"Switch!" Jonah yelled. Joe rolled away, and Jonah was in his place, just like they had practiced.

"Hello, guvna," Jonah said with a smile. The Werewolf of London dropped his weight back on his haunches to leap at the teenager. Jonah let the beast jump, deftly dropped to his knees, and lunged, meeting the lycanthrope in the abdomen with an heirloom butter knife. He plunged it so deeply into the intestines of the wolf his arm entered partially behind it, which pulled the beast down upon him. The creature turned to human form and died on top of the boy as the Wolfman launched his attack on Joe. Jonah struggled to push the dead body off him, so he could help Joe, but he was too weak.

Joe faced the Wolfman once and for all, man to animal. The werewolf was so terrifying – Joe was shaking uncontrollably. They circled each other, one of them afraid and one of them murderous and overconfident. "Make your move, mutt," Joe said.

The werewolf stopped and lunged toward Joe. Joe leaped aside, narrowly avoiding the swipe of a claw. As the evil beast landed on all fours, he was bitten in the upper back by the fearless little Black Dog with the silver tooth. If the Scottie had sunk her right fang into him, the battle would have been over, but the dog had latched on to the werewolf with the opposite side of her mouth. Although deeply imbedded in him, her bite did not kill the beast.

Black Dog was locked onto Wolfie like a Gila monster. The werewolf roared and shook, but he could not throw her off. He swiped at her with his claws but could not reach her. Finally, he brought his right elbow into Black Dog's poor little ribs with tremendous force, sending her flying and further injuring the cage of bones protecting her huge heart.

The werewolf could not have been more enraged if it had rabies. Things had not gone as planned for him. He turned to circle Joe again, digging his claws into his own palms in bloody fury.

"Whatcha want?" Joe asked as he circled, never letting his attention be swayed. "You want your wittle dwagon? That didn't work out so well, did it? Your Werewolves of London are dead, too. You will be next."

The Wolfman could take no more. He leaped at Joe E. – much faster than Joe expected. If it would have been a movie, the jump would have been a high, slow-motion arc. But this was not a movie. The werewolf had launched a surprise attack on a straight line vector directly at Joe's startled heart.

Joe had been stalling, not wanting to make the first move. He had goaded the werewolf to strike first, but it surprised the boy, nonetheless. As the Wolfman leaped at him, Joe dropped backward, flat on his back, then defensively lunged his wooden spear directly into the heart of the lycanthrope that had terrorized Stringtown for so many years.

The animal fell to the ground and landed hard on his side, skewered and spewing a fountain of blood from his mouth. The spear was still in the beast, having been wrenched from Joe's hands. Joe jumped up and pulled the lance free, not knowing if his enemy was dead or dying.

The Wolfman lay withering on the ground before the young man. Joe felt an overwhelming sense of pity wash over him as he stood over his vanquished enemy. For some reason, he felt no accomplishment. He felt sympathy for the werewolf – sympathy for the Devil.

The transformation process of werewolf death passed through the Wolfman, the opposite of what he had experienced many years before when he became a lycanthrope. A man now lay before Joe, face down. Joe stood over him, watching in anguish.

For reasons unknown even to him, Joe reached down and turned over the body, now fully human. He felt some compulsion to see the face of the person who had tried so hard to kill him.

Joe gasped at what he saw and cried out, "NOOOO!!"

It was his Uncle Ernie, pleading with his dying eyes for forgiveness.

"I'm so sorry. It wasn't my fault," Ernie said, blood running down his chin. Joe moaned and bent down to comfort his uncle for a brief second before the man was gone forever. He put his ear near Ernie's mouth and heard, "Please... forgive."

Ernie's final words were ushered by a long, last breath, then a great gasp, and then Ernie was walking with The Reaper.

Joe was stunned and in shock, attempting to understand what had just happened. He sat on his knees in the grass with a thousand yard stare. He had just killed Granny's son, his own flesh and blood uncle.

Joe reached to unlash the record needle from the top of the spear. He thought of stomping it into the ground, so it could never be used again, but changed his mind and slowly wiped the blood from it and placed it in the little bottle. He returned it to his right-front pocket, where it would always remain.

The record needle that had caused all this madness to occur had, ironically and rightfully, ended it. Joe wasn't sure the needle would serve this purpose when he made his weapon, but his sixth sense had guided him. His guardian angel surely had something to do with it, as well.

Joe had rightfully deduced that the needle contained some amount of silver, but had not known in his wildest dreams he would murder his own uncle with it. Jonah walked toward Joe, who was still on his knees staring into the heavens. Jonah place his hand on his best friend's shoulder and uttered simply, "It's over Joe. Ernie is at peace now. We all are."

From the brush behind them, something burst forth into the clearing, rushing toward the unsuspecting boys. This battle would never end, it seemed. It was Jack the Ripper, and he crashed across Joe's back, forcing him to the ground and knocking Jonah to the side in the process. Joe was stunned and unable to fight back, pinned to the ground by the weight of the murderer's wicked body. The Ripper smiled and lifted a rusty butcher knife over his head, intent on finishing the job the werewolf had not.

Suddenly, Aqualung burst from the trees at a sprint and waylayed the Ripper with a rugby tackle, knocking the knife from the murderer's hand. Aqualung locked his arms around his adversary as they fell to the ground together.

Collin had a choke-hold around the Ripper's neck from behind as they lay in the grass. "Ye been me nemesis for too long," he said softly into the ear of the scourge of humanity.

"Let me die for my sins, for once and for all," the Ripper answered. "I have lived with this guilt long enough."

"That will be my pleasure," Aqualung said. He loosened his hold around the murderer's neck and slit the throat of London's infamous serial killer with the letter opener. "May ye never rest in peace. May ye burn in Hell."

The Ripper's body slowly disappeared like the others. The dragon's form had done the same. All the supernatural enemies were now just a memory. The forest was absolutely silent. Joe and Jonah and Aqualung looked to each other, not knowing if it was really over.

Otis strode up and whooped, "Hootie-Hoo! We done it!"

One by one, each realized Otis was right. The nightmare was finally over.

The four of them stood up and met in a group hug, then crumpled to the ground, sobbing and laughing, until Joe thought of Black Dog. He jumped to his feet and raced to where the little girl lay, her chest heaving as if she were breathing her last breaths. Joe was terrified she would die and disappear like the others. He crouched over her and pleaded, "Don't leave me, baby!" He pushed his face into her neck. Losing her would be too much at this point.

Otis, Aqualung, Jonah, and Sugar gathered around. Jonah hugged Sugar's neck, praying she would not dematerialize like the other supernaturals.

A minute passed, seeming like only a couple of minutes for a change. Joe sat up and Otis and Jonah put an arm on each of his shoulders. The little dog lay motionless.

Otis spoke, "Joe, she done gave her life for you."

Black Dog lifted her head and looked at Otis like he was crazy. She bared her teeth in a strange smile and struggled to her feet. The ordeal was over. Things were indeed returning to normal. All the disappearing had been done, and Black Dog, Aqualung, and Sugar were going to be around a while. Joe picked Black Dog up in his arms and walked to the center of the clearing. The others watched.

Joe stood at the imaginary fifty-yard line and raised his face to howl at the bright moon above him, still holding Black Dog, who wasn't going anywhere. The howl was nothing like the Wolfman's. It was pure joy.

"WE DID IT!!" he yelled to the sky in a much higher pitch than he would have liked. "We did it," he said softly to Black Dog as he lifted her, so she could look at the moon and stars above. Joe turned to his friends and smiled. "We did it."

Sugar could not contain her joy any longer. She let out a whinny and raced to the center of the clearing, bucking and screeching happily, looking like a marlin tailing on the surface of the Gulf of Mexico.

Otis, Jonah, and Aqualung raced up, and they all hugged ecstatically.

Otis grabbed Jonah by the chin and yelled into the boy's face.

black 263 dog

"We done did it, lil' bruva!"

"We did it, homeboy!" Jonah exclaimed in retort. "I love you!!"

Aqualung jumped on Otis' back, whooping and hollering in his idiomatic way.

The Queen of Light burst a gigantic firework overhead, which showered down over the group. She was gone evermore, though her presence would be felt for the rest of the boys' lives.

After a bit more celebration, the men felt childish and stopped. Then, they simply looked to one another, occasionally surveying the battlefield. When two pairs of eyes locked, they smiled a little and nodded. Their eyes were doing the talking now, saying once again, "We did it." It was slowly sinking in.

CHAPTER THIRTY AND THREE

The boys and Aqualung returned to the compound, walking as slowly as possible, then led Sugar into the carriage house for the night. Otis drove his battered taxi from the forest, then through the front gate, and parked in the half-circle driveway. He would spend the night at the house. He couldn't be driving his ravaged cab around Stringtown without explanation – too many questions would arise.

Aqualung and Jonah were waiting by the front door as Otis turned off the battered car for what might be the last time. "Ya done real good tonight, Keisha," Otis said as he patted the dash of the old vehicle. Otis loved his old car like people love their dogs. He gathered his strength and opened the door to get out. "Errbody gots ta cry sometime. Upon us all a little rain must fall," he said to himself as he softly shut the door. He looked toward the house at Collin and Jonah and smiled, his gold tooth gleaming like the North Star. Everything was gonna be alright.

***

Joe E. had taken poor Black Dog upstairs and laid her in Ernie's closet on a soft padding of blankets.

Meeting in the kitchen, the men sat down to debrief and have a needed drink. They tossed back a couple shots of vodka. They said nothing, just looked at each other and shook their heads from time to time. They did not boast or re-tell details of the battle. They felt dirty, like real men do after real war.

Finally, Aqualung spoke softly, "Glad to finally get me revenge on Dirty Jack." He let out a whiskey laugh and his voice raised. "Sent him to Hell where he belongs, laddies! Thanks for giving me the opportunity, Joe."

"Well, I think I'm the one that should be thanking you, Collin," Joe said. "After all, you did save my life."

"You saved mine first," Aqualung protested.

"It's a chicken and egg thang, fellas," Otis said, as smooth as Lando Calrissian. "I think it's safe to say we saved a lotta lives. We be like Colt 45 – we work every time."

They all laughed, although Otis was the only one that

understood the joke. It didn't matter – they were just happy to be in each others company. They were happy simply to be alive.

Joe was noticeably less elated than his compatriots, though he put on a brave face. Jonah noticed that the vodka seemed to be ushering his friend into despair, rather than celebration.

"It had to be done," Jonah comforted.

"I know, Jonah, but I don't have to be happy about it. I killed my own uncle. I can't believe it."

"T'wasn't your uncle, young Joseph," said Collin.

"It was the werewolf that done terrorized this town almost three decades," Otis interjected. "It had to be did, son."

"You guys are right, I know that," Joe said. "Ernie needed to be put out of his misery. Just promise me that Granny will know none of this, okay?"

The others agreed to die with the secret.

"You know, you're exactly like your uncle, Joe," Jonah said.

"Yeah, I know we look alike. You've told me."

"I don't mean that. You lived parallel lives. Ernie killed the first werewolf – the one from 'Bark at the Moon'. Apparently, he got bitten doing it, though. He wanted to protect Granny and Stringtown, just like you. It just didn't work out as well for him. There's nothing to feel guilty about. Ernie didn't want to be a werewolf and kill people. He couldn't control it after it happened – after he changed. It controlled him. You did the right thing. You put an end to his agony and everyone else's. It was something that had to be done. Don't feel bad. Your uncle is in a better place."

"Might we pray for his soul and speak not of this again?" Collin asked.

"Bow heads," Otis spoke without waiting for an answer.

"Father, you created all that is good in this world, and we thank you for that. We know that you done blessed us in so many ways – most of all by giving us life. Oh Lordy, we do thank you for that! You delivered us from evil tonight, when we was in the shadows of the Valley of Death. And I do believe we did your bidding the best we could. We ask that you take mercy upon those we had to... kill. We ask that you see us not as murderers, but as redeemers. Those that we... that we killed, were not evil. They were unwillingly possessed by the Devil, and we only desired to deliver them from that evil and end this dark time on Stringtown. May they rest in peace in your holy arms, Lord. Amen in the name of Jesus."

"Amen," the others said.

Otis continued as they raised, then re-lowered their heads. He had been filled with the spirit – and by the many spirits of Stringtown he often spoke of. He began to sing softly. It was a song he had never sung before. In fact, Otis had never even heard it. It was one not heard in Stringtown since the days of slavery, long forgotten. It was delivered to Otis spontaneously, like 'Stairway to Heaven' was to Robert Plant and Jimmy Page.

"Mary had a silver chain. Every link said Jesus' name. Hold on. Hold on. You wanna get to Heaven, I kin show you how. Keep yo hands on tha Gospel Plow. Hold on. Hold on."

Otis sang the verse two times, and the others joined in one by one – first Jonah, then Collin, then Joe E. They joined arms and sang it over and over, crying and laughing as the bottled emotions of the last 175 years and the last forty days washed over them.

They weren't crying from anguish, but from pure joy. The four of them were in evangelical ecstasy. They were being absolved of their sins and baptized by their tears. By the end of this exorcism, they swayed back and forth in each others arms like overwhelmed hippies at Woodstock. God had delivered a message to them, and it was cool. Not so much fire and brimstone – more like Jimi Hendrix setting his Strat aflame at Monterrey. The burning bush can take many forms, but it always leads people to the promised land.

During the climax of the sing-a-long, Joe stood up and walked to the sink to dump the remnants of the half-gallon of vodka down the tubes. Collin gave him a distressed look, but found strength in the hymn and sang louder than before. Joe smiled happily. The last drop of alcohol had been consumed in that house.

"Mary had a silver chain. Every link said Jesus' name. Hold on. Hold on. You wanna get to Heaven, I kin show you how. Keep yo hands on tha Gospel Plow. Hold on. Hold on."

CHAPTER THIRTY AND FOUR

The next morning parachuted down over the old house with its usual blanket of dew. There had been so many next mornings this summer, the participants did not realize that this next morning was more special than the others. They had forgotten the battle, forgotten the drinking and singing in the kitchen, forgotten everything. Had it all been a dream?

Slowly, the men re-wound the VHS tapes in their brains and adjusted the tracking. It had been real. It had really happened. They smiled with satisfaction at the remembrance as they drifted in and out of consciousness.

It was time to enjoy life. There were only two short weeks to do so before the boys had to return home and prepare for the new school year.

"Wake up, sleepyhead," Joe said to Jonah, who was already awake. "We've got to police up this place until next summer."

"You got it, bro." Jonah smiled. "We did it, didn't we?"

"Last night wasn't a dream, that's for sure! Well, I guess it kinda was – a dream come true. Get your butt outta bed!"

The boys laughed their way down the stairs to the kitchen, intent on creating the mother of all breakfasts, 'platter' be damned. They sang together as they toiled, taking turns picking the song. They had never been happier, and they couldn't wait to wash the dishes.

The meal that morning looked like something from a Narnia-inspired hallucination. There was even a unicorn enjoying chocolate pancakes with blueberry syrup, for goodness sakes! Aqualung was cleaner than he had ever been, wearing clothes from Ernie's closet. He looked more like a Werewolf of London than Jack the Ripper for a change, which was nice. He had trimmed his beard and looked pretty darn good, except for his teeth. Otis tried to enjoy himself, but his worries about his taxi were obvious to the boys.

Joe pulled Otis aside for a private chat. It was strange to be celebrating over breakfast and even stranger for the teenager to be counseling the old man, but at this point... well, you know.

"Otis, you're concerned about your cab, right?"

"Sorry, son. I'm glad about everything, but I ain't got the money to repair ol' Keisha."

"Keisha?"

"Well, I never had a baby, so I named her. I mean, my ol' gullfriend named her."

Joe E. suppressed a smile.

"Don't worry, Otis. I've got a few tricks up my wizard sleeves. And if they don't work, I'm sure Granny would love to assist in getting the cab repaired."

"Well, if that don't beat all, Joe. You is sumpin' else. You gon' be president one day!"

"Don't wish that on me! I don't know why anyone would want that job," Joe said with a smile. "Enjoy yourself, Otis. We'll get you back in the driver's seat as soon as possible."

As the celebratory meal wound down, Joe carried a doggy batch of food on a tray up to Black Dog. He quietly opened Ernie's door and slid the closet door silently to the side. He paused to gaze down at his little girl. She was dreaming about chasing squirrels, her delicate feet moving in a syncopated rhythm. He was full of love and bent down to gently rouse her with an affectionate stroke of his hand across her wet nose and over her closed eyes with their soft black eyelids. She woke and looked up at Joe and smiled. She was so in tune with the boy. They were in love with each other.

As Black Dog attempted to rise, Joe gently pushed her back down. "Don't get up, girl. I'll feed you." The two of them spent the next fifteen minutes together, Joe feeding his pet by hand. She didn't wolf the food down like before – she ate slowly. She wasn't a ravenous, uneducated canine, after all. She was an ebony princess – Southern royalty. It would be unbecoming not to chew her food the appropriate number of times.

Joe talked absentmindedly as he fed her. "Guess we did it, girl. At least I hope we did. Who knows – there could be another wolf out there in that forest. I hope Uncle Ernie really did kill that first one, like Jonah said, but you never know."

After the last bite, Joe petted Black Dog until she fell asleep, both of them drifting into the subconscious. Joe began to sing softly, the song he would never go more than a few days for the rest of his life without singing to himself.

"*Mary had a silver chain. Every link said Jesus' name. Hold on. Hold on. You wanna get to Heaven, I kin show you how. Keep yo hands on tha Gospel Plow. Hold on. Hold on.*"

Joe looked down and saw his precious pet was sleeping peacefully. He snapped to and mentally said to himself, "Okay, time to get to work."

***

Joe went down to the kitchen to find Otis, Jonah, and Aqualung returning the room to spotlessness, singing the old negro spiritual, although it had undergone a transformation and morphed into a sort of jaunty sea shanty, courtesy of the influence of Collin James. It still worked, regardless – they had found their own special serenity prayer. The three men were uplifted, their feet dancing on the worn wooden floor. Sugar stood in the pantry with her eyes closed, the chocolate overdose having sedated her like the tryptophan from a Thanksgiving feast.

The men made their way to the back porch after the cleaning was done and took reclining positions upon the old wicker furniture. They fell into the peaceful slumber of a two hour nap, each dreaming satisfied summations of the endless summer – a summer that would never be relived in any other medium than dreams and memories and stories told by old men.

They were struggling a bit – not knowing what to do after expending so much time and energy to defeat the werewolf and his army. What next? It was like a college football team the day after winning the national championship. Coach Joe E. had a plan, though – start doing push-ups and getting ready for next season. After a nice nap, of course.

Waking before the others, Joe left the men to sleep. He returned to the record player. It had been the vehicle of incredible suffering, as well as incredible accomplishment. That's the way things are here on the third rock from the sun. Very few things are purely good or purely evil, other than God and Satan.

Joe plugged the needle back in and dug a record from the stack. It was not something one would expect to find alongside Ozzy

Osbourne platters, but it has to be remembered that Ernie had an older sister, Joe's eventual mother. The song was called 'Big Yellow Taxi' and was by a hippie chick named Joni Mitchell. Joe must have been confused about how the record player worked because he played the song backward instead of forward.

Joe E. hoped beyond hope he could make this work. If sheer willpower had anything to do with the outcome, he would find success. He knew a taxi couldn't be extracted from the cellar and worried that if it came through in the carriage house it would be possessed by some evil, like the car in the Stephen King novel, 'Christine'. What he was doing was risky, but Joe figured killing a stupid car would be way easier than going to war with all the evil that could be summoned from classic rock. Hell, a spike strip would probably do the trick, he thought with a laugh. Or some sugar in the gas tank.

After backmasking the song, Joe went downstairs and plopped down on the parlor room's couch, a little wary to see the result of his actions. He stared at the cannon ball in the wall and smiled. This really had been one helluva summer, he thought. He rose and walked over to the ordnance and rubbed it with his right hand. "Bring me good luck," he said out loud. He walked out the front door, unfettered by worry.

The sun overhead was at full power, not a cloud in sight, which made Joe squint his eyes to shield his retinae from the photons streaming from the sky. He walked around the corner of the house and saw a beautiful vintage cab, just like one from the TV show 'Taxi', parked on the grass directly above the underground tunnels of the cellar.

Joe said, "YES!" and pumped his fist like Tiger Woods used to do, pre-scandal. He raced around to the back porch, jumping as he ran, yelling, "Otis, wake up! Wake up, Mr. Otis!"

Hearing the turmoil and thinking something wrong, Aqualung, Otis, and Jonah leaped to their feet. "What is it, son?" Otis axed somberly, expecting the worst.

"Come here!" Joe barked. "Come to the cellar!" He was gone before the others could get the screen door unlatched.

They raced toward the cellar and stopped as they rounded the back corner of the house, stunned by what the saw before them. Joe leaned against the vehicle, grinning like a Cheshire Cat with a belly-full of magic mice.

Otis was overwhelmed. "Damn boy, you done did me a beautiful thing," he whispered.

"You deserve it, Otis. Let's go for a test drive – we need to pick up Granny."

Jonah and Aqualung transferred the license plates from the wrecked Cadillac Continental to the new cab, which had been custom made by the Checker Motors Corporation in 1978. The plates would do for the time being.

The four of them jumped into the car and marveled at the quality of the interior. Seeing a cab fresh out of the box, before it delivers thousands of people to their destinations, is a wonder to behold. Otis fought back tears.

Thankfully, the key was in the ignition. Otis took it between his fingers, turned to look at Joe with a smile, and rotated it 90 degrees forward. The motor roared to life with a statement, seeming to say, "I am here, and I own the road." Joe laughed and slapped his hand against Otis' shoulder over and over. Jonah and Aqualung were in the back seat, whooping and hollering. Aqualung had never been in a car and was manic with the excitement of the whole experience, like a dog on its first trip to the park.

Otis pulled the shifter into drive and slowly circled in the grass, guiding his new baby to the driveway and out the gate.

The crew creeped by the house across the street. The old man was in his front yard picking weeds. He looked up with a hateful gaze. Otis laughed and laid rubber, angering the octogenarian, who was oblivious to all that had taken place in the forest behind the house across the street.

"Dang hooligans!! What do you think, Poo-Poo?" he said to the aged poodle a few feet from him. Poo-Poo, being crankier even than his master, raised his leg and gave a few squirts, baptizing the old man's boots. "Dang it, Poo-Poo! You're going blind faster than me!" he said, kicking at his precious lawn in anger.

***

The entourage arrived at the old folks' home and entered

black 272 dog

through the front doors like visiting royalty. The administrator rushed to Joe and asked if something was wrong. "Heck no," answered Joe. "We've come to bring my grandmother home. How much do we owe you?"

"Well, I don't have the figures tallied, son. I'd guess it to be around $3000, ballpark."

"The service you have provided has been far more valuable than that, sir," Joe E. said. "I'll speak with my Granny – we can surely provide you far more. And please inform your guests they will have a catered dinner tomorrow night, featuring the finest barbecue in Alabama. Can we do that, Otis?"

"Shouldn't be a problem, Joe. Might need to out-source the dessert, though."

"Done," Joe said.

"We thank you so much for your generosity," the administrator answered with a smile. "Really – thank you."

Joe stopped and looked into the man's eyes, extending his hand. The administrator gripped Joe's handshake with both hands – he really cared about his wards. "I need to consult with my grandmother, but I feel confident your facility will be well taken care of for some time," Joe said.

The administrator's eyes lit up. Words escaped him in his joy. "Thank you, thank you," he managed through trembling lips.

"Lead us to the Granny!" Aqualung exhorted.

The man looked at Aqualung in his ridiculous seventies garb and let out a laugh. "Right this way! Follow me, boys! Ha-ha!"

The group slowed as they reached the room. Their escort made a slight motion to Joe to indicate they had reached their destination. Joe nodded and placed his hand on the man's shoulder to show his appreciation.

Joe walked to the open door and peered inside. Granny sensed his presence and turned to look at him, her face a question mark.

"We did it," Joe whispered, not wanting to wake his sleeping grandfather. Granny smiled and rushed to hug the boy, overcome with emotion.

***

black 273 dog

Hello again. Remember me? I've been here the whole time, but I've been laying low, waiting to see how things turned out. I'm not used to riding in the backseat, but it's been a great trip. Grandpa Joseph didn't wake up ever again, sadly. I had to take him shortly after the barbeque party at the old folks' home, but rest assured, he's in a better place. He held on so long – until he knew Granny was safe without him. That's the way love works.

The rest of the summer passed quickly, and many things were accomplished. Aqualung was taken to the barber/dentist that had outfitted Black Dog with her silver tooth and received a full-on gold grill, much to the delight of all. Otis was able to register his new vehicle, despite it having no vehicle identification number. Granny returned home, of course, but didn't spend her days asleep, like she used to. She spent her time gardening, singing Beatles songs all the while. She didn't care to drink vodka anymore, and spent very little time in the bedroom that had once been her prison.

The carriage house was burned to the ground, fueled by the kudzu the boys had piled up at the beginning of the summer and never gotten around to burning. The cellar was torn asunder by a heavy-metal backhoe and filled in with dirt and concrete, until a modern storm shelter had taken its place.

Black Dog's ribs healed during all this, and she took her place at Joe's side, guarding against any threat, though there was none. Sugar was loosed into the forest with the knowledge she could at any time drift back into the compound. Aqualung would be there to feed her – he had chosen to stay with Granny. He would care for the house, accommodate her needs, and protect her, if necessary. In time, a nice stable would be built for Sugar, and Aqualung would brush her and care for her for many, many years.

**

After the boys left for their senior year, Aqualung thrived as Granny's manservant, doing the necessary chores and repairs to keep the house in good form. He never drank on the job, but surprisingly came to assist the elderly man across the street with difficult tasks, often drinking beers in the kitchen after doing so, although he had to listen to long, complaining rants about the good old days each time.

Otis was always at the ready to assist, of course. He had taken great pleasure in helping burn down the carriage house. Aqualung could not obtain a driver's license, since he had no birth record, so Otis retained his job as chauffeur, dutifully tethered to the walkie-talkie.

The boys returned home to complete their public education, but were men among boys. They couldn't be bothered by petty high school cliques and other teenage crap. They never told anyone what they had done, but it showed. They breezed through their senior year and returned to Stringtown, Alabama, the following summer. Black Dog traveled hidden in a bag under Joe's bus seat. This time, they had a ride waiting for them at the bus station when they arrived in the middle of the night. They ate at least two breakfasts a day and did a ton of yard work. In the nine quick months they had been away, the kudzu had grown over everything in its path, like it had been possessed by some supernatural spirit.

CODA

Two 15-year-old boys are exploring the forest. It is summer, July 2. The year is 2032. One boy is obviously the leader – the one whose parents just purchased the old house from the man named Joe, whose grandmother had willed it to him. The other boy follows him through the trees, laughing.

Suddenly, the boy in the lead stops, and the second boy nearly collides with him. Their gazes track from the forest floor to the sky slowly, as they try to understand the weird tree towering above them. The first boy steps forward and pulls a vine from it.

"What is it?"

"Looks like a statue."

The boys run to the feet of the monument, grab handfuls of kudzu and pull, stripping the vines from the rusted figure.

"What is it?"

"A giant."

"A giant what?"

"A giant man – made of metal. An iron man...."

Roll Credits